Stories from

EPOCH

Stories from

EPOCH

The First Fifty Issues (1947–1964)

Edited by BAXTER HATHAWAY

Cornell University Press

ITHACA, NEW YORK

CORNELL UNIVERSITY PRESS

First published 1966

Library of Congress Catalog Card Number: 66-23557

PRINTED AND BOUND IN THE UNITED STATES OF AMERICA
BY THE VAIL-BALLOU PRESS, INC.

A Foreword

EVER since the first issue of *Epoch* was published, shortly after the end of World War II, its editors have been on the lookout constantly for exciting new talents and for significant new forms in short-story writing. They have given over a major part of the magazine's space to the stories they have discovered. The stories in this book, my favorites from the first fifty issues of *Epoch*, give a good picture of what the modern short story has been like. They show what new homesteads contemporary writers have staked out in the frontier territories of imagination, what new forms they have made as vehicles fit to express the aspects of experience with value for them, what the vital modes of thought have been while the world endured cold war, bomb threats, population explosion, and ever-accelerating change. The common notion is that an Americanized world is a pack of face-less robots, of cheerful idiots only vaguely uneasy with automa-tion and an expanding economy. Our serious writers show how much this is true and how much it is not true.

We can find a great diversity here. *Epoch*'s stories have never been tailor-made to a single pattern, nor held down to a mono-lithic idea of what an audience wanted to read. Writers have been urged to create their own worlds in their own way. Some of these stories are traditional in holding a mirror up to an ob-jective "nature," to that complex of perceived surfaces that we all agree is "out there." Such stories are usually called realistic, for we define realism as the composing of events observed in the common-denominator world, with a crowded canvas of particulars brought to us by our senses. Few stories in this century are, however, entirely objective, for above all else, ours is the century of psychological analysis. Daniel Curley, in "The Manhunt," gives us a surface of a sheriff's posse searching for a lost child, a realistic situation and setting, but our attention is focused upon the inner feelings of the fisherman who inadvertently has become the object of suspicion; Ken Marvin's manhood is brought to question, not his guilt—that and any community's vicious distrust of an outsider. The same pivoting of external action upon conflicts of the human heart is to be found in Harris Downey's war story "The Hunters," in Philip Roth's "The Contest for Aaron Gold," in the probing of the relationship between man and wife that R. V. Cassill provides in "Fracture," in Herbert Wilner's assigning his story "The Bandaged Man" to the boy, who has merely broken his leg in a football game, and not to the Italian gangster, who has killed a cop, to whom the title refers (this is essentially the same technique that Hemingway used in giving the story of "The Killers" to Nick Adams and not to Ole Anderson). These stories represent the main line in twentieth-century fiction following the pattern of the Joycean "epiphany" already established in *Dubliners*. Objective plot gives way to the structuring of the stream of thought or feeling of the central character. The Joycean epiphany was essentially an image-making art form, based solidly on portrayal of realistic details, framing the details, and giving them a center in insight or illumination. Symbols can function in an epiphany as they can in a Chekhov story, but they become part of the composition, or give enrichment to the realistic details that are composed. The grizzly bears in Ray B. West's story are symbols of this kind.

Whatever the continuing popularity of these stories of psychological realism may be, the literary critics who resent any departure from the modes of Chekhov, Joyce, Hemingway, and Faulkner fail to notice where a large part of the power and originality of contemporary writing lies. Our main battle is with abstractions, with facelessness. In depth psychology the outer shape of character was already lost. In a new kind of story, vaguely comparable to abstract expressionism in painting, the stylizing or conventionalizing of an action takes precedence over mannerism in the depiction of character. Stylizing is expressionism; our low-level sense of external reality is distorted by the more pervasive sense of what is meaningful in inner reality. The concretion of myth is substituted for the concretion of the photographic image. The characters of myth, it is true, are faceless, and the manneristic individuality of the human profile is lost in the machines of what is abstractly expressed. It is with ideas like these in mind that we must approach stories like George P. Elliott's "Sandra," James B. Hall's "A Spot in History," or Thomas Pynchon's "Mortality and Mercy in Vienna." In these, the dialectic of the mythic action takes precedence over the aliveness of the illuminated moment. These writers are in their own way, a way quite unlike that of the social-protest writers of the thirties, purveyors of theses—abstract concepts. George P. Elliott invents a myth in order to say things about the relationships that exist between men and women today. James B. Hall creates, not a realistic picture of carnival life, but a mythic projection of what the Protestant or Puritan ethic implies—that is, capitalism. Thomas Pynchon's title, taken from *Measure for Measure*, is a strong hint of how little his concern is with a photographic likeness of the behavior of bohemians in Washington, D.C.

In the tradition of the recent past, stories like these have been classified as "fantasies," a term that somehow makes too much out of the difference between their world and reality. In another tradition at least as old as Neo-Platonism, the myth created in stories like these becomes the reality—or the surreality. Kafka has apparently played an important part in the formulation of this kind of modern story, but these "fantasies" also differ markedly from Kafka's kind, especially in their greater use of realistic and nonallegorical fact. At the same time, action is not an engine for the creation of extra-meaningful suspense, and the Aristotelian "character" has disappeared into process.

But there are other kinds of stories here too. Some, like

Jordon Pecile's "A Piece of Polenta," create new dimensions by using flat surfaces of commentary on events that are indistinguishable from those of autobiography. Then there is the Freudian world; stories like John Logan's "Panic Round," or Julius Laffal's "Bake Plenty Bread," are built up so completely out of behavior traits of psychological or psychopathological import that reality must be defined in them in terms of a Freudian way of seeing. Some stories are written with tight economy, in grim-lipped severity of line. Others—like Douglas Fowler's "Tartarus," for instance—are lavish with expressive detail and high-flying diction. The modern world is a Byzantine age, exhibiting the paradoxes of Byzantium. We fluctuate between a spartan iconoclasm by means of which we try to defend ourselves against the disconcerting richness of possibility in daily life and, on the other hand, a yearning to partake of the complexity. Both kinds of expression fit our contemporary needs.

I have presumed to make this selection of stories from the pages of *Epoch* on the basis of the longevity of my connection with the magazine. But I must hasten to acknowledge my indebtedness to the insights and judgments, the enthusiasms and discriminations, of my many colleagues on the changing editorial staff over a nineteen-year period that led to the initial publication of these stories. I wish to thank each of the writers for permission to reprint their stories, and Russell and Volkening, Inc., for permission to reprint "Fracture" by R. V. Cassill, "Mortality and Mercy in Vienna" by Thomas Pynchon, and "Twelve O'Clock" by Harvey Swados. Daniel Curley's "The Manhunt" is reprinted by permission of the author and John Schaffner, literary agent. I especially want to thank David Ray, one of *Epoch*'s mainstays for four years, for encouraging me to make this selection and for the great amount of labor he went to in setting up the manuscript for this book.

BAXTER HATHAWAY

Ithaca, New York
April 1966

Contents

Stories from

EPOCH

The Manhunt

BY DANIEL CURLEY

IN the middle of the morning, Ken Marvin suddenly became aware that the stream he had been fishing since sunrise had already led him into the fringes of a swamp. He stood perplexed a moment with the water gently tugging at his boots. He thought at first of following the stream a bit farther, but when he tried to take a step he found himself up to his ankles in muck and sinking all the time. Although he had little difficulty in working his way back to better footing, he was shaken.

He sat on the bank to catch his breath and quiet the trembling in his legs. He glanced at his watch. Of course he hadn't wound it all week, but in any case the time was right for him to pack up his rod and take off across country for the logging road where he had left his car.

As he stood up, he noticed his billfold lying on the ground beside his pack. He reached for it and stopped with his hand extended: that might have been all that anyone had ever found to tell what had become of him, first the car and then this, and nothing more forever. That was rather more peace and solitude than he had bargained for when he came to the woods— certainly it was no improvement on the alternatives already facing him: to resume the role of the stranger who lies awake beside a peacefully sleeping wife and thinks of women, young and

1

passionate, or to disappear into the disguise of the man nameless and hiding, afraid to claim even a profession for himself.

He picked up the billfold and he picked up the pack. There
was still a long walk ahead of him. If he started at once he
could take it easy and calm himself on the long walk back, and
he could hold off until the very edge of the woods—and perhaps beyond—the haste and tension that usually accompanied
his turning home.

For just a moment longer he looked at the stream and he
looked at the trees. He listened to the water and the wind and a
frog and a cricket and a blue jay.

As he left the stream, the undergrowth was thick, but he
shortly found a footpath going in more or less the right direction, and, after a mile, the footpath turned into a cart path, and
that quite gently led him into somebody's back pasture.

He was well out into the clearing before he noticed the large
crowd around the house. He assumed there was an auction and
thought for a moment of stopping to buy a present for his wife,
just a little something to thank her for understanding how
much he needed this trip by himself. But he still had far
enough to go so that he was able to talk himself out of it before
he got close. It would be awkward at best, out here in the
Maine woods, to be the only stranger at a country auction. He
might buy the wrong thing anyway. His wife might even resent
not being taken to the auction herself—no, that really wasn't
fair. After all she wasn't the one being driven crazy by her
change of life.

But in any case it might be better if he didn't have to mention the auction at all, so he stayed as far away from the house
as he could. Besides, he wasn't ready yet to come out of the
woods, to start all that up again, to relinquish for good and for
all the possibility of circling back to the brook in the swamp.

Although he was careful not to appear too interested as he
was passing closest to the house, he was aware that a man was
walking down to intercept him. The man was dressed in tan
like a soldier and gave, even from a distance, the impression of
authority. When Ken could no longer pretend the man wasn't

there, he turned and saw him hung about with the signs of his trade: whistle, badge, handcuffs, and gun. He was a very large man.

"Good morning, sheriff," Ken said hastily. "Something I can do for you?" Ready or not, he was wrenched out of the woods.

"Routine matter," the sheriff said. "I see you been fishing. Mind if I check your catch?" His eyebrows twitched when he talked. They were enormous. Grizzled and tangled and wiry, they jutted a good inch and a half from his forehead, a positive thicket.

"As easily done as said." Ken smiled weakly. He had been very foolish to be alarmed. After all, sheriffs might appear anywhere, even here, little as he liked to think it. "I haven't so much as seen a fish," he said. "The streams are too high with all this rain. I've had a fine walk though."

"Well, that's something," the sheriff said. "But I might as well check your fishing permit while I'm at it."

"Of course," Ken said. "It's in my pack here." His pack was really his oilskins and sou'wester rolled up around his spartan lunch and an elegant silver flask full of whiskey. It was a hip flask he found few opportunities to carry but always kept full against contingencies that never seemed to arise.

"Nonresident permit. Seems to be OK," the sheriff said. "And did you hike in or drive?"

"Drove part way," Ken said.

"Well, if I check your driver's license and registration I won't have to do it next time I see you out on the highway," the sheriff said. "Ah, yes," he said as he examined the papers, "that clears that up. Your car was spotted in the woods over in back of the ridge, and we thought it just might be stolen and abandoned."

"You sure keep an eye on things," Ken said, laughing without reservation.

"That's what we're here for," the sheriff said. "And if you're headed for your car now, you're a little out of your way—not much, but a little. That where you're headed?"

"Why, yes," Ken said, "I am."

"All you have to do is go on along here—oh, half a mile or so—and turn right at the crossroad. That will take you straight over the ridge."

"Much obliged," Ken said.

"Don't mention it." The sheriff stepped back to give Ken passage. "But wait a minute," he said. "If you've been fishing through there, perhaps you can give us a little help." His eyes swept over the country Ken had been crossing.

"Glad to—if I can," Ken said.

"Well, did you by any chance see or hear anything unusual there?"

"No, I'm sure not," Ken said. "Something wrong?"

"The fact is," the sheriff said, "we're forming a big search party to go into the woods to look for a lost baby."

"Good Lord," Ken said. He glanced toward the trees. They were close together along the edges of the clearing, and there was much underbrush. Flecks of darkness showed everywhere.

"Some of us have been out all night, but now we're trying to go at it more systematically."

"Yes," Ken said, "that's bad country, some of it. Rivers, swamps, cliffs."

"Did you see any animal sign?" the sheriff said.

"I'm afraid I'm not much of a woodsman," Ken said.

"There's not too much to worry about from animals this time of year. There are bears around, though, and bobcats aren't unknown."

"It looks bad," Ken said.

The sheriff shrugged. "Thanks anyway," he said. "Straight along here and right at the crossroads." He began to turn away.

"Wait," Ken said. "I wonder if you could use me to fill a place in your line?"

The sheriff stopped and faced Ken again. "Why, that's very kind, I'm sure. We need every man we can get. Come on up to the house and have some coffee. It will be a little while before we can get started. I have to radio my deputy to stop watching your car. We need him for other things now, but it was just possible that the thief—if there had been one—would have come back to the car. And you must tell me if you saw any other fishermen in there this morning. They might be able to tell us something." He led off toward the house.

"I'm afraid I can't help you there," Ken said. "I haven't seen anybody since I drove in yesterday. I went back to sleep in the car, but I haven't seen a soul."

"Well, we'll just say you've scouted that section for us, and we'll start on something else."

The sheriff walked through the crowd of men to a police car parked on the lawn in front of the house. He unlocked the car and got in and began to use the radio. Ken had followed along in his wake and found himself close to the car and quite in the center of the group. As he waited for something to happen, it seemed to him that he was being stared at, but he decided that the men were really looking past him at the car. Even so, in order not to cross glances with them, a roughly dressed crowd, he magnetized himself to the car and stared straight ahead at an enormous red ear with a great dangling lobe. Among the messages relating to the search, Ken heard directions being given for taking the guard off his car.

Then the car door opened, and the sheriff stepped out. He had put on horn-rimmed glasses while he was using the radio, and he looked rather like a professor who might have been a third-string tackle once upon a time. "All right," the sheriff said. "This field has got to be searched." He pointed to a large hayfield south of the house. "Line up on the other side of the wall."

The sheriff started them off in a line that stretched all across the field. Ken was somewhere near the middle, and he could hear the sheriff close behind him exhorting them to keep the line straight and firm. They went slowly through the tall wet grass, silently, except for the shouts of the sheriff. At the end of the field they crossed the road and came back through two smaller fields there.

As they approached the house, Ken could see the sheriff talking on the radio in his car. He hadn't realized until then how very silent the search had become, only the swish of the grass against his boots and a muffled oath as someone stumbled. The sheriff was standing beside his car when they gathered around. "They're sending an airplane," he said. "We'll wait for it."

"What'll we do till it gets here?" a man behind Ken shouted. Ken looked at the ground so no one would think he had spoken.

"Wait," the sheriff said without looking up from locking the car door.

The group began to disperse, and Ken turned, not knowing where to go, and found himself standing beside a knot of men squatting at the base of one of the large trees on the lawn. As he glanced down at them, their eyes flicked over him and were at once veiled. He was acutely uncomfortable but couldn't move without at least being able to give himself a good excuse. He looked unhurriedly away and studied his surroundings.

The farm gave the impression that it was gradually dying, that some vital force was drawing inward from the boundaries. The more remote fields were filling up with juniper and pine. The outbuildings were in various stages of disintegration. One, at some distance from the house, had fallen down so long ago that it was now only a mound of vines. Ken couldn't begin to imagine what it might have been. Another small stone building was roofless. It might have been a smokehouse. The farmhouse itself, however, a large house, had surprisingly been painted not many years before—say, at just about the time somebody might have been putting in a lot of overtime in a war plant. There was surely nothing in the farm itself to explain such prosperity. Why, even the barn attached to the house had collapsed recently—at least it showed the same paint job as the house— and lay exactly as it had fallen.

Half a dozen men were poking along the edges of the jumbled timbers, which hadn't yet fallen so far they couldn't fall farther and snap a leg. A line of men sat along the edge of the porch swinging their legs and drinking coffee poured from blue enamel pitchers by women wearing men's jackets and sweaters. Ken wondered which of the women was the mother of the child. None seemed right for the part—no tears or struggle against tears, no words or gestures from the men. More women were busy in the kitchen, but there too he could see no sign. If the thing had happened in his family, his wife would have been either the one organizing the work on the vegetables for the stew or the one at the table with the field telephone. But neither woman seemed young enough to be the mother of a baby. He gave up the futile speculation.

Under each of the large trees on the lawn a small knot of men squatted on their heels and plucked grass-blades or scratched the ground with sticks. Others came and went around the corner of the house by twos and threes. And always more men were coming down the road to join the search.

They came from one direction only because, although the road didn't exactly end at the house, it did become the cart path which became the footpath which lost itself in the woods near the swamp. He glanced involuntarily back over the way he had come. There was a small party of men just disappearing into the scrubby cutover thicket near where he had come out.

"We can search the other field again." Ken, having completed his leisurely inspection of the place, looked down again at the group at his feet. The speaker was a bearded man, a young man with bright blue eyes and weathered skin. He wore a sou'wester like Ken's, but he wore it with a sort of ramshackle authority that Ken knew he could never attain. "If we need something to do, we can search the other field," the bearded man said. "I went through it last night in the dark and twice this morning, and I know how it is to have to sit still. I was here all night, and I stood in that field after everybody went home, and I listened. If there were anything to hear, I could have heard it. I was listening down beyond the far end of the field in the brush just before daylight. There was fog off the brook down there. A buck walked out of the fog, and I put my hand on his side—right on his side—and I could feel him freeze, and then he was gone. Right on his side, he was that close." He was laughing with excitement and his hand was extended so that Ken felt as if he had turned just too late to see the buck spring out from under the reaching hand.

"Every time a new gang gets here, they search that field," the bearded man said. "If the man who's on the west end of the line is a woodsman, they find some big cat tracks along the wall way up in the northeast corner. Mighty big cat tracks. A bobcat will jump a man out of pure meanness. Then they swing around by the barn and find the garden, and that makes them think about the boy—teenager from the village—that was hired yesterday to work in the garden. And while they're thinking about that, they come to a place in the orchard where somebody's been digging. So they send up to the barn for a shovel, and they dig up a calf that died a week ago. Three times I've smelled that calf: it's dead."

"What about the pigs?" one of the other men said.

"Ah, the pigs," the bearded man said, like Socrates, as if he had been thinking about the pigs all along. Ken hadn't thought about them at all and still didn't know what everybody was nodding about.

"Knew a feller had a stroke and fell in the pen and had his leg et off," another man said.

This was such a revelation to Ken that he set off to look for the pigs without wondering at all if he had a good excuse for leaving. As he turned away, the bearded man was saying, "Looks like that gang's getting ready to do something. Guess I better take them through the field."

Knowing there was no point in volunteering for that search party because he'd never be good at finding cat tracks, Ken wandered around to the back of the house and poked selfconsciously into trampled thickets and peered under a rickety boardwalk that ran from the kitchen door to the barn over a patch of marshy ground and some old foundations. He stayed a moment to watch a fire truck pumping out an abandoned well that had been remembered suddenly by an old man who had been a boy on that farm.

At last he found the pigs in the barn. He leaned on the partition and looked at them. They looked at him. With a stick, he poked through their litter for a rag, a tiny shoe, a doll. They rooted around, turning over the straw in a frenzy of protest. He looked at them. They looked at him.

"I say," the man next to him said, "that a strange car up in here would be noticed and remembered."

"I guess you're right," Ken said as if he had at last been convinced, although actually this was another entirely new idea to him. "If a strange car should ever find its way back in here."

"Which I doubt," the man said.

"It doesn't seem likely," Ken said, fighting to keep from putting on a phony Maine accent as he belatedly understood where the strange-car idea put him. It would clearly have been much better if he had gone on his way after the sheriff cleared him.

"Just what I say," the man said. "Mean-looking boar."

"Sure is," Ken said. He looked at them, and they looked at him out of their pig eyes, but he turned his head and went away because they seemed to know he didn't know which was the boar.

Crawling under the skeletons of tractors, climbing into the remains of truck bodies, he came to an orchard where two men were digging. The sheriff was watching glumly. A teenage boy was standing near the hole.

"It's only the calf," the boy said.

"Mmm," one of the men said and went on digging.

"I was right here in the garden all the time," the boy said. "She was talking to me awhile and then she went back around the house."

"Mmm," the other man said. They came to the calf. It was dead.

"Do you suppose," Ken said softly to the sheriff, "that if you took the calf out and dug under it—"

"I read them all the time," the sheriff said, "and I did that the time I dug up the calf: the ground hadn't been touched."

"It was a thought," Ken said.

"I appreciate it," the sheriff said

"They say the pigs are a thought too."

"There're lots of thoughts," the sheriff said, brooding.

"It was nothing but the calf," the boy said.

"Mmm," one of the men said, scraping dirt back into the hole.

The sheriff turned on his heel and started through the garden toward the house. The boy ran after him. "Any clues, sheriff?" he called.

"Not a one," the sheriff said. "This where you were working yesterday?" He stopped and studied the ground.

"Right around here," the boy said.

"She was out here, you say?"

"Her mother sent her out to bother me, and she was playing awhile on the grass under that tree." He pointed to the nearest apple tree. "And then she went around front."

"Around front?" the sheriff said. He looked off in the direction the boy indicated. The barn was between them and the house.

"She was bothering me, so I sent her around to her swing."

"I see," the sheriff said, "but you don't know if she ever got around front?"

"She was headed there," the boy said.

The sheriff headed there, followed by Ken and the boy, but once they were around the corner of the barn, they veered over to the well. A larger group of men was waiting near the pumper now. "How you coming?" the sheriff said.

"Should know pretty soon," a fireman said. "Don't know why they ever gave up this well. It's a corker."

The sheriff moved toward the barn. Ken went with him. The boy stayed at the well. "Think they'll find anything there?" Ken said.

"Not a chance," the sheriff said. "It took two strong men to move some of the junk off that well, and it hadn't been moved before in years."

"Why bother?" Ken said.

"Oh, you always pump out wells. People can see you're doing something, and a lot can happen in the time it takes to pump out a good well. I tell you, Mr. Johnson—"

"Marvin," Ken said.

"What's that?" the sheriff said. He stopped and turned toward Ken.

"Marvin," Ken said. He stood facing the sheriff. "You called me Johnson but my name's Marvin."

"Of course, it is," the sheriff said. "I saw it on your papers. That Johnson business is just something we say around here. We're always saying, 'I tell you, Mr. Johnson.' I don't know why we say it, but we say it all the time, and we say it to everybody. I can tell you your home address, your car registration, and the name of your employer if you want to test me."

Ken didn't make any response because he had a sudden vision of the sheriff sitting in his car while the men were finishing the search of the hay fields: and the vision, like a dream, told him without words exactly what the sheriff was saying on his car radio and exactly what the answer would be when it came: K. Marvin, this city, guilty of three traffic violations in the past four years, two overtime parking, one red light. Ken could even see the headlines: Local Man Grilled as Sex Fiend Suspect. That would look very good on his record.

"Don't think we don't appreciate your wanting to help," the sheriff said, "but the truth is summer people just don't turn out very much—no offense intended."

"I've got kids of my own," Ken said. He didn't trust himself to try a longer speech. He had all he could do to keep himself from whipping out his billfold and frantically offering up the photographs.

"Well, I'll tell you right out," the sheriff said, "there's one hell of a long line of parked cars back along the road there, and there's only one car within miles that doesn't have a Maine number plate on it, and it's my business to know how many summer families there are around here."

"Yeah," Ken said cautiously.

"I'm sorry," the sheriff said. He laid his hand gently on Ken's arm. "Here I am blowing off to the wrong guy. Isn't that just the way life is? Hell, man, I'm just the one who wouldn't want to face his own wife and kids if he didn't do his share up here on the mountain."

"Yeah," Ken said. "Especially since I know the area." The sheriff tried to be impassive but he didn't make it, and Ken knew at once that he had said too much. "I've fished through here a couple of times before." The sheriff managed to be impassive this time, but his eyes did flick toward the brush at the end of the field where the fog had been earlier in the morning. "Mostly on the other side of the ridge," Ken said and quit.

"Every experienced woodsman counts at a time like this," the sheriff said. Ken was through talking for a while, but the sheriff seemed not to notice. "I hope you won't mind if I ask a personal question," the sheriff said. Fortunately he didn't wait to see if Ken was going to be able to give the only possible answer. "I mean it helps in my work sometimes if I'm able to place a man by his accent, and I don't get much chance to talk to people from your state, you see what I mean? I mean is your accent typical of your state?"

"Good lord, no," Ken said. He rushed ahead, sensing an opportunity to make himself a little less foreign. "Why, I'm practically a local boy, born and raised not thirty miles from Boston."

"That's what I figured," the sheriff said. "And I wouldn't mention it if I were you. Just a friendly tip, you know, but we're too close to Boston here and get a lot of the wrong kind of summer people—no offense. There was a lot of trouble last summer with a gang of queers that rented a place on the lake. They went around with lipstick on and like that. I got them out of town before anybody got hurt. But Boston just isn't popular around here if you don't mind. A man like you, trying to raise a decent family, knows all about that."

They had been standing between the well and the barn. Now the sheriff dropped Ken's arm and they went on together into the barn. People made room for them as they stepped up to look at the pigs. "Mean-looking bugger, sheriff." It was the same man who had said it to Ken before, only now he had a long stick and was scratching the back of the pig he obviously meant. Ken looked at the boar, but the boar wasn't interested in him.

"Mean enough," the sheriff said.

"Going to butcher the lot or just him?" the man said.

"Not any of them for a while," the sheriff said. "Not until we get the well checked out anyway."

"Can't wait too long or it won't do any good," the man said. "You'll never know what they et." Ken was afraid he'd throw up, so he began to work his way out of the barn.

"Another hour won't matter," the sheriff said. "I had the ag department on the phone last night. We've got plenty of time."

"Any strangers been noticed up in here?" the man was saying. Ken didn't hear what the sheriff said in reply. He was already out of the barn. He wanted only to keep on going and get the hell out of there altogether and find his car and go home, but as he came around the corner of the house he saw how impossible it would be to sneak off.

The lawn was now entirely covered with men. Women were serving coffee and doughnuts on the porch. Ken wanted a cup of coffee, but he didn't take it because he was too flustered to be able to tell if it would look funnier if he did or if he didn't. Everyone seemed to be pretending not to watch him. He drifted back to the group around the bearded man.

"Henry knows pigs," the bearded man said. "What do you say, Henry."

"No," Henry said. He was dressed all in heavy denim and wore knee-length leather boots. His hair curled over his collar like a woman's.

"See?" the man with the beard said. "Henry says no."

"No blood," Henry said. Everyone waited. "A pig will toss," he said, "and a pig will shake, and a pig will splatter blood all over the walls. Rats, snakes, a dog one time. Always blood. No blood, no."

"There's a winter's eating on those pigs," the man with the beard said. "These people will be awful hungry by spring if we kill their pigs. Poor bastard lost enough on the hay we trampled. Kill his pigs too and he'll really have something to come home to—no pigs, no hay, lost kid, wife out of her head up there." He raised his eyes toward an upper window of the house.

"Where is he?" Ken said in spite of knowing he ought not to open his mouth.

"Hospital," the man with the beard said.

"How come?" Ken said.

"Cut off his leg with a chain saw," one of the others said.

"They better lay off the pigs," the man with the beard said. He started to get up.

"Sheriff knows it well as I do," Henry said.

The man with the beard stood up and turned, as if it had been his intention from the beginning, to watch a small yellow aeroplane that flew low over the house and out over the south field, slewing heavily through the air like a car in snow.

The sheriff appeared at the corner of the house, striding toward his car. He unlocked the car and reached in for the handset of his radio. "It's about time," he said, looking at the plane as if the pilot could read his face as well as his voice. "The well is dry and in another ten minutes it would have been the pigs and then God knows. Have him stay low and in sight of the house as much as possible." He put the handset away and locked the car. "Now there's one thing we haven't tried," he said, "and it's something they can't cover from the air. I mean the fence rows."

"OK," the man with the beard said.

"No," the sheriff said. "I want you to stay here, George, and be ready to lead a party at a moment's notice. This field's about played out."

"Gottcha," the man with the beard said. "That cutover land due north of here up to the foot of the cliffs. We stayed out of there because it's too thick for a man to force his way through very well, but a child down low might get through. There was a bear in there last fall."

"Henry—" the sheriff began

"Power line right of way," Henry said.

"Right," the sheriff said. "But not until I give the word. You'll need two big parties, and I'll need a small one. Hey, kid, come on and make yourself useful. Earn that cup of coffee." He spoke this time to the boy who had been working in the garden.

"I'm with you, sheriff," the boy said. He came over with his coffee cup in one hand and a stack of doughnuts in the other.

"See that you stay with me," the sheriff said. "I may need messages carried." He looked to see who else to take.

"I'll go with you, sheriff," Ken said. He didn't know what he thought he was thinking. Perhaps he wasn't thinking at all. Perhaps he just couldn't bear to discover that the sheriff really would pick him after the kid.

"OK," the sheriff said, as if it were a matter of no importance to him. He barely glanced at Ken before he went on picking his men. One of his men was the man who had twice called the boar mean looking.

"Why me?" the man said. "Why not some of these guys who haven't been out once even. Is that fair?"

"No," the sheriff said, "it's not fair. But that's the way it is. There's nothing fair about a kid being lost in the woods and God knows what else besides. And there's nothing fair about the stores that are closed today and the farm work that is piling up, but there are a lot of men who know that fair or not they've got themselves to shave tomorrow morning, and that's a pretty tough job when you can't look yourself in the face."

The man flushed. "OK," he said, "so I'll raise a beard." He was obviously trying to make a joke of the whole thing.

"Ask George Booth about beards," the sheriff said. "He'll tell you how much trouble they are." He laughed.

"I feel like a jerk," the man said under his breath.

"So what," the sheriff said, "as long as you aren't a jerk?"

Ken saw now that he had gained nothing by volunteering and wished he had forced the sheriff to make a move and perhaps, one way or the other, put an end to all this cat and mouse. Well, he wouldn't stand for any more of that. He knew how it would be in the woods, men straggling off in all directions and at all paces until he was left alone. It would be a simple matter then to straggle over to his unguarded car and be clear of the state before he was missed. Then he would very shortly be talking about this day with somebody, his wife perhaps, telling it as a funny story, perhaps, reducing it to words—but could he really, to his wife, of all people, ever say actually, "In Maine they thought I looked like—well—like a degenerate?"

The kid stood beside him while they waited for the sheriff to get ready. "I seen it all," the kid said, "only there wasn't nothing to see."

Even when the sheriff had his men picked out and had given final instructions to George and Henry and had inquired when the stew would be ready, he still hesitated. He said to Ken, "Look, I feel like a bastard, you having been so cooperative and all, but truth is, not knowing you, you see what I mean, but what I did was let the air out of one of your tires. That was before we knew whose car it was, and we didn't want it going anywhere while we weren't looking. I feel bad about that now, believe me, and what I'd like to do is have one of my men go by there and put on your spare for you."

"No, no," Ken said.

"No trouble," the sheriff said. "I've got to send a man over past there anyway."

"Please, no," Ken said.

"It would be very kind of you," the sheriff said, "to let me do this in order to make up for what I thought—in the line of duty, of course—but still I feel pretty rotten about it now."

"What can I say?" Ken said aloud to the sheriff and repeated silently to himself. At least the deputy would be finished there long before Ken could walk back to the car. It would still work out.

"Thank you," the sheriff said. "I'd have felt very bad if I couldn't have done anything."

"No," Ken said automatically, "thank you."

"I'll need the car keys," the sheriff said, "to get the spare out of the trunk. Don't worry, my man will be back with the keys long before we get out of the woods."

Ken silently handed over the car keys. It was just possible that the sheriff meant only what he said and that he wasn't simply confiscating the keys.

The sheriff turned with the keys in his hand and crossed the lawn to what looked like a state trooper. The two men spoke

together. Ken couldn't hear what was said, but he saw the
trooper nod and start back up the road toward another police
car. The sheriff came back empty-handed.

The sheriff led his group to the corner of the wall near the
garden. He put two men on each side of the west wall and
started them off to the north, and he put two men on each side
of the south wall and started them off to the east. Ken was on
the south side of the south wall with the kid. The sheriff himself stayed on that side of the wall.

When Ken got to the end of the first field, the sheriff was
waiting to offer him a cigarette. Ken took it and the sheriff held
out his lighter, snapping it as he reached toward Ken's face.
The lighter didn't work, and the sheriff withdrew his hand,
peering at the lighter and continuing to snap it. "Must be the
flint," he said. He put his hand into his pocket and pulled out a
fistfull of change and disintegrating Kleenex and keys. Among
the keys, Ken saw the keys to his own car.

"A dime will fix it," the sheriff said and picked a dime out of
the mess in his hand.

Ken didn't trust himself to say anything. He was afraid his
voice might show his terror or, even worse, his triumph as he
thought of the secret key stuck up inside a bumper guard.

The sheriff tried his lighter again. It flamed at once. They
both lighted their cigarettes. "You people continue along here,"
the sheriff said. "I'm going to go over and see how they're making out along the other wall."

Ken nodded. All he had to do now was lose the kid, and he'd
be off. He could change the tire in five minutes—if it really was
flat—unless, of course, the sheriff was making it too easy for
him to make a move. It might be just as well to wait a bit and
see what way the wind was blowing. And when he did make his
move, the sheriff, with the keys safe in his pocket, would never
be looking for that particular move.

It would be easy to lose the kid, Ken discovered, once they
got started again, because whenever the going got in the least
rough, the kid would make long detours away from the wall.
He'd miss fifty yards of wall in order to avoid a briar patch or a

blow down. Ken, who found himself caught up in the search, was irritated that he wasn't free to come down on him sharply and doubly irritated because he supposed the kid thought him a fool for looking carefully in even the most impossible places.

The going got rougher and rougher way down in back where the fields had long since been allowed to revert to woods— except for the walls there was no way of telling they had ever been fields. In fact, they had had time to grow a crop of timber and be cut over and grow up again in brambles.

He crawled and climbed and bulled his way through, often walking on top of the ruinous wall. Stones rolled under his feet, logs crumbled, vines wrapped themselves around his legs. He was soaked with sweat. He took off his windbreaker and began to get chilled. His legs were trembling when at last the entire party reassembled at the farthest corner of the last conceivable lot. Just beyond that wall the land dropped suddenly into a swamp.

The sheriff didn't look at the swamp, but he did look at his watch and said, "I guess that's it. The stew should be ready by now."

Ken was surprised that he hadn't made his break before this, but at the moment he was too exhausted to strike out by himself. The search had led them off in quite the wrong direction anyway, and he'd have to go back past the house to reach his car; so he stumbled along behind the others.

The fire truck was gone from beside the well. The barn stood empty. Ken ducked into the barn for a good belt of whiskey. The pigs lay sleeping in their pen. Someone had dragged an old fashioned grindstone out into the middle of the barn floor. As he tilted his head back and looked along his flask he saw the worn and darkened handle and part of the freshly burnished blade of a knife projecting from a timber not a foot from his head. Still holding the flask, he took the knife and hid it among some boards stacked off to one side. Then he had another drink and went around to the front of the house.

There was a long line of men waiting for stew, but Ken was able to get a cup of coffee without waiting, and he sat down to eat his sandwiches. He knew when he leaned his back against the tree that he'd had it. He was afraid he might not be able to walk all the way back to his car even if he got his chance.

Around on the other side of the tree, the sheriff was talking with the bearded man. "How'd it go?" the sheriff said.

"Just fine," the bearded man said. "They began going home just after you left. Can't be more than a hundred still here."

"Did you search over north and along the power line?"

"Didn't get to it."

"Then we've got that to do this afternoon," the sheriff said.

"Some Boy Scouts brought a St. Bernard."

"After all this rain?"

"It would just make a big circle in the field and keep coming back to the barn," the man with the beard said. Ken looked instinctively toward the barn where several men poked thoughtfully at the fallen timbers.

"That's an idea too," the sheriff said. "Things quiet otherwise?"

"Just fine." The Boy Scouts filed past with mess kits full of steaming stew.

"Here comes my old lady," the man with the beard said. "She's going to scalp me for all this time up here."

"Hello, sheriff," a woman said. "You getting any work out of him?"

"Couldn't do without him, Mrs. Booth," the sheriff said. Ken, who had lately felt a passion for scrutinizing other marriages, turned frankly around to see what the bearded man's old lady would look like. She was a very pretty woman, a little older than he would have guessed, which only meant he had been fooled by the beard into thinking the bearded man looked older than he was. Except for a gingham apron she was dressed for the woods: boots, jeans, and jacket.

When Ken turned around to look at the woman, the sheriff spotted him. "There you are," the sheriff said. "Feel up to tackling the power line this afternoon?"

"I'm afraid my legs are shot," Ken said. "I'm afraid I've had it."

"I tell you what," the sheriff said, "if you still feel like help-ing—"

"Of course," Ken said as quickly as possible.

"What I need is to have somebody stay at the radio this afternoon, somebody steady and reliable. I'll show you how to work it, and you can rest all afternoon and still be a big help, OK?"

"Of course," Ken said. "Glad to do what I can." At least he'd have a few hours, while he sat in his goldfish bowl, to try to make some kind of plan, to decide whether it would be worse to ask for a lawyer too soon or too late. He was already certain he couldn't prove his innocence of any charge that might be brought against him.

"I'm going to bring George some stew," the woman said. "How about you, sheriff?"

"Much obliged," the sheriff said.

Henry, the pig expert, was going off around the corner of the house together with the man from the barn—the one who had twice called the boar mean looking—and half a dozen other men. George's wife was already coming back with a bowl in each hand when everyone heard a horn blowing in the distance. At first it sounded like a short-circuited horn, but then they could tell it was someone making a racket. The car was clearly coming all the way to the house. They could hear the racing motor now. Men began moving toward the road to see. Some began running. Ken was literally unable to move. The sheriff stood up and came around the tree until he stood beside Ken. His bowl was just at Ken's eye level. It was a very real bowl of stew, steaming hot. The random size of the chunks of potato and carrot and meat was convincing. The color of the liquid was genuine, never made with food coloring. It looked like the stew they used to have at home.

A small black car careered up onto the lawn. An old woman was leaning out the window screaming, "The child is found," as if she had been waiting all her life to scream something out the window of a speeding car.

There was no more time. The steam from the sheriff's bowl

drifted gently between Ken and the car. "Let it be a bear," Ken said.

"What did you say?" the sheriff said.

"The child is found safe," the woman screamed.

There was a cheer. "Lucky kid," the sheriff said. He cheered. The kid stopped gobbling his stew long enough to cheer briefly. The man with the beard cheered with one arm around his cheering wife. Ken cheered. He picked himself up.

"Your keys," the sheriff said, digging in his pocket and bringing out Ken's keys. "Your car's all ready to go. My man even took the flat in and blew it up, so you're all ready to go."

"Thanks," Ken said. He felt expansive now that he had beaten the sheriff at his own game; besides there was nothing to be gained by calling the man a liar.

The old woman ran tottering from the car to where the sheriff stood. "The child is found safe," she gasped. "Just walking out of the woods. On the other side of the mountain." The old woman turned and waved her arms over the crowd. "Safe," she screamed, "safe, safe," and subsided without transition into an elegant Victorian faint.

Women rallied to her and hid her completely. Ken and the sheriff were elbowed into the background. "I almost forgot," the sheriff said. He reached into another pocket. "When my man was fooling around with the jack, this fell out of somewhere." It was the secret key.

"Thanks," Ken said with a difference.

"It was the least we could do after the way you pitched in," the sheriff said.

"Anytime," Ken said.

"Lots of people don't look at it that way. They don't like to get mixed up in things."

"Anytime," Ken said. But he was deathly afraid.

Take the "A" Train

BY DONALD DeLILLO

DOWN in the shallow light at the foot of the stairs he saw his shadow. He followed it down and across the floor and pushed stomach-first through the turnstile. The train was here: Lexington Avenue Express. He got on and got a seat. There were three others in the car—a man, two women. The lights blinked on and off, and two weary fans corkscrewed slowly. There was a newspaper on the seat across the aisle. He read the headline: YANKS SPLIT—his eyes steady on the paper as the lights flashed back: DROP TO SECOND—as they flared again. Now he closed his eyes and his head tumbled down, nodding, nodding, nodding, against his chest.

Cavallo was thirty-eight years old, a heavy hairy man, dark and simian: neckless, hump-shouldered, zoo-faced. He had three dollars in his pocket, nothing anywhere else. He had given his money to bookies and borrowed more from loan sharks to give back to bookies, and now he owed a lot to the ones he had borrowed from. An hour ago, climbing the stairs to his apartment in a garlic-and-oil Bronx tenement, he had looked up and seen the landlord waiting at the top of the landing. "Hey, Caval'," the old man said, "Ima joost on my way to calla the cops. Noomber one, eighty-five dollar I gotta comin' from you. You no pay, you no live here no more. Noomber two, two men was here to looka for you. Tree times they come today. They no look like they interested to play gin rummy with you. I no want trouble. You pay me now or I calla the cops." Cavallo had turned and gone down the stairs and out of the building. The neighborhood was dead; fish markets dry and padlocked, pastry shops dark, vegetable crates in off the streets for the night. He went south along Third Avenue all the way down to 149th Street. He saw the entrance to the subway. He knew he could sleep there. He knew he could stay underground and sleep.

Now, striking his mind behind closed eyes was the soft cyclic friction of white-black, white-black as the lights pulsed, faded, pulsed again. His thoughts, coming slow and blunt in glacial mass, were infused with sleep-heavy sounds. Whispering fan-blades paddled the air; from a rangeless distance doors opened on silence, held, rumbled, clamped shut with a sharp quick crack of finality; beneath him the train wheels, crackling acety-lene sparks, railsplitting black steel, ripped sleep up and out from the bottom of his mind. He stretched, opened overcast eyes. Grand Central, he thought. Then 14th, then Brooklyn Bridge, then Fulton. Then what? Chambers? Wall? Six or seven people got on, and the train started. Two of the passengers, an old man and a woman, started to talk; their words, slow and scaly, dropped to the floor like dandruff. He closed his eyes again, hearing voice upon voice, thought upon slumbering thought, thinking: what do I do now; where do I go; who will help me? He knew the answers. Nothing, nowhere, nobody. This is the way it begins, he thought. Before you know it you're a bum sleeping on the subway like the bums you see all the time in bars and in the street sprawled like dead men, and all at once you're one of them. Sprawled like dead men, he thought, as voices like voices in dreams sounded from a long way off. He had never done it before, slept on a train. He had never even thought about the possibility of doing it, in the way that you never really think of suicide until your temple beats to the touch of cold metal or the bedbug street comes up fast to close your bulging eyes. This is the way it begins, going to the last stop, to Brooklyn, and then back, and back in some part of your

mind seeing two men you've never seen, movie gangsters who
know how to hurt you just enough to keep you interested. So
you stay down, he thought; down in the dark: as now the voices
and tunnel sounds went dead, and sleep, vast and tidal, thundered through his mind; and then was stilled: and silence now;
now nothing.

Complexities of textures. Within the shapes inside the mind
he saw flurries of light, deadlocks in motion, a fast black face, a
folded newspaper beneath a short-sleeved arm—images separated from the shadow of a dream. He rubbed the back of his
neck to arouse complete consciousness. The car was crowded;
above him, people swayed from straps. Morning, he thought,
Rush hour. And he tried to remember the night before, but the
memory was a mirror veined with cracks. There was a time of
coming up out of sleep steeped in morphic visions deep beneath
the hearing of a voice: *last stop pal end of the line*; then a surrender again to brief sleep and a time of waking and walking
down steps, under tracks, up again, recalling now the reading of
signs: *Atlantic Ave., Flatbush Ave.*, not sure now which one it
was, or whether it was both or neither; and finally an obscure
dawn sense-impression of other trains, other sleeps, the nightmare cry of wheels screaming round the bend of dreams, and
the terrible feeling now of the mind opening on the prolonga-
tion of oblivion, like the opening of whisky-red eyes on the ruptured memory of a night in some sad Bronx bar.

Reading the street names at each stop, he realized he was on
a Seventh Avenue local, going downtown. What day is it? Friday: payday. But not for me, not for Angelo. It made no difference; one week's salary—especially his salary, maintenance
man's salary, maintenance man's salary who works in a Bronx
Department store—wouldn't even begin to get him out of the
hole. He got off at Times Square. People were everywhere, sleep-
faced, quickstepping, up and down stairs, in and out of trains,
everywhere, every inch. Cavallo bulled up a flight of stairs to the
next level. He found a food counter; had coffee and two doughnuts; left no tip. After going to the men's room, he got on another train. Just as he sat down, the woman next to him asked if

this were the train to New Lots Avenue. "I don't know," he said, and, thinking that she might consider him stupid, or unfriendly, thinking even that she saw through him, that she realized he didn't know where he was going simply because he was going nowhere, added: "This is my first trip to New York."

The woman, pale-blond and slim, a lean, high-cheekboned face, reminded him of his wife. Helen. He hadn't thought about Helen for a long time now. So now I'm thinking about her, he thought. So, so what? They had met in 1945, in England, where he was stationed during the war. When he was discharged they came to New York and were married. After the ceremony—they had to kneel outside the altar rail because Helen wasn't Catholic—everyone went to the banquet hall, a mammoth loft near the Bronx Zoo where the CYO fights were held every Wednesday night. Now, in the pure perspective of so many years, he saw the wedding reception as a smiling snapshot of everything he wanted his life to be: a good big slow meal with the wife, then maybe some of the family coming over to pay lotto or cards or something; good wife, good family, lots of laughs, lots of beer.

The antipasto came and quickly went; the soup vanished symphonically—great oceanic droolings and slurpings; next was the ravioli, son-om-a-gun, only five to a customer; nobody finished the rubber-breasted chicken—nobody ever did. Waiters carried in pitchers of beer, bottles of rye, cake, ice cream, coffee. Children got restless, ran through the hall in squirrel packs. Young men threw olives at each other, and the unmarried girls without dance partners went swift as lizards along the wall to the ladies' room where they stayed a long time. Now it was getting to be time for la tarantella and the band went into it suddenly, all brass and abrupt as a blowout. Everyone cheered, and the old men were up first, twirling their moustaches, strutting over to their wives like vaudeville dancemen. "Angelina, come-a dance la tarantell' con su amore." A coy squeal: "No no no no. Ima too fat. I fall down go boom." But after a few manly winks, some heftings of dead wifely weights and many sly pinches of bottom as big as planets, they were all up, the old and the fat, hands on hips, feet sedately tapping, arms entwined now, heads thrown back, hands clapping, feet stamping, the women's breasts careening like weather balloons, faster and faster they danced, circle within circle, up and down and around, a stampede of giggling elephants, ten, twenty, thirty couples whirling and wheeling as the young people laughed, clapped, got up and joined, and it was one big circle now, round and round, faster and faster, a merry-go-round of shouts and music and laughter, and Cavallo, watching, realized it was all for him, and he took Helen's hand and smiled an enormous white smile. This was the way it would always be. This was the way. Good wife, good family, lots of laughs, lots of beer. No, he would never forget that night. It was one of the few things left to remember.

There was a drunk sitting across the aisle with a bottle set between his feet. The train lurched, and it fell; a slim red river of wine coiled down the floor. The man sadly followed its course with his slippery eyes. Cavallo watched the other people in the car look away—to the floor, the posters, the ceiling. The bottle started to roll, and the man, trying to get up and go after it, bumped against the woman next to him.

"Be careful," she said; then, addressing a footnote to everyone in the car: "Some people belong in jail."

The drunk eased his head up and around and looked at her with the derelict's classic contempt for respectability. "Screw you, lady," he said.

The others, temporarily interested, looked away again—an instantaneous shifting of viewpoints. Cavallo got up, walked over to the man, looked down into his rusty face. A short left to the head and he'd go to sleep. But now the woman stood up, quickly, and went to the other end of the car. Cavallo, glancing into the dirt-smeared window above the drunk's head, understood the reason. His face, rippling in dim reflection as the train bucked and heaved, was a face belonging to something you find sitting in some doorway in the Bowery: eyes vague and far back; black stubble; dirty-little-boy's cheeks and forehead. He knew she considered them two of a kind, him and the drunk; she was running away from both of them. He was a bum, all right. Now it was official. At the next stop he got off.

He rode all day. He rode locals, expresses, shuttles; he went to places he had never even heard of: Hoyt Street, Zerega Avenue, Astor Place. At each stop he read the street name and after a while he started reading them backwards. lanaC teertS. dnarG esruocnoC. He rode with beach-bound kids carrying blankets and portable radios, with mortar-faced laborers who got off early, and, from 14th Street up, with the bargain hunters from Klein's, the female riot squad, women who you swore could play guard or tackle with any team in pro football, here using loaded shopping bags and bundles and an occasional lethal umbrella to get to the nearest seat. He stayed underground and rode, changing trains, even systems—IRT, BMT, IND—but never going up to street level, staying down below in his warm moist cleft within the anonymous press of bodies. At 42nd Street he got off and walked through a tunnel into the lower level of Grand Central Station. Commuters running for different trains crisscrossed in intricate football patterns, and the gates that clapped shut behind them locked them like the gates to the state pen in old Cagney prison pictures. He went past a bakery, a model home built to actual dimensions, through another tunnel and past a cocktail lounge, a clothing store, and a barber shop. As he walked down a flight of steps to the men's room, he realized that a man could live his entire life here, here in this compact civilization beneath the earth. It was something to think about.

You can never figure out where anything begins. You can never figure it out, anything, where it begins. He was riding again, chewing a sawdust hamburger he had just bought. The beginning of becoming a bum was what was going through his mind. After it happens you wonder where or how, not even knowing until it happens that there was a where or a how. But there was, he thought. Maybe it was Helen walking into the house at three o'clock in the morning one morning about six years after they were married. Cavallo was sitting drinking a can of beer, waiting. "Angelo," she said, "I don't love you any more. I love another man." Just like that. I love another man. He threw the beer can at her.

Maybe that was it. Maybe it was Helen. After the divorce he was no good. Single again—who needed it? She had been a barricade between himself and the end of himself; beyond that point was nothing but loneliness, and now, without her here, he had to walk into it. She was not pretty, and her taut, staccato accent made him think of toothpaste being squeezed in rapid spurts from a tube. But she was someone to talk to, listen to, sleep with, smile at sometimes, walk nowhere with, drink beer with on Friday nights when he came home from work with the big buck-and-a-quarter pizza from Luigi's, touch in bed at night—the things you forget the next day, remember ten years from now. Every empty minute was stretched unbelievably by the reality of not seeing her again. Then, slowly, like the fragment of a childhood dream that tilts from the memory and falls finally away to nothing, she disappeared completely. He started bringing home small pizzas. Seventy-five cents.

An old colored blind man came tap-tapping down the aisle with a tin cup in his hand. Again Cavallo watched the falling of faces; people studied the floor, their eyes sweeping its length slowly and tentatively, as though detecting land mines. Clink clink clink. Somebody dropped some change in.

"God bless you, son," the old man said, low.

Son. How did he know it was a man who had put the money in? Maybe the old bastard's a fake, not really blind. Gotta watch out for fakes. Never know who's blind, who isn't. If he isn't, that old man, would he say *son* to me? Do I look like somebody's son? Not to my father. A bum for a son. That's what he used to say. I got a bum for a son. That was another thing he had not thought about for a long time now. His father. Maybe he was saving his father to think about. Maybe his father was the beginning of sleeping on trains, and he was saving thinking about him until now, until he had something to hate him for. A few feet away, a fat woman clodding mountainously toward the closing doors collided with the blind man. The cup hit the floor, and scattering coins wheeled, spun, fell dead. A half dollar expired at Cavallo's feet. He thought of the money he had left, then quickly looked at the other people as they helped the old man gather his coins. He stepped on the half dollar and, simultaneously, his mind tried to divorce itself from that swift terrible movement. Thoughts, like carousel steeds, turned mechanically, going nowhere, then suddenly stopped at this: *a bum for a son.*

Helen was afraid of the old man, he remembered. Cavallo couldn't blame her. There was a lot to be afraid of, a lot to hate. "For why you come here?" he said to them once as they walked in for Sunday dinner, Helen strategically carrying the perennial peace offering—a box of Italian pastry. "For your mama's spaghetti because your wife no can cook? Or for your old man's money because you no can find good job? Some son, my Angelo. This country big country. Lots jobs. Even carpenter like me make so much money in one week that in old country I dropa dead joost to look at it. But you, my son, no can find good job. What you do in that big store full of crazy womans looking for bloomers? Ride-up-a-down, up-a-down, carry bundle, fixa lights, sweepa floor. Then you come to me, to old man, for money so you can buy perfume for the wife so she smell like bar of soap. Bull-a-shit. You my son. Figlio mio. But no more money you get from me. No more, goddamn."

Cavallo wanted to walk out, but he thought about the money. After dinner he would take the old man aside and explain the situation. Just two hundred, pa. We need a few odds and ends here and there. We'll pay you back. I'm due for a raise. Middle of next month. We'll pay you back then. Promise. Middle of next month That was what he would say. And, in the end, the old man would give. So he didn't walk out. Instead he sat down to eat, across from his father who was at the head of the table, the throne. Cavallo's mother set a plate in front of the old man. He took one look and then joined his thumb and forefinger and twirled them against his cadaverous white cheek. It was capozzela—the head of a lamb. Cavallo saw Helen wince as his father picked up the red, white-eyed skull and kissed it.

"Che bellezza!" he said. "The most beautiful goddamn lamb I
ever see." Then he scooped out one of the eyes, put it in his
mouth and started to chew. "Ahhh," he said, "joosta like one of
mama's big brown nipples." Helen got up and left the room.
"Whatsa the trouble with her?" he said. "In England, they no
teach young lady to say scooza me when she go take a leak?"

"Pa," Cavallo said, "why do you have to do things like that?
Why do you have to get her upset all the time?"

The old man stopped chewing. "Who get who upset? I no
can even eat in peace in my own goddamn house, goddamn.
How you want me to eat the eyes; with knife and fork? You
listen to me, Angelo. I tell you something. She is a stranger,
that woman. She is not of us. She no belong here. Why she no
give you kids? A woman is to give kids. She no give kids, she no
woman. She no even smell like woman. A bar of soap you are
married to, Angelo. She is to wash hands with, that woman.
Where you find her; on shelf in English supermarket? I do not
make joke. You want to come-a this house anymore, you leave
her home."

"But, pa," Cavallo said, "she's my wife. She'll give me kids.
All we need is a little money. I know you worked hard for what
you got, but what good's it doing you with cobwebs growing on
it in some bank?"

The old man pointed a long, granitic finger. "You shut upa
you face," he said, "you son-om-a-beetch."

All right. That was the end of it. He didn't see his parents for
three years after that. But something in him slammed to a halt.
His mother's face, round and brown as a meatball, spun down
the long alley of his dreams. His father—Cavallo thinking of
him gaunt and bent years ago down in their dark cellar whit-
tling a magnificent walnut chest for the living room—
hammered nails of remembering into his mind. He thought of
the long winter walks through the zoo, and much later, just before the war, sitting in the stadium bleachers watching the old
man's hero, Il Cinque, Number Five, the Serene and Classical
DiMaggio, drifting smooth as smoke toward a high high fly.
How do you forget the man who is your father? This was the

thing he thought about more than any other during the time of
not seeing him; this was the thing he could not do, the forgetting, because too many years went into the making of the memory, too many times of love and hate and fear and love again.
This is a turning away that some people can make, he thought,
as he lay in bed one night, a turning away that starts when they
are six and sent to some camp on some mountain every summer
until they are thirteen when they are sent to something called
prep school which lasts until it is time to be sent to college and
then to the army and then to marriage; and this is why they
never have a mother or father, only a two-headed thing called
parents who are only to write letters to, never to touch. There is
no love without touching and feeling, he thought. In their big
old bed when he was a child he hid warm between the two
warm big bodies that made him; his first time in church he
slipped beneath his mother's black dress that smelled like an
old stale sofa, clutching her mighty calves while apocalyptic
Italian women recited the rosary, their voices pessimistic as
stained glass; feeling the pulse of his father's hand on his chest
as he lay hot with scarlet fever, he heard the life-force in that
proud Sicilian voice: "My blood is yours, my little son Angelo.
My strength is your strength. I send forth life into your body.
Feel it fill you with my own manhood. Feel it, Angelo. Breathe
it in, figlio mio. It is yours. I give it to you. You are my son."
How do you forget the man who is your father? How many
nights, deep within the shipwreck of sleep, does he appear, like
Christ, with blood upon his carpenter's hands? His hands. The
touch and feel of his hands. There is no turning away from
flesh, he thought, remembering the afternoon of his thirteenth
birthday when his father, stooped like a question mark over his
worktable in the cellar, suddenly turned to him and said: "Come
here, Angelo, and I will give you the present for your birthday. It
is something which all men must give to their children, and
this is the time when you must have it. In this country they
read it to their young ones from books with long words. No
book I need to tell you this. Take down your pants." Angelo did
it. His father took the boy's organ in his coarse hand. It hurt.

"This is what makes you man. It is not just to go to bathroom
with. It is to put into woman. When you are close to woman
and touch her and move you hands over her, it will get hard as
fist, and burn red like torch. That is all you must know. That is
all there is. The rest is like eat or sleep or go to bathroom. You
do it because it must be done. Remember this day, Angelo. It is
the day of your becoming man. It is the day your father made
you man." And Cavallo, lying in bed, thinking of that hard
hand upon him, that fierce intimacy of flesh, rolled over toward
Helen, slipped his hand beneath her nightgown, up along the
inside of her thigh. "No," she said, moving away. "Not tonight." Again, he thought. Helen tired, Helen sleepy, Helen not
in the mood. The next day, Sunday, after three years, he went
to visit his parents. And a year after that, almost to the day, he
threw the beer can at his wife.

Tap-tap-tap came the cane, louder and louder. The old man
was coming back through the car from the other end. The loud-
speaker crackled: *149th Street, Grand Concourse next.* Cavallo
realized he was on the Jerome Avenue express; it would rise
above the street after the next station. He had to get off. The
blind man was getting closer. Cavallo watched his eyes; a pair of
zeros. He leaned over, still watching, then picked up his foot
and plucked the coin from the floor. The train slowed, and the
tin cup was rattling now a few inches from his face. His fist
clenched tightly, and he could feel the rhythmic substance of
the metal, cold and incredibly large, in his hand. The train
stopped and he got up; the doors skimmed open.

"Getting off," he said. " 'Scuse me. Getting off."

The old man, who up close now smelled the way a thousand
old things smell—old wet dogs, torn old back seats in old cars,
empty booze bottles, bags of garbage in Spanish alleys, a season-
ing of old age and sweat and the same clothes for two weeks—
got out of the way now, and Cavallo was out the door. He inhaled deeply and it felt good. He put the coin in his pocket. He
wondered how long it would be before he smelled like the old
man.

His sixth-grade nun told him once an animal was an animal

because it had nothing to love. God was good because He loved
man. Man was good because he loved God. An animal was not
good, was not bad, because an animal loved nothing, period.
Cavallo had never forgotten it, all about the animals, and sitting on a bench now on the downtown side—he had crossed an
overpass above the tracks to get here—he thought about it
again. He was close to it now, he figured, having nothing, and
having nothing to lose in acting the way an animal acts. It is
like a dream that you know is only a dream. You rape the first
woman you see. There is no retribution in a dream, no God.
But stealing from a blind man was not happening within the
soundings of sleep. Still, it made no difference, not now, not
anymore. There is no beginning to it, he thought. And no end.
Being born is the beginning. And the end is death, hell, eter-
nity, pain, alone forever, nothing. Alone. He had been alone for
nine years, ever since the divorce, too long a time. Who could
survive it? What things could you say to yourself to make loneliness bearable? After a while the quaint bachelor routine was
splayed across the night like a deck of cards. Try to survive the
nine-hour poker games in grim, smoke-gray kitchens; stranded
desperate faces circling the table, clock-tick, coin-ring nibbling
at silence. Survive the beer-stained nights in dead-end bars,
whisky philosophers, the fights on TV, the bartender's fat face,
a fat lone blonde with swampy lips saying, *How 'bout another,
baby.* Try to survive. He had survived the loss of his wife, but
not the loneliness she created, or what she said. *I don't love you
any more. I love another man.* It started when he went back to
seeing his father, borrowing money again. She hated him for it.
But he was weak, he knew it, and there was nothing he could
do. She even got upset when he stopped going to Mass; she said
it was his father's bad example, that everything his father did
was a bad example and bound to catch up with him in the end.
His mother, over a dish of lasagna, casually informed him he
was going to hell. His father waved a gravy-red fork. "Is no
difference," he said. "The females they go church all time because they want to seduce priest. But priest joost like woman.
Even wears black dress. Ha!" Cavallo had told the story to

Helen, but she wasn't amused. "That man is a tarantula," she said. "Step on him before he poisons you." But she did most of the poisoning, he thought now, not sure whether he really believed it. He stood up, hands in pockets, and walked slowly along the platform, trying to align his thoughts. They were jigsaw pieces that would not fit; to be able to sleep and forget, that's all, just to be able to sleep. Here it came now, the train. He got on and sat down; his right hand, still in his pocket, sifted slowly among riotous artifacts—handkerchief, matchbooks, keys—and then touched the cold quick coin. Impulsively he withdrew the hand. He was really blind, he thought. That was all he thought. Just: he was really blind. Then he closed his eyes.

And now, imponderably as wind stirs a curtain, he felt a subtle touch upon his thigh. He snapped awake. They leaped back like garbage-can alley cats. Now he saw them clearly, crouched, weaving slowly now, Puerto Ricans, three of them, just boys, smiling; there was no one else in the car. One of them had a knife; his thumb jerked and the blade flared swift and clean. Cavallo got up.

"Bastards," he said.

"Money," the switchblader said. "Geeve money or we cut you bad."

"Bastards."

They moved in now, slow and small and hunched, pleistocene warriors, not smiling now, their faces tense as pain. Now they came, fast, and he hit the switchblader, crack, square in the teeth. The other two were on him, all over him, and he felt himself going down, arms around his neck, a lightning knee in the groin. He hit hard on his hip, and all three were on him now, all knees and elbows, and he closed his eyes as the first fist hit him. It did not last long, just seconds, and now he felt the weight go away from his chest. The faraway monkey-chatter faded; it was quiet now. He tried to move and could not. He opened his eyes, and the first thing he saw was a big, happy poster above a window. It read: NEW YORK IS A SUMMER FESTIVAL.

Within the clockbeat of some personal midnight, time suddenly stops, and you are left swinging from a noose over a space deep as the lack of God is deep. Now there was nothing left. He was nothing. All that had been left was that he was a thief; it had been something, a name to call oneself. Now he was not even that; he was a thief who had been robbed, a nothing now, a man who was not a man. He did not know where he was. All he knew was the train, and its voice, and the beginnings of a new pain upon his face. He realized he was sitting on one of the seats; he did not know how long he had been there, or how he got there. It made no difference now. "Bury me in a plain coffin, Helen," he had said once. "These air-conditioned Cadillacs they bury people in nowadays are just a waste of money. When you're dead, you're dead. That's all." The people across the aisle were looking at him. He got up, legs cast in concrete, and went over to the door at the end of the car. He looked into the glass panel. The flesh beneath his eyes was distended, and his cheeks were scraped red. He felt far away, not here, not even himself, something cornered far from its hole or tree or cave, about to die; and there they were, tears skating down his reflection in the glass like sweat down an ape's face.

This was Saturday. Two nights and one day, he thought, as he walked slowly through the train, from car to careening car, vaguely aware of several upturnings of faces when he passed. So short a time, yet it seemed as long as all the previous days of his life combined. How much more to go? When will the breath stop short, the lungs surge gaspingly upward, the emptiness fill with tons and eons of darkness? In a far extremity of his mind, suicide glinted needle-hot. Throw yourself under a train. Stop service for a while. A minor inconvenience. Small item in the paper. Unidentified man jumps.

"Look out, buddy, I gotta get off." Cavallo moved out of the man's way.

From platform at. At what? Where is this? He looked out the window, but the train had already started and darkness slid backwards into darkness. No, he could not die that way. Too many years, he thought. Too many times of love. I was baptized. I received First Communion. I was a little boy with a white suit, my first suit, and I kneeled with the others and I said to myself: *I love you, Jesus.* I married a woman who loved me once, and have a mother and father. He remembered the wedding feast, the happy dance of the paisanos. For me they danced. For Angelo. Kill myself and I kill them all, all, forever, the ones who danced one night for me. No, he could not die that way. And his mind shifted sardonically to an additional reason. Animals do not kill themselves. Only things with souls know where to probe for the fatal vein.

On Saturday afternoon, late, down in the subway, nothing much happens. Cavallo sat staring at a spaghetti poster. He could not remember the last time he had eaten; he could not remember enjoying any meal at all since the last time he was at his father's house, two months ago. Before and after that, it had been frankfurters, hamburgers, TV dinners, nothing, nothing at all. He rationed his money carefully so he could play the horses. The only way to beat the horses was a lot of money, and plenty of time to make it work for you. During the week he bet with the neighborhood bookie; on Saturdays he went to the track. He lost steadily. It was just a bad streak; soon he would start picking them right. Wrong. And in the poolroom where he bet they called him Crystal Balls Cavallo. He went to a couple of loan sharks and borrowed money. He had to give the system time to work; bet heavy on the second or third choice to show. You don't win much but you win. Build up some capital and then really start to move. He thought of nothing but horses for two complete weeks. Figure the horse, the odds, the jockey, the weather, the last three times out, the post position, the horse's owner's middle name. Figure everything. He did, and it all went wrong and he lost it all, almost a thousand dollars, none of it his. Still, he did not realize how critical the situation was until last Thursday night, the beginning of the long ride nowhere, when his landlord said that two men were looking for him.

Now he was on the shuttle to Times Square, and it was later, late evening, and the train was full of teen-agers, young men with bacon-fat complexions and their rock-and-roll girls, Brook-

lyn madonnas with helium hips. Cavallo knew where they were
going; he had gone himself too many times, alone, on too many
Saturday nights. They were going to the Paramount, the Loew's
State, the Rivoli, and then they would walk the great white way
beneath the electrical bedlam of slogans, past the Metropole,
the penny arcades, the tango palaces (25 Beautiful Girls 25).
He knew. He had been there. He had seen them.

He got off and went down a long corridor past a subterranean
Nedick's, feeling hunger twitch again in his belly. He came out
in an open space ringed by flights of stairs, down into a lower
level, up into the street, into Times Square. Men were standing
against the walls, just standing, staring. Trains thunderclapped
in the tunnel below, and from above, from the street, he heard
the inflectionless insect swarm of the city: trillioned voices
adrift in the night, incessantly bleating car horns; remembered
street sounds sketching a still life of the mind—an intuition of
light within the dry catacomb. But who were these men? He
moved slowly among them; a cigar-counter sign blinked neon
into their eyes. Here was a pair of negroes dangling loosely
against a wall, finger-snapping a secret counterpoint. Here were
drifters with long-lost eyes looking for a fix; syphilitic reprobates
from all-night movies on the make for some smash: a nickel, a
dime, anything. Here were pushers and panhandlers, beards
and bop hat, hoods standing scratching themselves, trying to
score with the square chicks from the Bronx and Queens.
Around the corner the shooting-gallery guns sounded like dry
branches cracking. A wino lay face-down on the concrete, his
bottle next to him, empty; nobody stopped—just another bum.
Cavallo went into the men's room. He washed his hands slowly
and listened to the dialogue that pingponged back and forth
from within two of the stalls.

"Hey, uh, you know how we get to Washington Heights
from here?"

"The 'A' train, I think. I don't know."

"Take the 'A' train. Great, hey. What a cool train that must
be. Hey, you sure, man?"

"No. I don't know. Maybe not."

"Man, we gotta find out. What a party it's gonna be. Tonight the whole world turns on, man. Washington Heights.
Crazy place. Look out the window and, zoom, there's Jersey."

"Yeah, but we better find out. Could be a different train.
Could be a square train, like 'B' or 'C' like."

"The 'A' train. Too much, man. What a train."

Cavallo dried his hands and walked out, out into the open
space past the illegible faces of the abandoned, the gone, the
cool, the hip. He didn't know who they were or what they were
talking about. He knew if he stayed and spoke to them they
would laugh. They would know. Another square. He did not fit,
even in the mud, even among the worm-life beneath the
earth—in Times Square in the big city on a Saturday night.

Sunday: the end of the world. Nausea was palpable, a dry
tonnage in his throat. Beyond hunger now, he sat with his head
slumped between his knees. His arms plummeted straight
down, fingers scratching the floor. Think, he thought. Think,
animal. Think of anything, nothing, the wind. The fans were
still and silent; heat hung heavy in the car; a little girl wanted
some ice cream, mommy. She had an English accent, the little
girl, and Cavallo waited for her mother's answer, for Helen's
answer, but it never came. He tried to raise his head; it was as
though he had an oxcart on his back. Is this how it is to die?
Did God know that I would die in my sleep on a train? The
train goes to the last stop, the dead-end, and you wake up and
you're not you anymore, not anywhere anymore, somewhere in
the middle of nowhere, darkness, nothing but the mind thinking. If God knew (*God knows everything,* she said once saying
the rosary in the living room wearing the dress that was black as
sleep and smelled of old moldy dust when he asked her if God
knew when he would die), why did He make me? Who made
me? God made me. Who is God? God is God is (dog spelled
backwards: he said it once when he was seven, a wise guy, a little wise guy; she told him to go to confession or she would tell
Papa). Bless me father for I have. Father. Let me die now before it is too late and I must see him again, see that face cruel as
Christ's. Is this how it is? To die. How is it to be born? Nobody

remembers. Remember nobody, think of nothing now, just stop, stop, end the terrible sound (*bang bang bang* following him following her out the door leaving the old house and the old man downstairs in the house making a coffin, she said, to bury his son: him: walking behind her now wondering who she was; a bar of soap, he had said, a stranger, and what did it matter then, now, ever, what did it matter when he knew that never again, not then, not now, not ever, that never again would she spread those limey legs without knowing that the old man was coming in too), the sound of someone suffering, the dangerous silence that splits the mind. Remember who he is. I am you are He is. He is an old blind nigger with a cane coming down the road looking for a fix. The whole world turns on, man.

A single fan heaved its blades into ponderous motion. He heard them swish the air, round and round, turning forever, infinities of circles within the soul. The whole world. Turns. Finally he raised his head. The other fans started to move. He watched the blades revolve slowly, individually, then gradually faster, each one coiling into the other and now all of them spinning as one, stars within systems, systems within galaxies. The light came suddenly, right now, a flash of pain, and he knew at once. This was the wrong train; he was above the ground, outside, in the sunlight. He got up and looked out the window. There was Yankee Stadium, the upper deck, a million white shirts, speck upon speck. He ran through the train, toward the rear, from car to car, an immemorial desolate shriek unbending in his chest. As he ran, his right arm was stretched forth, high in the air. The hand was open, fingers straining, as though he were trying to seize one final handful of a darkness black as the universe.

The Hunters

BY HARRIS DOWNEY

PRIVATE Meadows was lost. He had no idea which way his outfit had gone, had ever intended to go.

They were moving into France from the north. Naturally, their progress would be to the south. But during their fighting from Cherbourg they had moved in all directions. He did not know how long it had been since they left Cherbourg—three weeks, four weeks. It was some long undeterminable stretch of time. Nor did he know how many miles they had come—forty, fifty, maybe two hundred. They had come through villages— slowly, ferreting snipers from the ruins that their own artillery made. Someone had named the names of the villages but he had not understood. He had asked the names again and again, feeling that he should establish something familiar in his memory, feeling that he might come to understand where he was going, what he was doing. But between question and answer, he would fall back into the torpor that his life had been since Cherbourg. The answer, like a fragment slanting a helmet, would strike his mind obliquely and deflect away into the noisy and flashing anonymity of war.

He had traversed plow-furrowed fields when silence, imminent with violence, weighted him down like a pack. He had traversed shell-pelleted fields when fear tangled his legs like a barricade. He had seen his enemy and his comrades sprawled grotesque and cold in the neutrality of death, as impersonal as the cows among them, angling stiff legs to the sky. He had thrown grenades at hidden men; and once, staring into wide stark eyes down the bead of his aim, he had sighed out his breath toward a union more intimate than love—and more treacherous than its denial. He had seen a dog, tethered at the gate, howl at the noise of destruction and die in terror; had seen bees swarm from their hives at the ground-shake of cannon and hang in the air, directionless. He had seen Frenchmen return to their villages to gesticulate the glory of victory and, sobering, to peer from behind a silly grin at the rubbish that had been their homes. But these things had not touched him. He had left himself somewhere, and the farther he walked the terrain of war, the farther he went from himself.

He heard the spasmodic eruptions of war. He listened to silence hissing like the quick fuse of a bomb. Yet, he felt nothing—unless it were weariness. He walked under the high fire of artillery as though it were a canopy against the rain. At first, he had been unhappy and afraid; and perhaps, in the static musing, in the constant but unapprehended memory that was himself, he was yet unhappy and afraid.

Casually walking, talking to his friends, or running, crawling, squirming on his belly, looking ahead for cover, he had followed his leaders from sector to sector. The sun had come up on his left, on his right, from behind him, had sheered through the odd geometry of fields and had slid down the high summer clouds behind him, in front of him—always in a new tangent to the hedgerow. Twelve times, twenty times. How many times had he seen the sun point a surprising direction that was the west?

That morning he had seen the sun come up in the direction they were to move. Lying against the massed roots, he had looked through an opening of the hedgerow over a pasture that ran a quarter of a mile to a wood.

There near the woods he saw a farmhouse with spindly trees growing around it like a fence. He lay still, watching the sun

slip above the treetops. To the right of him lay Barr, a replace-
ment who had been in the company only a week or so, a talka-
tive fellow who somehow managed to hold his happiness and
his identity about him. Beyond Barr lay Pederson, whose twin
brother had been wounded in his first skirmish and sent back.
To the left of him was Harrod, whom Private Meadows had
been with since induction. And beyond Harrod was Walton, a
slow-talking, card-playing soldier who had come in with Barr.
These men were his friends; by virtue of their position in the
squad, they were his friends.

All along the row men lay with their heads in their helmets.
Soon, from somewhere behind him, an order would be given
and everyone would begin to move. But he would not comprehend the order. Even when it was passed on to him and he in
turn passed it on, he would not consider its meaning. He had
given up trying to understand words—orders, directions, cau-
tions. He moved and lived in a channel of sounds, but his mind
took them in as involuntarily as his lungs breathed the air. It
was his eyes that activated him. He watched his leaders and his
comrades. He followed. He did what they did. He listened
acutely and unendingly but never accepted the meaning of
sound. Consciously, he heard only silence, that dead silence
which makes one feel that he has gone deaf.

As he looked through the hedgerow at the sun, he began to
hear the silence gather. Even the men behind him, the lieuten-
ant, the sergeants, had become silent. He could feel the silence
creep along the hedgerow, turning the heads of his comrades.
The sun, having cleared the trees, seemed to stick in the silence.
The silence grew heavy. He could feel it on his back pressing
him against the earth. The grass in the field was still, as though
the silence were barrier against the wind. The silence swelled,
grew taut, then violently burst.

It was the artillery from his own lines. The barrage was steady
and strong. From beyond the woods the fire was returned, its
shells falling short in the field. The cows in the field had lifted
their heads and now stood as still as stone. Two horses from the
farmyard thundered across the level terrain. A fox bounding

from the woods reached the clearing and raced round in a circle.

Private Meadows pulled his head away from the opening of the hedgerow and leaned back against the embankment of roots. His unit began to move down the hedgerow. He followed, on his hands and knees, dragging the butt of his rifle.

When they came to the end of the row, they bounded into the woods at the south. There in the woods they dispersed and moved to the east. It was there in the woods that he got lost. He had followed the others for a time and then, of a sudden, he was alone. The artillery had stopped. It was the silence that called him to consciousness. He walked on, listening. He could hear nothing but the crackle of twigs under his feet. There was no firing even in the distance. And but for the noise he himself made, the woods were quiet—no wind in the trees, no birds even. He sat down, leaned against the trunk of a tree, crossed his piece over his thighs, his finger on the trigger, and waited. He waited for a sound.

He had expected that other men would come from the direction he had come. But somewhere, skirting the trees, he must have got out of the line of advance, for no men came.

The woods were eerie. It seemed that all the men had walked off into another world. leaving him alone. He didn't like the silence. He got up and began to walk, taking a direction half left to the one that brought him to his silent place. He came to a cart path. But he would not enter it. He stayed in the woods, keeping the path in sight, following it; it was angling him again to the left. He walked slowly, cautiously, wondering whether he were approaching the enemy line. The woods were thick and dark. Each tree was watching him, listening to the sounds he made. Each step was a deepening into fear. It was not the sort of fear he knew under fire. There he was scared, but this was a worse fear—unrelenting and conscious.

He hardly moved at all, putting one foot carefully before him and looking about, listening with all his body to the silence, before he brought the other foot forward. Then he stopped still, like a man yelled into a brace. He had heard a voice. His heartbeat pounded the silence. Then, directionless, whispered, he heard distinctly: "Hey." It was an American word, he guessed. But German snipers used American words as traps. He started to walk on, and then a little louder this time: "Hey." The word spiraled through the silence like a worm in wood. He halted again. He was afraid to turn. He dared not lift his rifle. Whoever called had a bead on him. Tentatively he put a foot forward, took a step. "Hey." He was playing with him as a cat does a rat, teasing him before he put the bullet in his back or between his eyes, waiting for him to make some particular move—to run, or turn, or lift his rifle, or gaze up into the barrel tracing him.

His enemy was all around him, saw him at every angle. He stood motionless, as though immobility forstalled the shot. He felt the sweat burst on his forehead. He was weak. In his memory he reviewed the sound, trying to divine its direction; and the voice came again. While he was listening to the voice in his memory, it came again, confusing him: "Hey, there." It came from all sides of him, the voice of the forest itself. "Put down your gun." The command was clear and slow—behind him. He lowered his rifle to the ground, stepped backward, waited. "Turn aroun'." He turned slowly, holding his breath. He saw no one.

He watched the trunks of trees, expecting a head—and a gun—to slip round into the open. "Where you goin', bud?" At the foot of a tree to his left oblique, partly concealed under a bush, sat a man on his haunches, leaning forward on his rifle. It was an American: the helmet, the green jacket. "What'cha scared of, bud?" The man stretched a foot forward and rose clear of the brush.

Private Meadows stood still. Was it a joke? He rather expected others to appear from the forest—from out of the brush, from behind the trees; expected all his lost comrades to appear from the silence that had swallowed them. He wondered whether he had not been lost in meditation; whether, as he followed his comrades through the trees, he had not fallen into a fearful dream and was now emerging into reality as one of his

friends shook his shoulder, urging him on. He had been hypnotized by his fear. He wanted to cry but was too much exhausted
to cry. The man standing before him, touching his shoulder
with a thick hairy hand, was strange. He and the man were
alone. And the silence was real. "Come out of it, bud." But the
man was not concerned. A grin stretched over his fat face like a
painted mouth stretching over a tight balloon. He was enjoying
the joke he had played. "What'cha doin' here, soldier?" The
voice was as cold as authority.

"I got lost," Private Meadows said.

Then the voice was as hooligan as persecution: "That's mis-
behavior before the enemy. They'd hang you for that. That's
desertion."

Private Meadows didn't know the ensign of the man before
him. Nor did he attempt to surmise it. It would be whatever
the manner suggested it to be. In the man's manner there was
some kind of authority. So Private Meadows answered with the
only defense he knew: "I was lost."

"Me too," the man said. "*I'm* lost."

The man pointed to the gun on the ground. Private Meadows picked it up. Then he looked at the man squarely. Vaguely
in his mind were the questions: *Why did you make me put it
down? Why did you scare me?* But he never uttered them.
They hung wordless in his mind, expressed only as the straight,
surprised, and momentary stare. Then they faded into his real
being, that shadowy remote musing, progressively growing dark
since Cherbourg—and inaccessible. He looked off, into the direction he had been walking. "What are we gonna do?" he
asked.

The man walked forward. His answer was a command: "Take
it easy—till we know what's up."

Private Meadows put his arm through the sling, settled his
rifle behind his shoulder, and followed. He was over his fright
now, the weakness gone from his knees. He was safe again in
the guidance of the Army.

He saw the broad round shoulders before him humping the
air like an elephant's flanks and the heavy field boots scraping

through the brush, flushing the silence. The noise of their progress was to Private Meadows an easeful shelter, like a low roof on a rainy night. Then there was the burst of a cannon— the slamming of a door in the giant structure of war, shattering the silence of the endless chambers that, for a moment, Private Meadows had forgot.

"A eighty-eight," the man said. They had both stopped at the cannon burst, had looked at each other and then in the direction of the sound. The burst came again, then again, as they stood motionless, listening. Then came the sound of rifle fire, pelleting the continuing bursts of the cannon. "Well, now we know where we are." The man spoke softly, his head, poked forward on the thick neck, malling up and down—a mechanical ram impelled by words. "Let's go," he said. He changed the direction nearly full right. They came to a dirt road. "You been on that road?" he asked. Private Meadows shook his head. "Must be mined. Or we'd be using it," the man said. "Sump'n comin'." Down the road, winding out from the trees, came a cart. They drew back, settled themselves behind a bush, and waited. The cart came slowly by, going in the direction from which they had come. A man walked beside the horse and from time to time put his hand at the bridle. In the seat of the cart was a woman holding a baby. In the back, among some baggage, sat a child, leaning her head against a mattress.

After the cart was out of sight, the two soldiers went again to the edge of the road. "Guess it ain't mined," the big one said. His eyes, nearly obscured under the net-covered helmet, were two little mice peering from under a crib. His grin was the lifting of a rake, and the mice scurried back into their holes. "Let's go," he said. He jumped the ditch and ran across the road.

Mechanically Private Meadows followed him. "Ain't we gonna try to get back?" he asked.

The man turned sharply and looked at him distrustfully. "You don't wanna go now, do you?"

"I don't know," Private Meadows said.

"We getting back, see. But we takin' the long way roun'."

Private Meadows shrugged his shoulders. He was tired. The man had stuck his great round face close to his and was staring into his eyes. Private Meadows held his face against the stare but wearily closed his eyes. Sleep covered him like a breaker. His body swayed. Then he shook his head and opened his eyes. "Come on," the man said.

They walked through the woods, keeping within sight of the road. The distant rifle fire was continuous. The artillery had begun again, and from time to time a great cannon jolted all the other sounds to silence. Though they were walking oblique from the firing, Private Meadows wondered whether, on the tangent of their direction, they might not be approaching the enemy's lines. But this wonder was fleeting like the recurrent sleep that blacked him out whenever he closed his eyes. Responsibility had gone the way of his fear; he was automaton again. He was following.

The man, who had been walking ahead, jumped to cover behind a tree, at the same time wagging a fat hand around his waist in signal to Private Meadows. Private Meadows was behind a tree almost as quickly as the man and then, peering around, he saw the cause of alarm. A German soldier was coming toward them. He was unhelmeted, a cap pulled low over his forehead. Slung over his shoulder and hanging at his waist was a leather case. "Hey," the big man called in the whispering voice. The German was startled by the sight of the man even before he heard the voice; for at the utterance he had already stopped, gazing first at the face and then at the rifle pointing from the fat round hip. "Hey," the man repeated—needlessly—for the German was standing frozen in the first attitude of shock.

Without turning his gaze from the German, the man called out to Private Meadows: "Is it clear?"

"Looks clear," Private Meadows said, shuttling his gaze among the trees.

The man approached the German until he stood within a few feet of him. "Search him," he said.

Private Meadows, holding his rifle at the waist, came beside

the German, with his left hand felt the pockets of the uniform
and, walking behind him, lifted the leather case from his shoulder.

"What's in it?" the man asked still gazing at the German,
thrusting the muzzle of his gun forward. The German, who had
stood listless, his hands dropping to his sides after Private
Meadows lifted the case from his shoulder, stared at his victor,
as though in the uncomprehended words there was a new terror. Then quickly, as though guessing the meaning, he lifted his
hands shoulder high in surrender. "Higher, you sonofabitch."
The man motioned with the muzzle of his gun. The German
understood the motion and lifted his hands above his head.
"What's in it?" This time the voice was different. The German
understood that the words were not for him. He cupped his
hands behind his head.

"It's money," Private Meadows said. He held a handful of
the bills in front of his companion.

"Christ! Kraut money," the big man said.

"It's filled with it," Private Meadows said, sliding the money
back into the case.

"Where'd you get that money, bud?" the man said. The German became rigid. The terror returned to his eyes, but, with it,
there seemed to be another feeling—of impatience, perhaps of
injustice. "Where'd you steal that money, Kraut?" And at the
question there came into the German's face a sense of outrage.
The big man saw it. "You bastard," he said. "Can't you speak
English?"

"Nein," the German said quickly. And he shook his head,
"Nein."

"Nein, nein!" The man mocked him. "You dumb bastard."
He lifted the muzzle of his gun and twice thrust it forward in
the direction from which the German had come. "Get goin',"
he said. "Vamoos." The German was doubtful. He turned his
body slowly but kept shuttling his gaze from the gun to the fat
dark face above it. "Get the hell goin'." The German took a
step tentatively, looked once at the fair-faced soldier who was
adjusting the leather case at his waist. But in his eyes there was

neither help nor corroboration—only indecision and doubt as great as his own. He started walking slowly away, his hands still cupped over his head. Then, just as he took the first step that was quicker and surer than the rest, the shot cracked through the woods. He fell forward on his face.

The big man lowered his rifle. Private Meadows, his mouth wide open, watched him open the bolt and push it forward again. He looked down at the ejected cartridge case, awesomely, as though it were a rabbit out of a hat, surprising and not quite convincing.

"Let's get the hell outa here," the man said. He walked quickly past Private Meadows.

Private Meadows looked again where the German had fallen. He saw an arm lifted, like a swimmer's in arrested motion. He saw it fall forward. He turned and followed his leader.

They came to a clearing, a series of fields surrounded by hedgerows and forming a rolling terrain.

"Better not go out there," the man said. Yet, if they followed through the woods, along the edge of the clearing, they would approach too directly the enemy line. "We gone far enough anyways." He listened to the distant crack of the rifles. He sat down and pulled his rifle over his fat legs crossed like a saw-buck. "Let's see that money." Private Meadows handed him the case and sat down beside him. The man dumped the contents on the ground. There was a tablet of forms printed in German. He tossed it away. "Musta' been a pay-sergeant. . . . Suppose he was payin' men out on the goddamned *firin'* line?" The money was taped in seven tight bundles. "That sonofabitch was makin' way with somethin', you can bet your hat on that." He studied the numerals on the bills. He divided the money into two stacks and handed one stack to Private Meadows. He held up the case. "Want it?" Private Meadows looked at the case and then into the lariat eyes hesitantly. He shook his head. The man tossed the case beside the forms.

They both sat looking at the money in their hands. "Suppose it's any good?"

"It's German," Private Meadows said.

"Yeah, I guess so . . . but francs are good. We gonna get paid in francs. If ever we get paid."

"Maybe when we get to Germany—" Private Meadows said.

"Not me. I ain't go'n *get* that far," the man said. "Not me. Je-e-esus! Not me." He spread out his thick legs before him. "Look at them goats!"

In the clearing there were three goats. They had come through a break in the hedgerow or had climbed up some unnoticeable ravine, for they had not been there when the men first looked out. They neither grazed nor moved. It seemed that they were listening to the sounds of the firing.

"I'll take the one on the left," the man said. "You take the one on the right. And I'll bet you my stack of tens against it." He chunked out a bundle of the little bills.

Private Meadows spread the bundles of money fan-fashion, selected a bundle, threw it out, then turned toward the man— his look bending under the helmet to ask: *Now what?*

"We'll have to fire together or they'll be to hell and gone. Yours on the right." The man caracoled his arm into the sling and was adjusting himself to fire from the sitting position. Then Private Meadows understood.

"I . . . I don't think—" But the man was in position. Private Meadows thrust his arms through his sling quickly.

"Are you ready?"

"Say, do you think—"

"Are you ready?"

Private Meadows jerked himself to the kneeling position and slid the gun-butt into his shoulder, his face tight against the stock. He squinted his eyes as he leveled the sight. "OK."

The man muzzled against his gun, and each of his commands was whispered in the respiration of a breath: "Ready—Aim— Fire."

The rifles cracked. The right goat fell, its front legs bending before it. The left goat sprang into the air, like a horse rearing, then rushed forward and crashed face first into the ground. The middle goat lifted his head as though sniffing the air but did not move from where it stood.

"Look at that dumb bastard," the man said. He humped his shoulders over his rifle. "I bet I get him first shot." He turned his head towards Private Meadows, his chin sliding along the gunstock. "OK?" he asked impatiently.

"I—" But the man was straining in a flesh-taut position, ready to fire. "OK," Private Meadows said.

The man took aim. The goat started walking forward, his nose still in the air. The man shifted his gun, aimed again, fired. The goat bleated once, turned, and ran. The man shot again. The goat fell, gave three long trembling bleats, and was silent.

"Well, it's yours," the man said. He leaned back, picked up the money, and threw it to Private Meadows. "That bastard." He crawled back against the tree, put his gun on the ground beside him, and pulled a package from his knapsack. "Got a ration?" he asked.

"I got some choc'late," Private Meadows said. He stood up, holding the money out from him as if he might throw it back to the man or fling it into the woods. He looked down at the notes in his hand—thoughtfully, as though trying to recall how they came to be there. Then he slipped them into his jacket pocket. He sat down again and took out his chocolate. He took a bite of the hard cube, lay back on the ground, and immediately fell asleep.

"Hey. Hey, bud." The man was pushing his boot into Private Meadows' side. "Get up. The artillery's stopped."

Private Meadows sat up. The firing had almost stopped. "We must'a taken the hill," he said.

"It's a town," the man said. "A village. We were after a village."

Private Meadows stood up. "You suppose we really took it?"

"Sounds like it," the man said. "We better get goin'. We better start findin' ourselves." He started walking down the edge of the clearing. The hulking form, moored to some narrow gaze, rode the slow steps heavily, in strenuous swells and sudden falls. Private Meadows followed. To their right, the sun was halfway down the sky.

They came in view of a farmhouse. It stood in the clearing

about fifty yards away. "Looks deserted," the man said. They stood looking over the field at the small squat house. "We'll see," the man said. He lifted his rifle and fired. Then they waited but there was no sign of life from the house. "Can't tell if I even hit." He fired again. And as they stood waiting for whatever they expected might happen, an aeroplane loomed from the south. They ducked quickly into the woods and there from among the trees watched the plane. It was flying low and unsteadily. "Dammed thing's fallin'," the man said. And as he spoke, they saw a figure drop from the plane—and then another. A parachute opened and then fell into the jolt of full bloom. The second opened, leapt up at the hinges of the air, jolted. Then a third. They had not seen the third drop from the plane but there it moved, in echelon, with the others.

"Brother!" the man said, lifting his rifle. "I'll take the one on the left again. Same bet."

Private Meadows stared as the man pivoted his gun on the floating figure and fired.

"Quick, you bastard," the man said, stepping closer to him, his mouth curling down from the utterance in anger. The impatient words were command.

Private Meadows shouldered his gun and, while still leveling the figure into his sight, fired. He saw a body twitch, the hands fall from the cords, the head lean back. As he lowered his gun across his chest, he drew his heels together and stood straight and stiff, gaping at what he had done.

"Same again on the middle one," the man said. He lifted his gun but his target was already falling beyond the roof the house. "God damn," he said, dropping his gun from his shoulder. "He's outa sight 'cause you waited so long. What were you waitin' for?"

"You don't shoot men when they're parachutin'."

"My ass! You don't shoot *prisoners*, do you?"

"You sure they were Germans?" His voice was almost supplication.

"How do I know?" He started walking into the woods. "Let's get the hell away from here."

Private Meadows stood holding his gun over his chest, his hand on the bolt. He looked over the field. The two white chutes, now lying on the ground, were barely visible. He drew his bolt, ejecting the cartridge case, thrust the bolt forward again, and, yet holding the gun across his chest, followed the man into the woods.

"Suppose they were *Americans!*" he called out.

The man stopped, turned back—the accusing, distrustful look again in his eyes. "American, French, Kraut, whatever they are, they're fly boys, playin' games in the air and sleepin' in a bed at night." His helmet was almost touching Private Meadows' own. "Look, bud, you shoot first and *suppose* afterwards, or you'll get lead between your own eyes." He drew back a step. "Ain't you killed any before?"

Private Meadows remembered the terrified eyes staring into his own. He answered doubtfully, in the voice of conjecture: "But I knew who I was killin'."

The fat lips drew tight round a sibilant of contempt. Then, "Killin's killin'," he said. "How long you been in this push anyways?"

"Since Cherbourg."

The man looked him up and down. "It's a wonder you lasted this long.

Through woods, over the dirt road, and through woods again to the first fields. Down a hedgerow cautiously. Debris of the advance: cartridge belts, helmets, clips yet filled with bullets, a knit cap, a dog lying dead, a deck of cards scattered, and letters. The wounded and dead removed, but the signs of death in the wreckage. And then the main road, from which the night before they had deployed. Now an ambulance passing, now a jeep. A squad of soldiers, bearded, and fatuous with grime, shoveling dirt from an embankment to cover the carcass of a cow. Salvage of tanks and trucks. Trees broken and charred. A column of medics, walking with stooped weariness, into a side road. Trucks, filled with infantrymen, coming up from the rear. Then the village: "This town off limits for all military personnel." Really no village at all, only rubble: a tall mahogany armoire standing erect and unscratched among bricks and nameless jointures of wood like an exaggerated product in an advertisement; the horseshoe arches of four windows, like a backstage flat, signifying a church; the graveyard, a grotesquery of holes, stone, and up-turned coffins; and, sitting atop a fallen door, a yellow and white kitten washing an outstretched paw.

At the entrance of the village and even in the street beyond the off-limits sign, there were soldiers. They stood in groups, but they were quiet, looking over the ruins of the village or down the wreckage-strewn road they had traversed, staring vacantly at the interpreter talking to a group of five Nazi officers or at the Military Police helping a sergeant line up a lengthening formation of prisoners. The scene was almost still, like a rehearsal of a play where everyone waits for the director to reach a decision.

The two soldiers stopped by an off-limits sign and surveyed the scene. "I gotta find my company," the big man said. He went up to a group of soldiers. Private Meadows watched him a moment and then followed after. He saw one of the soldiers answering the big man's question, pointing away from the village. And before Private Meadows reached the group, the big man walked away. Private Meadows stopped, ready to lift his hand in farewell, but the man went lunging on without looking back —the heavy body, in its laboring gait, an enemy to the air it humped and to the ground it scuffed: the beast that walks alone, that—among all the animals of the forest and in the meeting of its kind—is yet alone, the stalker of secret places, the hunter. Private Meadows sensed the solitariness; but he thought it was the realization of his own loneliness that made him shudder.

He approached the group of soldiers and asked the whereabouts of his company. All the men looked at him blankly. And then one, interpreting the silence of the group, answered: "I don't know."

Private Meadows turned away. Beyond the formation of prisoners he saw some French civilians crossing the street. A fat woman, carrying a hamper, walked down the side of the formation, a little white dog following her, scurrying from one side to the other to sniff at the boots of the prisoners or at something in the rubble.

He was alone again. He was lost.

At home he had often had a dream of being late for school. The scenes of the dream were always different, but the dream was always the same. An unsuccessful effort to get to school: the determination, the hurry; running down the street, then caught in some void where time passed and he stood still; or still discovering himself at a strange corner, not knowing the direction, not knowing how he came to be there. The remembrance of the dream was fleeting but the familiar hopeless feeling of it remained. He felt that no one here would know his company, that his company would be in a distant place maneuvering through some different duty. He had left his company that very same morning after sunrise and only now was the sun beginning to set. But his calculation gave him no assurance. He felt that he had been separated from his comrades for a campaign of time. And this—this feeling—was his real knowledge.

He went from soldier to soldier, from group to group, asking the position of his company—his question automatic and hopeless, but persistent like a sick man's fancy. And when a soldier answered *Yes* and named the directions, his mind was filled with only the realization of the soldier's knowing, so that he had to ask again.

His company was bivouacked less than a mile from the village. It was still twilight when he walked among his platoon.

"Meadows! Man, I thought you'd found your number." It was Barr. He was sitting on the ground, leaning against the wood fence. He touched the ground beside him in invitation for Meadows to sit.

"What happened to you?" Harrod, too, was leaning against the fence. He was smoking a cigarette. His face was black with grease and dirt.

"Guess I must'a got lost," Private Meadows said. He leaned his gun against the fence, dropping his helmet to the ground, and sat down.

Without looking around, Barr stretched his hand to his left

and said: "They got Pederson." Private Meadows looked up at him. "And Walton was shot in the hip but he'll get all right, lucky dog." He put his feet out before him, crossed them at the ankles, said wearily: "We 'bout all would have got it if it wasn't for those bombers. Zoom. Bang. And not another eighty-eight booped after that."

"Those *what?*" Private Meadows asked.

"The bombers. The lucky dogs. Sleeping in England to-night."

"I got lost." Private Meadows said.

Harrod and Barr both looked at him.

"Well, you're home now, chum," Barr said. "Good ole Easy Company. Gonna have hot stuff tonight—out'a mess kit. And a sleep, I-hope-I-hope-I-hope, here against a soft warm fence."

"Wish they'd hurry with chow," Harrod said. "If I close my eyes, I'll never make it. . . . How much longer they gonna keep us in the line anyhow?

"Couple of more days, I guess," Barr said. His tone was now flat as if he had no interest in what he said.

"I wonder if I'll live that long," Harrod said. There was nothing in his voice; it sounded like a routine speculation, as if he wondered whether he would be in town long enough to send his clothes to the laundry.

It was almost dark.

Private Meadows was bent forward, his arms lying against his thighs, his eyes pressed against his wrists. Barr noticed that each hand clutched a stack of notes and, as he started to ask what they were, he heard the sobbing. It simpered like a fuse and then burst. The shoulders shook convulsively. "What the hell, kid?" Barr sidled close to him and put his hand on his arm.

Harrod looked over at him, then flipped away the dead cigarette that he had been absently holding between his fingers. A whistle blew.

"Snap out of it, kid," Barr said, rising. "It's time for chow." He stepped back and picked up his mess kit. Then he and Harrod stood on each side of Private Meadows and waited.

The Motion of Forgetfulness Is Slow

BY CHARLES EDWARD EATON

THEY met at the Atlantico, one of Rio's most popular night-clubs. They knew from the beginning why they were sitting next to each other, and this enabled them to dispense with the stiff and tedious preliminaries of conversation and be almost immediately easy and informal. Their hostess, Jacqueline Laurent, was a garrulous, masculine Frenchwoman of forty-five, a refugee, somewhat bitter about life, but still a great arranger of romance, an authority on the principles of life, although she had no lover at the moment, and it was doubtful whether she would ever have one again. Some said she was a Lesbian, but that was probably untrue since it would have been too easy and almost natural for her, and she was a woman who enjoyed what was most difficult for her to do. Her preoccupation with love had made her widely and ardently social, and she was a familiar figure of café society. Though people feared her, knowing that she could be vicious or benevolent according to whim, they were always glad to be entertained by her because she was never dull. With her love of intrigue, she never gave a party that did not have its implications of the destruction or arousal of a *liaison* between at least one of the couples present.

She had chosen the proper time for this particular conspiracy. A few weeks later, and it might never have happened. But to-night, success was probable. She knew it, they knew it, and, as a consequence, the surface of the evening moved rapidly. Since she liked them both so well, she had gone to some trouble to inform and prepare them carefully beforehand so that nothing would go amiss. Ingrid Lombard was an old friend from the prewar days in Paris, and Robert Atherton, a young journalist with the Office of the Coordinator of Inter-American Affairs, had won her sympathy not only through his personal charm but because he was a type which she liked, very blondly and brightly American, evoking sentimental memories of her life in the United States when she toured the country on the old Keith vaudeville circuit singing French songs.

Jacqueline knew, and she was satisfied now that they knew what she called the "circumstances." A week before, Ingrid's husband, Monsieur Charles Lombard, had left for Paris, recently occupied by the American army, and it was understood that he would not return. Monsieur Lombard was a handsome man of fifty, a painter of minor talent but much ego, possessed of the aloofness and confidence that are often so attractive to women. Ingrid had met him ten years before when she had come from Sweden to study art in France. Out of her respect and need for love she had made of him, in her mind, something he was not, but something she could love, and they lived rather happily together until his selfish possession of her was sated. Now at thirty-nine it was hard for her to lose him, and for the moment she had almost ceased to exist since she realized that the world of her invention, of which he was the center, had really never had any validity at all. There is nothing lonelier than living among the ruins of belief and because she could not bear this loneliness she had come to Jacqueline's party.

Robert Atherton had not known much about love when he came to Brazil. Like many young Americans of thirty, he had slept with a girl or two, but the relationship had always been of short duration, rather frantically and hectically physical—the kind of experience that later enabled him to understand what a

Brazilian friend meant when he said that love in America was usually a matter of athletics. The girls he had known at the university had been wholesome, usual in opinion and attitude, pretty but sexually rather dull, and he had lost interest in them quickly. Not long after his arrival in Brazil, he met Yvonne Vautier, who had come to Rio to visit friends and been stranded there by the outbreak of war. She was urban in manner and outlook, small, unathletic but firm and trim of figure, and had a very intense color of red-gold hair and brilliant blue eyes. She was two years older than himself, had been married once, and in love several times. She liked Robert, understood him quickly, and became his mistress after six weeks. They had a *garconnière* together, and Robert went through a complete experience of love, beyond the merely sensual, beyond the spirit of youthful adventure, and knew for the first time what Europeans meant by falling in love mentally as well as physically. Jacqueline, who was a close friend of Yvonne, had enjoyed every stage of the affair, thinking it a perfect union of Old World-New World. She foresaw what would happen to Robert when Yvonne found it necessary to return to her aging parents in Paris, was ready with comfort after the departure and, finally, the party and meeting with Ingrid.

They knew, and yet they had come, were studying, and were going through with it. They knew it was one of Jacqueline's little amusements, and that it might be desperate for them, but there was a chance it might not be, and nothing was worse than shutting the door completely and admitting that it was over, that one had been loved and now was not loved and might not love again since love was miraculous and even haphazard and accidental and not to be expected more than once in a lifetime. No, it was better to pretend that the door was still open in a place where self-deception was possible, where there were people, music, and motion—pretend, at least for tonight, that circumstances were still fluid, that it should and would happen again, that it might happen more beautifully than before.

The party of six couples, all foreigners, was masterfully engineered by Jacqueline, although she was not really interested in

any of them except Ingrid and Robert who were the nerves in
the body of the group. It was their presence alone that excited
and stimulated her and enabled her to play with skill the part of
the gracious hostess, knowing that the whole elaborate social
texture of eating and drinking, gesture and small talk had a purpose and center of intensity, a covert drama which was of her
own instigation. As they talked, they were conscious of the fact
that through the sound and action of others present, in intru-
sions and withdrawals, the unpredictable pattern and direction
of reciprocal speech, the sudden close-knit vocal unanimity,
Jacqueline was listening to them with a focus of attention, central and direct beneath its superficial digressiveness.

They knew that they were being used, and they did not care.
They knew that Jacqueline was increasing the sense of her own
power by finding them, for the moment, at least, pliant in her
hands. If things worked out as she intended, she would never
let them forget it. No, she would never let go of them.
But sometimes it is better to be used than to remain inert since
movement is life, and in both of them there had been a great
and sudden slowing down, so that memory receded into the
past hardly at all and the present was stagnant, as if the means
of extending feeling had been shut off within the blood, leaving
in the heart neither the possibility of death nor birth. Jacqueline promised to unlock this rigidity. So being used was moving
and better than being still at the point where one could not
move voluntarily, the point where someone outside had to play
Fate and free the congealing of circumstance.

Inside where there were music and light, and whisky had
loosened the tightness of thought, it was possible to feel the
surface of life moving, not quickly yet, but mobile again and
moving toward the old rapidity. It was possible to believe this
even more securely, knowing that Jacqueline was helping it
happen. Jacqueline, too, from the outside believed, and it is the
viewpoint beyond the personal which supports confidence.
Yes, she was very sure. When they left at midnight their sense
of identity which had been hard and stopped was fluid again,
lightened and diluted in the hazy but swirling suspension which

alcohol makes in the mind. The past did not weigh as much as it did, so that they felt that they could move through it or around it and that it was not any more one's self lying in a closed small place. And Jacqueline was standing there, telling them good-bye, sure of it, smiling and solicitous like an accomplice. The last thing they saw was her mouth with the heavy black down on the upper lip, smiling and obscene in the foreground, and if it had not been for the whisky they would have been embarrassed.

Then in the cab they were not so sure of motion, although the physical movement was there in the rolling of the wheels along the Avenida Atlantica, down the damp curve of the beach in the phantom-dim light. Through the open windows the rawness of the sea came in. The apartment houses were all dark and like a huge cliff on one side, and there was heaviness again everywhere. By contrast, the sea was loose and flatulent, having no thrust and incisiveness where it struck the ponderous earth, pouring on the sand a white spray without power. They said nothing and sat apart, strange and stiff, on either side of the seat. It was not a long drive, but it felt long and stretched out as though the pace of the moments had shifted again and was going slower and slower and might stop altogether. The driver sat at the wheel, rigid, tense, noncommunicative, strangely so for a member of his trade, and seemed to lean with intensity on the gas feed like a man who kept his feelings distended in order that they might remain fluent at all in a night of thickening dross.

Ingrid had an apartment in the hills above the city. Most of the foreigners lived there because of the long open view of the sea, the lighter air, and the feeling of being above the tropic languor of the beaches. But tonight the fog and sea mist were reaching up into the higher air and were curdling around the tops of the hills, and it was hard to imagine that morning would ever open the sky again and that the harbor would lie there below in a rippling scarf of blue, fluid with outward-going ships and racing light.

When the cab stopped at the top of the hill before the en-

trance of the apartment, laboriously and massively as though
the functions of the engine had finally been choked with night,
Ingrid said to Robert quietly, "Come in. Come in and have a
drink."

"All right," he said, and they went into the dark entrance
without looking to see whether the cab moved on.

Inside it was better with the rawness of the damp air leaving
their skin and the warm interior light, and they could forget a
little the strange solidification of the drive up the hills away
from the music and movement of the nightclub and Jacqueline,
glowing triumphant, transmitting impulse and impulse as
though her body were the channel for the current. But now it
was better again, although the house was not cheerful. It was
furnished as a foreigner might furnish a house, thinking of
home. There were things that recalled Sweden and Paris, and
they looked dead and rootless here, as they would have in any of
the fashionable apartments of the city where one always sensed
beneath the structure of modernity the jungle earth, unrecep-
tive to anything that was superimposed and of its own. But
more than this, the living room where they were sitting was
cheerless because of the things that were missing, little things
that had indicated two were living here, closely and intimately,
and whose absence now said one, and one alone, one, now and
perhaps forever, alone.

She had nothing in the house but gin, and it was bad to mix
it with the whisky, but there had to be somewhere to start from
and this was not like the nightclub at all but a sliding backward
to a point where the emotions were once more constricted, and
they would not have been able to start again without something
to drink. But as the gin awakened the ebbing, warm radiance in
their bodies, they wanted to talk and to knit the nightclub feeling and the feeling of now together. And he began to see her
for the first time through his own eyes, not remembering very
much of what Jacqueline had told him to think, and he wondered whether she were seeing him similarly.

The reddish hair and the blue eyes, he was thinking. *Like
Yvonne, and yet not like her, not like her at all. The red hair*

and blue eyes of Sweden. Not Paris. No, not from Paris. Not delicate and very slender-compact. Not small of shoulder and breast. Not the small mouth and the blue eyes with a film of the sea across them. But very kind and generous like her body, filling the sofa with abundance and the wish to give it and the feeling that her abundance lies fallow and unclaimed.

And now, perhaps she was thinking—still remembering partly what Jacqueline had said, not being able to forget the other one, the one before, as women are never able to forget the other one wholly—*he is thinking of her. And is needing not to think of her, not to remember because it hurts, but to touch and be touched, finding the under-depth and the inner, healing, pain-forgetting heart of touch. Wanting to forget, being young, and not yet all-despairing. Remembering and not wanting to remember how love suffers. But remembering and still remembering. Being young, uncynical, and what I would have wanted of love.*

Then they were speaking aloud, but it was difficult, for Jacqueline was not there, transmitting impulse and impulse, joining their diffidence through the force and confidence of her personality. It was difficult because there was a feeling of guilt beneath their being together. A feeling of betrayal and shame at trying to forget too soon, and yet, undyingly, the wanting and willingness to love, the furtive hope of filling the image in the heart with another image, of blending form, gesture, and word upon the memory of another form, other gestures, words that were now a consummation and a death, inert and final, forcing upon the mind the recognition of not-love, the fear, hardest to bear, that love lies in a compartment of the soul severed from current consciousness, suspended and immobile in the enslavement of memory.

The music of the *samba* came in through the open window, primitive, simply melodic, without rhythmic sophistication, unabashedly and unashamedly sensual. In the night that had seemed to be going solid and weighted it was a cry that said the darkness had not died, that the body of the night had heart-life still.

"There's a *batuque*," she said, singing the refrain. "*Quero chorar, nao tenho lagrimas*. I want to cry, but I have no tears."

"That's Brazil," he said. "More deeply Brazil than anything else I know."

"Yes," she said. "I'll miss it when I leave. I won't miss much else—not any longer. There was a time when I would have, but not now. How I hate the *gran finos* and their silly floating-flowers lives, the false front of the Copacabana, like a stage setting imported from Europe. And how I hate myself for ever thinking I wanted it all." She paused and listened to the music once more. "But I want to remember that crying. I don't ever want to forget that."

"They laugh so much here," he said. "No wonder in their music they want to cry and don't have any tears."

The women's voices carried the words, soaring and quivering, seeming to fall back into the deep and resonant under-boom of the talking, wanting to listen to the music.

"When Charles and I first arrived, I liked it better here than any place I had ever known," she said finally. "Somewhere in the back of the mind, all of us dream of a country that is love's. Perhaps it is because in the fairy stories we read when we are children love makes everything beautiful. The witch is really only a princess in disguise, the beast a Prince Charming. And, of course, where they live happily ever after is the most beautiful country on earth. We will always remember this country. It is the one place we can never forget. I suppose I thought I had found it once and for all when we came to Brazil. The mountains, the sea, the clear blue of the sky, were fabulous, the perfect background for what I was feeling. Finally, the landscape was not background but part of the feeling itself as though there were nothing antipathetic in the world and I could reach out and touch a rock, a flower, a tree, and know it to be love's. Now I don't feel that way any more, and I can't really see Brazil at all. I suppose that is why I want to leave it. I don't like hospitality, and I want to see again."

She spoke now without pausing, without even waiting for the conventional linking sentences that he might have inserted. It was not a monologue of self-absorption or indifference but of intense awareness of his presence, of an urgent sense of the need for fluency between them which she, being on the surface at least less constricted and diffident than he, must supply. Consequently, she talked steadily, intimately, and inclusively, lest a silence occur, as in the car on the way to the apartment, and an intangible thickness coagulate and make communication slow to a laborious stop.

"When Charles told me four months ago that he wanted to go back to Paris, I knew he would not take me with him," she said. "He did not say so then, but I knew that he would expect me to understand in time, and that I would not go. He was French all the way through, very passionate, very complete in love, and very sure when it was over. My use was a thing of time, neatly measured so as not to last one day beyond boredom."

"To be the lover who does not lose takes precision in judging others and the incapacity for regret, and Charles always saw things with a terrible precise clearness. He was very afraid of growing old, and I had begun to remind him of the fact that he would. No man wants to live in a museum of what he was. He can go back there in memory but not live there. Charles saw the future clearly. It was my fault that I kept it vague and undefined."

He was glad that she was talking, since he himself was not ready to talk, being closer to memory, and he knew that she would come, as she had, to that point in the past where the rupture was, the point from which they must, if ever, proceed. He was thankful for the flow of her words. The ample talkativeness of women, he thought, is often a thing to be thankful for. In a moment of tension, it will do its best to push remembering forward into not-remembering or spread it horizontal and thin like water on a dry field to be slacked up and lost from sight. Silence is the cause of much of our suffering, the keeping of grief within us, acute, perpendicular unreleased, and women, he felt, know this better than men.

But, though he had not spoken, he knew that she was aware

of the intensity of his response. It was she, ostensibly, who was moving them toward a starting point, but the tempo and extension of her conversation would not have been possible without his sympathy. Her words were the surface motion, but a hidden current, intuitive and deep, like a belt under a revolving tableau of figures and scenes, was moving them into conjunction.

When she paused at last for breath, they were once again, for a moment, silent, but the silence was not empty or formal but quivering with the reverberations of her words. She sat loosely against the sofa, her figure nowhere strict and taut, not fat but well rounded, the body of a woman, who, without fear of falling into excess, could stretch the sweetness of her sense a little beyond denial.

There are no rough edges in her, he thought. *She is gentle and hurt. Hurt and not able to hurt in return. The muscle of her heart is rich and strong but tired from loving, enduring, and not wanting to hurt. Now she is missing, needing the serenity of affection. Can I open in her the sealed-up power of touch again? Can I kiss her, touch her, taking the darkness of sensation into another darkness until there is warmth and the denial of darkness? To do this, to need to, to want to love again, to try in a passionate wanting.*

He moved very close to her and put his arms around her. He did not look into her eyes because of his embarrassment and because he was ashamed of his desperation, of his desire to commit so soon a betrayal, of his wish to flood his loneliness with sensuous oblivion. Suddenly he was hearing, "Slowly, Robert. Not so fast. Wait a little." Said gently, tenderly resistive, at the same time that she rose and went into the other room.

Before they lay down, she lit a candle and placed it on the table beside the bed. At first, he was shy about the light, but then he was not, for it left them visible to each other and yet indistinct, hardly familiar at all, more like dream figures, even strange to themselves, and perhaps this was better and easier for not remembering. The candle had been used before and was encrusted with its own wax flesh and relic-weeping, and he thought that everywhere you looked in the world, at any hour, there was something broken, torn, crying, or frozen in an attitude where the crying had stopped. It was right that she had lit the candle, alive again now and liquid with fresh tear-form droppings, gleaming through all its cylindrical shape, dully so at the base, tipped with a tiny, molten self-destroying crater where the flame, like an element antipathetic to the entombing wax, was almost disembodied from the wick. Without this light and its training it would have been impossible, at first, to have stayed in the room. The night would have been too dense and they would not have been able to endure the muffling darkness without the wavering, shadow-shimmering flare of the candle whose almost incorporeal lucence moved, probing and pliantly caressive over the walls, bed, table, over them where they lay, as though to enter once more the thingness, the body, that it would, but finally, death-fearing, could not leave.

She did not undress entirely but lay there partially hidden from the candle glow like one who knew light and the absence of light, not calculating the risks, being incapable of doing so, but not rushing toward them either, knowing the pitiless price one pays for wanting to possess the beautiful whose possession always quivers with not-possession, bringing the final soulless wish not to have possessed at all.

As he looked at her, very quiet and waiting, with the light on her reddish hair, everywhere on the broad surface of her face except the recesses of her eyes which were dark and closed, he knew that he would always remember her saying, "Slowly, Robert. Not so fast. Wait a little." Not harshly spoken, but gently admonitive, as those who have suffered will admonish others who have also suffered but not so greatly as they.

Then she put out the light, and there was a moment of strange waiting and perilous equipoise in the darkness. And when he touched her, the touch of another was there. And when he kissed her, it was illusive and unreal since he could not kiss though memory, since he could not touch her really at all, suddenly in the darkness remembering, not being able to forget, feeling that forgetting, in a life time, would hardly move fast enough or far enough to leave behind in silence one word of all that remembering.

And where his hand, his physical hand, reached—but without feeling—to accomplish the touch, he could imagine that she, too, would put her hand into another hand, and that their past lives were locked in a trance out of which they looked, as from emprisoned sleep, into the outrageous, shame-haunted, pent-eruptive world of dream to see the fictive motions of their present lives.

It was then that he remembered—as memory will always make you remember a clear indestructible moment of the past just when the present struggles toward freedom—the departure and final passage of the boat seen from the window of his hotel, the boat, white, compact, poised like a bird on the water. The realization and shock-vision that within the boat was the other form, the other face, the absolute evidence of love. Within that boat moving, at first, slowly, almost laboriously and reluctantly, then quicker, more quickly, quicker, more quickly, quickly, quickly, quickly, until the sky at the far end of the harbor cracked open and, in a moment and forever, the boat drained out of consciousness.

Afterwards, it was very quiet in the room. They lay there silently, unstirringly, as though in the darkness they were being watched hostilely from above. It was a long time before he dressed, and he began to wonder why she said nothing. But then he knew that her quietness was not anger, not silent reproach, not exclusiveness, not indifference, but deep patient waiting, the acceptance of not-possessing, the recognition of the vastness between one life and another.

At the door she kissed him softly, without passion, and he wanted to cry out and shake his body for its obtuseness and his heart for its backward looking, but he did not. He could not. The sidewalk toward the city was steep and damp, and he had to walk down through the thick fog slowly, very slowly, to keep from falling.

A Sense of Destination

BY FAYE RITER

GRANDMA Westerman surrendered to circumstances after she broke her leg in a fall on the short flight of steps leading down to the kitchen. She began the descent with the righteous irritation of one prepared to reprimand the housekeeper for filching secretly from pantry stores. And, one foot catching in the hem of her long black skirt, she had fallen with all the gracelessness of her age. A leg had twisted beneath her so that brittle bones cracked and splintered.

And she lay there almost the whole morning, for the housekeeper, having heard her approach, had snatched bonnet and shawl and hurried out of the basement door to do the morning marketing, Then she had met an intimate friend, quite by chance, of course, in the fresh, meaty atmosphere of the butcher shop and had been invited to step over to the coffee shop, where the remainder of the morning had vanished.

The housekeeper had screamed at finding her mistress lying as in death upon the floor. "Lord, help me," she babbled, trying to decide whether it was best to inform first the doctor so that he could attend the old lady, or to call the eldest son, who could at once take over the responsibility of the injured woman.

"There," she soothed distractedly, standing over the quiet figure.

At that moment Grandma Westerman opened accusing eyes. "Robber," she pronounced with finality, and closed them again.

"It is good, maybe, that you fell," the doctor told her later, scratching his neck reflectively. "For once you are pinned down, and one can look at you and see that you need attention for other things."

She snorted indignantly at that.

"You were dizzy, perhaps, when you fell?" he suggested.

"What an idea! I was in absolute health."

"Just like my mother," he commented, writing out prescriptions, "never ready to admit an ailment. Why do you have such pride?"

It was at this period, more shamed by the disease of her body than by the breaking of bones, that Grandma Westerman announced to her son, Albert, the eldest although the last of them to marry, that he might now move into the family home.

"It will come to you, anyhow," she said heavily from the brass bed. "I will not be in your way."

"We shall come to look after it," he agreed at once, stiffening his shoulders, "and you, too," he added in haste. "It will not do for you to be here alone now."

Afterward she declared that if nothing else good came from the disaster, at least she had got rid of a corrupt housekeeper and gained the devoted Clara.

Meanwhile, Albert and Leonie and the three children moved in, and Clara, whose duties were restricted to the dim bedroom and pocket-handkerchief of a sitting room and to the care of the grandmother, faithfully reported the changes that the household was seeing. Since she herself was elderly, and at once in sympathy with Grandma Westerman, Clara regarded the alterations with certain suspicions and even with jealousy.

"You will not know the ground floor when next you see it. They are throwing paint upon the walls with abandon— unpractical, foolish colors that will show every touch. And the fine heavy draperies have been taken down and packed away. There will be only glass curtains of silk, and the sun will shine

in to fade the flowers on the carpet. It is too much to expect
that they will close the shutters on the sunny side."

In the beginning Grandma Westerman did not feel much interest in the mysterious proceedings below. The shock of exchanging a vigorous life for a bedridden one was all she could
handle for a time.

"The young do not have the solid, conservative ideas that I
was brought up on," she told Clara gloomily. "Let them do
what they will."

After a time, when she had reconciled herself to pain and to
lying abed, she hunted ponderously in her mind for means of
passing the hours when her hands were tired with the weight of
the lace she was knitting, or her fingers stiffened after working
with an embroidery needle and thimble on the cut-work of a
bureau scarf. She would sigh and call out to Clara, "Did they
leave the painting of fruit over the sideboard?"

"That was carried off long ago," Clara would respond with
relish. "And in the bay that looks out on the garden she has
green things growing. Likely they will die soon."

"I suppose my good tablecloths are used for everyday," the
old lady would go on. "Finally they will fall to pieces in the
wash water."

"No-o-o-o," Clara would shake her head. "Mats she uses for
everyday. With children, too. They are more practical, she says.
But it keeps her girl polishing."

"I came here the same way," Grandma Westerman said
abruptly one day. "I made my changes, too, though not with
such speed. It is not easy to go into the household of another
without seeing what might be done."

"You have good understanding," Clara approved. "They
have taken out the hall trees, and your heavy carved table. They
had things of their own, too, she said."

By the time they were finished with the renovation, Grandma
Westerman thought, by the time the painters and carpenters
were gone and every pin was in place, then they would come to
sit with her longer. As it was, Leonie must answer every sum-

mons of the workmen and of Christine, the hired girl, to whom
the big house was confusing. The children were at school, and
Albert was gone all day. Save for the clumsy movements of the
workmen, the house was quiet; it was not quite as she had
visualized, living with three careless children.

Leonie, thin, sallow, sharp-eyed, her face softened only by
abundant, wavy hair, came in every day, naturally. She would sit
down a moment, but her eyes would wander restlessly away
from the bed as though contemplating brisk activity. "Do you
not want these blinds opened? I myself would become spiritless
in so dark a room." She might arise to straighten the bureau top
that was disorderly with medicine bottles, fancy work, and
newspapers. "At the pharmicist's I saw Belle Speas; she asked
for you and sent word her mother would come soon. She is
suffering from kidney stones—old Mrs. Bartel." And then, with
a sigh, "I must hurry down and make the noodle; that Christine
cannot make one fit for a pig, and Albert insists on the kind you
taught me when first we were married."

In the evening, Albert would come in for a short while, expansive after a heavy supper despite his thin, slightly stooped
figure, smelling of cigar smoke and faintly of the cologne applied that morning after shaving.

"Well, Mama," he would say without expecting an answer,
"have you had a good day? Business is something to make your
eyes pop, believe me. It was not like this in Papa's day. All the
forms and permits to be got!" He would shake his head and
cluck his tongue, sitting down then to talk about the business
for a time. "You will fall asleep if I speak longer of business, eh,
Mama?" He would chuckle paternally at his own jokes.

Once she heard him reminding the children that they were to
stop in every day to speak to their grandmother. "Every day,
mind you," he repeated.

"I do, Papa!" Elizabeth, the oldest, cried indignantly, so that
her father hushed her. "I do nearly every day, anyhow. Maria is
the one who sneaks out of it, and I am quite sure Theodore
doesn't go in more than once a week."

Curiously the old lady listened to the objecting young voices, and that of her son, leading them, then, like the concertmaster setting the pace and the tone, so that all three fell into the murmur habitual upon this floor of the house when one of the parents was near.

When spring bloomed into summer and she found herself promoted to a yellow wheel chair shiny with varnish, she asked Clara to push her into the carpeted hall, and it seemed that she entered another house upon leaving her own room. It was not merely the new brightness of the walls, nor the glimpse of the lower hall with its table and heavy mirror in place of the hall trees; it was that she had been gone from most of the house so long that it was unfamiliar and no longer hers. She was a stranger, looking at the home of another.

Surprisingly it was less painful than Grandma Westerman had anticipated; she was ready to admit that the house belonged now to Leonie, whom she did not know intimately and never would, and to Albert, who lacked the vigor of his parents. And it belonged, too, to the children. A tennis racket rested carelessly in a corner, and in the upper hall a doll carriage, its hood primly up to shield the occupant, stood against the wall as though possessing perfect right to its position.

With Clara she schemed clumsily to get the children, one at a time, into her room. It was like snaring animals that were neither timid nor sly; they were all absorbed in inconsequential activities more important to them than the turning of the earth.

Elizabeth, the eldest, was first. Fidgeting in the small rocker, she frowned at fleeting thoughts as though at ease and yet forgetful of her surroundings.

"You are old enough to begin a marriage chest," Grandma Westerman suggested. "Do you embroider well? Can you knit lace?"

"That's old-fashioned, Grandma," Elizabeth explained, rocking lightly and playing with the gold locket she wore. "I can hemstitch very well; Mama says I take smaller stitches than she can."

"Maybe you would like to learn to knit fine lace yokes for your nightgowns," the old lady ventured.

"That is no longer the fashion," the girl said with pity, and smiled as though her grandparent were a child still learning the ways of the world.

Grandma Westerman would not stoop to luring any of them with gifts or promises. No bribes, no candy bowl, no coins. Gifts were strictly associated with occasions—birthdays and Christmas, confirmation, graduation.

Theodore did not know what to do with himself when he was in her room. He studied the floor, described circles on the carpet with his shoes, played tricks with one hand upon the other, and labored with a frown to think of subjects for dutiful conversation.

"I know a boy that collects birds' eggs," he said with sudden inspiration. "He let me blow one out. A swallow's egg with speckles. First you punch a needle in each end, and then you blow. You barely blow at all, or the egg breaks."

"Your grandfather collected stamps," Grandma Westerman told him. "Do you like stamps? Someday they may come to you."

"I might collect wild animals," he confided, "some day." Then the look of faraway dreaming left his eyes, and he hurried away with complicated but vague explanation regarding a ball game.

Of a cool summer morning Maria could be heard lurking in the upper hallway, passing her grandmother's door without apparent reason other than curiosity or perhaps some half-murmured and mysterious game she played with invisible companions.

If Grandma Westerman called out to her, the little girl appeared shyly in wordless question, cradling a doll with battered face or carrying scraps of paper, bits of cotton material, a fancy box or some other subject worthless in the eyes of an adult.

"Will you let me see your leg?" Maria asked hopefully in an undertone at one of the first intimate encounters.

Grandma Westerman lifted the light cover, revealing the plump cast upon her old leg. And when Maria reached out exploring fingers to tap the cast, Grandma Westerman chuckled aloud.

"You find that interesting," she stated, watching the child's soft face, feeling a faint flush of pleasure as Maria stared long with respect and admiration.

"What do you do, now that there is no school?" the grandmother asked when the leg was modestly covered again.

"Oh—things," Maria answered vaguely, her eyes turning away and dreaming momentarily upon unseen vacancies. "Lots of things." A secret look of pleasure entered her eyes.

"All day you play," Grandma Westerman said wonderingly. "From morning till nighttime."

Maria nodded slowly in pleased agreement. "Sometimes I work, though," she spoke virtuously in afterthought.

"What work do you do?" the old woman asked indulgently.

Maria frowned in recollection. "One day I made a penwiper for Papa's desk."

"Very good," Grandma Westerman praised.

Maria shook her head in distaste. "It was ugly. Ugly, ugly, ugly. Mama would let me use only old dark cloth—so the ink would not show."

"That was sensible."

"I don't like to be sensible," Maria demurred. She rocked so hard that the chair moved over the faded carpet.

"Everyone must learn to be sensible. The earlier, the better." Grandma Westerman fell into an unexpected doze, and by the time she opened her eyes again Maria had slipped away.

It was the elusiveness of the household that caused Grandma Westerman to brood for slow, stuffy hours. She was outside the magic circle they occupied, and there was no way to step over the boundary. She was outside in time and in space, in person, even. There was no way to enter but with the assistance of a spiritual hand from one within, and that hand was not offered. They saw her, but they looked with shallow, absent eyes—those people within this one small magic circle. They saw the plump, old-fashioned little woman, lips disciplined, standing soberly outside, watching, ready to speak phrases of another world, an-

other time, phrases that were dull and stiff and hopelessly out-
moded. They felt sorry for her, sorry for the detached position
of her years and her physical being, but they did not feel compassion; their mental eyes could not penetrate that far.

They did not know, she would tell herself mournfully, that
they were all moving with unsuspected speed toward the very
position she held. The parents surmised it, perhaps, at shadowy
moments in the night's midst when they lay in uneasy wakefulness, but they would never speak aloud of it. As for the children, they had not one idea in the world that they would ever
proceed past a wonderful age of fresh adulthood where the
universe would open like a sorcerer's ball to offer dazzling beau-
ties.

"If they could but know—" she would speak to herself in
alarm. "If they could but know—" And she might utter a faint
sound of consternation that would rouse Clara if she were in
the room, and then Grandma Westerman would have to mumble that she had merely cleared her throat.

When Albert's birthday arrived, a celebration was planned; it
was as though, in taking over the family house, he had come of
age or attained a position of increased prestige, at least.
Grandma Westerman's other sons and their families came from
their homes in nearby towns to celebrate the occasion. When
the gala day arrived, two of them carried her from her rooms,
down the steep flight of carpeted steps, through the real hall
and the tiny conservatory, where a long table was set under the
chestnut trees. Her wheel chair was there, awaiting her, and
Clara fussed over her, shaking out a light shawl to cover her legs,
rearranging the lace collar on her black silk dress.

It was a drowsy summer afternoon; the languid wind played
with the corners of the white tablecloth without intent, and the
bees droned monotonously in the arbor. The families made a
fine showing, ten children and the half-dozen adults, the sister
of one of the daughters-in-law, and then herself, apart from the
others, eating from a tray upon which Clara high-handedly
placed some of the choicest morsels—the livers of chicken, the
most perfectly shaped little dumplings, the tiniest of the new
potatoes dripping with black butter.

Grandma Westerman's mind journeyed back to the times that she herself had been the one to plan such occasions. She it was who arose early to cook and bake, to turn out the richly seasoned dishes, to give orders to the housekeeper, choose the cloth to be used, cut the garden flowers, and lay the silver on the table. Now it was another; now it was Leonie. She had arisen when the dew still drenched the grass. The precisely decorated cake that stood before Albert now, bearing his name and birth date, was of her baking.

Albert cut it with a long silver knife, light-heartedly pretending for the children's sake to make a wish as the blade disappeared beneath the snowy icing.

"The first piece is yours," the smaller children repeated solemnly. "The first piece is yours, because this is your birthday."

He set to one side the plate holding the first slice, and when he cut a second, Clara, hovering over him, whispered in his ear. As he was about to hand her the second plate he put it aside and impulsively reached for the first. With a courtly bow in his mother's direction, he announced, "To Grandma I present the first slice with the birthday wish."

As Clara with a proud smile bore the plate to her, the children all clapped loudly in approval, and the women joined in for an indulgent moment. Their clapping was flat and hollow in the sleepy summer air. It was as though for a moment they were expressing all the half-spoken excitement of the day in the wild movements of their palms meeting, parting, meeting vigorously again. It was not Albert's act or the honor accorded the grandmother they were applauding; it was the summer day, the good heavy dinner, and the expectations and secret dreams of their age.

They toasted the day with sweet pale wine. The old woman became drowsy for a time; Albert's voice, as he arose to make a solemn speech, drew farther and farther away from her, and she awoke only when the air was quiet again.

With lazy whoops, then, the boys arose and went to assemble at the far side of the garden, and the girls followed them hopefully. Christine and Clara had cleared the table of all but the coffee cups and the wine glasses and the remains of the cake, and the parents reviewed news of the past months, relating what mutual acquaintances had died, what families had been blessed with births, describing illnesses and other misfortunes that had overtaken some. They spoke of old Mrs. Bartel dying suddenly, of the division of property, the quarrel between two of the children over certain land.

"She had nothing left," Grandma Westerman said unexpectedly.

From their positions at the table they all turned to stare at her, sitting aside in the varnished wheel chair.

"I myself am ready to go," Grandma Westerman continued calmly. "I am ready to die."

In abrupt shame and alarm the faces turned away from her again, all but those of the two older granddaughters, who, lips parted, watched her frightenedly.

"Now, Mama," one of the sons murmured uncomfortably.

"It is not right to talk so," another reprimanded gently.

All were silent for moments. Then one of the women spoke hurriedly, asking Leonie about the burnt-sugar birthday cake, of which now only a thin wedge remained.

After a while Grandma Westerman fell into a light, restful doze. And she dreamed that the sons and sons' wives had drawn into a clandestine group at the end of the table to speak of her in deep whispers.

"Grandma is failing so fast; I could not believe it when I came yesterday. . . . She is becoming a different woman— fleshy still, but quiet and watchful, with little to say. . . . She is slipping—slipping slowly away. Leonie says she sleeps more and more—little naps here and there. . . . And what she said a while ago. 'I am ready to die,' she said; I thought my heart would turn over. . . .'"

Afterward she did not know if they had really spoken such words or not. Perhaps she had not even slept but had withdrawn into a cocoon apart from consciousness but not remote enough for unconsciousness.

The thought fretted at her brain. If she were going to die, she

wanted the quitting to be abrupt, not lingering. She wanted to
move rapidly from one world to another without having time to
think about it, to be fearful of the moment, and to conjecture
as to what internal strength she might have.

Above all, she desired to be heard before departing. How
could she tell them what occupied her thoughts? They did not
have time to listen. They were, in addition, deaf and blind to
what was to be heard and seen.

Her own mother had died without speaking of what lay
within her heart, but she had been unwarned of death. One
hour she had gone about household duties; the next hour she
had been carried to her bed to draw final breath. Yet there had
been her paternal grandmother, who lived with them for the
long years of her widowhood. She had calmly bade them draw
about her bedside. Grandma Westerman had huddled there
with her brothers and sisters, terrified into wordlessness, yet
bound by a terrible curiosity for the labored breathing, the
ashen face and the determined voice speaking solemnly, almost
wistfully, but still commanding them so that the hour remained
in her mind all this time.

"Honor thy father and mother," the old woman had said
hoarsely to the frightened children. And to the parents, "Above
all, live prudently. . . ."

But it was not enough, Grandma Westerman told herself. It
was as though her grandparent were bidding a stern farewell before making a visit elsewhere, or merely giving reprimand for
some misdeed. The young should learn what lay before them;
knowledge of that kind would give purpose to their lives, con-
templative wisdom to their youthfulness. How could they live
prudently when the reason for prudent living was unknown to
them?

And how could she tell them except at such a moment as
death, when they would gather round with respect upon their
faces and respect within their beings, respect for death first, and
then for the one about to close her eyes forever to the world? It
was too plain that she could not command from the weak position she held now. To them all she was but an ailing old woman

with a crippled leg upon which she would never walk again, a sick old grandmother who was classified nearer the children than the adults.

She had lost the independent vigor of being that had been a foremost quality. It had begun slipping unnoticed from her long before she fell upon the stairs. And now she had ceased expecting its return, ceased caring, even. Yet it was better that way; if she had known it was dwindling into nothing, she would have been angry and frightened. Now it was gone, and she was ready to accept the loss just as she had accepted whatever came.

Yet there remained this one desire, this yearning to reveal to her children and her grandchildren the direction in which they walked.

She began dwelling upon what she would speak to them. Beneath the sky, she must tell them, the earth turns slowly. No one feels the motion of its turning, but there it is. The seasons follow one another; the years tread softly on each other's heels; the generations are born and given maturity, and the movement is the same. The universe operates by cycle; every element depends upon a cycle.

"As I move away," she said in the darkness of quiet night hours, "you move up. We walk slowly, all of us, away from the sun, that gives life." There was another thought that caused her to digress then. Did they walk away from the sun, or did they move toward this representation of God? She could not tell. But whatever the focus, they walked blindly. They had little sense of destination until all of a sudden it appeared before them, ready to swallow them whole, to add them impersonally to all who had gone before into the vast, solemn brilliance of the unknown world after.

That was not all. There lay, in the invisible air, the unspoken bidding to serve the world in some manner, to extend the eye and the hand beyond the fairy circle of family and friends, to touch what seemed near untouchable. It was more than duty: it was a spiritual bidding of a universe in which all souls were equal in need. All were frail and open to pity; all must, despite weak and transparent qualities, give of themselves. She herself had not become aware of this until age had crept quietly, stiffly upon her.

She lay thinking upon all this, repeating until the thoughts wore grooves of their own upon her mind and crowded out the tiresome details of the physical world. The season changed, but she hardly noticed. She was on her way; despite the old limbs quiet in the bed, she was taking the last, dragging steps. Sharply she attended to that one activity; when she could step not once more she must take a stand and speak.

The sons came regularly, one by one, to sit near her, but she scarcely noted their presence. Only Clara was left of reality, Clara whose bent shoulders and slow, steady steps appeared without being summoned. Grandma Westerman would look at her with fondness, at the patient eyes and wrinkled, ministering hands.

Sometimes in the heavy night hours, when Clara would pour her a drink of water or let medicine trickle into a silver spoon, they would speak in spare phrases with an intimacy that comforted her.

"You will have a home here," Grandma Westerman murmured. "I have spoken to Albert."

"It is wicked to imply—" Clara reprimanded as a child. "You will be better one day soon. The medicine is slow when one is heavy with years."

"I see the truth," the old lady said stubbornly. "At my hour nothing obscures the eyes."

"One must always hope," reminded Clara. "There is nothing in the world if not hope."

"When the time comes," Grandma Westerman spoke, "you must call them in—Albert and Leonie, and the children."

"Yes, yes," soothed Clara. "You have told me a dozen times. I have promised."

"There is something I wish to say to them," the old woman said dreamily, "something they must know."

Day by day a great eagerness for the hour came over her. Sometimes she feared to fall asleep, thinking it might come unbeknownst, and be lost to her. "If you see sometime," she instructed Clara, "that the time has come, rouse me. Do not hesitate."

But in her awaiting, in the alert core of her mind, she watched stealthily. The triumph of recognition was almost overwhelming. Such eagerness flowed through her that she lost awareness. In the dazzling, blinding swirl of unconsciousness she forced her way determinedly back and held a position divided only by a dimness of physical perception.

There was confusion in the doorway; she endured it with patience, holding proudly to her command of the hour; such strength seemed to resurge she thought herself able to wait for long. Anticipation brought exquisite pleasure so that she trembled violently and Clara held to her while still crying to the family, "Hurry now!"

It was Elizabeth who was responsible for the commotion. Hysterically she tried to pull away from her father. "Don't make me," she wept.

"She is too sensitive for this," Leonie defended her daughter. "And at the delicate age, too."

"Nevertheless she must enter," Albert pronounced. "This is Grandma's last wish. Slap her cheeks and bring her to her senses."

When the old lady opened her eyes again, the room was quiet but for Elizabeth's muffled sobbing as she stood pressed within the circle of her mother's arm. She could see the two small children standing beside Leonie, and she frowned at the absence of Albert.

"My stomach aches," Theodore whispered, and Maria looked at him as though he were a stranger.

At last Grandma Westerman discovered that one hand was being fondled, and that at her side was Albert, his eyes pink, his face damp. Finding his nearness distasteful, she looked at the children again. It appeared that two large tears stood on Maria's cheeks, that they had come unbidden from the round, wondering eyes to roll gently only a little way. She wished Maria were beside her rather than Albert; the child would be less disturbing than the man, but there was not time to request the change.

Clara she could not see at all, but sensed that the elderly woman was close to her. Sighing, prolonging the moment a bit, Grandma Westerman wet her lips with unwieldy tongue, and spoke.

"The universe turns slyly, and unseen," she said. In a little the church bells would be tolling ponderously for her; she and her brother had run swiftly down the street to the church when their grandmother departed.

"She is out of her head," Leonie murmured. "She does not know what words she speaks."

"As I move away," the old woman went on softly and deliberately, as if repeating a lesson, "you move up into my place. . . ."

Blinking her eyelids, she looked at them long. What she had already said was beginning to penetrate; she could tell by the increasing mistiness of the faces as though the spirits had arisen to the very surface.

Exultation flowered as she bid the next phrases come to her lips and tongue, and she could not speak at all for a moment. But she had only begun. Her triumph must carry her through to the end of the precise revelation.

"We are all walking faster and faster," she wanted to say, "to our destination. . . ."

But with a rude rush it all receded from her—the words, the faces, the brilliance, the universe. And she was alone.

At the Crossing

BY JAN WAHL

EVEN now, comfortably sheltered in hard-won sheets, when I hear trains litter the night with their sad warning whistles—stealing out of the dark, merging again into deep vasty stillness like needles threading time and far-flung cities, speeding, though somehow barely inching by, mournfully hooting their song—I try telling myself there is a hand at each throttle, gloved, but perceptibly of flesh-and-bone; yet there was an instant, long past (that is, "long past" as we reckon apple-dropping, artery-stiffening, ordinary time), when I, out of need or fear, or maybe conscience, believed an agent of unknown powers, destiny's tool, whether sinister or angelic I was never completely to resolve, to be hurtling straight toward me, uncompromisingly, shatteringly, with so solemn an impact that it thrust me headlong into the future, into inevitable manhood; oh God, such a terrible swift machine.

To begin with, I was early an orphan. . . .

Before I'd no more than unveiled my eyes, Mother and Father (names never to be abbreviated, for me, fondly or by habit, into *Mom, Ma, Pops,* or *Dad*) were snatched supernaturally away, drawn upward into "ethereal bliss." The latter I was promised by some obscure, smiling face that leaned over my crib—some distant cousin or shirttail relative, who, having thus discharged the duties of kinship, removed herself from view, now remembered chiefly as a figure culled from the past, a messenger of unearthly tidings. I seem to accompany this visitation with a musk compounded of sweet cloves and pungent mothballs, as if, whoever she was, she were kept in storage in a closet, to be let out solely upon the occasion of momentous news; and having related it withdrew again into her dim, sacheted limbo.

Thereafter I was shuttled between two sets of unwilling, tight-lipped grandparents, handed over at regular intervals like a package which no one presumed to claim for very long.

At the first house, in town, I was let loose to roam upstairs the whole day, dressed in my Dr. Denton's; there was an airing deck which turned itself into an island, fighting ship, or iceberg. I used to collect acorns and throw them from this tower at the passing, fat honey-man, whose shout, "Made by bees, buy it puh-*leeze!*" was the signal for me to catapult my ammunition. Getting stung on the ear by a flying seed, he'd gaze upward, in pain, to the airing deck, where I would strike my fists against the eaves trough, instantly grieved. Yet the next time he passed I repeated my mischief: and again, and not until then would he, slowing his bell-harnessed pony, look up at me. Marooned, I used to hoist appeals of distress (a stocking tied to the plumber's friend; or a diminutive rocket, secretly hoarded on Fourth of July, which I dared not shoot off but could only wave at the end of its stick), to nobody in particular; once I thought of flinging myself down from my deck, smashing myself like a pancake in the yard—and *then* they'd be sorry, I said, the "they," I suppose, signifying my "town" grandparents. Else I toyed with stowing away on a freight train as it lingered beside the dusty Granary, hoboing it to sheik-filled deserts or mermaid seas. There was the station office, small and forlorn, rarely occupied, whose Master flagged sleek diesels down, when it happened bona fide passengers had purchased regular tickets; but I had no such hopes for formal departure, tutti-frutti ice-cream sundaes (double-heaping dip with fudge, bought while my grandmother was having, next door, her wispy hair curled and strangely

blued) being the manageable limit of my escape. My grandfather, who owned a hardware store (everything in the house
was fitted with a Yale lock, even the cupboard for gingersnaps
and raisins), spent afterhours practicing archery in the back
yard, a sport to which I was never invited, though my aim, as the
honey-man knew, was pretty fair. Besides, it was my trembling,
constant notion that if my bow-and-arrowed grandfather had
indeed summoned me down, it would be, due to his increasing
passion for trick shots, to perch an apple on my head. He also
had a workshop, a sturdy tar-roofed annex to the garage, where
he enthusiastically strived to make what he called the "Table
Ideal." Saws spun, the lathe whirred, the power drill screeched;
you could smell varnish and sticky glue. These wobbly-legged
products of his leisure became his annual Christmas gifts. The
neighborhood was gradually flooded with slightly lopsided tables; but you guessed if he ever achieved his goal, the lathe
would stop. Unfortunately, the lathe didn't stop soon enough:
one day he sliced off his favorite (right-hand) index finger, a
tidbit pounced upon at once by the bulldog, Chum, who scurried around the yard with it teasingly clenched in her jaws. My
grandfather, amazed, spouting precious blood (peering down on
the scene, I was sure I observed his normal ruddy color oozing
away), chased her under a set of fragile, crackly bushes, where
she selfishy transported her treasure; driven to a frenzy, torn between the desire to confiscate the finger and the fear of ruining
first-class garden-club bushes, he grew white, not only from the
blood-letting but from sheer vexation. However, Chum had un-
wittingly saved the day (persuaded at length to swap the trophy
for a nice beefsteak patty, upon later reflection she felt grossly
cheated), for the digit, having been warmed in her salivaed,
panting mouth, was usable still: the doctor who practiced
around the corner, like a top-hatted wand-waving conjurer,
quickly pressed the severed piece back into place, where even-
tually it mended, becoming stiff, less serviceable than before, yet
a triumph, to me, of the surgeon's art—proof that the most mys-
tifying things were possible. I lived a shadowy life in that house,
now and then bending over the polished red-oak banister, peek-

ing into the living room, where my grandmother served tea in handleless cups ("Chinese," she declared; thus, for a long time, I assumed the people in China were not equipped with hands) to three other ladies, all of whom sat laughing, with bright bonnets on, around a wicker card table, playing a game which went by the name of Pepper. I had prepared an answer in case they ever invited me to join their group—"I'm sorry, it might make me sneeze!" but, since the invitation never came, that attempt at wit ruefully went to waste. I was the family skeleton, doomed to traipse no farther than the reaches of the upper hall. I was the black, unlucky penny, nourishing the theory my father and mother had been a gangster and his moll, shot down at the height of a glorious career. (Unless they had shot each other.) Later I decided, with less romanticism, that neither set of grandparents cared for ghosts, and, in a way, I was one, a feeble reminder of the children they so soon had been deprived of. Since it was impossible to discover what my mother and father had been like (with tantalizing exceptions; for instance, once I was taken on a rare walk by my grandfather, who kept nervously flicking the drooping daisy in his buttonhole with his patched finger, and when we passed the Main Street saloon, the town drunk came tumbling out the door, throwing a wild salute, asking, "Hey, isn't that Big Gooseneck's boy? Hello, Little Gooseneck!" my grandfather propelling me angrily away; however, thereupon I persistently tried, by means of various exercises, to elongate my neck, in the vain hope of increasing the resemblance), I had little, you see, to pattern myself after. One day I found the medicine cabinet in the bathroom by some miracle unlocked; with the aid of a new, glittering tube of toothpaste I was able to write my name wherever I chose—so that you could even sit on it. The tube at last exhausted, I tried yelling down the warm-air vent to Chum, who was obliged to pass her days taking frequent naps in the basement. My grandmother's cronies were immersed in their usual round of Pepper, and, being bored silly (having gotten no reply from Chum), I decided to swallow, and pretend it was poison, a bottle of devil's-skulled iodine. I didn't, it seemed, need to pretend, and fled downstairs with throat aflame, interrupting the cardplayers, who turned four shades of green. My grandmother objected to scenes of violence, sticking her nose ostrichlike into the smelling salts, while one bonneted lady forced upon me, whether for punishment or remedy I wasn't positive, a lump of fat yellow butter. When the wand-waving doctor appeared, to work his mesmeric spell (aided by what I took to be an innocent bicycle pump), and they knew I would survive, there was an inarticulate farewell; I was hustled immediately out of town, delivered to my grandparents in the country. I was never sent to the ones in town again, thus never to learn if that grandfather found the table he was avidly searching for, out in his shed, to display it elatedly when he was done; nor if someday I might be elected to take a hand at cards.

On the farm, I fared no better. Collecting, washing by hand then candling eggs, pulling or planting beans, carrots, red beets, squash, okra, turnips, green-topped onions, radishes and (considered a newfangled, city-eating crop) broccoli—my domain strictly confined to the rows out behind the kitchen (the man-sized, Herculean fields lying beyond, ineffable stretches of corn, alfalfa, winter wheat, being prodigiously outside my ken), co-priest of sorts at innumerable baptisms of fatally slaughtered hens (their creepy, defiant, twitchy death dance made a stark spine-tingling spectacle: you never knew if they intended to hop after *you*) in tubs of steaming water, plucking scalded feathers, tossing endless loops of entrails to the cats (mostly fed on a gruesome diet of coffee grounds and leftover mashed potatoes, after which the innards probably came as a delicacy), hapless victim of the stern unwritten country code that while the sun was out, from rise to the drop at day's end, no decent bones were at rest—I perpetually juggled these homely products in clumsy, unfeeling fashion. Whatever my origin, I was clearly not bred out of the soil and was overjoyed my mother (if this were indeed my mother's house) had spirited away. If I, endeavoring to call it quits, slipped off to bed with hands unscrubbed, the following morning I was privileged to fetch and prune my own birch switch and had to grab my ankles and lower my knickers.

Eggs were intended for the market, not for the table; for the sake of economy, diluting was done on a grand scale—even oyster stew stretched and thinned to the point where ingredients had to be seasoned with bold imagination—you had to satisfy yourself with flavor. My grandmother put up long-lasting, rubbery, sour preserves, and in the evening, her bifocals hooked over her wart, patiently rocked away and mended, repeating religiously under her breath, "A stitch in time saves nine." There seemed to be a great distrust of idleness, my grandfather almost never dragging himself indoors, except, as in a daze, to step wearily across the threshold when ordered in for meals (the farm was marked with invisible boundaries; it was unseemly to cross beyond your place, and my grandmother ruled the hearth), and then his mind was outside, on pig litters or punctured Sears & Roebuck tires, or alternation of crops to save the soil. I don't know whether they lived in peril of having the sheriff foreclose, but they constantly felt in danger of sudden hail or swift tornado, or some vague terrible vengeance of the Lord that might sweep the place to ruin, though I believe they feared the poorhouse more than Hell. Yet there was one extravagance—which was not even that, to be truthful—a hired girl named Arlene Trietch, who, because of weak crossed eyes (Arlene, literally, however hard she struggled, could not see past her nose) could command no more than five dollars a month plus board, a sum for which she turned things upside down and swept and faithfully scoured, as if we were readying the place for inspection, to meet the Day of Judgment. On Saturday nights Arlene used to stand out on the back stoop and count the stars, and hum to herself and dance with the broom, and fly up to her room, which was cold, and secretly wail; till once my grandmother came out and caught her, announcing fiercely, "Wicked sins make wicked sinners! I know! It's happened before!" and Arlene, troubled, cried aloud; and I was left to make of that what I could, fitting it into the puzzle of who I was. The Saturday "dances" were cancelled, and Arlene fell into a decline, now and then gazing with blurred, limited vision, off into the blue with a worried desperate look, grabbing the business end of her broom and sweeping the varnish off the floors; she no longer hummed, nor made a game of pretending to number the stars; and if she so much as smiled, whirled around, haunted by the idea my grandmother would claim she harbored evil demons. Life on the farm being pretty much puritan matter-of-fact, only out in the privy, with the slatted door safely bolted, rules and chores behind me, could I speculate about the universe. At night, I heard trains howling far away, melancholy and wonderfully enticing; and in the dark I suppose I shared some of Arlene's electric dreams—like wanting someone to bend down, and plant a comforting kiss on my brow. Out in the privy, I became fascinated by the bottomless-seeming hole. Nearly accessible, yet forbidding, it promised, within its depths, admission to worlds mysterious and explorable, though the only possible entry was too small to accommodate me. Suddenly inspired, I decided if I couldn't go myself to appoint a proxy. I ran to fetch one of the kittens—in fact, to keep him company, scooped up all four and dropped them ceremoniously in. They disappeared one by one, sinking out of sight with unhappy squeals, drowning. I sensed the tone of things had changed, and raced out of my orbit across the fields to locate my grandfather who was pitchforking hay. He followed me back, strapping on hip boots, and tore the privy violently apart, spewing boards and stepping into the opening, which, exposed to view, gaping wide, looked horrible and glamorless. My grandmother washed off the bodies he retrieved; three had suffocated and the fourth lay dreadfuly gasping, and he too died, taking his secrets with him. I remember the official county sedan that whisked me soon away, and when it quickly wheeled off, onto the sun-baked road, no one came forth to shout good-by, though, when we were at a distance, I thought I saw, at an upper unpainted window, Arlene's tousled head—with her half-blind eyes semaphoring in vain, trying her best to make me out.

Uncle Nick and Aunt Ida Grove had never been blessed with children—a bed of unfortunate tulips lined their stucco cottage, a granite birdbath sat empty in the yard. It seemed they could never make things grow, nor, though they changed the water, could they attract the dusty, flying birds. The county board attempted to palm me off on them. I was received with open arms. They bought me the Book of Knowledge, and handed me a dollar to spend each week. I, in return, gave Uncle Nick his heart medicine daily, and for Aunt Ida stirred cake batter and laid out the heirloom knives and forks. I got anything I wanted, and soon I asked for a dollar and a quarter a week.

Uncle Nick, semiretired (he delivered the rural morning mail, piloting his cargo through cinders, tar, and clouds of sand), polished energetically his car. Aunt Ida used to stick her head out the side entrance, advising, "Let the boy do it, now! You've got to take it easy!" So I assumed the work and rubbed until my elbows ached, and Uncle Nick would hover over me, smoking a forbidden cigar. My meager arms, strained and sore, labored manfully. I derived a certain pride from watching him back the gorgeous, glinting car out the drive; with a smile, he always returned my wave. Aunt Ida would load my lunch box with peanut butter and thick slices of ham, and frequent surprises like twisted "lickrish" ropes and even jumping beans (which you dared not eat, to be sure, but which my schoolmates unfailingly envied). I would line up colored beans along the sloping top of my desk, letting them race downhill into my lap. I don't know why, but I found, with practice, that red beans generally won, a fact that entertained me more than long division. I had a shiny bike, while the other children went by foot. This way, the Groves said, I came home "in advance," though I sometimes vexed them by taking a meandering, circuitous route—along the creek and three times around the waterworks, inhaling the awful fumes. When I arrived, Aunt Ida was usually half-dissolved in tears, as if I might have been stolen, or worse, as if I were really too good to be true, being no more than a wished-for phantom.

When I had lived with them approaching a year, mollycoddled and fussed over, lavishly satisfied, and my sets of unindulgent grandparents had nearly sailed out of recollection, Uncle Nick mentioned intending to take me to the Ridge Church's

Fathers and Sons Banquet, and for the occasion bought me a suit, far in advance; he could hardly wait, and weeks ahead started marking Thursdays off on his insurance calendar.

We often drove out, just beyond town to the B & O crossing, to watch the new streamliner dash through. It passed like a great gray bullet, toward dusk, its piercing beam illuminating the tracks for a hundred yards. The locomotive's eerie horn (the old, conventional trains whistled) hooted miles before it ever appeared, and we used to count the towns and highways— three in all, within our range of hearing—through which it cut before we laid eyes on it. I hung onto Uncle Nick's hand tightly, meeting the coming monster. So did Aunt Ida; and when it lightninged by, with an overwhelming avalanche of sound, the ground under us trembled. "What won't they send out next?" Uncle Nick quietly would reflect after this symbol of the modern age sped out of view again, back into the future— and our car, spruced up to a fare-thee-well, nevertheless seemed out-of-date and diminished, and we rode our relic home.

An albatross so long, I scarcely knew what to make of the Groves's barrage of affections: I had never developed the faculty to respond. Once I came out on the sun porch to find Aunt Ida shelling peas, and having been initiated in this art on the farm, I sat beside her with the dishpan, culling fresh green pods. Pink-cheeked and cheery-eyed, she bent over to pat my arm, softly. Taken by surprise, I knocked my pan to the floor, and in my clumsiness squashed a dozen peas, but what I wanted to do was to bury my head, with thanks, deep in her apron lap.

Another mishap occurred upon my birthday. Aunt Ida and Uncle Nick had laid out, on the mantlepiece, a parade of fine lead soldiers, identically plumed and uniformed, including a tent to place the hopelessly wounded in; it was a handsome gift, painted by hand (later I learned *he* had done the painting, because I discovered his kit of oils), but I failed to be pleased, having long set my mind on a Lone Ranger outfit (I had visions of myself doing good deeds, while masked). I sulked and at once stormed off to my room, leaving them hurt and empty-handed.

Oh God, my sphere having been an airing deck and a poor back stoop, I was cast at sea, in the dominion of unrehearsed, actual love. I hadn't got the knack of playing the son, I used to tell myself—how could I ever grow up to play the father?

Uncle Nick often sat at the table late, tallying his bills. One night, before bed, I brought him the heart medicine (I wondered if that was what I needed, to fertilize my love capacity, but it tasted discouragingly rancid). He was sharpening his pencil with a pocket knife; I envied him the beautiful point. "Looking forward to the banquet?" he asked, measuring the calendar, which on the bottom border stated,

WILL YOU LEAVE YOUR FAMILY PROVIDED?

"Oh, yes!" I replied, faking enthusiasm, holding brightly the spoon. The banquet then meant nothing to me except the first opportunity to show off my suit, but for him, I now see, this meant the realization of a long-held, marvelous dream.

As it happens, I must reveal, he didn't enjoy that pleasurable meal.

Aunt Ida having inspected us, I believe, one thousand times, we were pronounced absolutely elegant. She tied my spotted bow tie, tucking a handkerchief in my pocket so that miniature rabbit ears hung out.

She fixed me, finally, with a jeweler's appraising eye, removing last-minute lint. Suspendered Uncle Nick was reshining his shoes, nervous and joyful. I think what I regret most about that evening—the remaining events must be approached in a fatalistic light, otherwise it turns out gloomily tragic—is all the wasted effort, the useless attention to detail. Aunt Ida continued fussing over me, then turned her gaze on her husband. I went to get his jacket, hanging on a hook in the hall.

"Ida, did you ever guess I'd make the Fathers and Sons Banquet? By George, it hardly seems possible!" I heard him chortle, his voice quavering. The full import of it—that I was to act as a full-fledged son—was just dawning on me, trickling into my consciousness. I picked up the jacket and felt an attractive lump inside, the lump identified as his worn leather wallet: and when

I unsnapped its catch and lifted back the "hider," I counted
five five-dollar bills. As if observing the fingers of an old pro, I
watched mine seize the crispest of the five like a pair of pinch-
ers, and I folded it hurriedly, slipping it into my pants pocket. I
thought of myself donating tutti-frutti sundaes to the whole
class, or at least walking out of Robinson's Five & Ten wearing
the Lone Ranger suit. I might even buy Aunt Ida a cat from the
pound; I heard tabbies were available as low as fifty cents
apiece—for Uncle Nick I'd get tobacco. I never considered he
might discover the loss; it seemed to me that anyone carrying so
much as *five* five-dollar bills should never miss one. With this
logic on my side, I brought the jacket in, and he stuck his fists,
trembling, inside the sleeves. Aunt Ida walked us out to the
car, which I had polished that afternoon. Its body, shelllike and
smooth, seemed armor invincible. Uncle Nick undertook to
paint out every scratch that marred its surface; and since he
drove through rough country roads, delivering the mails, he was
often busy. We dusted the windshield anew, Aunt Ida shedding
a few tears. "My two boys," she said, hugging us both good-by;
and we got in and locked the doors ritualistically. "Don't eat
too much!" she laughed, and we laughed back, heading out Mc-
Kinley Road toward the Ridge. In the distance I heard a train's
hoot.

"Three!" we both chimed, winking, then settled down.

At the Ridge Church we were to fulfill important roles. We
began to ponder the significance of our journey, and what lay at
the end, and each lapsed into thought.

We passed the newspaper editor and his wife, napping on
their porch. The light was fading, another day falling. I was becoming hungry. I was going to ask whether it was true chicken
barbecue was to be served, but suddenly I felt the five dollars in
my pocket, eating a terrible hole. I squirmed in my seat. We
heard the train again. "Two!" we said, driving on in silence. I
noticed Uncle Nick had turned vivid crimson, flushing in the
face. I was sure he suspected what I had done. "Do you need
your medicine?" I volunteered, edging guiltily forward; and
while he reddened, I grew pale. I thought I could hear the five-

dollar note unfolding itself, trying to spring out of my pocket. Uncle Nick slumped forward, leaning against the wheel, his foot pressing heavily on the gas pedal. We gained momentum. The train sounded its horn, down the line. We had cleared the edge of town; the road to the crossing was wide and straight. "*One*," I cautioned, under my breath. Uncle Nick stared, without faltering, ahead. The warning signals blinked steadily. I could feel the tracks reverberating; there was a queer buzzing in the air.

"Uncle Nick, it's here," I said, maneuvering toward the door handle.

His hands were locked to the wheel, and though we had crossed the yellow line to the left side of the road, we were accurately mounting the raised incline, between the two flashing lights. He seemed to be bent on a solitary mission, to aim straight for the Ridge. "I stole five dollars," I whispered, glancing at the approaching train. The powerful engine was racing to meet us squarely at the intersection. "Stop, I took the money!" I called, but nothing could have prevented the driver from heading the car, now slackening a trifle, over the looming tracks.

"Please!" I added, clutching his sleeve.

He sat immobile, like a plank of wood, his eyes stubbornly glued ahead. "FATHER!" I urged, as a last resort—yet I already knew everything was too late, I was obliged to suffer on my own; to survive, I understood, you have got to become independent, you have got to free yourself totally. . . . I left him stiffly, grimly guiding the wheel (alive or dead, he would not abandon ship), and as the train bore thunderously down, a second before the ear-splitting impact—the train seemed to be screaming inside my head, making me choose between oblivion and the chance to prove myself—I opened the door almost against my will and dived out alone, far out into space, plummeting to I didn't know where. . . .

Sandra

BY GEORGE P. ELLIOTT

A FEW years ago I inherited a handsome, neo-Spanish house in a good neighborhood in Oakland. It was much too large for a single man, as I knew perfectly well; if I had behaved sensibly I would have sold it and stayed in my bachelor quarters; I could have got a good price for it. But I was not sensible; I liked the house very much; I was tired of my apartment-house life; I didn't need the money. Within a month I had moved in and set about looking for a housekeeper.

From the moment I began looking, everyone assured me that I should get a domestic slave. I was reluctant to get one, not so much because of the expense as because of my own inexperience. No one in my family had ever had one, and among my acquaintances there were not more than three or four who had any. Nevertheless, the arguments in favor of my buying a slave were too great to be ignored. The argument that irritated me most was the one used by the wives of my friends. "When you marry," they would say, "think how happy it will make your wife to have a domestic slave." Then they would offer, zealously, to select one for me. I preferred to do my own selecting. I began watching the classified ads for slaves for sale.

Some days there would be no slaves listed for sale at all; on Sundays there might be as many as ten. There would be a middle-aged Negro woman, 22 years' experience, best recommendations, $4,500; or a 35-year-old Oriental, speaks English, excellent cook, recommendations, $5,000; or a middle-aged woman of German descent, very neat, no pets or vices, good cook, recommendations, $4,800. Sensible choices, no doubt, but none of them appealed to me. Somewhere in the back of my mind there was the notion of the slave I wanted. It made me restless, looking; all I knew about it was that I wanted a female. I was hard to satisfy. I took to dropping by the Emeryville stores, near where my plant was located, looking for a slave. What few there were in stock were obviously of inferior quality. I knew that I would have to canvass the large downtown stores to find what I wanted. I saw the ads of Oakland's Own Department Store, announcing their January white sale; by some quirk, they had listed seven white domestic slaves at severely reduced prices. I took off a Wednesday, the first day of the sale, and went to the store at opening time, 9:45, to be sure to have the pick of the lot.

Oakland's Own is much the largest department store in the city. It has seven floors and two basements, and its quality runs from $1,498 consoles to factory-reject cotton work socks. It has a good, solid merchandising policy, and it stands behind its goods in a reassuring, old-fashioned way. The wives of my friends were opposed to my shopping in Oakland's Own, because, they said, second-hand slaves were so much better trained than new, and cost so little more. Nevertheless, I went.

I entered the store the moment the doors opened, and went straight up to the sixth floor on the elevator. All the same I found a shapeless little woman in the slave alcove ahead of me picking over the goods—looking at their teeth and hair, telling them to bend over, to speak so she could hear the sound of their voices, stick out their tongue, like an Army doctor. I was furious at having been nosed out by the woman, but I could not help admiring the skill and authority with which she inspected her merchandise. She told me something about herself. She maintained a staff of four, but what with bad luck, disease, and her husband's violent temper she was always having trouble.

The Federal Slave Board had ruled against her twice—against her husband, really, but the slaves were registered in her name —and she had to watch her step. In fact she was on probation from the FSB now. One more adverse decision and she didn't know what she'd do. Well, she picked a strong, stolid-looking female, ordered two sets of conventional domestic costumes for her, signed the charge slip, and left. The saleswoman came to me.

I had made my decision. I had made it almost the moment I had come in, and I had been in agonies for fear the dumpy little shopper would choose my girl. She was not beautiful exactly, though not plain either, nor did she look especially strong. I did not trouble to read her case-history card; I did not even find out her name. I cannot readily explain what there was about her that attracted me. A certain air of insouciance as she stood waiting to be looked over—the bored way she looked at her fingernails and yet the fearful glance she cast from time to time at us shoppers—the vulgarity of her make-up and the soft charm of her voice—I do not know. Put it down to the line of her hip as she stood waiting, a line girlish and womanly at once, dainty and strong, at ease but not indolent. It's what I remember of her best from that day, the long pure line from her knee to her waist as she stood staring at her nails, cocky and scared and humming to herself.

I knew I should pretend impartiality and indifference about my choice. Even Oakland's Own permits haggling over the price of slaves; I might knock the price down as much as $300, particularly since I was paying for her cash on the line. But it wasn't worth the trouble to me. After three weeks of dreary looking I had found what I wanted, and I didn't feel like waiting to get it. I asked the saleswoman for the card on my slave. She was the sixth child of a carpenter in Chico. Chico is a miserable town in the plains of the San Joaquin Valley; much money is spent each year teaching the people of Chico how to read and write; chico means greasewood. Her father had put her up for sale, with her own consent, at the earliest legal age, eighteen, the year of graduation from high school. The wholesaler had taught her the rudiments of cooking, etiquette, and housecleaning. She was listed as above average in cleanliness, intelligence, and personality, superb in copulation, and fair in versatility and sewing. But I had known as much from just looking at her, and I didn't care. Her name was Sandra, and in a way I had known that too. She had been marked down from $3,850 to $3,299. As the saleswoman said, how could I afford to pass up such a bargain? I got her to knock the price down the amount of the sales taxes, wrote out my check, filled out the FSB forms, and took my slave Sandra over to be fitted with clothes.

And right there I had my first trouble as a master, right on the fifth floor of Oakland's Own in the women's wear department. As a master, I was supposed to say to Sandra, or even better to the saleswoman about Sandra, "Plain cotton underwear, heavy-weight nylon stockings, two dark-blue maid's uniforms, and one street dress of conservative cut," and so on and so on. *The slave submits to the master:* I had read it in the FSB manual for domestic slave owners. Now I find it's all very well dominating slaves in my office or my factory. I am chief engineer for the Jergen Calculating Machine Corporation, and I have had no trouble with my industrial and white-collar slaves. They come into the plant knowing precisely where they are, and I know precisely where I am. It's all cut and dried. I prefer the amenities when dealing with, say, the PBX operator. I prefer to say, "Miss Persons, will you please call Hoskins of McKee Steel?" rather than "Persons, get me Hoskins of McKee." But this is merely a preference of mine, a personal matter, and I know it and Persons knows it. No, all that is well set, but this business of Sandra's clothes quite threw me.

I made the blunder of asking her her opinion. She was quick to use the advantage I gave her, but she was very careful not to go too far. "Would you like a pair of high heels for street wear?" I asked her. "If it is agreeable with you, sir." "Well, now, let's see what they have in your size. . . . Those seem sturdy enough and not too expensive. Are they comfortable?" "Quite comfortable, sir." "There aren't any others you'd rather have?" "These are very nice, sir." "Well, I guess these will do quite well, for the time being at least." "I agree with you, sir."

I agree with you: that's a very different matter from *I submit to you.* And though I didn't perceive the difference at the moment, still I was anything but easy in my mind by the time I had got Sandra installed in my house. Oh, I had no trouble preserving the proper reserve and distance with her, and I could not in the slightest detail complain of her behavior. It was just that I was not to the manner bred; that I was alone in the house with her, knowing certain external things to do, but supported by no customs and precedents as I was at the plant; that I found it very uncomfortable to order a woman, with whom I would not eat dinner at the same table, to come to my bed for an hour or so after she had finished washing the dishes. Sandra was delighted with the house and with her quarters, with the television set I had had installed for her and with the subscription to *Cosmopolitan* magazine that I had ordered in her name. She was delighted and I was glad she was delighted. That was the bad thing about it—I was glad. I should have provided these facilities only as a heavy industry provides half-hour breaks and free coffee for its workers—to keep her content and to get more work out of her. Instead I was as glad at her pleasure in them as though she were an actual person. She was so delighted that tears came to her eyes and she kissed my feet; then she asked me where the foot basin was kept. I told her I had none. She said that the dishpan would do until we got one. I told her to order a foot basin from Oakland's Own the next day, along with any other utensils or supplies she felt we needed. She thanked me, fetched the dishpan, and washed my feet. It embarrassed me to have her do it; I knew it was often done, I enjoyed the sensuous pleasure of it, I admired the grace and care with which she bent over my feet like a shoeshine, but all the same I was embarrassed. Yet she did it every day when I came home.

I do not think I could describe more economically the earlier stages of my connection to Sandra than by giving an account of the foot washing.

At first, as I have said, I was uneasy about it, though I liked it
too. I was not sure that as a slave she had to do it, but she
seemed to think she had to and she certainly wanted to. Now
this was all wrong of me. It is true that domestic slaves usually
wash their master's feet, but this is not in any sense one of the
slave's rights. It is a matter about which the master decides, entirely at his own discretion. Yet, by treating it as a set duty, a
duty like serving me food in which she had so profound an interest as to amount to a right, Sandra had from the outset made
it impossible for me to will not to have her wash my feet. She
did it every day when I came home; even when I was irritable
and told her to leave me alone, she did it. Of course, I came to
depend upon it as one of the pleasures and necessary routines of
the day. It was, in fact, very soothing; she spent a long time at it
and the water was always just lukewarm, except in cold weather
when it was quite warm; as they do in good restaurants, she always floated a slice of lemon in the water. The curve of her
back, the gesture with which she would shake the hair out of
her eyes, the happy, private smile she wore as she did it, these
were beautiful to me. She would always kiss, very lightly, the
instep of each foot after she had dried them—always, that is,
when we were alone.

If I brought a friend home with me, she would wash our feet
all right, but matter-of-factly, efficiently, with no little inti-
macies as when I was alone. But if it was a woman who came
with me, or a man and wife, Sandra would wash none of our
feet. Nor did she wash the feet of any callers. I thought this was
probably proper etiquette. I had not read my *Etiquette for
Slaves* as well as Sandra obviously had. I let it go. During the
first few weeks, all my friends, and particularly all my women
friends, had to come to observe Sandra. She behaved surely and
with complete consistency toward them all. I was proud of her.
None of the women told me that Sandra was anything less than
perfect, not even Helen who would have been most likely to,
being an old friend and sharp-tongued. After the novelty had
worn off, I settled down with her into what seemed to be a fine
routine, as one does with a mistress. To be sure, it was not long

before I would think twice about bringing someone home for
dinner with me; if there was much doubt in my mind about it,
the difference in Sandra's foot washing alone would sway me
not to bring my friend along, especially if my friend was a
woman.

When I would come home late at night she would be waiting
for me, with a smile and downcast eyes. I went, in October, to a
convention in St. Louis for a week. When I came back, I think
she spent an hour washing my feet, asking me to tell her about
the physical conditions of my trip, nothing personal or intimate
but just what I had eaten and what I had seen and how I had
slept; but the voice in which she asked it! One night I came
home very late, somewhat high, after a party. I did not want to
disturb her, so I tried to go to my room noiselessly. But she
heard me and came in in her robe to wash my feet; she helped
me to bed, most gently. Not by a glance did she reproach me
for having disturbed her sleep. But then, she never reproached
me.

I did not realize fully how much I had come to depend on
her until she fell sick. She was in the hospital with pneumonia
for three days and spent six days convalescing. It was at
Thanksgiving time. I declined invitations out to dinner, in
order to keep Sandra company—to tend to her, I said to myself,
though she tended to herself very nicely. I was so glad to have
her well again that the first time she could come to me I kept
her in my bed all night—so that she might not chill herself
going back to her own bed, I told myself. That was the first
time, yet by Christmas we were sleeping together regularly,
though she kept her clothes in her own room. She still called
me sir, she still washed my feet; according to the bill of sale I
owned her; I thought her a perfect slave. I was uneasy no
longer.

In fact, of course, I was making a fool of myself, and it took
Helen to tell me so.

"Dell," she said over the edge of her cocktail glass, "you're in
love with this creature."

"In love with Sandra!" I cried. "What do you mean?"

And I was about to expostulate hotly against the notion, when I bethought me that too much heat on my part would only confirm her in her opinion. Therefore, seeming to study the problem, I relapsed into a brown study—under Helen's watchful eye—and tried to calculate the best out for myself.

I rang for Sandra.

"More Manhattans," I said to her.

She bowed, took the shaker on her tray, and left. She was impeccable.

"No, Helen," I said finally, "she does not make my pulses race. The truth is, I come a lot closer to being in love with you than with Sandra."

"How absurd. You've never even made a pass at me."

"True."

But Sandra returned with the drinks, and after she had left we talked about indifferent matters.

As I was seeing Helen to the door, she said to me, "All the same, Dell, watch out. You'll be marrying this creature next. And who will drop by to see you then?"

"If I ever marry Sandra," I said, "it will not be for love. If I have never made a pass at you, my dear, it has not been for lack of love."

I looked at her rather yearningly, squeezed her hand rather tightly, and with a sudden little push closed the door behind her. I leaned against the wall for a moment and offered up a short prayer that Helen would never lose her present husband and come looking in my part of the world for another. I could have managed to love her all right, but she scared me to death.

I thought about what she had told me. I knew that I was not in love with Sandra—there were a thousand remnants of Chico in her that I could not abide—but I could not deny that I needed her very much. What Helen had made me see clearly, was the extent to which I had failed to keep Sandra a slave. I did not know whether it was her scheming that had brought it about, or my slackness, or whether, as I suspected, something of both. Some of the more liberal writers on the subject say, of course, that such development is intrinsic in the situation for anyone in our cultural milieu. It is a problem recognized by the FSB in its handbook. But the handbook advises the master who finds himself in my predicament to trade his slave for another, preferably some stodgy, uninteresting number or one who is deficient in the proper qualities—in my case, as I thought, copulating. The trouble with this sound advice was that I didn't want to get rid of Sandra. She made me comfortable.

In fact, she made me so comfortable that I thought I was happy. I wanted to show my gratitude to her. After she had straightened up the kitchen that evening I called her into the living room where I was sitting over the paper.

"Yes, sir?" she said, standing demurely on the other side of the coffee table.

"Sandra," I began, "I'm very proud of you. I would like to do something for you."

"Yes, sir."

"Sit down."

"Thank you, sir."

As she sat, she took a cigarette from the box, without asking my permission, and lighted it. The way she arched her lips to smoke it, taking care not to spoil her lipstick, annoyed me, and the coy way she batted her eyelids made me regret I had called her in. "Still," I thought, "the Chico in her can be trained out. She's sound."

"What can I give you, Sandra?"

She did not answer for a moment. Every slave knows the answer to that question, and knows that it is the one answer for which he won't be thanked.

"Whatever you wish to give me, sir, would be deeply appreciated."

I couldn't think of a thing to buy for her. Magazines, movies, television, clothes, jewelry, book-club books, popular records, a permanent wave every four months, what else could I get her? Yet I had started this offer; I had to follow up with something. In my uneasiness and annoyance with myself, and knowing so well what it was she wanted, I went too far.

"Would you like freedom, Sandra?"

She dropped her eyes and seemed to droop a little. Then tears rolled down her cheeks, real mascara-stained tears of sadness, of profound emotion.

"Oh, yes, sir," she said. "Oh, my God, yes. Don't tease me about it. Please don't tease me."

So I promised her her freedom. I myself was moved, but I did not want to show it.

"I'm going for a short walk," I said. "You may go to your room."

I went for my walk, and when I came back she had prepared my foot bath. She had burned two pine boughs in the fireplace so that the room smelled wonderful. She had put on her loveliest dress, and had brushed her hair down as I liked it best. She did not speak as she washed my feet, nor even look up at my face. All her gratitude she expressed in the tenderness with which she caressed my feet and ankles. When she had finished drying them, she kissed them and then pressed them for a time against her breast. I do not think either of us, during these past few years, has ever been happier than at that moment.

Well, I had my lawyer draw up a writ of substantial manumission, and Sandra took the brass ring out of her left ear, and that was that. And that was about all of that, so far as I could see. She was free to go as she wanted, but she didn't want. She got wages now, it is true, but all she did with them was to buy clothes and gewgaws. She continued to take care of the house and me, to sleep in my bed and keep her own personal possessions in her own room, and to wash my feet as before. The manumission was nothing it itself, only a signpost that there had been some changes made. Continually and slowly changes kept being made.

For one thing, we began to eat together, unless I had guests in to dinner. For another, she began to call me Mr. Oakes. It seemed strange to have her go where she wanted, without asking me about it, on her nights out. I became so curious about what she could be doing that finally I asked her where she went. To night school, she said, learning how to type. I was delighted to hear that she had not been wasting her time at public dances, but I could not imagine why she wanted to learn typing. She had even bought a portable typewriter which she practiced on in her room when I was away. "Why?" she said. "My mother always said to me, 'Sandra, they can't fire slaves.' Well, I'm not a slave any longer. That was one nice thing about it, I wasn't ever afraid you'd fire me." "But, my darling," I cried, "I'm never going to fire you. I couldn't possibly get along without you." "I know it," she replied, "and I never want to leave either. All the same, I'm going to learn how to type." She had her own friends in to visit her; she even gave a bridge party one evening when I was not at home. But she never called me by my first name, she never checked up on me, she never asked me the sort of intrusive, prying question which a man hates answering. She kept her place.

Then she discovered she was pregnant. I immediately said I would assume all the financial responsibilities of her pregnancy and of rearing the child. She thanked me, and did not mention the subject again. But she took to sleeping in her own bed most of the time. She would serve breakfast while still in her robe and slippers. Her eyes were often red and swollen, though she always kept some sort of smile on her face. She mentioned something about going back to Chico. She began serving me canned soup at dinner. I drove her off to Reno and married her.

Helen had been right, I had married Sandra; but I had been right too, it wasn't for love. Oh, I loved her, some way or other, I don't know just how. But I married her simply because it was the next thing to do; it was just another milestone.

Nothing much happened for a while after we were married, except that she called me Dell and didn't even take the curlers out of her hair at breakfast. But she hadn't got to be free and equal over night. That was to take some months of doing.

First of all, as a wife, she was much frailer than she had been as a slave. I had to buy all sorts of things for her, automatic machines to wash the clothes and the dishes, a cooking stove with nine dials and two clocks, an electric ironer that could iron a shirt in two minutes, a vacuum cleaner, one machine to grind the garbage up and another to mix pancake batter, a thermostatic furnace, an electric floor waxer, and a town coupe for her to drive about to do her errands in. She had to get other people to wash her hair now, and shave her legs and armpits, and polish her toenails and fingernails for her. She took out subscriptions to five ladies' magazines, which printed among them half a million words a month for her to read, and she had her very bathrobe designed in Paris. She moved the television set into the living room and had a teardrop chandelier hung from the center of the ceiling. When she had a miscarriage in her sixth month, she had a daily bouquet of blue orchids brought to her room; she had to rest, and pale blue orchids are so restful. She became allergic to the substance of which my mattress and pillows were composed, and I had to get a foam-rubber mattress and foam-rubber pillow, which stank. She finally insisted that we go to visit her family in Chico, so we finally did, and that we go to visit my family in Boston, so we finally did. The visits were equally painful. We began to go to musical comedies and night clubs. Helen had been right: my friends did not drop by to see us, and they were apt to be sick when I invited them to dinner. Still we weren't all the way.

One night I came home late from work, tired and hungry. Dinner was not yet started, because Sandra had been delayed by her hairdresser. She fixed pork chops, frozen green beans, and bread and butter, with canned apricots for dessert. I had done better myself. After dinner, after the machine had washed the dishes, I asked her if she would bathe my feet. I was so tired, I told her, my feet were so tired; it would be very soothing to me. But she said, in an annoyed voice, that she was feeling nervous herself. She was going to go to bed early. Besides, the silence she left behind her said, besides I am your wife now. She went to bed and I went to bed. She was restless; she twisted and turned. Every time I would shift my position or start to snore a little, she would sigh or poke me. Finally she woke me clear up and said it was impossible for her to sleep like this. Why didn't I go sleep in her former room? She couldn't because of her allergy, she had to stay in the foam-rubber bed. So I moved into her room. And then I knew that she was my equal, for most of the equal wives of my friends lived like this.

Another night, I came home wanting very much to make love

to her. She had avoided my embrace for a long while. She was always too nervous, or too tired, for the less she worked the tireder she became; or she was busy, or simply not in the mood. But tonight I would admit of no evasion. She was beautiful and desirable, and I knew how well she had once made love to me. Finally, I held her in my arms. She knew I wanted her, and in a way as odd as mine she loved me, too. But there was no sensuous pressure of her body against mine, no passion in her kiss. She put her arms about my neck not to caress me but to hang like an albatross against me. She pressed her head against my shoulder not for amorous affection but to hide her face, to shelter it, in loneliness and fear and doubt. She did not resist me, or yield to me, or respond to me, or try to avoid me. She only went away and left me her body to do with as I pleased. And then I knew that she was free, for most of the free wives of my friends were like this with their husbands.

I had four choices, as I saw it: divorce her, have her psychoanalyzed, kill her, or return her to slavery. I was strongly tempted to kill her, but I was an optimist, I thought she was salvageable. Besides, who would do my housework for me? I made her a slave again.

It is a wise provision of the law that says no slave may be completely manumitted. Even substantial manumission provides for a five-year probationary period. Sandra had not passed probation. I had the necessary papers drawn up, told her, an hour before the men came, what was happening, and had her sent to the FSB Rehabilitation School in Colorado for a month.

She came back with the ring in her ear, saying sir to me, and the very first night she washed my feet. Furthermore she made love better than she had done for a year. I thought we were to be happy again, and for a week we seemed to be. But the machines are still there to do most of the work, and she still has her allergy. She does what a slave is supposed to do, but it is an effort, she has to will it, it exhausts her.

One evening six months ago, I came home to find no dinner cooking, no foot bath waiting for me, no sign of Sandra in her room. I found her lying on my bed reading *McCall's* and smok-

ing with a jewel-studded holder I had given her when she was
my wife. She flicked an ash onto the rug when I entered the
room, waved a langorous Hi! at me, and kept on reading. I had
my choice; she had clearly set it up for me. I hesitated only a
moment. I went down to the basement where I had stowed
away the three-thonged lash which had been provided along
with the manual of instructions when I first bought her, and I
beat her on the bed where she lay.

I think I was more upset by the beating than Sandra was. But
I knew I had had to do it. I knew I had neglected my duty as a
master not to have done it long ago. I think now, that all this
trouble could have been averted if formerly I had only kept a
firm hand, that is to say, had beaten her when she had risen too
presumptuously. For the truth is, Sandra is happiest as a slave.
That beating did her good, it kept her in place, and she knew
where she stood. It is no doubt all right to free exceptional
slaves, but not one like Sandra who is happiest when hoping,
when wheedling and pleasing, when held to her place.

But the beatings I should have given her formerly would simply have hurt; she would simply have avoided getting them.
Now, I am not so sure.

For she repeated the offense, exactly, within a month, and I
repeated the punishment. It wasn't so bad for me the second
time. She began seeing just how far she could go before I would
bring out the lash. She cooked more and more badly till I gave
her a warning one evening. When I finished speaking, she sank
to the floor, pressed her forehead against my foot, looked at me,
and said, "Your wish is my command." The irony was all in the
act and words, if irony there was, for there was none in the
voice or face. The truth was, as she discovered the next evening
when she served me corned-beef hash and raw carrots for dinner, my lash is her command. She seems happier, in a way, after
these distasteful blow-ups, comes to my bed voluntarily and
with the welts still on her back, does her work well, hums sometimes. Yet she falls back into her old stubborn mood, again and
again. There seems to be nothing else for me to do but beat her.
The FSB manual supports me. Yet I find it repugnant, and it

cannot be good for Sandra's skin. I had to lash her a week ago, and already, from the dirt she is allowing to collect on the living room rug, it looks as though I'll have to do it again. This was not what I had wanted. Of course, I have learned how to make the lash perform for me, how to make it sting without really damaging, how to make nine blows lighter than three. But it seems a pity to have to resort to this, when it was all quite unnecessary. It's my own fault of course; I lacked the training, the matter-of-fact experience of being a master, and I did not set about my duties as a master so conscientiously as I should have. I know all this, but knowing it doesn't help matters a bit. Sometimes I think I should have killed her, it would have been better for both of us; but then she will do some little act of spontaneous love, as now bringing me a cup of hot chocolate and kissing me lightly on the back of the neck, which makes me glad to have her around. Yet tomorrow I shall have to beat her again. This is not what I had wanted, and it cannot be what she wants, not really. We were uneasy and felt something lacking when she was a slave before, though we were happy too. We were altogether miserable when she was free. Yet this is not what either of us had ever wanted, though we are both of us doing what we must.

A Story of Infidelity

BY STEVEN KATZ

FEW people will acknowledge that the lions before the library are warm; but if one watches them closely and for some time, he can see the haze made on the late autumn air by their breath. It takes more watching than most people can afford, however, for stone lions breathe slowly, even in New York. There is no reason to believe that the lions haven't spoken from time to time, in their slow booming tones; but few, if any, can hear them. They extend to us the special tenderness of stone. "Come to us when you're alone." With diffidence the sphinx offers us repose, a caress over the centuries; and the great Florentine palazzi show us the possibilities of strength, as a hand against our backs when we are fatigued shows us how far we might go. "Be loved by us," they say, one looking to the north and the other to the south on Fifth Avenue. How they displace our emptiness; for where was that space before they arrived? In what direction did it gaze? The lady could wander about in it and take her mirror from her purse and examine herself, not for long. "We are more than friends to you," the lions say; but no one listens. People pass, going north or south, following the great avenue to their commerce; and the sound of the lions is like the traffic during the day, or the silence at night. There are some journeys we have never made, reader; and some we shall never make, alas.

Our vision tells us little of the presence of stone. It's a dampness in the air sometimes, or a desiccation sometimes, always a
displacement. People lean against the flanks of the lions and
find them warm; but they believe they've brought their own
warmth to the lions. They speak to each other and reach out for
a moment into the distances beyond the lions. A cold wind
wafts them down the steps of the library; they tremble and drift
off into commerce again. Lovers know the lions and in the evenings come to lean against the manes. They embrace, and nestle
in the stone, and believe that the softness they feel, eyes shut,
trembling, is the softness of each other. The lovers descend
from the lions believing they have found each other. They accept each other, and find each other hard, and they have already
forgotten the lions.

Of course Massimo Lint, the jeweler, never forgot the lions.
He would visit them ritually each night on his walk, tired as he
was after a long day of cutting or setting or fitting.

"Tonight again?" his wife would ask automatically.

"Yes, dear, just for a walk." He would set out as his wife was
starting the dishes. He had met his wife by the lions, of course.

She removed her hands from her cheeks and saw in the mirror how the dampness made them shine as they had once in her
youth. What had been an ample beauty in her youth had meta-
morphosed into the lines and attitudes of patience. It was a
sure thing she had to be patient with Massimo Lint who wasn't
a mean man but gave her no love any longer, and no consolation. Perhaps the water would whistle through the faucet or the
woman above would rattle the steampipe or glass would shatter
and she would get to the window in time to see the children
running down the street; but what was there for her? Perhaps
there could still be something, a lover for her, in a world that
seemed a feast of small pleasures. Even Massimo had a pleasure,
it seemed; his quiet evening walks. Perhaps he had a lover.

The night was foggy and cold; one of those sensual late
autumn nights in New York when one lusts for warmth. The
street lamps were negligeed in light and each brown hallway
puckered into the street. It was one of those nights in New

York when a young man desires everything: to find something palpable in the fog, to spend himself all at once in a few great hours of collision. He closes his book and puts on his oldest pants and a zipper jacket and disrupts his hair with a comb. He leaves his familiar posters on the walls and the kitchen with its remnants of visiting friends and steps into the street to chance the gangs and to meet, perhaps, one restless girl tired of the office.

"Excuse me," she says, as they brush each other, turning an unlit corner.

"It's all right," he replies. "It's dark out." They each pause a moment and look past each other in the fog. They step toward each other as if they want to see what there is over the other's shoulder. Their lips meet, and their mouths open, and their tongues brush each other in the fog. Their arms find themselves warmer within one another's coat. Their hands apply various pressures to each other's flesh. The subway rumbles through a nearby grating. It wasn't the fog they had come out for after all.

"What's your name?" he asks her; and she lies to him. "I'm a student," he says, lying also, and he doesn't tell her his name. They disengage and walk together. She takes the support of his arm. It is as if they have known each other for a long time, these adventurers; and they seem to know their way through the fog. He softly hums a tune that he can't entirely recall, and she supplies the words to a different song entirely. They laugh and stop by a subway entrance and look at each other quizzically, and then descend into the humming and white light. A man removes a ten-cent root beer from a machine on the platform.

Massimo Lint kissed closed mouth, however, because he was never a man to seek adventure. Never, even to greet the shy thrustings of his wife, has his tongue ever ventured forth from his mouth. It wasn't that he held it back, it was just never inclined to leave. It might have meant new devils to cope with, new dreams of heaven and hell, new adjustments. He knew he wasn't the adventurous sort. He was a shy man who didn't

thrive on new experience. If it weren't his habit to take a walk
every evening he would certainly have stayed at home, out of
the fog and cold. He was no young man with husky desires. He
would meander in the same way every night, with his eyes to
the ground, as if he were looking for something. Perhaps it was
a sense of loss that brought him each night to the lions. He
had first known Clio at the lions, and that had been, he often
thought, his only adventure.

"Do you come here often?" He had seen her every night for a
month by the lions, and she had aroused his curiosity. She
didn't respond to his question at first; but she didn't move away
from him. "Do you enjoy it here?" Again she didn't respond.
He wiped his brow. He hardly had courage for another question. It had taken two weeks of planning to approach her at all.
"Are you fond of the lions?" he finally managed.

"I certainly am," she said. "Otherwise you wouldn't see me
here every evening." She left abruptly, fixing her hair. Her response was not disheartening. At least she had noticed that he
too came every evening.

He approached her boldly next evening. "I take it you've enjoyed your walk this evening."

"Yes, I have been enjoying it," she replied caustically, with
the disdain of a woman protecting her virtue.

"I always enjoy coming here at this time of night when the
lions are lit up. They seem to pale, as if they're lonely." He put
a great deal of poetry into those sentences.

She softened. "I like to watch them too," she said. Their eyes
met for the first time. Hers green, his pale blue. "What do you
do for a living?" she asked.

"I'm a jeweler," he responded with pride, for it was a skilled
trade.

That was enough for her. They met every subsequent night
and would lean against the lions. They went to dinners and
dances and to their various beds, and ultimately to their marriage in the warmth of the lions.

He still remembered her as she had been when he met her by
the lions. She was a metamorphosis of air and sweet scents. Her

arms, bending gently like ferns, extending toward him as if they asked his support; and he would feel always inadequate and flattered. He would take her hands in his and caress their softness with his skinny fingers.

"I waited all day to see you," he would say, breathlessly. "I could hardly work."

She would seem embarrassed in her feminine way. "You're just telling me a story." She would squeeze his arms. "But I thought about you too."

They would blush together and gaze at each other lovingly. It was a wonderful time for Massimo. "Where will we eat tonight?"

She would shrug her shoulders and he would bravely suggest a place. He liked to take her to well-lit places where he could watch all her gestures. Each of them was an adventure. She was a bit mysterious then and hard to comprehend; and she frightened him. But he gorged himself on the adventure of her. He felt then that his whole being was one great palate for the tasting of her, and that there was more variety in her than he had the ability to comprehend. What had she been then? He would ask himself this as he walked to the lions in the evenings. He would try to recall his former gluttony. His appetite had shriveled so, and the woman Clio had become now affected so little of his palate. He would look at her, trying to remember what she had been, but she was always there, her face pared by the years, her arms extended toward him like withering branches. His love had been of huge dimensions, and still was, but it embraced nothing any longer.

Mrs. Lint also felt the loss. A woman needed children and a flower garden. She could anticipate only her husband's two arrivals each day, from work and from his evening stroll. His habits were comfortable to live with, but if a woman didn't have a family she wanted more than comfort out of life. She wanted a bit of excitement, some little adventure for which she could be useful. Even a wicked husband, or one who had some juice in him and could turn her inside out, like a fig. She wasn't yet without desire. She knitted and watched television and each

night he came home she would vainly try to make him look at
her again as if he desired her. She would fix her hair, or use a
new scent, or speak of love. She listened to grocery carts rattling
in the street.

Massimo Lint leaned on a bus-stop sign and watched the
lions. His breath poured vapor into the fog. The lions were
hardly visible in the fog, but he could feel their repose; it was
that attitude of repose he could never attain. It wasn't disdain
they had, but the grand indifference of lions, as if they waited
for one great moment, worthy of gesture. Neither of them
looked at him, no matter what distance he stood from them.
They both stared beyond him.

An unlit bus passed. A group of youths, arguing loudly, with
their collars turned up, hurried up the avenue. The street lights
went from red to green to red again in lumbering rhythm. It
was time to go home again, he thought, with the vague dissatis-
faction he felt every night at the apogee of his walk. "What do
I have to return to?" he would wonder. "The shadow of a
woman." He sighed, and released the bus-stop sign, and stepped
off the curb toward home. He paused. He sensed something
behind him. He didn't want to turn. He was frightened by the
things that could happen in New York City. But his curiosity
turned him and he took hold of the bus-stop sign again. There
was a form between the lions. It was a young woman emerging
from the fog; and what's more she was coming toward him. He
looked up and down the avenue: nothing. The red lights of
cars retreating. The young girl was walking toward him, sugges-
tively. He mustered the arrogance to return her stare. He would
wait for her. He certainly would; this was New York City after
all. He took a few steps away from his bus-stop sign. The
woman was almost upon him. The fog seemed to have deepened, and he could hardly see the lions, but the woman seemed
to be sculptured out of the fog itself. She was almost upon him
now. She was quite large, almost a foot taller than Massimo
Lint. Her face.

"Massy dear, I thought you'd never come tonight," she
addressed him familiarly and huskily. It was Clio's voice, his

wife's, although more youthful. He looked closely at the face that offered itself for a kiss. His lips met hers in moisture.

"You look about tired out, Massy dear. Did you run all the way here for your Clio?" She stroked his chin. She was quite large.

"I'd almost forgotten we had an appointment," said Massimo Lint, trying to be casual.

"That's how much you think of me," she pouted largely and took his trembling thin hand in her oversized grip.

"But I think about you all the time, Clio; every day." He reached up and placed his hand on her shoulder, as he had done once.

"I can't stay long tonight you know, but I did want to see a little of you before I went to my parents. Sometimes I'm not sure you'll be here when I come."

"It's good that you think of your family and visit them. I respect that in you." Massimo Lint could hardly feel his lips move as he spoke. It wasn't he at all. She was gazing at him with real love, and he tried to smile at her but was afraid to reveal the wrinkles at his eyes and mouth. His youthful Clio had come back all at once, and larger than life. This was the woman he had married.

She took his hand and led him off a few steps to lean against the pedestal of a lion. "You know I love you?" she said.

"And I love you," he replied. She gathered him in an embrace that emptied him of breath, and a huge kiss filled his years of longing. Then she left, and he shouted after her, "I'll see you tomorrow," and she shouted back that she'd be there. He started his walk home again. He was attentive of the little things that scuttled about the streets in the wind: leaves and wrappings and billowing newspapers. The fog was lifting. How strange it was. The streets were glistening like sand at the edge of the waves. He stopped before a car window to look at himself. She hadn't even mentioned that he had grown older. As strange as it was it didn't seem impossible because he knew all these years that his real love was still alive somewhere. And it had come back to him in such great proportions. He stepped into his elevator and rose toward his older Clio. What a poor, tattered bit of shrivel she was. He pitied her suddenly and felt generous toward her. He would have to do something for her, a bit of consolation.

She could see the difference in him as soon as he entered. He looked at her so attentively and didn't immediately give his brusque order to turn off the television. She began the conversation she had planned anyway. "They were married today despite it all and they showed pictures of it on TV." She smiled at her husband. He seemed suddenly to take so much notice of her. She nervously touched her hair. She knew it was unkempt. He came over to her and measured her face with his hands. "Did something happen on your walk?" she asked.

"Nothing happened to speak of," said her husband, still regarding her strangely.

Some men, she recalled reading, became more affectionate toward their wives when they had mistresses. But his salary would hardly afford him a mistress.

"I'd like some hot chocolate," he said; and she could feel him watch her as she walked across the room. It was a sudden change in him, she thought.

She didn't know what to think of his new affections. He even kissed her twice in the course of the evening. She didn't know whether to be happy or not, it was so strange. She went to bed with him and dreamt that night about flowers. She was a small girl in a garden of huge flowers. She ran about looking at the blossoms from beneath. She could see mostly the sepals, curled and green beneath the blossoms, and got only hints of the colors; but she was sure the colors must have been glorious. She looked up at them and wandered about. Her dreams were never very complicated.

Mr. Lint couldn't fall asleep. Not only had he seen his larger Clio but his wife had shrunk. She went to get his hot chocolate and was a whole foot and a half shorter than he. She could hardly reach the shelf. She seemed a little less substance and shape also, as a snowflake that begins to melt.

"Did you do anything while I was gone?" he asked her. He

touched her as much as he could to see if he could remember her former proportions. She was certainly smaller.

"I watched television is all." Her voice too was smaller and higher pitched. He went over to kiss her lips in order to imitate affection. It was a pitiful small embrace after the one he had endured earlier that evening. They went to bed, and after she was asleep he removed the blankets from her and examined her carefully. He knew that people began to shrink as they got older and he thought that perhaps it was happening to her, but she wasn't quite that old yet. There was an attitude of serenity and happiness about her as she slept that made him feel a bit guilty for his transgressions earlier that evening. He thought of his younger Clio. It wasn't really a matter of infidelity to spend time with her. There was no reason for him to feel guilty, for he would be more faithful to his true love if he spent his time with the younger Clio than if he endured the older one. He covered his wife over again and lay back against the pillow. It was comforting to think that he would see his love by the lions again.

He did see her again, and again. The pace of his stroll had picked up as the weather became colder. He felt quite lively. He would meet his Clio and they would embrace, and laugh, and speak of felicity. Would think to travel together, to make nice friends. Would giggle over a little turn of phrase. He wanted to take her to restaurants, to dance with her, to be alone with her all the time. It was a foolish streak of propriety in him that kept him from this; and his propriety made him feel a bit guilty still when he returned to his wife, with the last kiss of Clio still fresh on his lips. His guilt made him superficially more attentive and affectionate toward his wife, although each little affectionate gesture he offered her became more offensive to him. And what was worse the wife had become more affectionate toward him. Each night after his stroll she would erase the memory of the younger Clio's kiss with her own desiccate lips. His wife, as small as she had become, was more and more of a burden on him. He didn't want to put up with her at all.

"Let's go out some night again," the older Clio said one night, wearing lipstick in a moment of frivolity.

"Where can we go?" Massimo said, suddenly surprised. "And why?" He had such dreams of doing these things with her younger counterpart.

"We could go to a restaurant, like we used to; or just for a walk back to the lions." She laid her little arms upon his shoulders.

"Yes. I'll consider it," he muttered. He began to tremble slightly. What a terrible thought it was to think of confronting the younger Clio with the older. He looked at his shriveled little wife. She was nothing he wanted to go about with, to restaurants or places. He had to do something about her. He had to carry her about like a spool with the thread wound off.

He could hardly concentrate at work the next day and nearly ruined a stone by cutting across a flaw. He stopped working and paced about. All his colleagues removed their eyepieces to look at him. He knew he had to make a decision.

"What's wrong, Massy?" asked one of his friends.

Massimo didn't reply.

"If I didn't know just how old you are, I'd say you had love troubles." The friend took Massimo's shoulder. "Are you in love at your age?" Massimo smiled weakly and tried to lift his eyes to his friend's face. "Why don't you take off for the rest of the day. I'll make your excuses."

He walked immediately to the lions and sat on the steps. Everyone could see it in him. There was no reason to hide it anymore. His wife had become nothing for him, and his reborn love had become everything. He might as well declare it, he thought. He thought of his wife's request to go out and shuddered. He would begin to live again with his younger Clio. His love was now greater than his propriety. He would take her places and enjoy every bit of her. He wouldn't worry any longer about the little old Clio at home. He sat all the rest of the afternoon by the lions, hoping his young Clio might come a little early. He would take her to dinner that evening, and then they would dance. There was a bit of the sprite left in him yet.

Massimo Lint was in for a surprise, of course, as all adventurers are in New York City. Perhaps he had stayed too

long by the lions. He wasn't accustomed to desire and had neither the patience nor experience to sustain it. It was a shock to
him, therefore, when after dozing a bit he finally heard his
younger Clio's voice.

"I thought you'd never get here tonight, after you'd promised
me dinner." Her voice was like the roaring of a kettledrum.
"You're getting later and later," the roar remarked.

Massimo Lint looked about and at first saw nothing. The roar
made his spine freeze. He thought that it couldn't be, and then
he looked closely at the southern lion and it was, there she was.
She had grown to the proportions of the stone lions and was
nearly a part of them. She lumbered toward him down the steps
like some great animal and lifted him to her huge mouth. Her
breath was foul, and her lips slapped his face like a mop.

"It's almost too late to have dinner," she rumbled.

"I thought I got here early," he said meekly. "We can still
have dinner," he mumbled, a lump forming in this throat at the
thought of maneuvering her now outlandish proportions
through a restaurant door. He stepped back several yards to sur-
vey her. She was as beautiful as she had ever been, though there
was a great deal more of her. At least she wasn't lost. It might
be said, in fact, that he had gained a great deal.

"I'm famished," she bellowed. "Let's go to Maurizio's."

Massimo Lint closed his eyes. What could he do? How could
he explain her to the waiters? How could he pay for all that
she'd eat? "I don't think I can go tonight," he tried to say, but
she was already moving down the street in front of him. He
wanted to run away, but he knew it was wrong to leave a girl
unescorted in the evening on the streets of New York; and he
was in love with her besides.

The food wasn't exceptionally good that evening and they
didn't eat a great deal. To Massimo Lint's surprise no one
noticed his oversized Clio, or those who did were too sophisti-
cated to mention it.

"I'm stuffed to the gills," she thundered at him.

"I guess we can leave," he shouted at her.

The sky was quite clear for New York and some clouds shone

bravely through the haze. He had come through that in good
shape, he thought; and he was still left with his love. He felt
himself transported suddenly toward the stars. Clio had taken
him in her large hands and lifted him to her mouth again. His
face was mauled by her coarse tongue. She held him away from
herself and sighed. The sour wind lifted his hat from his head.

"My love for you grows with every day," the voice moaned
from her cavernous mouth.

"And mine for you," gasped Mr. Lint, turning his face from
the wind and stench.

She placed him back on the ground, and the couple bid each
other good-by fondly. Massimo Lint returned to the lions and
looked at them some more. He couldn't really adapt himself to
things cut in such huge proportions. The lions seemed to be
smiling at him now in the yellow light. He began to feel grate-
ful to them, for it hadn't been a catastrophe at all. "As large as
she is she's still beautiful," he said to the lions. "And I want to
thank you because some men never see the second time what
they had once loved." The lions probably took a while to reply,
and Massimo Lint was already on his way home.

He wanted to tell someone of his experiences. He wanted a
test of their credulity. He hadn't heard of a similar thing happening to anyone else. As chance would have it a young boy
with a grocery cart passed him by and that in itself was strange
because it was late to be delivering groceries. Massimo Lint
beckoned to the young man pushing his cart. "Hey, there, will
you listen to me?" The boy rolled by with his cart. "Hey, there,
do you know what just happened to me?" Massimo Lint asked.
But the boy turned a deaf ear, not caring for any problems but
his own. Mr Lint watched him a while down the street. The
young man wouldn't have believed him anyway. He would have
to tell his wife, he thought. She would at least listen to him.
That was her virtue.

A moisture filled New York and the stars dissolved into the
haze. He turned the corner of his street. The exhilaration of
these days of love's renewal had told on him, and he was beginning to feel the strain. It was good to see his home again. Any

adventurer, amorous or otherwise, longs for familiar comforts from time to time: the proportions and ease of a bed he has slept in before; a hand offering familiar caresses; the particular density of a room in which he has spent a good deal of time. Mr. Lint looked through the doorway toward the elevator where a young couple embraced, waiting to ascend. He too was in love again. He had his own Clio, and he no longer had to feel lonely as he once had in the presence of lovers. He entered the hallway, reluctant to interrupt the young couple. But he hadn't interrupted them. They embraced as the door of the elevator closed. His old desires were upon him again, more strongly now. He needed to tell someone about himself. He turned to the young couple that was embraced in the brown light of the elevator. "I'm in love again, you know," he said. They paid no attention to him. One could hardly tell that they had just recently met on the street, the way they fondled one another. He could speak only with his wife who was accustomed to listening.

"Do you know what happened to me this evening, dear?" he shouted to the older Clio who was sitting with her television and knitting.

"No dear, what did happen?" his wife replied in a strange new falsetto.

Mr. Lint entered the living room and turned on the light. His wife disposed of the television. "Well, I saw . . ." he began, and immediatley stopped. He stared at his wife again.

Mrs. Lint felt stuffed with smiles. She was feeling her happiness again. The extra attention her husband had been paying her of late made her conscious of her looks again. She had gone that day to the hairdresser for a more youthful styling, and she had bought, on the way home, a crystal necklace that glimmered like the necklaces of her youth. She was wearing the necklace, and she touched her hair from time to time, and she felt a new youth coming on her. "What did you see, dear?" she asked.

The high tones of her voice were like the squeakings of a door. He could barely make out the words. The dimensions of his younger Clio were certainly no stranger than what he was seeing now. She had become absolutely tiny, like a girl of six.

"What was it you said you saw?" she squeaked, and scurried about like a mouse.

"Nothing, dear," he replied, trying not to seem to have noticed the change in her.

"But you said something happened to you," she insisted.

He touched her hair, which had become fine as silk from shrinking. "What I meant was a joke, that nothing at all happened to me, as usual."

"Did you notice my hair?" she asked.

"Yes, I did," he replied. There was no chance now that he would confide in her about his great-sized Clio. She had problems of her own. He felt suddenly as if the key had turned on his life, and he was left in it. He was full of loneliness again. He could speak with no one of the immensity of his love. The men in his office would use him for gossip. His wife was too small. Delivery boys wouldn't stop to consider him. Other lovers had no time. He would have to speak with young Clio herself. His love for her kept growing.

Her husband's affections were too much for Mrs. Lint; she was melting in them. He had lifted her to her feet and had carried her to bed. She never realized he had so much strength left. She lay beside him that night and touched his thigh and kissed his arm from time to time. She felt a great tenderness toward him again, as she had once when she first became his wife.

"Clio," he called when he didn't find her immediately next evening at the lions. He had been anxious about her all day. "Where are you tonight?" he shouted. He was trembling. His love for her had grown even as she herself had grown. He listened for her, worried that she might not come that evening. He had taken this meeting for granted. "Clio," he called again, and heard this time, as if in response, a roar that was almost too deep to be audible; various, like planes at high altitudes, or a waterfall. He called again, and heard the roar again, as if it were really a response to his calling. The very ground seemed to vibrate with the roaring. Perhaps it had all been a dream, he

thought. He had assumed she would be there. Perhaps the
vision was lost forever, if it had been a vision. He felt hope
draining from him. He thought of the bit of nothing he would
be left with, his older Clio at home. The roaring pulsed about
him and seemed to shake the very pediments of the lions. Perhaps the lions were roaring somewhere within themselves. He
looked at them, and then into the sky to see if it might be some
planes passing above. There she was. She wasn't flying at all, but
she was a huge building of a woman, his Clio. She sat on the
library building as if it were a stone bench; and her features
were softened with fog, and altitude. She was still beautiful.
This was how his love had grown. "I love you," he shouted to
her, and he could see this time her huge mouth move, and he
felt the roaring again, and this time a strong wind followed that
nearly blew him into the street. He struggled back toward the
library again. Her head leaned toward him gently out of the
fog. He shouted, "I love you. I need to speak with you." He desperately tried to make her hear. Then he felt himself rising, as
if he were a rocket launched, and he heard a great smack, infin-
itely more loud than the waves in the rocks, and he felt a great
moisture upon him suddenly. He was on the ground again. He
had been kissed by his love, and he felt utterly weak. He trembled by the bus-stop sign. It was more than he could take. He
looked up to where she smiled down on him like an oriental
shrine. He wasn't a young man any longer. He couldn't handle
all this love alone; he needed to tell someone.

He started home, weakened. He would have to speak with his
wife no matter what size she had become. He thought of her
size. "What size could she have become?" he wondered aloud.
His younger love was so huge. He rushed home even more
quickly than he had come to the lions. He threw open the door
and called her name and ran into the living room. The television set was still on. He turned on the light. His wife was gone.
She no longer made even a shadow on the chair where her knitting needles lay by what used to be her side. "Are you here,
dear?" he whispered, for he remembered the terrible effect his
huge love's voice had had on him. He listened for even the

tiniest screeching but heard nothing. The house was empty as far as he could tell. How gray the walls seemed. "Am I a murderer?" he wondered. He took a plaid woolen scarf from the closet and wrapped it about his neck and left the house. The city thundered with his guilt and with the roar of his love. Guilt hung upon him like the moisture of a caress, and he arrived at the lions again in tears because he had no place else to go. How those stone beasts smiled at him now. The enormity of his love was still there, larger than she had been before, her features lost forever in the high haze. He climbed as high as he could on her shoe and embraced as much as he could of her calf. Her skin was coarse and cold and smelled strongly of urine. He leaned his cheek against her roughness and sobbed for his love.

Mrs. Lint had been feeling fine and had decided to step out herself that evening. It smelled like spring to her although winter was well upon the city. She was hardly herself since her husband had begun his new affections. She noticed everything. This was the sort of evening young ladies like to take to their ample and throbbing bosoms; and they wander out alone among the meadows and wildflowers. They absorb each scent that is mingled with the special moisture of the evening. They think about young men who hunt for owls in the pine woods that surround the meadow. They run to the edge of the meadow and hoot, sounding not too much like owls. The young men discover them, and everything is embraced and kissed.

Mrs. Lint didn't feel young this evening, nor ample-bosomed, nor did she consider New York a meadow; but she was out nevertheless and quite happy to look in the windows of the closed shops. It might have been a lucky coincidence if she could have happened upon the lions that evening for she might have assuaged her husband's misery. She might have found him there embracing his love, or a column of the library, or the lion's rump. She might have offered him then a little tenderness.

Bake Plenty Bread

BY JULIUS LAFFAL

KEOGH, my eyes were on him as he walked here and there, a small potbellied man with a scar from navel to groin, swinging one hand against the wall and holding his trousers with the other. I heard him sing, and I said to him as he passed:

"Keogh."

He stopped and raised his head.

"Who's talking to me?"

"I am. Mr. Fuller."

Without moving his body he twisted his neck until he was looking at me. His eyes were large and yellow like oysters, and he wrinkled his narrow forehead so that the lines of his crewcut hair almost touched his eyebrows. The nostrils of his thick nose were dilated. Then he came to my chair, leaned over, and whispered in my ear:

"Let's go get something to eat before someone sees us."

"What was that song you were singing?"

He started back.

"I wasn't singing no song," he said.

"You sang it last night too."

"I was in Perth Amboy, New Jersey, last night, so let's get something to eat. You and me. Let's sneak off so nobody else'll know."

"Why don't you wear a shirt," I said. "You look like hell without a shirt."

"You ain't my mother," he snapped.

"That scar on your belly," I said. "How'd you get it?"

He looked down and touched it tenderly. Then he scratched it. Standing in front of me, he scratched it hard, and slowly the pink flesh became bright. I heard the grating of his fingernails on the flesh, like a file on wood.

"You'll hurt yourself," I said.

"My brother gave it to me."

His eyes were on me, huge seabottom eyes, as he scratched. I felt all their eyes turned toward us, all those shadows hugging the wall, with their legs drawn up to their bellies and the meaningless magazines in their laps.

"That was a hell of a way for your brother to treat you," I said.

His fingernails dug in, and flecks of blood appeared.

"That's a hell of a way for *you* to treat me," he cried.

The doctor came out of the windowed nurses' station and quickly, although with seemingly unhurried steps, approached and took Keogh's arm. The blood was not running free, but all the length of the exacerbated scar, the skin was torn.

"Why did you do that?" asked the doctor.

Pulling away his arm, Keogh went out of the dayroom to the porch. He locked the fingers of his free hand in the heavy wire screen and pressed his face against the mesh. Segurski and Loomis were throwing a baseball in the narrow confines of the porch, and Freddie Jarvis was lying on the flagstones with his head on one of the leather seat cushions. They stopped playing ball when the doctor came on the porch and watched him. I too went to the window of the dayroom and watched.

He was a tall, thin doctor, with horn-rimmed glasses and bushy hair. His coat reached only to his knees. The doctor spoke to Keogh, but Keogh said nothing and looked out through the wide mesh at the world which was ten stories down, a world of housetops and shrunken trees and narrow roads and pigmy figures making their way about in boundaries

beyond which we but not they could see. I watched the doctor's
face, his puzzled eyes, his hesitantly moving lips, and the way
Keogh turned his back on him as if he were no more than the
murmur of the airplane which was passing above. Then the
doctor became silent and put his hand on the steel screen and
looked out too. Segurski said, "Come on," and began to throw
the ball again, and I went to the door of the porch and leaned
against the jamb, aware how at this moment Keogh was the
center of our world. After a while the doctor dropped his hand
from the fence and turned to go. Then Keogh said:

"Let's get something to eat."

The doctor smiled and said, "It's almost lunchtime. You'll be
having something to eat soon. But I'll get you some cookies."

"What's the difference between a mess hall and a restaurant?" asked Keogh.

Freddie Jarvis raised his head and shouted:

"Damn you, you ain't in the army any more."

Keogh answered calmly:

"You stand up in the army, and you sit down in the navy."

Freddie told him what to do with himself.

He swung his free hand against the wall as he left the porch,
his head tilted to one side. He pushed by me and, when the
doctor came near, I said:

"He's crazy, that Keogh."

The doctor gave no sign that he had heard and walked away.
I heard my futile voice echoing against the walls and the eyes of
others pointing at me like heatless flames. I could stand in that
iron cage and look out across the sunken world and watch people crawling lost and lonely on the streets. I had no need of
Freddie Jarvis, or Loomis, or Segurski, or the tall thin doctor, or
Keogh. Why was it then, that the unanswering look, the curt
nod, and the disdaining world could do so much hurt to me? I
went out on the porch and looked over the miles of houses,
woods, and fields that stretched to the horizon. Keogh came
and stood beside me munching cookies. I said to him:

"Why don't you tie the damned strings together so you don't
always have to be holding up your pants?"

He said, "He gave it to me so's I would remember him."

"Damn you, Keogh. The next time the doc comes to talk to you, don't you go wandering off down the hall. He wants to help you."

"Who says so?"

"I say so."

He smiled, revealing his rotten teeth and the crumb mash over them and over his lips.

"Your hair is white," he said.

"I'm older than you, Keogh. You listen to what I say."

"I listen to you."

"You let them put a bandage on it, then," I scolded him.

"What are you saying?" His voice rose suddenly.

"You let them bandage it," I repeated.

"You want to let them take it away from me? My brother gave it to me!"

"Why did he give it to you?"

"He baked bread all his life, and I ate the bread. He said to me, you eat the bread, but you don't bake none, and if you do, I'll give you something to remember. I ate the bread, and he came and gave me this."

"All he did was hurt you," I retorted. "He was mad because he wanted you to work."

"Don't tell me that," he shouted as he stumbled away in his slippers, holding up his trousers. "He gave it to me so's I'd have it. He gave me something not to lose."

In the dayroom, although the door of the porch swung shut after him, I could see that he was still shouting. All the others, in their chairs, stared at him, for he stood in the center of the room. After a while he stopped shouting and with his shoulders bowed and his bullet head cocked he walked off through the corridor.

Old Mr. Ellis had my seat in the corner. I knew he would get up pretty soon and show the nurse his colostomy bag, then I'd get my seat back. Meanwhile I watched for Keogh, and he showed up in the corridor several times. He would look at me, then turn around and march out of sight. But once again he came back and glared at me, baring his teeth. I stared right back at him hard, and he shook his fist and shouted:

"Blood is water and water is milk."

Freddie Jarvis marched over and planted himself before me with his legs spread. He was a big fellow, over six feet, with a shock of red hair and muscular arms. He was full of bravado, and I had seen many of them shrink from the threat of his hand, although he had never yet raised it against me.

"Why don't you leave the goof alone," he said. "All you do is argue with him. If you want to fight, fight with someone who can fight back."

"I won't run from a fight," I said looking straight into his eyes. "You may whip me today and whip me tomorrow, but the day after that I'll whip you."

He scowled and his face became flushed. I had not budged, and I sat as I was, with one leg drawn under my chin, and my eyes plumbing his own which were weak and shifty.

"All he does is run around and yell," he whined. "They ought to send him somewheres else. And you too."

"I suppose you don't belong in here," I said.

"Hell no, there ain't nothing wrong with me. I got a job to go back to. I feel good. I'm getting out of here. I'm no nut."

I picked up a magazine and looked at the pictures.

When the new shift came on at five, I saw the doctor in the nurses' station. Miss Karakas came down the corridor, and I asked:

"Who is that new doctor?"

"Dr. Walters? He's the new resident."

I stayed on my feet even though Mr. Ellis went after my chair, because I wanted to talk to the new doctor. I estimated he was no more than thirty years old, but he knew a lot in this world. I could tell from his eyes. They were eyes that tried to understand, eyes that could be hurt, as I had seen Keogh hurt them, wandering off clutching the strings of his trousers, leaving him empty-handed with all the tenderness he brought. He was talking to Dr. Gerhardt, my own doctor. He had a wide mouth, and once when he laughed it was not merely a movement of his mouth but of all his face and body. He swayed back and forth and bent over as if to bring him closer to Dr. Gerhardt who was a small man. When he came out, I was standing near the door, and I said:

"Dr. Walters, could I have a couple of minutes of your time?"

"Certainly," he replied.

I knew that Freddie was watching me, and Mr. Ellis, and all the others. Fortunately, Keogh was not there to see. I said:

"I mean, in private."

"Why don't we walk down here in the hall," he said.

We walked along the corridor, and he looked at me and waited, and I finally said:

"Would it be possible for you to be my doctor?"

"Dr. Gerhardt is your doctor, isn't he?" he asked.

"Yes."

"Has something come up that makes you want to change?"

"No," I said quickly. "Nothing has come up. Dr. Gerhardt is a good doctor. Only I thought you might be able to help me more, being a new doctor."

He put his hand on my shoulder, and I was all at once tearful and angry, and I scarcely knew any longer what was happening. He said to me:

"Why don't you try to talk about it with Dr. Gerhardt? I'm sure he'll understand and be able to help you."

He opened the door with his key, and I saw the last of him through the little rectangular light.

At night Keogh went around banging doors and everyone screamed at him. The aides took him off to seclusion, and his voice behind the thick doors and walls was only a distant murmur, like the clatter of birds, for after a while he was not shouting, but singing. I got up and looked through the window in the seclusion ward and saw him sitting on the floor. I knocked on the door, but he did not look up. Then Johnnie Parker, the aide, came along and said:

"Mr. Fuller, why don't you go back to bed? You need the rest."

"I don't like to see him all alone," I said.

"He'll be all right, Mr. Fuller."

"Did Dr. Walters say to put him in seclusion?"

"The doctor said to put him in seclusion if he got upset."

I took one last look at Keogh. He had become silent and was stretched on the mattress on the floor. I went back to my bed. They were still talking, demanding angrily among themselves that he be sent away. I wanted to shout at them, "Would you, if that happened to you, want to be sent away?" But I recognized after a moment that their voices were also expressing this fear, and soon enough they fell silent. Morning came. I got up with the first light to avoid the jam in the bathroom, and I got my shower before the stalls became sodden with the smell of sweating bodies and the steam. Keogh was still in seclusion, pacing the narrow hall with his head bowed. He had undressed himself completely, and his clothes were in a heap on the floor beside his mattress. I located the aide and demanded Keogh be let out. The aide, who had come on in the morning, said he would be, then went back to sort sheets in the closet. I knocked on the door of the nurses' station, and Miss Karakas came out.

"Keogh ought to be taken from seclusion," I said. "I don't think Dr. Walters would want him there all morning."

"Oh, is he up?" said the nurse. "Thank you, Mr. Fuller. I believe he can come out."

I was sitting in my chair waiting for breakfast when he appeared in the corridor. My eyes were on him, but he did not look at me. The aide came through the dayroom, saying, "Breakfast, breakfast." They stirred out of their seats with a kind of hungry lethargy, and they came out of the bathroom wiping their faces with paper towels and lined up in the corridor. The aide went down his list of names.

I was watching Keogh on the porch, his fingers locked in the fence. The aide went to the door of the porch and said, "Breakfast." Keogh did not turn. We went to breakfast without him. When we got back, Dr. Walters was standing on the porch with Keogh. I saw Keogh look in the pocket of the doctor's coat and take out a gingersnap which he popped into his mouth. After a while he looked into the pocket, but all of the cookies were gone.

At lunch he would not come to the mess hall. While we were eating, an aide carried a tray out of the kitchen, and I knew it was for Keogh. But when we got back from lunch the tray was sitting untouched on a writing table, and Keogh was lying on the porch in the sun, shirtless and with his trousers open. His eyes were shut. I got a light for my cigaret from the aide and sat on one of the porch chairs near Keogh. His eyelids flickered once and opened for a moment, then shut again. Freddie Jarvis sat down beside me and asked for a light. I held my cigaret to his, and when he had his light he put his feet up on the concrete ledge.

"Look at him," he said. "What a sight for sore eyes."

I didn't answer.

"He'll come right up to the visiting room with his pants wide open. How stupid can they get? He ought to be locked up in a cell by himself. He's just an animal."

Dr. Walters came out on the porch.

"He's not asleep," I said. "He had his eyes open a minute ago."

"What did you have for lunch?" Dr. Walters asked me.

"Roast beef," I said. "And sherbet. It was excellent."

Keogh raised his head, then sat up, blinking. He got to his feet, and his trousers slipped down, leaving him stark naked.

"God," said Freddie.

Keogh stepped out of the trousers and shuffled away.

"Keogh," said Dr. Walters.

"Don't talk to me," cried Keogh.

"I brought a sandwich for you," said Dr. Walters.

Keogh searched in the doctor's pockets and took out the sandwich. It was wrapped in wax paper. He tore off the paper and stuffed the sandwich in his mouth. Bits of bread and cheese fell to the ground. When he was through, he picked up the crumbs and ate them too.

"I'll help you put on your pants," said the doctor.

Keogh got into his trousers, and the doctor tied the strings.

"Why are you angry?" asked the doctor.

"I didn't ask for words," shouted Keogh, putting his face close to the doctor's. "I didn't ask you to come when the green peas were boiling in the kettle. I wanted green peas in the kettle. Peas are blood and blood is milk. You tell me bake plenty bread, Keogh, but don't eat none. You come to tell me peas are in the kettle, but I want blood in my belly, like I saw it come out. . . ."

Dr. Walters grabbed Keogh's wrist as he dug his nails into the scar, and he pulled away suddenly, screaming:

"My brother gave me it."

He turned and stumbled through the door.

"I'll see that he doesn't hurt himself, doctor," I said jumping up.

"Leave him alone," he said sharply.

I stopped in my tracks. The doctor walked by me, after Keogh. I went into the bathroom and cried. Johnnie Parker, the aide, found me there and asked me if I was all right. I said to please tell Dr. Gerhardt I had to see him. But a half hour later when Dr. Gerhardt came, I had nothing to say to him and had to hide from his eyes because their power terrified me. Later in the day, just before supper, when I was sitting in my chair, Keogh came and sat beside me on the floor.

"Mr. Fuller," he said, calling me by name for the first time, "don't let him come near me."

"He wants to help you, Keogh," I said.

When suppertime came, he locked his fingers in the iron fence, and the aide couldn't pull him away, so we went to supper without Keogh. He got so weak in a few days that he crawled around on all fours, for he would not stay in bed, nor would he sit in a wheel chair. He would lie out on the flagstones of the porch in the hot sun, and Dr. Walters would come and sit beside him on the stones. We would all stop talking and listen as Dr. Walters spoke to him. He was not violent or vile-mouthed with Dr. Walters, although afterward he would beg me not to let the doctor come near him. I said to him:

"Keogh, the doctor only wants to help you."

He shook his head and said:

"My brother loves me. He gave me something to remember, he gave me blood. Tell him to go away."

I told the doctor what he said, and the next time he came to talk to Keogh he said:

"You want me to hurt you, Keogh."

"Blood makes brothers," said Keogh.

"There is love without blood," said the doctor.

"Blood is milk," said Keogh.

"Love is milk," said the doctor.

"Love is blood and blood is milk."

The doctor held his hand close to Keogh's hand. There were a saltine and a wedge-shaped piece of cheese in it. Keogh looked at the food, and for a moment his hand trembled, then he drew back and turned away. He looked strange now, with his ribs sticking out, his eyes protruding like light bulbs, his cheeks sunken, and his lips thin and dried up. The doctor kept his hand extended and slowly Keogh turned back, and he took the cheese and the cracker and brought them to his mouth. His lips parted slowly, and he bit the cheese. His throat worked, and he swallowed. We laughed and cried out:

"That's the boy, Keogh."

Dr. Walters went out and spoke to the nurse. Soon an aide came on to the porch with a tray on which were some slices of toast and a glass of milk. Dr. Walters sat there breaking the toast for him and holding the glass of milk to his lips as he drank. We were all happy that evening, but Keogh was silent, and at bedtime he came to me and took my hand and murmured:

"Mr. Fuller, tell him to go way. Don't let him come near me."

"Why are you afraid of him?" I asked.

"He wants to take me away."

"You mean away from here?"

"From me."

"He wants to help you, Keogh."

Keogh looked long at me.

"He wants to be my brother," he said.

"Yes," I replied. "He wants to be your brother. He wants to help you."

"Can he be my brother?"

"He can help you," I said.

"Can he be my blood brother?" asked Keogh.

"Not your blood brother. But he can help you."

"Then he hates me."

"No, Keogh, you're wrong."

"How can he be my blood brother?"

"He is your brother, Keogh, because all men who love each other are brothers," I said.

"If he is my blood brother, he will love me."

"He will love you anyhow."

"Blood brothers love each other."

Keogh was shouting throughout the night, and the aides carried him to seclusion. But he did not lie quietly, nor did he sing. He beat against the door and shouted curses. In the end the doctor on call, a broad-shouldered, businesslike man came, and soon the nurse hurried out of her station with a syringe. After a while Keogh became quiet.

In the morning Keogh went to breakfast with us. The aide stood beside him and watched him carefully as he ate, and all the time Keogh ate, he kept rolling his eyes upward, gesturing with his shoulders, shaking his head, and occasionally shouting things that we could not understand. As we left the mess hall I put my hand on his arm. He started back yelling:

"Get away from me, I don't talk to no woman."

"Keogh," I said.

"Your blood is rotten," he shouted.

"Come on, Mr. Fuller," said the aide. "Let's get back to the ward."

As we walked back, I felt their eyes on me, like fingers pointing, and I would have heard their snickering voices, but I shut them out. Let all the flames out of the eyes of all the world be pointed at me, and I will shut them out. Only, when we got back I couldn't wait for the doors of rooms to be opened for the afternoon nap, and I buried my head in my pillow and cried. After a while the aide came around tapping on the door with his key, and saying:

"Time to get up, fellows. We're going out to play ball."

I arose and went to my chair in the dayroom, and when the aide said, "Come on, Mr. Fuller, we're going to play a little ball," I shook my head.

Miss Karakas came out and said, "Don't you feel well, Mr. Fuller?"

I said, "I think I'd like to stay in today, Miss Karakas."

"Is something wrong?" she asked.

I shrugged.

"You're sure now, you wouldn't want to go out?"

"Thanks, Miss Karakas. I'd like to sit here."

The aides herded the others out of their chairs into the corridor, and they went off. I was alone in the dayroom, and my eyes were on Keogh through the window. He was standing in the middle of the room shirtless. I knew what he was looking at—Dr. Walters, who was in the glassed nurses' station leafing through a chart. When Dr. Walters left the station and walked in his slow pace through the dayroom, I said:

"Dr. Walters. . . ."

The doctor looked at me.

"Keogh is upset," I stammered.

He noticed and went on to the door of the porch. Keogh lurched to the door and pressed his bony shoulder against it as Dr. Walters stretched out his hand to open it. Dr. Walters hesitated, and Keogh pushed with all his might. As he did so, the power seemed to go out of his body, and he slid to the ground, until he was lying huddled against the door, but still he kept his hands against it, and stared up with his bulging eyes at the doctor. I wanted to run to the doctor and tell him not to go on, but he pushed gently on the door, and despite Keogh's desperate efforts the door opened. The doctor went out on the porch, and Keogh rolled over on his back. I couldn't sit there, I had to go to the window and look at them. I wanted to call the doctor, but I was voiceless. He leaned over Keogh, extending his arms to raise him up. Like a striking snake, the one coiled hand of Keogh sprang off the ground and struck at Dr. Walter's face. I saw his glasses fly off and shatter on the flagstones, and when he staggered back I saw only the deep flush of red on his face, but suddenly the blood welled out of the jagged lines made by Keogh's fingernails, and his hands flew up to his face. The blood poured between his fingers, and he stumbled against a chair, and groped with one hand for the door. The blood poured down his white coat, and I ran screaming and pounded on the nurse's window until Miss Karakas came out. She rushed to the doctor and took his elbow and led him into the office and out of sight. I went into the bathroom, and I leaned down over the bowl, and every last bit of my guts came out, yet I could not get out of my mind that bleeding eye of his.

I have decided not to look at the world. They try all sorts of tricks to get me to see, the offer of gifts I will choose, the inducement of beautiful pictures, the reassurance that I have nothing to fear, even ridicule. But I can find my way around the ward and out to the porch; my world is small enough. In blindness, I can enjoy their voices more, the aide Parker, Miss Karakas, the new people who have come since Dr. Walters left. Keogh talks to me, and we stand on the porch, with our fingers in the wire mesh, and sometimes he sings. His voice is sweet and high, like a bird's, and the words are always different.

The day of the accident I groped all through the ward listening for Keogh's voice, and I did not hear it, and when I found the door of the seclusion ward locked, I kicked it and yelled his name, knowing he was in there, but he did not answer. The aide put his hands on my shoulders and led me back to my room. But at night I returned and called his name again and again. Many hours later, while I was sitting beside the door, I heard his voice, clear bright, in song, and I could go back to bed and sleep. I was sitting in the dayroom the next morning when I heard his soft shuffling step. He sat down beside me, and the leather cushion sighed as he settled into it.

"Keogh?" I said.

"Mr. Keogh," he said.

I wanted to tell him how what he did was wrong, that Dr. Walters was his friend. At that time I thought Dr. Walters might return. Then Keogh spoke:

"Let's get something to eat," he said. "Just you and me. We'll sneak down to the mess hall or the canteen and get something to eat, and nobody'll know the difference."

"Why did you do that to the doctor?" I demanded.

"Come on," he whispered in the same enticing tone. "Just you and me, while no one else is looking."

"Damn you, Keogh, listen to me," I cried.

"I'm listening," he said.

"Why, then, why?"

He was silent for awhile, then he got up and shuffled away. I lost the sound of his steps in the noises of others talking and moving around the dayroom. I fumbled for a cigaret in my pocket, and called out:

"Does anyone have a light?"

I heard his voice from somewhere in the room:

"Light is fire and fire is blood."

Panic Round

BY JOHN LOGAN

NEVER there more than a half hour at a time, he leaves the bad bachelor home of the guard hut. No uniform yet, having only worked at the plant three nights. In fact knows he may not get one and does not care, for he works only the summer and goes back to college in the fall. The watchman's heavy keys bag the pocket of his corduroy jacket. The leather-covered time clock bangs and sways at his skinny hip. He carries a very long flashlight but does not turn it on. He starts the one o'clock round, the third of nine he will make, if he makes them all, if he stays awake; he doesn't care, alone now in the huge plant since twelve o'clock. Walks slow, is very tired, not having yet learned to sleep in the late-June heat of day. Has only half slept, with the help of pills, which he still feels, and much beer, which however makes him more hot, dreaming a lot, hearing the play of kids and their high laughter, hearing the chatter of mothers and the sounds of the cars. There is one car in the plant lot, past the lamp, a long walk down the cindered, shadow-laced parking space.

He thinks as he walks now that he does not know why he himself does not drive, and he thinks of his father, dead, and of his father's high, blue car in which he rode when he was a boy, outside of town, coming suddenly out of the hills in the bright

141

fall or into new towns, him singing over the wheels, his eyes not heavy.

His first key on the clock round is in the railroad shed and beyond the car in the lot, in which a man lies sleeping.

He feels in his pocket, walking through the dark, empty lot, the badly spelled note left by the earlier guard, named, not believably, Irons, a tough likeable huge man who always talked of his young daughter's bastard twins whom he and his wife were raising, or of the men in the plant he had known for the ten years he had been a guard, the cook who drank too much and who once seared some of his fingers in the french-fry basket, the drill operator who always gave everybody a hard time until he killed his brother-in-law with a shotgun blast that rocked him, Irons said, through the screen of the front porch. He had not been convicted, had become quiet, and never got huffy when he was asked like the other men to open up his lunch kit and show it on the way out of the plant. This had to be done at twelve when the heat-treat crew got off, and it was an uncomfortable part of the job. You never knew what you would see, and what if one had something in there he shouldn't have. What would you be able to do about it? Better not to look. God, this being a cop. He moves into the light, gaining shape, a slight figure, limping a bit. Kneels by the post under the lamp, takes off his shoe and empties a cinder out of it. The blue mercury lamp flashes in his hair about the rims of his glasses. He goes again into the growing dark, approaching the car.

"Visting Forman sleeping in car to save hotel," the note said. Under it a second message. "Check generator after twelve. Be careful the points is off a little. He had heard about the generator and trembled now. This round he would have to stop. At the first round he had not known which car contained the sleeping man, but at twelve the other cars were leaving and it proved to be the one farthest from the lamppost toward the railroad shed. It was a Nash. He had looked in it and had seen after his eyes adjusted to dark that the seats were changed into a bed and the man was there, lying on his side, dressed, no blanket over him. He was barely visible in the blue light from the parking-lot lamp. Had wondered what the man looked like, whether his face was old and calm, or young and anxious, or what; whether he slept peacefully; but dared not flash his light and had passed on. He thought the man was young. Something in the man's shape had touched a memory, and he had thought of him during the last hour, the figure coming into his mind when he dozed off resting on his round or in the guardhouse. The noise of his steps seems to increase in the gravel crunch as he walks toward the car, and he goes more softly, and looks in again. The man has not changed position. But the moon has changed, or his eyes see better in the dark this hour, or something has happened, because he's certain now the man's hair is gray in the blue lamp. Who is it? A great tenderness grows in him unaccounted for as he stands there. He wishes it were himself he sees asleep, wishes so much that he too slept, or that the man who sleeps were waked, so that he is not alone again tonight. There is a drunk feeling in him from lack of rest, and his hand moves on the handle of the door which begins to turn before he remembers what he's doing and takes his hand away and walks on into the dark, disappearing completely into the huge shed.

He trips a little over the raised doorjamb. Inside, he is suddenly dwarfed by a diesel engine lit by a bulb in the rafters. The ball of his foot forms hard on the rail as he steps on the further one to cross to the clock. These inside rails bother him. The door of the shed is closed on them, and he is alone with the great single-eyed, square-faced engine, in which everything is turned off. He opens the small door of the time key, raises up the metal bar, inserts it in the opening of the leather clock and pushes on the key until he feels the click against his stomach. Moves back, and the key flops, and he doesn't slam the little door but goes on out into the yard and dark. The grass is tall beside the railroad track and wets the cuffs of his pants. He feels the damp above his sock on his right leg. His eyes pull to the lit sign on the top of the central building, "Gulliver Plant No. 3 Quality Farm Machinery."

There are two other large buildings, three stories, on either

side of the long, lower, central one. And there is a small concrete shack in his path toward the nearest of the three main
buildings. It says DANGER in block letters over the door. The
power generator is in there. He opens the door and goes in. The
generator is running, and there is a high hum that fills up the
room, mixing with a brilliant naked light that is sharpened by
yellow paint on the rock walls. The first time he has had to turn
off the generator. This job is usually done by the foreman of
heat-treat, but he is off this night each week, and then someone
else has to do it. He is unsure and afraid because Irons has told
him the points are worn, whatever that means, and that it has
scared some of the new guards. There are many dials and
switches and a rheostat or some such thing. Shaking he begins
to move with his bare hands what he hopes is the right switch.
As the knife leaves the points, a blue arc of fire strikes between
it and them, and he leaps back crashing his head and shoulders
against the bright concrete wall, his arms spread out, in the sudden silence. The breath is gone out of him and he slumps, kicks
at the switch, weakly moving it further, and hopes it is all right
now, and leaves the shack. After the yellow light the dark is
cool, and he is glad for the grass and stars after the electric
flame.

The third of the five noises of the plant comes to him from
the wing building he walks toward. The first noise was the immense silence and height of the railroad shack, the second was
the power hum. The fourth is in the heat-treat lab and the fifth
in the other wing building where he knows continually a giant
is chasing a boy. The third sound strikes at him full as he hauls
open the door. A low sound under the stars, it gains at once
now, and he is gone into it. Just inside he pauses to push the
second key, and walks up a concrete ramp to a mammoth open
two-story, city-block-square room where nothing is clear, all the
shapes covered. He knows they are forms for making guns, not
used since the war, and that they are covered and the deafening
blowers kept going over them because they may be used again.
A form for making a gun is worse than a gun he thought. The
first night he had turned off all the blowers, eighteen buttons he

hunted for around the walls, brushing against the covered
shapes in the near dark, hoping perhaps something would get
warped if the temperatures were uneven a while. They were all
back on the next night, it was last night, and a note on his desk,
signed by the guard superintendent, told him to leave them on.
Now he walks around the edge of the covered machines, track-
ing his fingers, occasionally pinching them, along the metal
rollers of the conveyor. He stops at an engine for a drink, pop-
ping a no-doz pill into his mouth, though he knows they don't
work any more. Takes one each round, but usually further
along, so he won't sleep too much when he gets back to the
shack. The water here is warm, and he remembers it has not
been used for weeks or months or perhaps since the end of the
war.

Weary he climbs unpainted, cement stairs, turns left, and
pushes another key. It is in the men's room. When he has
moved the clock on the key, he forcefully puts it down, because
it is caught or stuck in its box, erect. All the machines in here
are useless, and their bowls are covered with dusty brown paper,
and the urine is years old. He walks back across the stairwell toward the women's restroom. In there is the only couch in the
whole plant, except for the beds in the first-aid quarters. Irons
has told him he slept there on day duty Sundays. Thinks perhaps he could catch a wink there now. The lights do not go on
when he flicks the switch. It is very dark, there is no window,
and he shines his flash. He sees the bulb is missing from the
ceiling, perhaps changed to a room that is used. Light strikes
the couch, a kind of daybed. He looks around for someplace to
set the flash and he upends it in an old deodorant container
hanging from the wall and lies down. There are many tiny holes
in the wall container, and the light is dim and fragments eerily.
He turns on his stomach and sees that the couch smells of dust.
It is hot in there, and he takes off his jacket. His eyes are heavy.
The Nash in the lot shapes in his mind. He has no car but
wants so much to sleep. He turns on his side. Turns on his
back. He feels afraid of something. Thinks perhaps it is the
incessant noise of the blowers and gets up and closes the door

and lies back down. It is immediately stifling. He takes off his shirt and opens his belt and lies still for a minute again. It is dusty and hot. He takes off his clothes except his shoes and socks and is naked against the plastic of the couch. Thinks of those who have lain there before, and he feels weak, his heart racing, running, or trying to catch. He touches himself briefly, tries to be reassured. Begins to tremble gently, his body humming low as the muffled noise of the fans. He looks at himself in the shattered light playing along his limbs and sees that parts of him are uncertain, in shadow. He identifies himself more strongly now, angrily, sweating, insisting, until his heart stops banging and swaying against his thin ribs and he feels more easy.

And immediately he begins to fall asleep and into a dream. He stands on a platform by the power generator. It has great, erect switches on it that need to be put down; some of them are double, some triple, with crossbars joining. There is a great humming in his dream. Many dials with trembling arrows in them, one large one in the great, square, center panel. There are four huge wheels with levers to be pulled along them. Now, again, they are the wheels of a car. He walks to the end of the platform and sees there is a man asleep in the car. The man is old and sleeps calmly in a mottled light from the ceiling fixture. It is his father's face. He calls to him to help, to show him what to do with the generator switches. How to run it. His father sleeps on, and he tries to move from the platform holding out his hand to open the car door but cannot move, and then he sees, shocked, that the gray-haired man is now an elderly woman whom he doesn't recognize, small metal clips in her ears. He turns back to the generator, shaking out of control, and forces a great switch down in the center panel. Blue flame breaks from the generator, playing over all the switches like a grotesque hand on the keys of a mammoth instrument, soundlessly. The fire chars the bars that connect them. The dials smash and the whole center panel bursts. His fingers begin to burn with blue light. His hair flames. His clothes flame blue and fall in smoking shreds from him. He stares at his hand from which the fingers are burning away each in its own blue flame, and he stares at his burning belly, which now tapers from him flat. His skin shreds, steaming, the muscles of his legs cook and curl, and his bones break with the blue heat. He wakes screaming and sits up on the couch a few minutes holding his skull in his hands, weaving.

He dresses and leaves the room forgetting his flashlight glowing in its fixture until he is nearly down the ramp into the tunnel to the central building, and goes back for it.

The tunnel is cement, square, with square pillars, and a few bulbs scattered through its length of about a block. He seems to be walking slower. Seems to be listening to his own feet as they sound. Goes faster by black alcoves with signs over them: "Obsolete. Do not inventory." All of the parts in them are useless even for the counting. Some are packaged neatly, squarely, in yellow wood.

Halfway down the tunnel he pushes himself against another key. The fourth of nine. His mind goes to the fifth which is above in the heat-treat lab, to the sixth in the great drill-press room, the seventh by the paint shed in the far wing, the eighth by the nurse's office at the front door. The ninth, home plate, the guardhouse. Toward the end of the tunnel the walls and the floor are wet from a cause he hasn't been able to find, and the noise of his steps alters as he crosses the boards laid across the brown-water pools, white at their drying edges. He sways on the boards, nearly asleep in the tunnel, now turns up the steps past a sink with gray soap in cup and on either side of it several anonymous hanging shapes of stained overalls, and comes up from the moist, filthy tunnel to the heat-treat rooms where the furnaces run all night and the lights are all left on. It is the only place in the plant where there are people on his earlier round, stowing with gloves the glowing pieces or dragging them out of the stoves with long forks or tongs, being busy about the cocks of water and oil at the furnaces, joking and sipping coffee as they rest on the bench. Now the only sound is the fourth great one, the noise of the fire in the furnaces. He eyes the corners at the tops of the stoves to be sure the oil drips. Looks at the two-

foot dials where the hands have to be in place or he must call
the superintendent. Walks hurriedly out on the loading platform in the coolness, seeing with longing the lights of a neigh-
boring plant and a light on in a far house, and flashes his own
light in the power meter there to read it. He returns and peers
into the burning furnace interiors, which are shapeless in the
heat, but contain now only color and burnt air, which curls blue
at the edges of the red and forms ghosts stretched out on the
glowing grills. Walks by a vat of oil where he has seen earlier
the red-hot parts plunged in to cool them. He turns and moves
against a key. And sits for a moment on the bench where he
has seen the men laughing with their coffee, and begins to
drowse and dream of cars, wakes anxious, and gets to his feet
again; walks on into the long dark room of drill presses. He
hears from the far wing, louder as he moves, the fifth great
sound of his plant round, the noise of the air compressor
which is in two cycles, one heavy, slow, a strong rhythm, with
an occasional explosive noise, a grunt or shout, the cycle of the
giant, and another very rapid and light, with a kind of whispering quality as of tall grass on bare legs, the cycle of the boy
running. Sometimes it seems to him the boy is running toward
not from the giant, the lighter sound preceding the heavy. He
feels the energy of the boy as from a distance and with a certain
compassion, and always it is there even during the other cycle.
He himself is very drowsy and knows he would be easily caught
and that he could not catch. His legs are tired from the round
now too and his shins ache. He pushes a key. The two cycles
are very loud as he enters the last wing where the machines are
assembled and sees the unfinished tractors with no wheels, like
great mutilated bugs brightly painted green and red and the
grills yellow, arrayed for a futile war. The yellow fronts are narrow, marked with gilllike lines, the headlights like the dispro-
portioned eyes of embryos, the whole melancholy and undone.
He passes the air compressor in a blur of racket of boys and
giants. Ahead, unpainted tops of the tractor cowling with round
openings for exhaust and fuel or for something of the kind are
piled up against the wall like heroic shields with great holes in

them, rust-colored, or like wounded torsos with perfectly formed gaps as for several monstrous limbs which are broken out or waiting to be screwed in. He pushes against the seventh key by a metal paint shed, open at one end with a track for transporting machines into it.

Now he hears a gurgling sound as of a baby, coming from the enclosure, and he steps across a rail, tripping a bit, and stands in the shed. He feels like an unfinished bug. He faces the closed end and turns on his flash. At once the whole thing is a terrible, overwhelming, painted yellow. He reels back from his own light, catches himself, looks about for the bubbling. A gun at the corner of the shed by his feet leaks yellow paint from a ruptured hose; it oozes like the blood of insects, like urine old and thick and clotting as the blood of men. Watching, listening, the smell suddenly makes him ill, and oddly he thinks of the danger fresh paint brings to pregnant women. It seems right he should head for the next to the last key by the first-aid room at the front door, the nurse's office. He passes the plant offices, trying the doors to be sure they are locked. Stops and buys a bar of candy from a food machine and drops the wrapper between it and the wall where he moves weakly on one more key. It does not click, and he tries again with more effort, until he feels it.

Sits on a bench by the first-aid offices munching the bar, fighting his eyes, thinking only cops and whores have a chance to grow so tired. Four days earlier he sat here before his examination. Inside the doctor had told him to take off all his clothes, and he'd taken them off, except for his shoes and socks, and laid them on a bench like this inside and had sat there a minute smelling his own sweat, the wood hard against his skinny buttocks. The doctor had called him then and, looking at his feet, had shaken his head and said he couldn't figure out why people didn't understand what was meant by "all your clothes." The doctor had told him at the end of the exam that he would not qualify for regular work either on the machines in the plant or as guard but that he could be OK'd for summer employment; had not told him what was wrong. The nurse had been very kind. His mind goes to her as he struggles to keep awake, sitting

on the bench, too tired to get up yet. The nurse's name was
Murphy. She was gray-haired and wore a flower, a daisy, held in
place at her breast with a metal brooch. She kept smiling and
talking so that he had to say little. The doctor had not arrived.
She had called him by his first name and had taken him by the
arm into the different rooms for preliminary tests, even helping
him out a bit with the eye business, and had sat him in a white
metal chair with artificially placed and adjustable arms and back
for the blood test. He hadn't expected this one. He didn't like
having something taken out of him and he was not prepared.
She was very gentle and didn't hurt him as she pushed her glass
key into him and opened up his arm. But he had begun to
faint, and he told her, his voice growing distant, that he didn't
know what was the matter but he felt sick and was sorry to be-
have this way. He could feel his vocal cords move on the last
few words but could not hear them for the roaring, as of blowers, in his head, and he was moving way out away from her as
she touched him and worked on him, dropping the back of the
chair, putting a cold cloth like a washrag to his face. His eyes
had found the colors of the room fading until only red and
white remained, a double outline at the edges of the tables and
cabinets, then these separated slowly like two negatives or patterns that only make sense when imposed together, and the objects were lost to him. He was asleep awhile in the machine and
came back to find her beating him about the wrists, sweat flowing cold against his limbs. She got him to his feet and half hugging him, talking tenderly to him, encouraging, had walked him
to one of the beds and put him in, taking off his shoes, loosen-
ing his shirt and belt and heaping blankets over him, and he
slept.

Now he sleeps again on the bench outside the office and
dreams he's on the bench inside, holding his arm in the air bent
to hold the cotton in place where the vein was punched. The
doctor tells him to take off all his clothes except his shoes and
lie on the table, which has a plastic cover and smells dusty. He
strips before him, using only one hand painfully, the fingers of
that hand aching as from burns, and the pain makes him weak

so that he moves to the table half fainting, swaying, thin, one hand cocked above him in a grotesque dance. The doctor stares at him on the table, shaking his head, a metal shield on his cap flashing like the light on the front of the train. Suddenly the doctor takes a small paint gun out of the white jacket pocket and begins to spray his naked body with yellow paint which is sticky and cold, and he wakes up, still sitting but hunched forward, the leather time clock hanging between his thighs.

He gets up and walks from the building, his feet crunching in the gravel drive toward the guard hut, the prodigal returned, impoverished, to his small home without people. He pushes the ninth key and feels it click in his gut and in his brain, and he puts his head on his arms and, falling asleep immediately, begins to dream of starting another round, as he will in twenty minutes, another dance of hours, another cycle of bad dreams, walking wearily toward the machine that holds the sleeping or dead man or giant or boy.

Face like an Ikon

BY LEONARD CASPER

THE Baltic: then.

Where the northern sea came farthest into the land, fog
spoiled up from the Rack-of-Jarrow in shapes of flung spindrift,
and there was a sound making in those early hours like the
creaking of birds, when the waters bent upward. No one expected it to be a good day for burning Cove's body. They sat,
dimly seen by one another, on the cold rocks above the village
while the mist kept tumbling over the windy headlands; and
there was moisture forming in the crinkles of their garments. At
the foot of the painstaking trail down the cliff head their fishing
boats were grouped in heavy shelters; and after that there was
the whole whaleback hump of the beach itself between their
land and the surging Rack: although they knew these things in
their minds, even on the leeward side of the cliff they felt salt
water on their skin and shook with disappointment. There was
nothing to see, not their own hands; and no one felt like talking.

The four guests from the Fira tribe, which owned the secret
of freezing the dead, quietly sought one another in the grayness.
They had come, expecting to be feted for keeping the young
man's body preserved these six long months while the ritual

was being served; but now, fearing that they would be blamed
for the sea chill itself, they shivered openly, so there would be
no mistake. Each time they found someone on the rocks, their
eyes flinched because it might be the sisters, Loretto and
Rainier, come out to curse them for the festival's failure.

As the weight of the day pressed down, the salt fog became
unbearable; the ransack of wind tore at the rock crannies, even
skimming chips into the air and finally blowing up a squall that
drove the villagers back to their huts. As they scattered, they
avoided the clearing where the pyre stood, and the hut where
the body lay; but in passing, they heard the heavy twinge of the
gut-harp that Loretto's husband played, and they felt glad that
their sorrow, for the spoiling of the funeral games, was being
shared.

Loretto sat on a stool across the corpse from Fin-Cove, her
husband. Although she knew that his fingers were too thick for
the gut-harp and he had run out of words to sing, she was proud
of him because he had found the hot baths here on the inlet
three years ago, and the tribe had followed him down the coast;
he had built himself a dwelling from ancient stone walls, and
even if he was not one of the elders, no one complained about
his taking the best of the stone—though stories about the last
battle with the Comers on the beach probably came from envious tribesmen; and he had married Loretto during the half-
year's wake because he said her eyes were far apart and she had a
good back for cooking. She rose now to place more fish within his
reach, so that he would not need to leave the corpse of her
brother. Tribal law said that a man's remains were to be
watched over by his kinsmen for as long as their wealth could
endure, the body passing from one relative to another, wherever
his blood lay, until at last he should be burned and his goods
distributed. Rainier, the younger sister, had begun the rite because she had discovered the body; afterwards, Cove had passed
from door to door, where straight faces took it on themselves to
mourn his loss; and now this last day it was Loretto's turn. She
was proud, as she set forward the plate of fish, that her husband
had stayed to mourn with her, even though on that last foray

the Comers had made their way as far as to the bottom of the trail because young Cove had broken ranks and fled. She smiled at her husband.

Fin-Cove's big hand brimmed over the gut-harp strings with desperate boredom. . . .

The sound made Rainier tremble where she lay in the other chamber with her brother's dog who, even in the rain, was going to die that day. Her hands found shelter on Kemp's warm belly under the long cold shag of hair; and she thought of her father's hut where Cove's body had first lain and of the night that the old man had died helping her take the corpse from the suddenly burning shelter; and she thought of Loretto accepting Fin-Cove then, of whom her father had disapproved—out of convention, Loretto said—and of Rainier's going to live with them until this day of the pyre, after which she would be expected to marry. She thought of these things, and no more than fragments of what she *wanted* to recall.

When morning came, after rocks had been rolled down all night on the invader and the last Comers had been driven into the prows of their nailed ships and had fled, the village women had descended by the trail and walked among the ashes of their staked ships and stumbled through the buffling edges of the tide to claim their dead. No one had spoken to Rainier; and so the thought had taken her to leave her father and sister and wander alone down the breaking shore. There among small rocks and the roots of trees, still a mile from the valley which they said later he was riding to reach, Cove lay in skewered flesh. His veins were a strange blue, hollow under his skin. Rainier called his name and knelt; she thought aloud, "Now he stinks!" despite herself and despite the fact that the water had washed him all night. There was sea salt in his lashes, salt sea in his ears. Then she touched his open eyes and there was music in her armpits. A sacred joy worked in her as she folded his hair back away from his forehead, like *her* hair, the darkest in the village; and she placed her hands on his wounds. It was only later, when they told her he had broken from the battle line—many of the men had seen Fin-Cove struggling to pull Cove off the side of a horse behind the fighting—it was only then that she was reminded of the touch of leaves in the clump where Cove had lain and thought how they had shrunken her skin like the touch of wet fur; she was not sure; nor had she seen any sign of a horse. . . .

Her mind kept blurring; only the uncertainity remained. She felt Kemp's warm belly, as warm as a year ago; but he was gone in the teeth and there was mucus in his eyes; was he still Cove's dog then? And she was afraid that her memory was like this; changed; like the memory of a battle; and perhaps it would be a good thing to see them both die today, the dog and all the left-over fragments of her mind. After the burning of her father's house she had refused to attend any other wakes; she had not looked at her brother's face since that time, and even now was afraid to walk into the death room nearby where Fin-Cove's eyes were waiting for her, and where Loretto whose hair was another color would smile at her angrily because Rainier wouldn't believe how Cove had died; Loretto would say that Rainier was jealous—she would say that right in front of Fin-Cove and she would be looking at him—that she loved her brother too much and right after the funeral celebration there would have to be a wedding. . . . Fin-Cove would bury his laughter and wait.

Rainier was afraid to get married, and not just because she had not married before: but men had called her brother a coward; she had been so close to him—Cove making her feel tall by putting her young thoughts into grownup words, even before she could know her mind, much less speak it—so close that perhaps she too had to be a coward now. With him to give her comfort of same-words, Rainier could face herself; without, she could face no one, nothing: her wisdom was gone with him. She was even afraid to look at Cove, because he might be dead (she could believe it of her father but not of *him*); or visibly guilty, and deserving of death. She wished that the last words of Cove would come back to her, so she would know what she was thinking and feeling.

Fin-Cove looked across at his somewhat pregnant wife and said with a glint of eyes, "Coin and corn! coin and corn." It was an idea that had come to him on his last trip to other nations, although he was not yet ready to explain it, even to himself. He knew, however, that the words had strange effects on Loretto; he smiled, seeing how they made her flesh crawl as if she were embracing him as she had been trained. . . .

Rainier crept away from the sound of that voice, to the door flap where the inborne air seemed warmer now. She slid back the hide, moved the wooden door farther away from the stone jamb, and was amazed to be able to see all the people running toward the village clearing. Kemp brushed against her and stood, his eyes closed, suffering the new air to enter his nose. The same wind that had blown the fog onshore, had blown it away and across the mountains now. She stepped outside and watched the shredded sky clear; birds moved inland again along the broadening flyway; back along the ridges she could see goats stepping down to watering places, their polished horns making a circuit of many suns around them. Children were coming out of hiding in the hot baths; their elders stood in the doorways, buckling on ceremonial robes, while the young girls brought wood out into the open and began to lay the pyre. Over all the sun swept, over the wet green headlands, raising steam and rubbing faces into smiles; the excitement of the funeral had begun.

Still the elders did not come to get the corpse. Rainier wondered if they had forgotten: she was afraid, when she judged her own feelings, that the time of waiting had not been six months of keeping Cove in mind, but six months of pulling each recollection to bits and scattering them. If any of the men in charge of this final ceremony left a bone unburned, they would be beaten with it unmercifully and be shamed: Cove was gone. Rainier felt fragile; the warm air pushed her against the door, although she was as large as her sister now, or as any woman; she wondered how young she was; and should she be married? For the first weeks she had named her brother Bear, in hope of his resurrection; but that hope was over; now she would be satisfied just to remember what he had to say to her, his final words. . . . But how could she? Cove had been dead when she came upon him! She was being as forgetful as the elders.

Still, she had put her fingers on his open eyes. . . .

The men from the tribe of Fira were chasing each other play-
fully through the high grass, raising hackles of laughter as they
ran. One stooped suddenly and made another bowl over him,
and as they knelt there, shouting and pretending to spar with
their elbows, Rainier recognized the tusk-colored face of the
smaller man. It was Herron, the minstrel whom Fin-Cove had
driven from the village with his own spear because at the pyre
of the first man to die in that battle (a poor man, burned
soon), Herron had chanted in his lay that it was Cove who
fought and Fin-Cove who fled; and he refused to confess later
that he had made a mistake, although Fin-Cove gave him every
chance to, pressing him to admit to drunkenness and then, in a
rage, putting out one of Herron's eyes. The minstrel was well
liked, despite what he had said in his chanting, and only a dis-
coverer of hot baths such as Fin-Cove was could have driven
him from the village.

She was reminded that her brother had once said, "It is
enough to have only one truth to a face"; but those were not his
last words, and why should they come to her now? He said
things that she thought she heard, but forgot, and things that
she didn't know she had heard but, until today, had not been
able to forget. Cove had been a boy as happy as any of these
playing, as happy as the Fira tribe, but he could not help saying
serious things sometimes, letting his face slacken so that the
laugh wrinkles hung like age. He would surprise himself with
words; and then he would smile again and be gone, unchal-
lenged, as swiftly as Herron himself had disappeared now, before her eyes, even while she was thinking. Herron had liked her
brother; he had known him.

She felt blown open by the wind.

The horny beaks of Fin-Cove's hand had bitten into her arm.
"Where is your brother's treasure?" he was asking. "What did
he own? It's time for the race, and you have kept everything
hidden long enough." His lips lifted and his voice changed:
"You can't hold on to it any longer, Rainier."

If she turned at all, their faces would be together. She let her
eyes close.

"Loretto will stay with the body until they come," he con-

tinued, hard again. "The sun won't last forever. Where is it?
The games are ready."

Still she seemed to be waiting.

"You know that this has to be done."

The pulse under her chin beat against the pulse in her
throat, but when she moved, it was as if he had not pushed her.
He walked behind while they were in view of the other huts,
but when Rainier entered the tree line behind the dark hunting
lodge, she was aware of his sliding hands.

My brother was a young man longer than anyone else, she
thought desperately; the last time I saw his face the lashes
scraped against his cheeks, wanting to open his eyes. We used to
run on the beach and pretend to help pull the boats onto the
log runners, and he said the wind smelled green. Or we stuck
our tongues into the air when we heard bird calls after a feast of
fish, and we tried to taste *with* them. He would think very hard,
with his long fingers locked, and I would rest the side of my
head against his and try to overhear him.—Did it ever happen?
How is it true?—He was a good listener, and people liked to tell
him stories but never the truth, I think. He had eyes that made
them sorry, but they wouldn't tell the truth. I could never be
certain. Then he would laugh anyway. He would hunt a great
deal and come home bloody and laughing, and he would say his
words, "I am Cove and I have the faith of joy"; and we discovered those words together. But he ran away from the Comers.
Didn't he run? . . .

She pulled away from Fin-Cove's cheek; angrily she showed
him the boughs and rocks that had to be moved, to reach the
scooped-out shelter. It was a big digging, almost like the hole of
a bear, she realized, as the muscular hands exposed it; and it was
rich with arm rings that Cove had won, and war trappings,
horns for drink, and hammered swords. Some of these were her
father's; Rainier had cached them together and was surprised
that she could not tell them apart.

Fin-Cove was squatting on one powerful leg while the other
pointed outward full-length, and his opposite arm reached
among the treasure until his fingertips could move softly along

the bronze, now gold, now iron surfaces as if they were metal
strings on a harp he played. As he touched them, his eyes
pressed together and he looked at Rainier as if she were still at
the end of his hand. His words came carefully. "I have waited a
long long time," he said.

"I don't belong to my brother's hoard," she answered; but
her voice wasn't harsh enough, and his smile merely deepened,
so that she wasn't sure after all, that he was answered.

Finally he said, "You are always in my best thoughts. You
have my best wishes. My intentions are the best for you. My
thoughts of you are always best"; in a hundred different ways, it
seemed, he tangled the same words in and out among her limbs
until she couldn't move. But she refused to listen and thought
instead of her father's final words, as their hut burned down
and the linden tree with it that had spread leaves over its roof.
"Herron will teach you," the old man had said, "trust Herron";
but it was foolish to waste his breath like that, because Herron
had already been driven from the village and besides it was no
good for a woman to learn to sing and play the gut-harp because
only a man could speak the moments of truth. Not her father,
however; but Cove, yes. He had studied with Herron, while she
listened alongside in the grass. She remembered the sight of
Cove leading the return from the farthest point of navigation;
he had leaped from the prow into the breakers, and his tunic
had come open, showing that the new hairs on his breastbone
were darker than his head because the arctic sun had bleached
even his eyebrows; and he had picked her up and said, "Nothing is completely imaginary, Rainier," and he had kissed her
eyes vehemently, so that the horizons closed for an instant overhead, and she could not forget the handsome tone of his voice
and how self-assured he was. She remembered his laughter even
later in those rare blackenings of his secret face when the look
was on him of one who has crawled a long way through veins.
This—these—were the Cove that others had never known and
that Fin-Cove would like her to forget. But each breath of hers
tried to pull him back.

She turned suddenly away from the crouching man's words.

"There's too much here for one man," she said proudly. "I'll
send others from the village to help you carry this hoard to the
race. . . . My brother once killed a man named Longo," she
added, "and another named Brawner who came in the dark."
Without waiting for what he might say, she walked alone back
to the village and the reaches of sunlight; nor did she think of
Fin-Cove, but only of her growing loss and loneliness.

A beachcombing party burst from the trail and, swinging
conch shells and driftwood they had brought from the scruff of
the waves, ran down from the high ground; they were greeted
by the crowds that had already gathered for the games: naked
wrestlers, layered with mud, circled one another on the flat
stretch that served as an arena. Over their heads Rainier could
see the bearers lifting Cove's straight body onto the pyre in the
full pouring of the sun, a cadaver under the noon of day.

She sent boys to carry the treasure because she knew how
they would enjoy it; then she went to Loretto, expecting to find
her weeping for herself and her unborn. But at the outer door
she met Herron kneeling beside the dog; as he rose, two falcons,
one brown and one mottled gray, swooped suddenly and
perched on the shoulders of his leather shirt; he brushed them
away, but again they came, and again.

"They're Cove's," he explained in his harsh-music voice.
"When I left, I took them, and today I set them free. But after
the fog lifted, they followed me. What should I do?"

It was as if he had said, Answer your name when called. She
felt compelled.

"Nothing living can be given away." Rainier spoke very
calmly: her first pronouncement, as if she were giving a golden
ring.

Herron nodded, unsurprised, and still nodding, walked away
with his hands in his belt. The falcons clung to his shoulders,
the dog was close to his heel.

Then Rainier went in to her sister Loretto, who, since they
were alone, leaned into her arms and said how much she
needed Rainier and forgave her younger sister for being jealous;

she wept and touched her stomach and asked what good she was to anyone.

Rainier felt possessed with strength. She knew only one song that Cove had made up, and not even all of that; but as it came back to her, it seemed to be the story of a girl lying dead in the courtyard, with grass growing throughout her abandoned hair as she slept so dreamlessly between the near forest and far-off song that the singer never spoke to her again. Rainier felt that she was that girl; whatever the chant meant, she had a share in it; she was almost the singer herself because the words moved her so; and even if Cove was dead by the time she came upon him, so she couldn't know his last words, still if she felt they were important to know, why shouldn't someone else say them for him, why couldn't she? And she knew this was her duty, and she felt quickening power take shape inside her, although as yet she didn't have the words themselves. She had just finished saying something fine, she thought; and even if she could not think what it was, as this dreamless state descended on her, still with all the sinking effort of her body she felt confident that she could speak again. She kissed Loretto's hair and helped her outside so that they could watch the games.

The wrestling and dancing had stopped. At that moment the high-rank voices of the elders were directing everyone to the course being prepared on the far side of the village where the boys had deposited the last properties of Cove in six piles within the space of a mile. As the crowd moved, the contestants themselves appeared, cantering their horses from many directions; except for loincloths they rode naked, with their fingers tangled in the manes of their bareback mounts. They were a dozen, some on short-legged heath-steppers that lumbered at the joints, some on flyblown studs and forked ponies; only a few had horses that were a pride to the eyes, and everyone breathed aloud when Fin-Cove came from the forest on a tall brown gelding whose head and tail were lofty and whose knees moved with more poise than was necessary. The crew from his vessel grinned at one another, and the rest of the assemblage guessed

that Fin-Cove had brought back this handsome animal, such as
no chieftain owned, on his last trip to far nations. They slapped
the muscles of their arms in applause and good cheer because
this was "Fin-Cove the warrior who stayed."

Four miles from the village and out of sight of the strongest
eyes, the horsemen gathered. A horn sounded, ravens burst
from the ripe trees along the way; sunshine on the ground broke
as the wind of the riders tossed aside the high grass, and dark
mud clapped against the horses' bellies. Soon the crowd waiting
at the first and richest pile could feel their own legs trembling
from the downrush of hooves; and although the riders' heads
were lost among manes, they recognized the gelding's rocking
neck and lifted foreknees ahead of all the others. Such a thing
of beauty and triumph was the gelding, coming into that stretch
that flattened out before him like a battlefield or any beach,
that no one dared cheer. They let the rider stop; they watched
astonished as the gelding circled the pile of trappings once and
his chest moved less and less, and then he seemed to dance on
one hoof at a time.

Someone broke from the line and, taking Fin-Cove's leg,
tried to pull him, victorious, from the horse, and the rest of the
crowd surged inward, too. But there was quick fear in Fin-
Cove's eyes; he drew up his knees onto the gelding's backbone,
and for a moment it seemed that he would stand there. Then
the people had to give way, because the other horses were coming up, and they narrowly escaped being trampled.

Rainier turned quickly to look at Loretto, and the elder sister
seemed to expect her eyes; but then Loretto's own spurted tears,
and whatever could have passed between was lost. Nor could
Rainier look back at Fin-Cove, now on the ground, smiling,
donning her brother's garments. Instead, puzzled again, she
pushed through the talk of onlookers and walked toward the
pyre.

Sunlight reeled from the ring-mail coats and handled spears
of the gathering. The chieftains sat on the long rocks that
would decorate the barrow after the ashes had been covered
with dirt: they played with the ends of their robes, admiring the

dyes. Around them stood the retainers, squeezing their fists
from time to time so that their biceps would swell in their gold
arm rings. The old men were drinking from their horns; the
young were watching one of the Fira demonstrate, with a jar of
water and another of fermented honey, how either could be
frozen: he spread powder, shuffled his feet, and spoke the
charm in a foreign tongue, and while they watched, a skim of
ice appeared, grew white and solid, and the heavy jars were
broken into shards; then with another pass of hands he let the
ice blocks melt. Rainier found wet spots on the ground afterwards.

Now the whole village was in place, and women were roasting
rabbits on little spits beyond the clearing. At last the horsemen
came up, each attired in his brand-new properties. Slowly they
rode around the corpse of Cove, now lifting their helmets by
the horns, now swinging their latest ornaments of twisted gold
in the sunlight, or warming their swords with a thrust; but no
one spoke. Although they were expected to sing this warrior's
praise, so that he could be burned, there seemed to be nothing to
say, especially since the authentic warrior Fin-Cove was present
and in his gleaming mail looked deathless and brave. The horses
moved slower and slower, the thrusts of the riders grew forced.

In their midst, Rainier felt the restlessness of the crowd. She
saw how the memory of her brother had been divided like so
many goods among these people; or so many single words which
could make sense only if they were all brought together again in
sentences and uttered by his living mouth; but separately they
would be forgotten—as they already had been; as she could feel
them being forgotten even by herself because she lacked the
stamina to keep her own remembrances of Cove together. She
had known Cove—the wise, who said right things; and now was
a time for saying. Someone should sing for him; should tell the
past and future; explain. Or he would be dead, and in him some
part of them would die, too, because they had shared one another.

Rainier wanted to speak, but lacked words. She looked at
Herron but he seemed to be smiling inside the withdrawal of

his mouth. The people waited. And then at last Fin-Cove himself, in a generous voice, began to raise a song, extolling the heroic life and the fall of warriors, how companions carried on, though the end of things was bloodshed. His voice was very loud. In a great swelling release, other voices joined with his, singing the conventions so resoundingly that pieces of kindling were jarred from the funeral pyre. Now the whole crowd had taken up the dirge, until the ring of spear on linden shield could not be separated from the sound of many throats. The very energy of their emotion made tears stand in Rainier's eyes and shocked her mind into silence, but she heard no one mention her brother's name.

Herron was beside her, his lips moving; even so, she did not realize at once that he was speaking. The ends of his mouth were calm, however concerned. Loretto joined them and looking into the tusk-colored face screamed above the dirge, "How dare you be here?" But he took their garments in his hands and led them aside until he could be heard.

"I know," he said to them; "I know! They are killing him. But I have been with the Fira, and I have been with the Magus. And I can bring your brother back to life."

The words lay with them a moment, while the uproar of the ritual stormed among their thoughts. Then the crowd opened to let the horsemen out, and the dirge subsided except for an occasional wordless cry. "Tell me to do it," Herron said sharply. Rainier began to walk back through the opening before the spectators could come together again.

Her sister threw up her arms. "Comfort me!"

Rainier wanted to see her brother; she began to climb over the kindling, while the people around her grew quiet.

"Comfort me!" Loretto cried.

"Come forth, saying!" Rainier called as she reached his side. Was the Bear asleep; and could he be made to talk again? His limbs were very straight, but even under the white windings they seemed full. She was heir to this body; somehow a woman had come out of man; yes; she had known him, touched his strength; and if one lived, the other would. Her hope took her up beside him.

"Comfort me!"

"Come forth, saying." Just for a moment she knew that Herron was at her back: "Tell me to," he whispered: then she was aware only of the face below her—Cove; her brother.

The face was like an ikon. It was more solemn than this moment; it would not accuse or prophesy again. What did it have to say?

In her youth she felt unutterably old.

"Don't insult our suffering!" Loretto cried, with great formality. The words lapped about Rainier like the makeshift of ebbing water.

It was not Cove's face. She could not remember. Had he been a boy once; did they ever play together: had they been alive?

Herron had only one eye and so probably he shouldn't be taken seriously. How had she been deluded into thinking he had two?

She could not even weep.

Seeing Herron, Fin-Cove had suddenly set a torch against the kindling. His new clothes which fit so well made him look very handsome. When the people began to shout again for "Fin-Cove! Fin-Cove!" the pressure was so great on her ears that Rainier had to open her mouth, and found herself shouting with the others.

She could not even remember her brother's name.

At last she reached the foot of the pyre; already the wood reck was mounting, the dark flames like long hair that blew upward and disappeared, leaving tumult, leaving the ponderous crackling of flames, and the bitter smell.

Rainier stood by herself because she had no one who belonged to her.

Herron had flung the dead falcons onto the dead man's chest. Now he opened the dog's jaws and, plunging with his knife, slashed the throat from the inside; the carcass he flung over the dead man's burning feet. Then he would have lain down among the flames himself; but the crowd took hold. ". . . are killing. . . ," he started to say, but they ground his mouth with the heels of their hands and broke him onto the grass until Fin-Cove arrived.

Before the pyre was consumed the crowd turned back to the foot races and swordplay. It was growing late. From time to time, as the sun dropped down, the people fed on the rabbits being cooked, and the little ones chewed on the bones.

A Spot in History

BY JAMES B. HALL

BECAUSE there could be no jump today, and because Carney
had stood withdrawn in the middle of his ropes and canvas and
produced the keys from the secret pocket of the trousers, and
because the buckskin pike outside Wilmington exploded from
the dark tree tunnel and opened out again into the purple of
back country toward the low hills and river, and because the
house was the kind where gravel tracks end abruptly inside a
barn yard, he tracked the boy.

The Deputy said at the end of the gravel tracks. And here
past the cattle's tongue-swept block of salt, and up the flagstone
walk with the iron handrails on each side leading to the back
stoop, the door. Behind him the monkey cage. Not a cage, but
an exerciser built of odd lengths of pipe upward and extended
until the whole jungle was passages to walk through, grasping
first one pipe then pulling along to another. The pipe collected
for quarters and dimes from every junk yard in the county, wired
together sometimes, but now crazy and rusting against the sky.
One piece of bedquilt stuffed in a windowpane fell out, so he
knocked again and louder to bring down the roof of the house
upon the inside footsteps.

Even before the father opened the back door he knew the
kitchen: split wood and the metallic smell of nutmeg. Past the

vacant wood box and into the front room where all blinds except one were down, and in the diagonal of that light the man had been rocking alone. Now the father sat down again, heavily, and rocked in his grinding country way. Nor heard the flight of starlings alight and yammer and fly away again from the pine trees outside: that tied-up bundle of clothes in the front seat of the Sheriff's car beside the deputy . . . yesterday.

". . . From that carnival," the father said, "I presume."

"Condolences, yes." He knew this was good because Carney would be pleased: this was Building For the Future, this was getting Public Relations.

"And was there, I presume?"

"Oh I'm always there. But yesterday I was watching with the others. I'm only a mechanic, you might say."

Before the father could lead up to the details—those things more than the deputy would say since elections were yet two years away—the woman called. From behind which of the seven paneled, black-oak living-room doors that opened off his room, he could not tell for the cry was the wife when the motordrome rider went over the top of his track and the brace cable across the top of the pit cut through a new six-ply tire and snipped his head off, then the wife had cried out and fainted except not this loud.

The farmer led the way through one of the dark oak doors and down a corridor into her own wing of the farmhouse. At first he could not see her, or the effects. But her wicker chair squeaked: she was in the darkest corner of her parlor, bundled in the smell of mould.

There was no canopy over the chair now, but she was upreared in the darkness. The wicker squealed when she twisted the big muscles in her shoulders, but her legs remained without motion, blanketed in that darkness.

"Oh *you* saw him. I can *tell*," she said. "Oh blood of that boy be forever on your head. Amen."

The farmer did not ignore her but he hesitated, then stood aside.

Her voice spread out across the room between them like some purple foot-thick layer of consuming noise.

". . . The first *fruit* of my *toil! Comfort of my age* (pause) *and* the sole survivor of *my own* family. A noble line Sirs (she rocked).

". . . Remembering everything: all the Kings of England, in their order. *Bonaparte's Retreat*, and all the choruses. And most of *Hiawatha*: 'Oh, by the shores of gitchaguma!' "

"A fine boy," the mechanic said, "But. . . ."

The farmer stepped forward into the dead air between them toward the watch pocket, where the check was, in the corner.

She smashed his toes with the root end of her sassafras cane. The father stepped back nimbly. He had been watching that stick. The mechanic thought he's going to kill her, now, but the farmer stepped back just beyond the end of that sassafras root and watched patiently.

She pointed the stick as a hunter might point a shotgun into a brush pile. She nodded along the stick towards the mechanic. He walked on tiptoe towards the corner of the room as though the stretched-out trousers and the jacket might twitch. The boy's check in the watch pocket felt like warm folded money in his hand.

In his own front room the father rocked again in his stifling air. The mechanic saw the farmer clearly, now that the last ray of light was going. He saw the boy's other things would remain in the attic upstairs: the half-kept baby book with the curious, full-blown angel pictures on the paper cover; the clipping of the newspaper which said about the baptism; the three Tom Swift books (*and The Airship, and The Searchlight, and The Giant Cannon*); the one scuffed-out baby shoe; and yet underneath all those attic feather beds the boy's grandfather's flintlock rifle, black and rusted and forgotten. But still loaded. He saw the farmer would sell out and move to town, there to sit out his time on a bench in front of some grocery store that gave credit to country people. But now he was only shut-mouthed and alone.

The scream and rattle-wing of the starlings in the pine tree made almost night fall. Outside, the monkey cage was reared against the sundown. He could imagine the boy leading the woman through the maze of pipes, trying to help her get the use of her legs again, since she had not walked since the birth of the boy, but no: not even a strap attached to each leg would bring the feet forward except at a drag, while she held on to the pipes.

The barnyard was behind and he drove back through the tunnel of the trees toward their fairgrounds. Carney's Packard was a big dog running the highway, belly low, and growling at the slabs of concrete.

Inside the fairgrounds and inside the race track the braced ladders of the high-diver platform seemed to spear the moon. He sensed but could not yet see the humped trailers and the curved humped tents anchored by ropes and by the Model T Ford axles sledged into the hardpan. He squirmed on the automobile seat for a minute so that the eyes could begin to see in all this darkness. He heard a foraging breeze make each brace and guy wire creak as though—secretly and all through the night—this carnival was growing, reaching out slowly, capturing more and more of this wet undefended grass. Across the race track in the regular fairgrounds he heard the hysteria of a small refrigerator motor, racing as though to cool all of that August night.

There was the smell of dew on greasy rags near the motor-drome where the riders of motorcycles chased each other inside the wooden silo ten times each day. At the far end of the area was the jumper's cannon pointed toward the sky; the net was low in the darkness in front of the grandstand. He labored to put up that net, but from one hundred and eighty feet in the air Consolo always said it looked like a bull's-eye. No bigger. Consolo, the jumper when the show ran like some fatal clock-work, when offers came in to take the show all over the world, when the audience never stomped or called More! More! By listening under the sputter of the mantles of a gasoline lantern he knew Consolo had come from the high trapeze, a catcher in Italy. The whole family had been with a show for years, then Consolo dropped his brother over the middle ring in Milan and after that he left the family act and came to America to Ringling's. Finally Carney got him. Consolo always worked in a

white helmet, and when the talker stopped Consolo climbed
the ladder to the cannon, to hesitate, to look. He would stare at
the crowd and he would pull them down inside with him. Then
the pulled lanyard, and he would be above the trees and rising.
At the top of his jump he could jackknife, and fall into that
spread-out net. Everybody thought that day he was faking, but
when they carried him to his trailer and said get up now, he did
not move. Above the net, just as he bounced once into the air,
after he landed, he died. Then Carney telephoned ahead to this
Wilmington to insert the ad.

One mauve light bulb where Carney kept the other blue suit,
where he made deals with county commissioners, where he
withdrew to lie down at night; parked around this one mauve
light the parts truck and the power plant and the cook shack:
all that canvas bulged forward regularly to breathe. Inside the
hot innermost room of Carney's trailer he saw the upended
orange crate and the bottle of beer and the cot. Carney raised
from the pillow and scooted back over the cot until he was resting his back against the bulkhead of the trailer. The undershirt
was the color of the hardpan dust that had blown across all
those summer fairgrounds. From under the pillow his teeth:
Carney plopped them in his mouth, like eating a doughnut.

The mechanic laid the Packard keys on the orange crate beside the bottle of beer; inside the breast pocket of his tan mechanic's shirt he could feel the warmth of the boy's folded-up
check.

"I wasn't out in your car with any girl, you know. I been out
making you some money."

Carney only let his eyes drop wider open. The arms were rolls
of white unbaked dough, but the hands and the wrists and the
neck were like hardpan. The dark wrists and hands dropped to
the floor of the trailer, and the cot began to shake. Then Carney rolled his head and face forward out of the shadows of the
corner of the truck. There were two big fish-bowl tears, from his
laughter. The cot sagged and the uneasy trailer yawed. Oh
Jesus! Jesus—awhoo! Awhooo! Then he stopped.

"You're smart, sonny," he said across the orange crate. "You

are intelligent!" (Ohhh awhoooop!—the split-throat nicker of
an old stallion.)

"No! No! Sonny," and then Carney was in control of his
wobbling body.

"Well," the mechanic said, "I thought you would be glad to
buy it back for fifty."

"Twenty years. That's what the sheriff told me, if it's en-
dorsed by forgery. Because when I saw you leave I just picked
up at-ere telephone to ask The Law. Yop."

"But you would have paid out $100 to his parents."

"Yop, *if* it was ever found—not burned or buried with his
clothes—and *if* they asked, and *if* it was a real check and not
just a carney check see? No, all of Greater Shows is right in that
black safe. And I'm Mr. Cash. That little old black safe don't
need to be opened tonight for you."

He turned to go out of the trailer, ashamed and feeling like
one of the briar-hopper hicks that tromped each day into the
grandstand or tromped ten times a day up the motordrome
ramp. After all the years of talking like Carney and acting like
Carney, and almost thinking like Carney himself ("I'm sorry, I
made a mistake") and forgetting gradually his old home, the
farmhouse outside Cincinnati. Carney let him get to the door.

——Hold on! It's just that you try so hard sometimes. Now
stand here beside this cot, Sonny Boy—I say—and answer up:

——You put out your forty dollars and a big story for a check
that was only paper but looked all right, forty dollars?

——That's right, Carney.

——Here is your forty dollars, forty dollars (takes this in
plain view).

——Hold on! You used my Packard automobile. Hand over
twenty dollars car rent I say, twenty dollars.

——That's right, Carney.

——Insurance and for gas: twenty dollars more, I say, now
you give me.

——That's surely right, Carney (hands over in plain view).

——Hold on! You were working overtime. So I give you back
twenty dollars for you to go *out* there. AND twenty dollars

more to return from the country (passes the last twenty, in plain view).

——Hold on! . . . I say, hold on!

"Oh Jesus, we ought to be in Vaudeville: Carney and Stupid: or, The Big Exchange."

Now in the middle of the nets and canvas he was even, except for the time on the road, but that time he knew was all Carney's anyway. Except that he was a hick, now, after all these years of forgetting. Carney had tossed him back his forty dollars for being a joke, just to show that Carney was like a father to him. Except now he did not want to be a mechanic anymore. He wondered exactly about that black safe in the corner, in the shadows. But he still liked Carney, and he still wanted to be kidded a little once in awhile, as long as it was all right.

"Sit down, my boy," Carney said. "Now we got a deal. You are in it. Everyone is in it."

Carney leaned back on the bulkhead of the truck, relaxed now. His belly curved outward and upward like the side of a tent.

"The show business. Now you wouldn't get this, but that high diver is *passé*. The bucking Ford is out, too."

The mechanic sat down on the orange crate and listened.

"So I sell out. Everything. I cut everyone's wages (except yours, Sonny). I buy up lots of scrap machine guns and tanks and we will mock up a portable pillbox. At night we will sell them a battle: Ypres, or Stalingrad, or Berlin. (Around New York City we can even mock-up a Buchenwald.) While the flame throwers warm up, the Grays slip out of the pillbox. Then a frontal assault with the Blues firing everything. We blow up the pillbox, but *they* don't know all the Grays are out but will hope so. Then our commentator says neither the Ins or the Outs were hurt. Now you wouldn't get that, Son, but *that's* show business.

"And Herbert, you lead the Blues. You carry the satchel charge. You'll give them a full-fledged battle, for one dollar."

Carney lay back on the cot and placed the big cigar delicately between his dry lips. In the heat of the summer night it was a long time ago when he joined Carney, just outside Cincinnati. It was in a country filling station where his father had put him to work when his father left town again: Barney had walked into that filling station and had asked to have a quick Packard washed. Now during the winters he watched all the equipment while Carney went to Miami to play the horses. Now he was someone Carney could pat on the shoulder if the business was good. And though he acted like Carney and though he wore black glasses even at dawn, he was not comfortable with the jumper's cannon because he would not jump, and yet it seemed the thing he should do. Perhaps he couldn't bear to find out if Carney would quickly fire him, if he ever got hurt. Or perhaps it was the thought of a crowd. . . .

And yet the day before yesterday was noon and county fair when the band music of sunshine made the ferris wheel turn white-spoke and seat-rocking above treetops. Noon, and the merry-go-round turns faster to calliope for the carved horses are riderless and all the children are eating from a family basket and white napkins under the maple trees. And on the track at noon the bay horse pulls a yellow sulky plop-plop-plop half around the track and then back, warming up. And at noon the fair is chromium and bright windshields in the sun, and the high diver tests his brace wires and the turnbuckles and sights his ladders for alignment, for he will climb slowly by band music to the platform and will sight down at the shallow tank framed in the triangle of light formed by the edge of the platform and his heels. He will sight steadily through that small triangle. When the drums roll he will hold his breath. Then tip the head back slowly. The shoulders overbalance into space. And down.

The mechanic was beside the cannon when he saw the boy coming through the glitter of driven steel stakes and the reflection of the sun on strings of light bulbs. The mechanic did not look up from the windlass crank for he was drawing back the acutator spring. Nor did he take off the black glasses, but he knew who was standing beside the windlass crank listening to the *creak, creak, creak*.

"You the crew chief?"

"Yop. And I'll bet you got a message from Garcia."

The boy was really twenty-three. His farm shoes were covered with the dust of a gravel-track road. The necktie was the Christmas four-in-hand, pretied at some factory, and the mechanic knew it fastened around the neck with elastic and a black hook.

". . . I have already signed my release."

So he explained again to the boy exactly how to stand on the two sponge-rubber pads inside the barrel. He would call the break . . ."and don't relax the knees—"

"Don't you think the place to begin is jumper, sort of at the bottom? Build a better mousetrap my mother says."

He did not take off the dark glasses but he paused and looked as sharply as he could into the boy's red face. He realized and rejected that he had also thought—when he left the filling station—that *he'd* be a partner someday.

". . . So I'm going to jump. He says show him I'm a real live wire and bring 'em in and produce."

He saw the wispy wet red hair fall below the rim of Consolo's old helmet. Carney had tossed this goof Consolo's old white jacket. The sleeves were too long but Carney said you will have to wear it anyway.

"I'm going to do it. I knew it when mother read the ad. It's in the blood."

He wondered if this boy would really jump. He had seen these country boys before: they came walking down the road, maybe limping from the time they were first sent out to work with a scythe when they cut themselves badly on the foot, but they came to join up as though there were nothing left now among the gravel tracks and cattle salt in the sand-briar hills that always stretch out toward the rivers from such a place as Wilmington.

"So I've got to jump," the boy kept saying. "I'm tired of sleeping in the loft and reading my correspondence lessons on steam fitting. And I'm tired of being badgered about making a man of myself."

He stared at the country boy through his dark glasses, but

now he could feel neither one way nor the other. By the noise he knew this was a Friday crowd. They were stamping the grandstand to pieces with their big shoes. They were people just off work from up-the-alley garages and from the gun factory and from the County Highway Department. And, of course, the farmers. They were laughing at the bucking Ford. Then the high diver, and this jump.

The boy was concealed behind the cannon. He stepped out, erect, when the talker called his last act of the day and of the season in Wilmington. When they saw him step out they laughed just a little. Because of the ad they knew he was not the regular jumper and besides he kept hauling at the chin strap of the helmet. The lower part of the costume was plainly over-alls. They thought he must be a local boy but none of them had seen him before; he had simply read the ad and had come out of some of the last of the back country, to get ahead. Or per-haps there was someone who said he was from beyond Villar's Chapel, and that they knew his Daddy. Then the band played "On the Mall."

"Hold your knees stiff. I won't trip it until you are ready." This with the lips averted from the crowd. He saw the sweat was running from under the white helmet. He saw the boy look up the long slender ladder as though the rim of the sheet-metal cannon was one mile away.

When the crowd saw the boy put the first foot on that ladder they settled down. They had not expected this one to take even that first step. He climbed rapidly, almost at a run. Quickly he threw one leg over the rim of the gun—slid down, out of sight.

The amplifier made a faint hum from the trees where the loud speakers were concealed:

. . . *And now, he is in position*—

The white helmet popped up over the rim. "I want to see the net. I can't see my net from inside."

He climbed up the ladder toward the helmet. The boy was holding on to the rim, his knuckles on the edge like a row of small white eggs.

"What's the trouble. Didn't we set it up to suit you?"

"Lower it. I want it lowered. I'll give them a real show."

"Consolo used this setting. You will land pretty close."

"Lower it. Or I won't jump."

Carney was below on the ground, looking up. "What's the matter. That guy yellow?"

"No, I'm not," said the helmet. "Lower it down."

"OK," said Carney. "Give 'im a couple of notches."

The mechanic climbed back down the ladder and turned the set wheel on the quadrant. He lowered the aim perhaps one inch.

 . . . *And now the management has approved that aim. Imagine yourself, my friends, inside that gun.*

The helmet popped up again over the edge.

The crowd laughed and booed. The timing was all wrong. Carney would really be sore now. But he couldn't fire the guy either.

"I can't see my net. I want it away down. Or I won't jump."

"Fellow, you better go along with . . ."

"Like he says," Carney called up to the rim, "He's the jumper. You ain't. *You* could have that job you know."

The mechanic climbed back down. The helmet disappeared. The voice from inside the gun kept calling, More! More! until the cannon was aimed flat at the net. The crowd stopped yelling and stomping. Some thought the guy was yellow. Some wished now they had not come at all. Then all of them were very quiet like children. Noiseless, now, except for the *plop-plop-plop* of the bay horse warming up on the race track, and the small refrigerator motor in the fair grounds still running.

Inside the cannon the echoes, *In the blood. The blood.* Inside there was the perfect hoop of daylight at the muzzle and the flat rope net set squarely in front of the eyes.

Carney fifty yards away on the steps of his trailer, standing in the sun. Carney nodded. 'Yes.'

He pulled the lanyard. Hard. The helmet hit the ground in front of the net. The white jacket disappeared into the wires and the glittering metal stakes. The whole net was a cloud of dust. That was all he could see because of the legs of the policeman running.

That had been Friday and the next day he had borrowed the Packard to drive through that dark tunnel of trees toward the back country where he'd found the fierce woman and the old man who—though he never knew it—was already broken by the depression, and the depression before that. Now he sat on the orange crate in Carney's trailer listening, watching Carney reach under the cot for another bottle of beer, seeing him drink half and seeing him pass over the last of the warm beer to his own receiving hand. This was the end of the season. Soon they would strike the canvas; then he and Carney would wait alone for another spring, in some other county. Then there would be the Blues and the Grays and the satchel charge. Just at dawn there was a knock on the door.

Carney rolled quickly out of the cot with that lithe movement that an old bareback rider never loses, even in flesh. He put on his black glasses and walked to the front of his trailer.

"Who the hell are you?" Carney said, as though he had run into a tax collector.

Outside in front of the trailer this kid was wearing silk coveralls, with white patches of parachute silk stitched all over the legs and shoulders. This kind was short and blocky like Consolo except he was blond and not sullen. He couldn't stand still. He kept hopping round like a little boxer warming up. He carried a staff made out of a piece of old airplane tubing. Inside his bundle, fastened on the end of the tubing, you knew there was another pair of tight-rolled blue-silk coveralls.

"Saw your ad," he laughed. "You should know I won't jump for cash. Only on percentage. I got an angle."

"You don't say," Carney said. "Say, where did you come from?"

"I'm from the Big City, man. I just rolled off a freight train and hit a-running."

The kid did two back flaps and then dusted off his hands. Then the kid reached down at the sides of his coveralls and pulled up folds of cloth that were sewn into the seam. He stretched his hands above his head. The web of cloth was reinforced with metal ribbing. They were outstretched, taut, white canvas wings.

"Y'see, I drift right over their heads and then break into the net. It's fancy."

"Nope," Carney said, and the mechanic was glad. "I got other plans. This jumping is finished."

"Suit yourself," the kid said, and he picked up his staff made out of airplane tubing. "See you in the money. At the Garden. Ha!"

Carney hesitated only a second. Then Carney ran off after him. He called the kid back. This kid was the type. He would pull them all in. Carney put his hand on the kid's shoulder as they walked along . . . very friendly, patting him (*pat, pat, pat*).

The kid broke for the cannon and began to crank the windlass. He did not have to be shown. Carney trotted across the area to the grandstand like a young stallion. No one else was awake. Carney was a one-man private audience. Already he was gaping at the cannon. His neck was red as any country hick's. He was waiting to see his new little jumper.

Therefore the mechanic went back into Carney's room and stole the car keys out of the secret pocket of the other trousers. He sneaked the Packard around behind the trailer. That little black safe wasn't so heavy as he had always thought. It fit very nice into the trunk of Carney's own automobile. He drove, with no dust, out of the quarter stretch and out of the fair grounds.

Now someplace down the buckskin pike take the drill and a tire tool and open up that safe. Reach inside and feel that slick greasy money, the season's take that no horse in Miami will ever get. Then drive and drive and drive: spend all that money at the towns along the way, driving always south. For behind there is only that expense of innocence and ahead there is sunlight and the great winking hotels where salt waves lick all night at the white and slumbering beach.

And he thinks, they will catch me. Perhaps in the Poinsettia

Grille, in Georgia. But Carney is a goner, so are the motor-drome riders and the high diver, and especially that new blonde jumper from the big city who would change everything. That big door will slam.

Yet pictures will be in every paper, and even perhaps in the books on history. And what else does a man want?

Mortality and Mercy
in Vienna

BY THOMAS PYNCHON

JUST as Siegel got to the address Rachel had given him it started to rain again. All day rain clouds had hung low and ragged-edged over Washington, ruining the view from the top of the Monument for the high-school kids on their senior trips, sending brief squalls which drove tourists squealing and cursing in to find shelter, dulling the delicate pink of the cherry blossoms which had just come out. The address was a small apartment building on a quiet street near Dupont Circle, and Siegel dove into the lobby, in out of the rain, clutching the fifth of scotch he was carrying as if it were a state secret. There had been times—during the past year, in the Avenue Kleber or the Viale delle Terme di Caracalla—when there had been a briefcase where the fifth was now, clutched under the same tweed-clad arm against rain or a deadline or some bureaucratic necessity. And most of these times, especially if he were hung over from the night before, or if a girl fellow junior diplomats had sworn was a sure thing had turned out to be so much more than sure that in the end it had not been worth even the price of drinks, he would shake his head like a drunk who is trying to stop seeing double, having become suddenly conscious of the

weight of the briefcase and the insignificance of its contents
and the stupidity of what he was doing out here, away from
Rachel, following an obscure but clearly marked path through a
jungle of distrainments and affidavits and depositions; wondering why, in his first days with the Commission, he should have
ever regarded himself as any kind of healer when he had always
known that for a healer—a prophet actually, because if you
cared about it at all you had to be both—there is no question of
balance sheets or legal complexity, and the minute you become
involved with anything like that you are something less—a doctor, or a fortune-teller. When he was thirteen, a little less than a
month after his bar mitzvah, his cousin Miriam had died of
cancer and perhaps it was then—sitting *shivah* on an orange
crate in a darkened room high over the Grand Concourse,
gaunt and looking a little like a John Buchan hero even at thirteen, gazing fixedly at the symbolic razor slash halfway up his
black necktie—that this awareness had begun to grow, because
he still remembered Miriam's husband cursing Zeit the doctor,
and the money wasted on the operations, and the whole AMA,
crying unashamed in this dim hot room with the drawn shades;
and it had so disquieted young Siegel that when his brother
Mike had gone away to Yale to take premed he had been afraid
that something would go wrong and that Mike whom he loved
would turn out to be only a doctor, like Zeit, and be cursed
someday too by a distraught husband in rent garments, in a
twilit bedroom. He would stand, therefore, out in some street,
not moving, hanging on to the briefcase and thinking about
Rachel who was 4' 10" in her stocking feet, whose neck was
pale and sleek, a Modigliani neck, whose eyes were not mirror
images but both slanted the same way, dark brown almost to
fathomlessness, and after awhile he would drift up to the surface again and be annoyed with himself for worrying about
these things when the data inside the briefcase should have
been at the office fifteen minutes ago; and realize, reluctantly,
that the racing against time, the awareness of being a cog, the
élan—almost roguery—of the playboy element in the Commission which went well with his British-staff-officer appearance—

even the intradepartmental scheming and counterscheming which went on in jazz cellars at two in the morning, in pensions over brandy and soda, were, after all, exciting. It was only when he forgot to take vitamin-B pills the night before to ward off a hangover that these funky periods would come at all. Most of the time the bright-eyed and bushy-tailed Siegel would assert himself and then he would look on the funky days as only brief aberrations. Because when you came down to it, it was fun to manoeuvre. In the army he had lived by a golden rule of Screw the Sergeant before He Screweth Thee; later in college he had forged meal tickets, instigated protest riots and panty raids, manipulated campus opinion through the school newspaper; and this was the part of him inherited from a mother who at the age of nineteen had struggled with her soul one night in a railroad flat somewhere in Hell's Kitchen and, half drunk on bootleg beer, had ended up refuting Aquinas and quitting the Roman church; who would grin fondly at her husband and refer to him as an innocent slob who never had a chance against her female cunning, and advise Siegel never to marry a shiksa but to find himself some nice quiet Jewish girl because at least there you were given a running start. For this his roommate at college sophomore year had called him Stephen and taunted him mercilessly about the still small Jesuit voice which kept him from being either kicked around or conscious of guilt or simply ineffective like so many of the other Jewish boys on campus seemed to Grossmann to be. "Also, Grossmann," Siegel had retorted, "it perhaps saves me from being a schmuck like you." Grossmann would laugh and stick his nose back in a textbook. "It is the seed of your destruction," he would murmur. "House divided against itself? You know." Well, here he was, thirty and on the way to becoming a career man, and not particularly aware of destruction mainly because he was unable to give it a name or a face, unless they were Rachel's and this he doubted. With the bottle under his arm he climbed up two flights of stairs, the few raindrops which had caught him glistening in the shaggy tangle of his tweed coat. He hoped she had said sevenish—he was pretty sure, but it would be awkward if he

arrived too early. He rang the buzzer in front of a door that said
3F and waited. It seemed to be quiet inside, and he was just
beginning to wonder if maybe she hadn't said eightish when the
door opened and a wild-looking, rangy man with fierce eyebrows, wearing a tweed coat and carrying what looked like a pig
foetus under one arm, stood staring at him, an empty room
behind him, and Siegel, annoyed, realized he had goofed and
that thirty years was a long time and that this might be a first
indication of senility. They faced each other like slightly flawed
mirror images—different patterns of tweed, scotch bottle and
pig foetus, but no discrepancy in height—with Siegel experiencing a mixed feeling of discomfort and awe, and the word
Doppelgänger had just floated into his mind when the other's
eyebrows shot up into twin parabolas and he stuck out his free
hand and said, "You're early but come in. I'm David Lupescu."
Siegel shook hands, muttering his own name, and the spell
broke; he looked at the object under Lupescu's arm and saw
that it really was a pig foetus, caught the faint scent of for-
maldehyde, and scratched his head. "I brought some booze," he
said. "I'm sorry about this, I'd thought Rachel said seven."
Lupescu smiled vaguely and closed the door behind him.
"Don't worry about it," he said, "I've got to put this thing
someplace." He motioned Siegel to a seat and picked up an old-
fashioned glass from a table, a chair from nearby, dragged the
chair to the entrance of what Siegel presumed was the kitchen,
stood on the chair, took a thumbtack from his pocket, stuck
it through the umbilical cord of the pig foetus and tacked it
onto the molding over the entrance, hammering with the bottom of the glass. He jumped down off the chair and above him
the foetus swung dangerously. He looked up at it. "I hope it
stays there," he said, and then turned to face Siegel. "Fetching,
isn't it?" Siegel shrugged. "Dada exhibit in Paris on Christmas
eve, 1919," Lupescu said, "used one in place of mistletoe. But
ten to one *this* group won't even notice it. You know Paul
Brennan? He won't."

"I don't know anybody," Siegel said, "I've been sort of out of touch. I just got back from overseas last week. All the old crowd seems to have drifted away."

Lupescu stuck his hands in his pockets and looked around the room, brooding. "I know," he said grimly. "Big turnover. But the types are constant." He moved toward the kitchen, glanced in, paced back again to the French windows, then suddenly turned and shot out a forefinger at Siegel. "You," he almost roared. "Of course. You're perfect." He advanced toward Siegel menacingly, stood looming over him. "Good grief," Siegel said, cowering a little. "*Mon semblable,*" Lupescu said, "*mon frère.*" He gazed at Siegel. "A sign," he said, "a sign, and deliverance." Siegel could smell alcohol fumes on Lupescu's breath. "I beg your pardon," Siegel said. Lupescu began pacing around the room. "Only a matter of time," he said. "Tonight. Of course. Why. Why not. Pig foetus. Symbol. God, what a symbol. And now. Freedom. Deliverance," he screamed. "Genie. Bottle. Century after century, until Siegel, fisher of souls, pulls the cork." He began running around the room. "Raincoat," he said, picking a raincoat up off the sofa, "shaving gear." He disappeared into the kitchen for a moment, came out with an overnight kit in his hand, wearing the raincoat. He paused at the door. "It's all yours," he said. "You are now the host. As host you are a trinity: (a) receiver of guests"—ticking them off on his fingers—"(b) an enemy and (c) an outward manifestation, for *them,* of the divine body and blood."

"Wait a minute," Siegel said, "where the hell are you going?"

"The outside," Lupescu said, "out of the jungle."

"But, look, hey, I can't make this. I don't know any of these people."

"All part of it," Lupescu said airily. "You'll pick it up fast enough," and was through the door and out before Siegel could think of an answer. Ten seconds later the door opened again and Lupescu stuck his head in and winked. "Mistah Kurtz—he dead," he announced owlishly and disappeared. Siegel sat staring at the foetus. "Well now, what the hell," he said slowly. He stood up and strolled across the room to where the phone was and dialed Rachel's number. When she answered he said, "Fine friends you have."

"Where are you?" she said. "I just got back." Siegel explained. "Well, I'm glad you called," Rachel said. "I called your place and you weren't in. I wanted to tell you, Sally's brother-in-law's sister, a winsome little brat of fourteen, just blew into town from some girls' school in Virginia, and Sally is out with Jeff, so I've got to stay here and entertain her til Sally gets back, and by the time I'm able to get away the liquor will be all gone: I know Lupescu's parties."

"Oh for God's sake," Siegel said irritably, "this is ridiculous. If Lupescu's friends are anything like him this place is about to be invaded by a horde of raving lunatics, none of whom I know. And now you're not even coming."

"Oh it's a nice crowd," she said. "A little curious maybe but I think you'll like them. You ought to stay." The door was suddenly and violently kicked open and through it lurched a fat florid adolescent in a sailor suit, carrying a girl piggy-back. "Lewpayskew," the sailor shouted. "Whay aw yew, yew mothuhlovin Roumanian."

"Hold on," Siegel said. "What was that again," he asked the sailor, who had deposited his passenger on the floor. "Mayun ah said whay's Lewpayskew," the sailor said. "God," he babbled into the phone, "they're coming, they're filtering in already. What do I do, Rachel, they can't even talk English. There is some nautical-looking type here who is speaking no language known to man."

"Darling," Rachel laughed, "stop acting like a war flick. That's probably only Harvey Duckworth, who comes from Alabama and has a charming southern accent. You'll get along wonderfully, I know you will. Call me tomorrow and let me know everything that has happened."

"Wait," Siegel said desperately, but she had already said "Bye-bye," and hung up. He stood there holding the dead receiver. Harvey Duckworth was stomping around in the other rooms, yelling for Lupescu; and the girl, who was very young and had long black hair and big hoop earrings and was wearing a sweatshirt and levis—who seemed to Siegel a perfect parody of the girl bohemian of the Forties—stood up and looked at Siegel. "I want to go to bed with you," she intoned dramatically, and all at once Siegel cheered up. He put the receiver back on the hook and smiled. "I'm sorry," he said suavely, "but statutory rape and all that, you know. Can I get you a drink?" He went into the kitchen without waiting for an answer and found Duckworth sitting on the sink trying to open a wine bottle. The cork popped out suddenly and the bottle slipped and Chianti splashed all over Duckworth's whites. "Gaw damn," Duckworth said, staring at the purple stain. "Mizzable Guineas can't even make wahn bottles raht." The buzzer rang and Siegel called, "Get that would you, beautiful," and picked the Chianti bottle up off the floor. "Still some more," he said cheerfully. He was beginning to feel jovial, irresponsibly so; a light-headedness which he realized might be one of the first stages of hysteria but which he rather hoped was some vestige of the old nonchalance which had sustained him on the Continent for the past two years. In the other room he heard what sounded like a chorus of roaring boys, chanting dirty limericks. The girl came in and said, "My God, it's Brennan and his friends."

"Oh goodo," Siegel said. "They seem to be in fine voice." Indeed, they were. In his suddenly amiable state it seemed to Siegel that this account of the young fellow named Cheever who had an affair with a beaver took on Deeper Human Significance, was gilded with a certain transcendental light which reminded him of that final trio from *Faust*, where the golden stairs come down and Margarethe ascends to heaven. "Really lovely," he mused. The girl looked with disgust at Duckworth and then smiled brightly at Siegel. "By the way," she said, "I'm Lucy."

"Hi," Siegel said. "My name is Cleanth but my friends call me Siegel, out of pity."

"Where's David, anyway. I ought to give him hell for inviting that oaf Brennan."

Siegel pursed his lips. Hell, this was impossible. He had to trust somebody. He took her hand and led her into the bedroom and sat her down on a bed. "No," he said quickly. "Not what you're thinking." He told her about Lupescu's sudden departure, and she shrugged and said, "Maybe it was a good thing. He would have cracked sooner or later, he was going native."

"That's a strange way to put it," Siegel said. After all, going native in Washington, D.C.? In more exotic places, certainly, he had seen that. He remembered a Peter Arno cartoon in the *New Yorker* he had always liked, showing a girl in Apache costume, sitting on the lap of a depraved-looking Frenchman in a sidewalk cafe; and the girl's friend, obviously an American tourist, armed with camera, shoulder-bag and guidebook, saying, with a scandalized expression, "But Mary Lou, you mean you're not going back to Bryn Mawr, *ever?*" Still, stranger things had happened. In the two semesters he spent at Harvard Siegel had witnessed the gradual degeneration of his roommate Grossmann, a proud and stubborn native of Chicago who denied the presence of any civilization outside of Cook County and for whom Boston was worse even than Oak Park, was in fact, a sort of apotheosis of the effete and the puritan. Grossmann had remained unmarred, majestically sneering, happy-go-lucky, until one Christmas eve he and Siegel and some friends and a group of Radcliffe girls had gone caroling on Beacon hill. Whether it was the booze they had brought along or the fact that Grossmann had just finished reading not only Santayana's *The Last Puritan* but also a considerable amount of T. S. Eliot—and so might have been a little more susceptible to tradition in general and to Christmas eve on Beacon hill in particular—or merely the bothersome tendency Grossmann had to get sentimental in the company of Radcliffe girls, he had still been touched enough to inform Siegel later on that night that maybe there were a few human beings in Boston after all. And this had been the first tiny rent in that midwestern hauteur which he had carried up to now as a *torero* carries his cape; after that night it was all downhill. Grossmann took to strolling in the moonlight with only the most patrician of Radcliffe and Wellesley girls; he discovered a wonderful make-out spot down behind the minuteman statue in Concord; he began carrying a black umbrella and gave away all his loud clothes, substituting flawless and expensive tweeds and worsteds. Siegel was mildly disturbed at all this but it was not until one afternoon in the early spring, when he entered their rooms at Dunster and surprised Grossmann standing in front of the mirror, umbrella under one arm, eyebrows raised superciliously and nose arched loftily, reciting "I parked my car in Harvard yard," over and over, that he was struck with the extent of his roommate's dissipation. The strong nasal r's Siegel had secretly admired were now enervated and pallid; and in that classic shibboleth, Siegel recognized poor, innocent Grossmann's swan song. A year later Siegel got a letter, the last: Grossmann had married a Wellesley girl and they were living in Swampscott. *Sit tibi terra levis*, Grossmann. But Siegel wondered how in the hell it was possible for anyone to sink roots in a town at once as middle class and as cosmopolitan as Washington. You could become bourgeois or one of the international set but this could happen in any city. Unless it had nothing to do with the place at all and was a question of compulsion—unless there was something which linked people like Gaugin and Eliot and Grossmann, some reason which gave them no other choice; and this was why, when it had happened in Boston and now maybe even in *Washington*, for God's sake, Siegel felt uneasy and unwilling to think about it too much. This little Jesuit thing, this poltergeist, would start kicking around inside his head just as it had done with the briefcase, and call him back to the real country where there were drinks to be mixed and *bon mots* to be tossed out carelessly and maybe a drunk or two to take care of. It was doing that now. So all he did was look at Lucy quizzically and say, "Well, I don't know. He seemed sort of under the weather. Also maybe a little neurotic."

The girl laughed softly, not trying for rapport any more, not even the bedroom kind; but anxious now for thoughts of her own which Siegel was neither ready to be curious about nor confident he would be able to cope with. "A little neurotic," she said, "is like being a little bit pregnant. You don't know David. He's well, Siegel, he's the only one of us who is." Siegel smiled. "I shouldn't talk," he said, "I'm a stranger. Look, Lucy, would you help me out a little with this group?"

"Me help *you*?" Suddenly weak, she answered with something that was so curiously both impotence and scorn that he began to wonder how well she was herself. "All right, I'll make a deal. Mutual aid. The truth is I need a shoulder to cry on." Siegel threw a quick glance behind him out into the kitchen, a glance which she caught. "Don't worry about them," she smiled, "they'll take care of themselves for awhile. They know where the liquor is and everything." Siegel smiled in apology, pushed the door shut, and settled back on the bed next to her, resting on one elbow. A Klee original was on the wall facing them; two crossed BAR's, hunting rifles, and a few sabres hung around the other walls. The room was sparsely furnished in Swedish modern and carpeted wall to wall. He looked down at her and said, "OK, cry away."

"I don't really know why I should be telling you about this," she began and it was as if she had said, "Bless me father for I have sinned," because Siegel often thought that if all the punks, lushes, coeds in love, woebegone PFC's—the whole host of trodden-on and disaffected—who had approached him with that opening formula were placed end to end they would surely reach from here back to the Grand Concourse and a timid spindle-shanked boy in a slashed necktie. "Except," she continued, "that you look like David, you have the same kind of sympathy for anybody who gets kicked around, I feel that somehow." Siegel shrugged. "Anyway," she said, "it's Brennan and that bitch, Considine." And she went on to tell how apparently this female economics expert named Debby Considine had returned a week ago from an expedition to Ontario and right away Paul Brennan had started chasing her again. There was a tree outside her apartment house on P St. and Brennan had climbed up this tree and waited for her to come out and whenever she did he would proclaim his passion for her in loud and improvised blank verse. Usually a small crowd would collect, and finally one night the cops came with ladders and hauled him down and dragged him away. "And who does he call to come down to the precinct to bail him out?" Lucy said. "Me, is who. Right before payday too. The bastard still hasn't paid me back. And to make matters worse he already had a record. Krinkles Porcino, that's Paul's roommate, got engaged to this girl Monica back around February. The two kids were really in love, and Paul was fond of both of them, so that when Sybil—she was living with David at the time—started running after Krinkles and threatening to break the thing up—well, anyway, she finally threw this big bitch scene with Paul in the lobby of the Mayflower, and Paul ended up slugging her with a vodka bottle he happened to be carrying, and they got him for assault. And of course David had a bad time of it because he hates to get involved in anything, but Sam Fleischmann, who's hated Paul's guts ever since Paul sold him $100 worth of phony uranium stock, felt so sorry for David that he started writing poison-pen letters to Sybil, dumping all over Paul. He'd write them in the morning right after we got up, while I made breakfast, and we'd both laugh and laugh because it was so much fun."

"Oh," Siegel said, "ha, ha."

"And then when Paul got out," she went on, "what should happen but Harvey had to fly into a rage at Paul because he knew I was in love with Paul and was sending him cigarettes and cookies and things while he was in stir, and he chased Paul for seven blocks through the theatre district one night with a boatswain's knife. That was sort of funny too because Harvey was in uniform, and it took four SP's finally to bring him down, and even then he broke the arm of one of them and sent another to Bethesda Naval Hospital with severe abdominal wounds. So Paul is out on bail now and threatening to get Monica because she's living with Sam but what the hell else can she do when Krinkles has been out of town for weeks trying to kick the habit and all. The trouble is that damn junkie doesn't know how really *good* she is, Siegel. She pawned Krinkles' baritone sax only a couple of days ago because poor Sam had just lost his job at the Smithsonian and was actually starving before she found out about it and took him in. The girl's a saint." She went on in the same way for fifteen minutes more, laying bare, like a clumsy brain surgeon, synapses and convolutions which should never have been exposed, revealing for Siegel the anatomy of a disease more serious than he had suspected: the badlands of the heart, in which shadows, and crisscrossed threads of inaccurate self-analysis and Freudian fallacy, and *passages* where the light and perspective were tricky, all threw you into that heightened hysterical edginess of the sort of nightmare it is possible to have where your eyes are open and everything in the scene is familiar, yet where, flickering behind the edge of the closet door, hidden under the chair in the corner, is this *je ne sais quoi de sinistre* which sends you shouting into wakefulness.

Until finally one of Brennan's friends, whom Lucy introduced as Vincent, wandered in and informed them that somebody had already walked through the French windows without opening them; and Siegel realized wearily that it was going to be that kind of a party, and having committed himself anyway by the very act of lying next to a girl he did not know and playing the role of crying towel for half an hour, resolved in true British-staff-officer style to bite the jolly old bullet and make the best of a bad job.

In the kitchen were a couple seated on the sink making out; Duckworth, horribly drunk, lying on the floor and hurling pistachio nuts at the pig foetus; and a group of four or five people in Bermuda shorts sitting in a circle playing Prince. In the other room somebody had put on a cha cha record and a few couples were improvising freely. Presumably intelligent talk flickered around the room with the false brightness of heat lightning: in the space of a minute Siegel caught the words "Zen," "San Francisco," and "Wittgenstein," and felt a mild sense of disappointment, almost as if he had expected some esoteric language, something out of Albertus Magnus. Beside the pig foetus there was only one other really incongruous note in the whole scene: a swarthy-looking person in torn khakis and an old corduroy coat who stood in one corner like some memento mori, withdrawn and melancholy. "That's Consi-

dine's latest," Lucy said, "an Indian she brought back from Ontario. Boy, what a hunk."

"He looks sad," Siegel said. Somebody handed Siegel an
ambiguous mixture in an old-fashioned glass and he sipped it
automatically, grimaced, and set it down. "His name is Irving
Loon," she said dreamily.

"Irving what?" said Siegel.

"Loon. He's Ojibwa. Oh there's Paul. Talking to Considine,
the bastard." She led him over to a corner where a diminutive
junior-executive type was eagerly haranguing this serpentine
brunette with heavily mascaraed eyes. At his first glimpse of
Debby Considine, Siegel drew in a low whistle and let the four
fingers of his left hand wobble to and fro a few times, forgetting
about Irving Loon, Prince players, and drunken sailors. "*Mar-
rone*," he whispered. Lucy glared at him. "Not you too," she
said furiously. "Goddamn all these sex machines." He was introduced and after awhile Lucy managed to haul Brennan away
on some pretext or other, and Siegel was left alone with the lady
economist. "And how were the boondocks of Ontario?" he said.
She looked at him from under lowered lashes. "So fascinating,"
she murmured in a husky, detached voice. "Do you know the
Ojibwa?" Siegel began flipping over a stack of mental IBM
cards frantically. There was something he knew, something he
had had in college. It irritated him not to be able to call the information up because most of the courses he had taken had
served no other function—at least such had been his undergrad-
uate protests—than to provide material for conversation at
parties like this one. Ojibwa Indians. Somewhere in Ontario.
Something weird, even funny, but he was damned if he could
pin it down. "You look compassionate," Debby said suddenly.
"Is there somewhere we can talk?" and Siegel, pulled away from
the IBM cards, thought, Jesus Christ, here we go again. He led
her into the bedroom, which was beginning to look like some
perversely decorated confessional, and wondered whether this
had been David Lupescu's place for listening to bent souls. He
had a hunch it was. She stood close to him and played with his
challis tie and gave him the demure bit with the eyelashes

again. "You're the same," she whispered, "you have this monumental Lupescu coolness. You're sure you're not his double-ganger."

"No," Siegel said, "I'm not sure. Go ahead." She hesitated and he prompted her, "Bless me father. . . ."

The eyelids flew open. "David said that too. Who are you, Siegel?"

"For the moment, a father confessor. What seems to be your trouble, my child."

"It's Irving Loon," she said, sitting on the bed and playing with the empty highball glass she had brought in with her, ignoring the irony, "he was so happy back in Ontario. At ricing time, you see, all the families are together, everyone happy, Togetherness in Ojibwa land. Blasts, brawls, sex orgies, community sings, puberty rituals. All kinds of wonderful local color to fill up notebook after notebook with. And Irving Loon, ten feet tall with fists like rocks and enough to make even a jaded heart like mine uneasy." Then, surprisingly—and, for Siegel, embarrassingly—she began reeling off a list of the affairs she had had in all the underdeveloped areas she had visited for the State Department; several pages of unofficial statistics which sounded a little like the catalogue aria from *Don Giovanni*. It seemed she had this habit of picking up male specimens wherever she went and bringing them back with her and dropping them after a few weeks. Her exes either assimilated in with The Group or found a niche in some other group or dropped out of sight completely and forever. But Irving Loon, she insisted, was different. He had this brooding James Dean quality about him. "He's been standing in the same corner all evening," she said. "He hasn't spoken a word for two days. I feel"—and her eyes gazed over Siegel's shoulder, out into God knows where—"that it's not only nostalgia for the wilderness, but almost as if somehow out there, in the hinterlands, with nothing but snow and forests and a few beaver and moose, he has come close to something which city dwellers never find all their lives, may never even be aware exists, and it's this that he misses, that the city kills or hides from him." I'll be damned, thought Siegel. This broad is

serious. "And this is just what I can't tell Paul," she sighed.
"He makes fun of Irving, calls him ignorant. But it's a divine
melancholia and it's what I love about him."

Good grief, *that* was it.

Melancholia. Just by accident she had used that word, the
psychologist's term, instead of "melancholy." Little Professor
Mitchell, perched like a sparrow on his desk in anthropology
lecture, hands in his coat pockets, a permanently sarcastic smile
twisting one side of his mouth, talking about psychopathy
among the Ojibwa Indians. Of course. The old memory bank
was still functioning after all. "You must remember that this
group lives forever at the brink of starvation," Mitchell said in
that deprecating, apologetic tone which implied that for him all
cultures were equally mad; it was only the form that differed,
never the content. "It has been said that the Ojibwa ethos is
saturated with anxiety," and simultaneously fifty pens copied the
sentence verbatim. "The Ojibwa are trained, from childhood,
to starve; the male child's entire upbringing is dedicated to a
single goal: that of becoming a great hunter. Emphasis is on isolation, self-sufficiency. There is no sentimentality among the
Ojibwa. It is an austere and bleak existence they lead, always
one step away from death. Before he can attain to the state of
manhood a boy must experience a vision, after starving himself
for several days. Often after seeing this vision he feels he has ac-
quired a supernatural companion, and there is a tendency to
identify. Out in the wilderness, with nothing but a handful of
beaver, deer, moose, and bear between him and starvation, for
the Ojibwa hunter, feeling as he does at bay, feeling a concen-
tration of obscure cosmic forces against him and him alone,
cynical terrorists, savage and amoral deities"—this time a smile
in self-reproach—"which are bent on his destruction, the identification may become complete. When such paranoid tenden-
cies are further intensified by the highly competitive life of the
summer villages at ricing and berry-picking time, or by the
curse, perhaps, of a shaman with some personal grudge, the
Ojibwa becomes highly susceptible to the well-known Windigo
psychosis." Siegel knew about the Windigo, all right. He re-

membered being scared out of his wits once at camp by the
fireside-yarn image of a mile-high skeleton made of ice, roaring
and crashing through the Canadian wilderness, grabbing up
humans by the handful and feeding on their flesh. But he had
outgrown the nightmares of boyhood enough to chuckle at the
professor's description of a half-famished hunter, already
slightly warped, identifying with the Windigo and turning into
a frenzied cannibal himself, foraging around the boondocks for
more food after he had gorged himself on the bodies of his
immediate family. "Get the picture," he had told Grossmann
that night, over mugs of Würtzburger. "Altered perception.
Simultaneously, all over God knows how many square miles,
hundreds, thousands of these Indians are looking at each other
out of the corner of their eye and not seeing wives or husbands
or little children at all. What they see is big fat juicy beavers.
And these Indians are hungry, Grossmann. I mean, my gawd. A
big mass psychosis. As far as the eye can reach"—he gestured
dramatically—"beavers. Succulent, juicy, fat."

"How yummy," Grossmann had commented wryly. Sure, it
was amusing, in a twisted sort of way. And it gave anthropolo-
gists something to write about and people at parties something
to talk about. Fascinating, this Windigo psychosis. And oddly
enough its first stages were marked by a profound melancholia.
That was what had made him remember, a juxtaposition of
words, an accident. He wondered why Irving Loon had not
been talking for two days. He wondered if Debby Considine
knew about this area of the Ojibwa personality. "And Paul just
won't understand," she was saying. "Of course it was a bitchy
thing to complain to the police but I'd lie awake nights, thinking of him crouched up in that tree, like some evil spirit, waiting for me. I suppose I've always been a little afraid of something like that, something unfamiliar, something I couldn't
manipulate. Oh yes," she admitted to his raised eyebrows, "I've
manipulated them all right. I didn't want to, Siegel, God knows
I didn't. But I can't help it." Siegel felt like saying, "Use a little
less mascara or something," but was brought up short by an
awareness which had been at the back of his mind since

Lupescu had left: a half-developed impression about the role Lupescu had occupied for this group; and it occurred to him that his double would never have said anything like that. You might give absolution or penance, but no practical advice. Tucked snugly in some rectory of the mind, Cleanth Siegel, S.J., looked on with approval. "Changing the subject for a moment," Siegel said, "do you know, has Irving told you anything about the Windigo?"

"It's funny you should mention that," she said, "it's a nature god or something, that they worship. I'm not on the anthropology end of things or I could tell you more about it. But the last time Irving was talking—he speaks English *so* well—he said once 'Windigo, Windigo, stay by me.' It's this poetic, religious quality in him that's so touching." And right about here Siegel began to feel really uneasy, to hear this tiny exasperating dissonance. Poetic? Religious? Ha, ha. "I'm afraid," she was saying. "I get so depressed, so exhausted. Even as a little girl I used to be scared of being hit by a meteorite, isn't that silly? This terror of the unfamiliar, this sort of arbitrary Act of God or something. It got bad, very bad, two years ago, and I tried to straighten everything out with an act of Debby Considine, by taking rather more than the prescribed amount of Seconal. Then when it didn't work I rode up on another crest and I've been there for two years and I guess now I'm about due for a trough again."

Siegel sat up suddenly and glared straight ahead of him, at the crossed BAR's on the wall. He was getting fed up with this. Lupescu was wrong: you did not pick this sort of thing up quickly at all. It was a slow process and dangerous because in the course of things it was very possible to destroy not only yourself but your flock as well. He took her hand. "Come on," he said, "I'd like to meet Irving. Say for your penance ten Hail Mary's and make a good Act of Contrition."

"Oh my God," she murmured, "I am heartily sorry. . . ." and apparently she was, but probably only because the interview had been cut short. They threaded their way between several inert bodies in the kitchen. The cha cha side had been replaced by Bartok's *Concerto for Orchestra* and Siegel smiled grimly because of its appropriateness; because he knew he could listen to anything else but this mad Hungarian without getting bugged, but at the sound of an entire string section run suddenly amok, shrieking like an uprooted mandrake, trying to tear itself apart, the nimble little Machiavel inside him would start to throw things at the *mensch* who had just cast off adolescence and who still sat perpetual shivah for people like Debby Considine and Lucy and himself and all the other dead, trying to goad it into action; and he wondered if perhaps Lucy's diagnosis of Lupescu's trouble hadn't been correct, and if someday he, Siegel, might not find himself standing in front of some mirror with a pig foetus under one arm, reciting Freudian cant at himself to get the right inflection.

"Irving Loon," Debby said, "Cleanth Siegel." Irving Loon stood motionless, seemingly unaware of their presence. Debby put her hand on the Ojibwa's arm and caressed it. "Irving," she said softly, "please say something." Damn the torpedoes, Siegel thought. Full speed ahead. "Windigo," he said quietly, and Irving Loon jumped as if an ice cube had been dropped down his neck. He looked intently at Siegel, probing suddenly with black, piercing eyes. Then he shifted his gaze to Debby and smiled wanly. He put his arm around her waist and nuzzled her cheek. "Debby," he murmured, "my beautiful little beaver."

"Isn't that sweet," Debby said, smiling over her shoulder at Siegel. Oh my God, Siegel thought. Oh no. Beaver? Now wait a minute. Somebody was tugging at Siegel's coat sleeve and he turned swiftly, nervously, and saw Brennan. "Can I see you alone for a minute," Brennan said. Siegel hesitated. Irving Loon and Debby were whispering endearments to one another. "Sure, okay," Siegel said absently. They crunched over the broken glass from the French windows and went out on a small balcony, which was just as well, because Siegel was beginning to get a little sick of the bedroom. The rain had dwindled to a light mist and Siegel pulled his coat collar up. "I hear you're a pretty sympathetic guy," Brennan began, "and I guess you

know how it is with me and Debby. The truth is I'm worried
about that Indian."

"So am I," Siegel started to say and then caught himself.
This theory about why Irving Loon was not talking was based
only on suspicion; and this whole absurd, surrealist atmosphere
had after all been working on an imagination known occasionally to go off the deep end. So instead he said, "I could see
where you might." Brennan turned crafty. "I think he's using
hypnosis on her," he confided, darting quick glances back inside
to see if anyone was listening. Siegel nodded profoundly. Brennan went on to explain his side of the tree-climbing episode,
and by the time he was through Siegel, who had not been paying attention, was surprised to find, on looking at his watch for
the first time that evening, that it was almost eleven. A few
people had left and the party was showing the first signs of
slowing down. Siegel wandered out into the kitchen where he
found half a fifth of scotch, and made a scotch on the rocks, his
first drink, as a matter of fact, since he had arrived. He stood in
the kitchen, alone, trying to assess things. First stage, melancholia. Second stage, direct violence. How much had Irving
Loon been drinking? How much did starvation have to do with
the psychosis once it got under way? And then the enormity of
it hit him. Because if this hunch were true, Siegel had the
power to work for these parishioners a kind of miracle, to bring
them a very tangible salvation. A miracle involving a host, true,
but like no holy eucharist. He was the only one, besides Irving
Loon, who knew. Also, a sober voice reminded him, he was apparently the only one who had the Windigo psychosis as his
sole piece of information about the Ojibwa. It might be a case
of generalization, there might be any number of things wrong
with Irving Loon. Still, perhaps . . . a case of conscience. Vincent came up to him and wanted to talk but he waved him off.
Siegel had had about enough of confessions. He wondered how
his predecessor had managed to remain as father confessor for
as long as he had. It occurred to him now that Lupescu's parting comment had been no drunken witticism; but that the man

really had, like some Kurtz, been possessed by the heart of a darkness in which no ivory was ever sent out from the interior, but instead hoarded jealously by each of its gatherers to build painfully, fragment by fragment, temples to the glory of some imago or obsession, and decorated inside with the art work of dream and nightmare, and locked finally against a hostile forest, each "agent" in his own ivory tower, having no windows to look out of, turning further and further inward and cherishing a small flame behind the altar. And Kurtz too had been in his way a father confessor. Siegel shook his head, trying to clear it. Somebody had started a crap game in the other room and Siegel sat down on the kitchen table, swinging one leg, looking in at the crowd. "Oh you're a fine group," he muttered.

He was beginning to think that maybe he should tell all these people to go to hell and go drop in on Rachel after all when he saw Irving Loon come dreamlike in under the pig foetus, eyes staring straight ahead, unseeing. Siegel, paralyzed, watched Irving Loon go into the bedroom, drag a chair over to one wall, stand on it, and unhook one of the BAR's. Rapt, entirely absorbed in what he was doing, the Indian began rummaging around in the drawers of Lupescu's desk. Gingerly Siegel edged himself off the table and tiptoed to the bedroom door. Irving Loon, still singing to himself, produced with a smile a box of .30 caliber ammunition. Happily he began putting rounds into the magazine. Siegel counted the rounds as he put them in. The magazine would hold twenty. All right, Siegel, he said to himself, here it is. Moment of truth. *Espada* broken, *muleta* lost, horse disemboweled, picadors sick with fear. Five in the afternoon, crowd screaming. Miura bull, sharp horns, charging in. He figured there were about sixty seconds to make a decision, and now the still small Jesuit voice, realizing that the miracle *was* in his hands after all, for real, vaunted with the same sense of exhilaration Siegel had once felt seeing five hundred hysterical freshmen advancing on the women's dorms, knowing it was he who had set it all in motion. And the other, gentle part of him sang *kaddishes* for the dead and mourned over the Jesuit's happiness, realizing however that this kind of penance was as good as any other; it was just unfortunate that Irving Loon would be the only one partaking of any body and blood, divine or otherwise. It took no more than five seconds for the two sides to agree that there was really only one course to take.

Quietly Siegel strolled back through the kitchen, through the living room, taking his time, unnoticed by the crap shooters, opened the door, stepped out into the hall and closed the door behind him. He walked downstairs, whistling. At the first floor landing, he heard the first screams, the pounding of footsteps, the smashing of glass. He shrugged. What the hell, stranger things had happened in Washington. It was not until he had reached the street that he heard the first burst of the BAR fire.

The Contest
for Aaron Gold

BY PHILIP ROTH

THE camp was hot. Two birds jabbered, and in the distance
Werner could hear a droning sound. As he trudged up the path
the drone became louder until ahead of him he saw a half
dozen men milling around a squat, shivering, black machine.
The men were at work on the road. For the first time Werner
noticed that he was walking not on dirt or grass but asphalt. He
set his bag down.

"What the hell do you think I'm running here, Angelo?" one
of the men was shouting. He wore a plaid, peaked cap, a white
polo shirt that had CAMP LAKESIDE scrawled across the
front, and rust trousers. "There's going to be—Angelo! Do you
hear me!"

A dark, dumpy man in work clothes answered him. "Yea,
Lionel, I hear you, I hear you."

"There's going to be parents bringing their kids. In five days,
Angelo, five goddam days!"

"I hear you, Lionel, I hear you."

"I want them to drive their cars all the way to the cabins,
Angelo. And if you can't finish the job, I'll get somebody else.
You understand me, Angelo?"

"I understand you, Lionel. I hear you, I understand you."

"Five goddam days, or I get somebody else!"

Angelo shuffled off to the other side of the machine.

"Yea, five goddam days, Lionel. OK. All right. Five goddam days. . . ."

"Mr. Steinberg," Werner called.

"Werner, Werner Samuelson!" The man in the peaked cap jogged over and swung a sweaty arm around him. In his sporty outfit he did not seem the gray-suited businessman who had stepped unexpectedly into Werner's Philadelphia ceramics shop back in March and offered him a job. "How are you, Werner?"

"A little hot."

"Get out of those clothes and get down to the lake for a dip. For christsake, you're in the country—" Mr. Steinberg suddenly pulled his arm from Werner's shoulder. "Angelo!" He started racing after the dumpy man. "Werner," he yelled back, "I'll talk to you later . . . Angelo, for christsake!"

With some difficulty, Werner found the new ceramics shop that was to be both home and classroom. After he had showered and unpacked, he sat down at the potter's wheel that was on the porch of the brown log building and began to toy with a lump of clay, turning it from a vase to a dish to a teacup and back again to a vase by way of a saucer. From the wide porch of the shop he could see the lake, big and blue, and beyond the lake the hills and the smooth green Berkshire mountains. Not since 1940, he remembered, when the Germans had chased him from his studio in southern Austria had he spent a summer in the country; for the past fourteen years the money from his Philadelphia shop had just been enough to scrape ungracefully along on, let alone to allow for vacations. In fact, had not Steinberg offered six hundred dollars plus room and board to be ceramics instructor at his summer camp, Werner suspected that once again, during the hot, customerless, summer months, he would have been on a one-meal-a-day diet. Finally, he might well have had to toss in the one thing he still had left, his shop. Now, however, when September came, with six hundred dollars and a little luck, he could give the shop one last try. It might

mean nine weeks with a hundred screaming boys, but nevertheless, Steinberg's offer was a godsend.

Across the lake on a high, white, wooden tower Werner saw a
figure in a white bathing suit waving an arm at him. The figure
looked as though it had been held by its hair and dipped in
bronze. Mr. Steinberg had mentioned that Werner's salary was
to be second only to a Mr. Lefty Shulberg, the swimming
instructor—that must be him. Lefty Shulberg had been a professional basketball player, Steinberg said, and once, in a Tarzan
movie had an underwater battle with Johnny Weismuller.
Werner watched the figure stop waving, push up on its toes,
and then from the tower plunge headlong into the lake, more
an airplane, Werner thought, than a gull.

The ceramics shop was at the far end of the camp, more than
a half mile from the entrance. As the days flicked by, Werner
could hear the asphalt machine moving noisily from the entrance road into the camp itself. Mr. Steinberg had granted five
days but in four Angelo had the road flattened and finished.
The noise, however, did not stop. So many parents had praised
the idea, that Mr. Steinberg sped to asphalting the other major
arteries of the camp: immediately, Angelo's boys were to begin
on the road that twisted down to Lefty Shulberg's lake. Werner
was pleased that it wasn't to be the dirt path that led to the
door of his ceramics shop.

The drone was still comfortably distant the first day a group
of twelve boys invaded Werner's shop. The previous evening
Werner had learned that the schedule was such that every boy
in camp visited the ceramics shop three hours a week, no more
than one hour a day. He had finally decided (and he knew he
was hedging) that the first day he would let them browse
around. Halfway through the hour, however, when it seemed
that the boys were restless with browsing—one had just cracked
a companion on the skull with a bony elbow—Werner herded
them around the wheel and began showing them how to work
with clay. As he worked, their twelve blank faces stared rigidly
up at him. It was a little upsetting.

"This," Werner told them, "is called a potter's wheel."

Nomenclature taken care of, he slipped uncertainly into history. "Men have used it for many hundreds of years to make beautiful and useful things." Unimpressed, the twelve stared on. He cleared a throat that didn't need clearing. "With the potter's wheel and their own hands, people have made vases and pitchers, cups and saucers, pots and pans, vessels and—and gourds. They've made vessels big enough to put two of you boys in." A fat boy in the second row looked disturbed. "But they put grain into them, sometimes water," Werner said quickly; "never boys, I don't think." There was relief.

"The men"—whoever *they* were—"always tried to make these vessels more beautiful and shapely." Somebody giggled. "They painted them red and gold, and blue and green, and they painted their sides with stories and legends. It took hundreds of years until men saw how much happier they could be if they surrounded themselves with beautiful—beautiful objects of art."

"Hey," shouted a boy in glasses and a too big baseball cap, "hey, can I work that wheel, Mr. Werner?" The giggler triggered off again.

"Yes," Werner said. "That is, no. Not right now." The giggles subsided into rhythmic thirty-second hiccups. "It takes time to learn what to do."

The boy in the baseball cap answered with a disgusted duck-like sound, moderately obscene, and Werner, concerned, quickly suggested that instead of working the wheel, each boy could grab a handful of clay and sit at one of the benches scattered around the porch and shape whatever he liked. The clay grabbed, Werner stole around to the opposite side of the porch for a smoke—he needed one; somehow twelve boys seemed like more than twelve boys.

He lit a cigarette, flicked a match out into the dirt path, and then to calm himself, he began counting the yellow, buggy sunflowers that slopped across the path. As he counted he inhaled long and deep on the cigarette; with the smoke, ever so faintly, he thought he could taste asphalt.

He was halfway through his second cigarette, when he heard

three urgent blasts from a whistle, then three more. Suddenly, on the other side of the shop there was bench-banging and foot-scuffling, and by the time Werner raced around to see what had happened, half of the boys had already scrambled off, and the rest were leaping from their benches and high-tailing it away.

Werner managed to grab one boy by the seat of his blue short pants.

"Where are you going?"

"What? We got swim now, Mr. Werner. Uncle Lefty just now blew his whistle. We got swim."

"Oh."

"Hey, lemme go, will you?" The boy jerked his head toward where Werner was still clutching at his pants.

"I beg your pardon."

The boy zoomed off, taking the five wooden steps in one leap. Werner looked out toward the lake. Astride the tower Lefty Shulberg raised his megaphone to his mouth and aimed at the ceramics shop.

"You guys in the clay factory, let's go. Swim! On the double!" The megaphone followed the boys. "Last one here gets a swat across the behind!" A yelp went up from the boys, and Lefty laughed into his megaphone.

Werner turned and looked at the benches: there were four of the twelve lumps of clay as lumpy as when they had been grabbed; five others scattered alongside had been expertly rolled into spheres—baseballs, obviously. Two of the original twelve were pancaked against the bench. One was supposed to be a pancake, the other had initials carved into it. Either it was an ashtray without a tray, or, possibly, an initial pancake. Unable to find the twelfth lump Werner gathered all the pieces to-gether and started to the supply room. In the furthest corner of the porch, however, there was something standing upon the floor, and so he walked to it. It was a small clay figure, a knight apparently, whose chest was covered with armor and whose spindly legs wouldn't have done him much service against a good, fast dragon. Werner mashed all the baseballs and pancakes into a wad, and mounting the wobbly knight in his right hand, he carried everything back to the supply room.

A few sunny days later, when the same twelve boys swarmed into the shop, Werner did not ask who had made the knight. He just gave out the clay and then strolled casually about. Sure enough, in five minutes there was a boy in the corner squatted Indian-style on the floor, the back of his frayed polo shirt to the others. When the whistle blasted six times, and everybody broke for the lake, Werner went to the boy and asked to speak with him a moment. He asked the boy's name.

"It's Aaron," the boy said.

"Aaron what?"

"Aaron Gold, Mr. Werner," the boy admitted. "I'll play with everybody else from now on, promise."

"You'll what?"

"You gonna report me?" Aaron said.

Werner told him that he merely liked his knight and wondered if he might not want some help.

"Can I play alone?" Aaron asked. "Uncle Irv says we gotta learn to play together."

"Who's Uncle Irv?"

"He's the head—the head counselor, I mean. He says we gotta not play alone. Uncle Lefty says so too. It's no good for you."

Werner looked the boy up and down. He was about eight years old, bony, underfed, a little tired-looking. He had thin yellow hair like tinsel, large brown eyes, and the most curious yellow peach fuzz growing down his cheeks that Werner had ever seen.

"You better go to swim."

The boy didn't move, except for a swoop of the head enabling him to scratch the hollow in his chest with his chin.

"Go ahead, go to swim."

The boy remained still.

"Oh," Werner said, "I won't report you—I promise."

That night it was hot and the air was gluey and so Werner

strolled along his dirt path. He was figuring out how to push some of the boys beyond the baseball-pancake stage, when he came upon Mr. Steinberg and Angelo. Mr. Steinberg was pointing and thrashing his arms as though he might have been a little angry with the moon, and Angelo had his hands deep in his pockets.

". . . if parents want to drive, then I want them to drive, for christsake. If you can't understand me, Angelo, maybe somebody else can. What the hell you think I'm running here?"

"A camp, Lionel, a camp. I'll get it done, Lionel." Angelo shuffled away. "Let me go home, will you?"

From the shadows Werner called hello to Mr. Steinberg. "Werner." Steinberg said. He hastened over to him. "Taking a walk, Werner?"

Werner said yes, that was what he was doing.

"Good, Werner, good," Steinberg said. "I've just finished speaking to Angelo. He's going to start asphalting your road so it'll be finished for visiting day. Would you do me a favor, Werner; when he starts, would you detour the kids through the grass?"

Werner nodded.

"Good," Steinberg smiled. "By the way," Steinberg said in an un-by-the-way tone, "Lefty Shulberg was a little annoyed this morning. Seems the Gold kid came down to swim fifteen minutes late. Would you see if you could do something about that, Werner?"

"What?"

"I don't mean to say you held him up, Werner. I know kids —they dawdle, play around. Just remind him to get down on time." He dropped his voice to a confidential octave. "Lefty tells me that the kid is kind of peculiar. Having a helluva time teaching him to swim."

"Peculiar?"

"Yea. You know, if there's one thing parents want to see visiting day it's their kid swimming around like a goddam fish."

Werner said that was probably true.

"But you know, Werner," Steinberg started away, "even old Lefty can't teach them if they're not there."

"Mr. Steinberg—"

"Damn near forgot," Steinberg called back. "Every kid's going to have something finished by visiting day, Werner. Parents want something for their money."

Werner thought of baseballs and pancakes. "I suppose so, Mr. Steinberg."

A week passed and the machine began blackening its way up the path to the ceramics shop. Inside the shop Werner had laid down his first law. He considered the wisdom of dispensing laws, but near his wit's end, he finally had to dispense: no more baseballs, no more pancakes. By now most of the boys had individual modeling projects under way. Snakes were the favorite, turtles a close second. Aaron was the only one who tried a human figure. He puttered with several knights for a while, then embarked upon a large one, a warrior knight standing and aiming his sword at something. For a while he couldn't decide what that something was. Werner said that since the something wasn't to be shown it didn't matter, but Aaron insisted that it did. Werner suggested a purple dragon with six heads and two tails. Aaron shook his head no. They discussed it. Finally they decided on a purple dragon with six heads and three tails. That seemed satisfactory.

It was on Thursday of the following week, about twenty minutes after the boys had dashed for the lake, that Werner stumbled over Aaron crouching under a bench, at work on his warrior knight.

"Aaron, didn't you hear the whistle?"

"Yes."

"Then why didn't you go to swim?"

"I was working."

"Uncle Lefty will be waiting. Suppose you go now. Quickly."

"But I can't, Uncle Werner. Look." He stuck the clay figure under Werner's nose. The legs, wobbly and undeserving of knighthood until then, were now solid and finely shaped.

"How in the world did you do that?" Werner said.

"Last night in bed, Uncle Werner, I just started to feel my own legs. They weren't nothing like the ones I was making, so I changed these. Can I stay and finish my legs, Uncle Werner?"

Werner didn't answer.

"Can I finish them, Uncle Werner?"

"Of course," Werner finally said, "of course—what do you think, I'm on the dragon's side?"

Werner feared that he would have a visitor that night, and he did.

"Werner," Steinberg stood framed in the doorway of the shop, "you're lucky it's me who's calling on you and not Lefty."

"Come in, Mr. Steinberg," Werner said. "You're letting in the bugs."

Steinberg slammed the screen door. He had to start again. "I tell you, you're lucky it's not Lefty. He's raging mad about that Gold kid not coming to swim today. He bawled the living hell out of the kid and now he wanted to get at you. I told him I'd take care of it."

Werner said nothing: could taking care of *it* mean firing *him?*

"Look, Werner, let's get squared around. It's good you're taking your job seriously, looking after the kids and all. But if there's one thing we don't want here it's one-sided kids. That's what I tell the parents and that's what they want, an all-around camp, you understand? But if you're going to let one kid play potsy with clay all day, Werner, what the hell are his parents going to say to me? For christsake, let's be practical—they're not going to be satisfied with nothing but a clay pot."

"The boys aren't making clay pots." From a shelf Werner took down Aaron's knight, what was finished of it.

"That's fine, Werner, fine. But don't tell me that should take a forty-hour week to produce." Mr. Steinberg smirked.

Werner didn't know whether to answer. "Why not?" he said finally.

"For christsake, we asphalted the whole entrance road, the whole thing, and the parking lot besides in seven days. Seven days, and you stand there and ask me why a kid shouldn't take forty hours to make a pair of goddam legs. Don't kid me, Werner."

It was said before he knew it. "I'm not trying to!"

"Goddamit, what the hell do you think I'm running here! Just let's not hold this kid back any more—I won't stand for it. Lefty tells me he sees how you hold the kid back." Mr. Steinberg paused a second. "I'd hate like hell to tell you what he said about you and that kid." At the door he turned around. "Look, as long as every kid has something by visiting day, we all finish out the summer together. If Gold has a what-do-you-call-it with real pretty legs, that's all the better!" He slammed the screen door, and the light bulb over Werner's head trembled.

It began to rain that night, a cold, miserable rain, and it rained for four days until the lake was a murky brown. The first rainy morning Werner watched from his porch as a single-file column of raincoated, rain-hatted boys marched to the recreation hall for "rainy-day activities." Lefty Shulberg, bareheaded, his trousers tucked neatly into brown combat boots, marched at the front; so close beside him that he might have been chained, was a boy in a bulky, yellow slicker and a black rainhat. In both arms, like a wet infant, the boy cradled a basketball. He was out of step.

"Sound off," Lefty bellowed.

A gleeful chant went up. "One . . . Two . . . Three . . . Four . . . One—two . . . Three—four." And then a barrage of giggles from the marching boys.

"Suck that gut in, Gold!" The other boys howled. Aaron almost dropped the big basketball.

When he awoke the morning of the fourth day, Werner knew it had stopped raining: the asphalt machine was droning up the road. Not wanting to run into Mr. Steinberg, Werner did not go to breakfast until late. Steinberg and his speed-up instructions had been on his mind these past four days, and he had finally reached a decision: after all, Steinberg was his employer, paying the check, and he was the employee. This was just no summer to get fired.

At the close of the hour that morning Werner told the boys that he was going to ask them a favor. "It's not a big favor," he said. "I just wonder if some of you who have been working slowly, couldn't work a little faster. Just a little." He put his back to Aaron. "We all want something finished when our parents come up on Sunday. . . ." He felt foolish for using the plural. "Don't you?" he added. Nobody seemed appalled by the news.

Before he could say more there came the three blasts, then three more, then the bellowing voice: "Swim! You guys, let's go. On the double!" The boys started dropping things and running. "Swim! That means *every*body. You too, Sir Lancelot!"

Werner looked quickly up and across the lake. From the high tower, Lefty Shulberg waved an arm at him. Then he raised his megaphone. "Get that lead out of your pants! On the double!"

Werner watched as the boys screamed and ran away. He watched as the two fat-ringed legs of the last boy vanished around the bend of the lake.

"Uncle Werner?"

Werner turned. "Aaron. Aaron, you're supposed to be at swim. Now get out."

"Uncle Werner," the boy said sharply, "I can't work *no* quicker."

"Look, Aaron, no time for explanations. Lefty's waiting."

"I can't finish by Sunday, Uncle Werner. I just can't!"

"You have to. Now go, Aaron!" Werner pushed him in the direction of the lake. The boy spun around.

"Hey, whose side you on, Uncle Werner?"

"What?" Werner snapped.

"Whose *side*—me or the dragon?" The boy's eyes looked like two brown egg yolks.

Werner smacked him on the behind. "OK. OK. *Don't* work no quicker. Now get down to Lefty. And on the double!" Werner turned, mumbling to himself, "For crying out loud. . . ."

"Thank you kindly, Mr. Werner," came a bellow from across

the lake. Werner swung around—from the corner of his eye he saw Aaron running away—and there was Lefty on the tower. With one arm across his middle, Lefty Shulberg bowed deeply, gratuitously, towards Werner's ceramics shop.

Sunday was visiting day, but by Friday the asphalt machine buzzed in Werner's ear like a horsefly. After lunch he looked out to see how far along Angelo's workers were. A short man with a scythe was down the road a few feet whisking away the sunflowers with wide, slow strokes. It was Angelo himself.

"How soon you think you'll be done?" Werner said to him. Angelo peeked over his shoulder like a nervous squirrel.

"Yea, sure, I'll tell you. If Steinberg gets his way"—he peeked over his shoulder—"we'll have the goddam thing done in ten goddam minutes."

"I see."

Angelo peeked again. "Yea, sure, then we can start paving the goddam lake." Mr. Steinberg suddenly appeared up the road. Angelo spit in his palms and went back to guillotining sunflowers.

Werner didn't make it inside in time.

"Werner, Werner," Mr. Steinberg shouted, "Angelo's going to have this road finished up for you by the end of the day."

Werner looked at him and said that was fine.

Two steps at a time, Mr. Steinberg hopped on to the porch. "I want to thank you—Lefty says all the kids been on time lately." Mr. Steinberg chuckled. "Kids are funny—got to stay on them, else they'll dawdle."

Werner turned to go inside. Mr. Steinberg followed him. Werner had been praying that Steinberg would keep away until after visiting day; Werner wanted to make sure they finished the summer together.

"Stuff looks all right, Werner, all right." He was at the shelves handling the boys' finished projects. This was no accidental visit.

"Damn nice ash tray," Mr. Steinberg said. Werner made believe he was doing some work of his own.

"Damn nice snake, Werner, damn nice."

There was silence while Mr. Steinberg checked over the rest of the shelves.

"What's this? What's this thing?"

Werner looked up. "That's unfinished."

"Unfinished? Whose is it?"

Werner waited. "Aaron Gold's," he said.

"When's he going to finish?" Stienberg turned the headless, armless knight roughly in his hand. "Tomorrow?"

"He doesn't come tomorrow."

"Well, what in hell is he going to show his parents?" Mr. Steinberg jutted his head forward. "Well, what?"

"That."

"That! For christsake, Werner, what the hell kind of game are you playing, anyhow! Look, I'm a busy man. I pay good money to see the work gets done." He clutched the unfinished knight in his fist. "Angelo gets his roads built on time. Lefty gets those kids in there swimming on time. I don't have to tell them what to do, for christsake." He slammed the knight down on the table. "Wait'll Lefty hears about this goddam thing. Look at this goddam thing!" He stared right at Werner. "Werner, I'm just about fed up. . . . What kind of game are you and that little queer trying to play anyhow!" Suddenly, he walked out of the screen door, bouncing it after him; he yelled a word back through it.

"Forchristsake!"

It was over. Werner lit a cigarette. Mr. Steinberg was fed up, but he hadn't fired him—he hadn't even mentioned it. Werner twisted the unfinished knight in one hand, trying to figure out Mr. Steinberg. He pondered for several minutes—and then it dawned: it was too close to visiting day. The camp wouldn't be all-around if there was a new ceramics shop without a new ceramics instructor. So. Mr. Steinberg had nearly for-christ-saked him into the floor, but he hadn't fired him. And after visiting day, the incident cold and no deadlines to be met, he certainly wouldn't fire him. At least Werner's six hundred dollars seemed safe.

Werner stared at the knight. What *would* Lefty say when he heard about the goddam thing? What he might think was that as far as the contest for Aaron Gold was concerned—for, apparently, that was what it had become to Lefty—he had lost. Lefty probably didn't like to lose, but Werner had had his way, and if that wasn't a loss, at best it was a tie. Ties probably wouldn't do for Lefty either. Maybe he would come over and punch him in the mouth. No, Lefty wouldn't settle up that way. It was too simple. No, but he would think of something. What? That didn't take too much pondering: probably Lefty would make Aaron Gold the most miserable kid in the world. He seemed capable.

Werner rolled the knight from one hand to the other. He heeled out his cigarette, and then he got up and went over to the clay cabinet and grabbed off a big lump of clay. He walked back to the table and picked up the knight. He began to work on it. In ten minutes he had grafted a neck and head on the figure. Then he started on the arms; he stopped first to ask himself at which one of the invisible dragon's invisible heads he should aim the sword. There was room for a choice. "OK," he said aloud, "don't get cute. Just aim at his goddam stomach."

By nine o'clock Sunday morning it was a steamy eighty-five degrees. Werner perspired as he arranged the boys' projects on the shelves for exhibition. When he turned to get a drink, there was Aaron Gold standing in the doorway of the shop; Werner hadn't seen the boy since the day before Steinberg's visit.

"Hello," Aaron said. He had on a laundry-stiffened camp polo shirt and shorts, and his yellow hair was matted to his head with water. He looked starched.

"Aaron, you're supposed to be at breakfast."

"I snuck out."

"Why?"

"I felt like it."

Werner went to the sink. "Want some water?"

"No."

Werner took a long drink. "If they miss you, you'll get into trouble," Werner said. Aaron widened his eyes and stared on a line towards Werner's navel. He jiggled his head first yes, then, ferociously, no. He was feeling skittish. Werner went to the shelves, a skinny line of perspiration oozing up along his spine. Finally, he turned his head to Aaron.

"Come here a second."

Aaron made believe he skated over to him, on ice skates.

"What?" Aaron said. The boy smelled from tooth paste.

Werner pointed a finger at the shelf. "Look."

In the center of the top shelf there was a lined index card, and on it,

A KNIGHT FIGHTING A DRAGON
By Aaron Gold

Next to the card stood a knight, whole. Aaron looked at the knight, then he looked up at Werner, then he looked at the knight. Werner's polo shirt felt like wet flannel.

"He got arms, Uncle Werner."

"Uh-huh."

"He got arms."

Werner nodded.

"Who put them arms on?"

"I did," Werner said.

"He got arms," Aaron said.

"Well," Werner said, watching him, "you didn't expect him to fight without arms, did you?"

Aaron didn't move an inch. Werner reached a hand towards his shoulder and, instantaneously, Aaron leaped back, as though it were a game of tag and if Werner touched him that would make him "it."

"Aaron—"

"You ruined him," the boy suddenly shouted, pulling at his yellow hair. "You ruined him," he ran to the screen door and began kicking at it. "You ruined him, you did, you did. . . ." And then he ran out the door and off along the edge of the lake, like a small wild animal who gets out of a blazing forest just as fast as he can.

Werner flopped down in a chair. He smelled his own perspiration. He was gripping the knight in his hand—and he
didn't even remember picking it up. He set it upon the table
before him, contemplating it as one might contemplate a rare
piece of sculpture. He stared a full minute and then like a
mace, he pummeled his right fist down upon it. It shattered,
but he pounded and pounded at it with his fist. He pounded
until it was a mess, and even then he didn't stop. It was a better
job than the dragon himself might have done.

Within an hour Werner had thrown all his things into his
suitcase and put on a clean shirt and his old cord suit. He had
already kicked open the screen door and started out, when he
saw that his right hand was grimy with clay. He went back in
and scrubbed it clean and then, once again, he picked up his
suitcase and left the shop.

The camp was hot. Above the new, black, sticky road the air
squirmed from the heat. Car noises rumbled from around the
lake, and as he walked, suitcase in hand, Werner squinted that
way. Black cars, red cars, tan cars were twisting slowly down
toward the lake and parking near the boathouse; and beyond,
astride the high tower, there was Lefty Shulberg in his white
bathing suit, talking through his megaphone. Lefty, it seemed,
was about to give a special diving exhibition for any parents
and kids who might be interested. Loudly, through the megaphone, he was welcoming his audience.

"How you doing, Mike. Sit your parents down right there.
That a boy . . . Jeff-boy, what do you say, kid." The names
snapped out like sparks, and then, a moment after Werner
heard them, they were muffled in a woolly heat. "Artie, that a
boy . . . Hey, Joe, how's my—Hey, what do you know! Goldy!
How are you doing, Goldy—buddy! That your parents? Good,
sit them right down front. What do you know!" Lefty waved
his megaphone at Aaron Gold's parents. Mr. Gold, in white
shirt and gray Bermuda shorts, waved back; Mrs. Gold nodded.
Lefty was treating their boy all right.

Werner just kept walking along the hot, squirming road and
out of the camp.

Fracture

BY R. V. CASSILL

"I WON'T have him in the house any more," she said. "I know that sounds like I'm getting old and mean and middle class and all that. But I simply don't want him here again. Is that unreasonable, hon?"

And the odd, characteristic thing about Margaret's ultimatum was that it didn't climax a discussion with her husband, who sat among the papers he had brought from the office, quiet as a well-fed Buddha. They didn't argue. Had they ever argued seriously? He couldn't remember a time. The ultimatum came at the end of an interior discussion so detailed that one suspected a regular little courtroom inside her head, where the advocates of conflicting views were allowed to confront, scowl, and grimace at each other.

So Worth thought. He had mentioned Harold at dinner. "Don Carpenter had a time with Harold yesterday," he said. "Seems Harold was coming over to his place for something. Well, Harold called to say that he'd got stuck in a bar on 83rd and wondered if Don would pick him up. When Don got there Harold was out in front heckling a parade of school children. I guess he was in wild shape—not shaved and you know how he looks with a beard on that green depraved face of his. Everytime a bunch of kids in costume would pass him he'd say loudly, 'Ain't that gawd dam cute?' Don says that there was a big circle around him, an empty place where women had pulled back away from him with their babies, kind of watching him uneasily out of the corners of their eyes."

"Oh good Lord," Margaret said.

"Then—this is the rich part—Don took him home and it seems that Don's uncle had just dropped in too. Don went out to the kitchen to mix a drink. Harold followed him out and said in a very loud voice, 'Where'd you get that ugly ball-headed sonofabitch? Uncle huh? Uncle Shmunkle.' Don's mother came tearing out and made Don get Harold out of the house."

"I admit," Margaret said, "that I don't see what's funny about it. Harold's just pathological. He ought to be locked up. There's nothing funny about a sick man. Harold is disgusting."

"Oh well," Worth said. The matter seemed to drop, but he knew it was being argued further in her mind. Since they had left the table and come to the living room, sitting with Margaret had been like sitting in a theater where the curtain for some reason is not yet raised. The action has evidently begun and sometimes the curtain is bulged or fretted by the movement of the actors. There is suspense but no sound until suddenly the stage manager resolves the conflict, says, "I won't have him in the house," banishes the contentious pleader so that when the curtain does go up the stage is vacant—but very orderly. Reason has swept it clean. The closed session has found results which may be published. Margaret has made up her mind.

"Whatever you want," Worth said. "I can take Harold—usually I can take him—or leave him alone. If you don't want him here. . . ." He shifted in his chair to settle back in contentment with her and the life they worked out together. She makes up her mind, he thought, just the way she set about fixing up this apartment, considering each of the rather drab possibilities and finally imposing sweet reason on what had been a hodgepodge of dowdiness when they moved in. Two years ago when they came to the city they had no choice but to take this fantastically old-fashioned apartment in a gone-to-seed neighborhood. And now look at it. The brown and purple drapes were gone. The lighting was rearranged. Painting the walls in the best modern way, working their furniture into place so it seemed to fit not only the dimensions of the room but the very habits of their living together had transformed the grotesqueness that seemed, God knows, to have been built into these rooms to a gray, white and ivory order in which their large Braque reproduction fitted as smoothly as the parts of a gyro compass. When he came home in the evening there was a kind of soothing each time he passed from the battered street to the precision of their apartment. This orderliness was Margaret's way with all things. His comfort was all her doing.

Of course it was all her doing, and yet it was an important part of her orderliness that she should ask, when the question had really been tied up and disposed of, "Is that unreasonable?" Her arrangements would be incomplete without his approval. And of course he gave it.

"It isn't at all, darling. There is no point in injuring ourselves trying to be courteous to Harold. He doesn't live in a mental world where courtesy makes any difference anyhow." Worth yawned. "You're the one to say. It's your home. He's your family friend."

"Well," she said, and obviously this was a point she had dispatched far back in her silent debate. "I don't think his coming from the same town makes an obligation at all. No . . . there are so many things about him that I can't stand. Like the change he picked up in the bar the other day. I don't think he was so drunk he didn't know whose it was. I would have called him to book for that."

"I should have," Worth said. "My fault, dear. I could have pointed out to him quietly that it was ours. It didn't seem worth mentioning at the time."

"How much was it?"

"Seven or eight dollars. I should have. . . ."

"I won't have you blame yourself," Margaret said. "It simply isn't your fault. You always act in a good sane way. But there goes Harold with our seven or eight dollars. So. . . . Then his harping at the Courtneys. 'The Courtneys are sonsofbitches, the Courtneys are sonsofbitches.' I think I told him rather stiffly that the Courtneys are friends of ours. He didn't pay any attention to me. That's too much. He says the same things about us to other people, for no reason. Did we ever give him any reason? I admit nobody believes him, but it scares me to know he's talking like that about us."

"I doubt if he talks about us," Worth said.

"How can you be sure?"

"I think he likes us. Poor Harold."

"OK, Worth. There's no way to be sure. Let's drop that point. But about a month ago—I didn't tell you this—I caught him stealing a bottle out of the closet right there. He looked like a mean little kid. I thought he was going to hit me when I caught him. I was truly scared. You were in the kitchen and I almost screamed."

"Oh not Harold. Harold wouldn't hurt a fly."

She came over and sat on the arm of his chair. Her plaid wool skirt rubbed his arm. He smelled the briskly clean smell of the wool. "Is it really all right with you if we don't have Harold here again? I mean not let him in if he comes? He'll be here knocking at our door sometime and we'll have to tell him he can't come in. I'll do it. I wouldn't expect you to because you're so softhearted. But is it really OK if I tell him NO he can't come in?"

"Sure." He smiled, pulled her down to him so he could rub her forehead with his nose. "After all, our marriage would be a poor partnership if we couldn't talk and arrange things like this. Let Harold go."

"You're so good," Margaret said. "You're good to everyone and I'm not like that. I'm just not made that way," she said in a childlike voice. He pecked happily at her cheek.

Presently when she had gone to the kitchen he had a pleasant vision of her in this part of her self-created setting, her blade-slender figure among the gray and white planes of the kitchen furniture. The warm brown gray of the walls was one of the colors that Margaret had mixed herself. A real triumph of taste.

Thinking of her in her simple and spotless kitchen and thinking how much the simplicity and severity of it pleased her, he wondered what had got into him that evening when he had thought of buying her the bracelet. Her thirtieth birthday was not very far off. This year he had not known what to get her. Since he'd come back from the ETO, birthday presents had been quite simple for her. Clothes that she had halfway picked for herself—pausing just far enough short of actual selection so he'd have an area of choice to make it his gift—or something for the apartment. They were settled now and her wardrobe was well rounded. It would have to be something different this year. Still the bracelet had been been a wild impulse, clear off the track.

The jewelry she liked was the sort which had the plain beauty of a microscope or a camera or some other instrument of precision. Her jewel box looked like an instrument case. Silver went with her clothes. He supposed the cool color of silver was really meant for her.

The bracelet fitted none of these conditions. He had noticed it in the window of a shop just at the edge of their neighborhood. The shop window was stuck full of junk, bracelets and rings and necklaces that were completely tasteless. At first glance this bracelet was the same kind of thing. There were spars of gold angling out of the band like the grains in a head of barley. It was oddly made. There were three coils of gold wire ending in the spars and the clasp fastened by wrapping these coils together like a spring. When his eye had stopped on it among the other junky pieces it had occurred to him that it had a quality of its own. It looked genuinely like a savage ornament, and it seemed to him Margaret might like it for its outright contrast to the other jewelry she owned.

Now that seemed a bad idea. Still he would not make up his mind. A bit of contrast quite unexpectedly given might please Margaret more than he knew.

Later that evening they talked more about Harold. She had passed judgment and even the specter of him should have been banished out of the apartment. It hadn't gone yet. She was restless. She might have been feeling that in her efforts at justice something had been overlooked. At last she said, "About Harold. Do you really agree with me? I can't be sure of myself. I knew Harold when he was a little boy, and I used to remember that I thought—after I left home, I mean—that he wasn't like the rest of the Parsons, not so stuck up. Maybe now that I have the chance to be nasty to him I'm paying back the Parsons family for the way they used to be. And if he's the only good one in the lot. . . . He is awfully poor, don't you suppose?"

"I suppose."

"And he is an artist."

"Not really. I don't think he works at all. He talks big about a book he's writing. Nobody has ever seen a page of it."

"I don't want to hurt him because there's something malicious in me," she said. "I want to be right."

"Now, darling, you gave your reasons like a little lawyer. They seem adequate. You could probably find more if you thought longer."

"Only, am I sure?" she said.

"Hon, it's all settled. Good-bye to Harold."

She sighed her contentment, twisted down in the couch so the breeze from the window would not touch her head any more.

"Thank you for keeping me straight, friend. I couldn't stand to have him come here any more," she said.

Thursday evening on their way home from the movies they stopped in the neighborhood bar and found Harold there. He had been waiting for them, it turned out, after he had called their apartment and got no answer.

They had not noticed him when they came in; they had taken their usual table back by the empty dance floor and had been served their drinks. They sipped and then there was a moment of silence. Worth was wondering if he ought to give his wife the bracelet which he had, after all, bought for her birthday. That odd gold bracelet was right now in his inside coat pocket, wrapped in a tissue-paper parcel. There were only two more days until her birthday and they had never made much of waiting to show the presents they had for each other. Now he was feeling that he might be able to explain well his reasons for buying something so out of character—so garish—for her. He might make a few amusing observations on the subject which she would remember and which would associate themselves ever after with the gift.

Then all at once Harold was standing over them. His shocking face peered down at them woefully. "Hello. I know I made a big ass out of myself the last time I saw you," he said. "Gawd. I can't drink decently and I know it. What's that got to do with it? No excuse. I made an ass out of myself. Period. See? I don't even know how to apologize decently. Oh forget it. Jesus." His face in the bar lights looked decayed and his clothes smelled with a combination of wet wool, urine, and tobacco smells. "Can I sit down?" he asked. "Or do you want me to get the hell away from you?"

Worth threw a smile to his wife and said, "Sit down, please. What will you drink?"

"Listen," Harold said doggedly, like a child who drives himself to say something which is not only painful but which seems to him to verge on nonsense as well. "May I sit down, Margy? I know what I did, too. I know I got some of your money the other night. God. I don't know how I did it. Did I . . . ? I guess not. Forget it. I know I didn't have any and then the next morning right in my breast pocket I found six dollars. How much was it now? I want you to tell the truth." He pushed a handful of dollar bills across the table, fifteen or twenty of them, wrinkled so much the pile stood an inch thick. "Please now, tell me."

"Never mind," Margaret said sharply. "We've forgotten about it."

"No, no, please tell me."

He's going to cry, Worth thought, and that isn't necessary.

"Here's the whiskey. Drink up, everybody. It was change from a ten, Harold, about eight and a quarter," he said.

After he took the money they drank in silence. A boy and girl left their stools at the bar and came back to the dance floor.

The boy put a quarter in the jukebox, turned to the girl with an almost imperceptible shrug of invitation. Her body rose to meet him as the music began. She went on tiptoe against him. The music had been chosen for the season—to say it was April, to make blatantly clear what the wind on the streets was all for.

"Jesus," Harold said. "Too much noise. We can't talk here. I hate to ask. . . . Forget it. Can we go up to your place for a nightcap? Here's the pitch. I've got to talk to you people tonight. That's not a joke."

"Well. . . ." Margaret seemed to be deliberating.

"I know what you must think of me," Harold said.

"We'll do it this way," Worth said. "Margaret's tired, but you and I will run down to your place for a while. For one drink. I've got to be at the office tomorrow and that's no joke either."

The street, when they went out with Harold, seemed by accident or miracle to have changed from what it was twenty minutes before. Perhaps because the bar was so dark, there seemed to be a luminosity in the air that they had not noticed, as if the air were full of a million sequins. When they had come from the theater the street was empty. Now a whole parade of boys and girls moved up the block—not exactly conjured by magic, because it was time for intermission at the Y dance, but magically making the night big and disquieting.

"I'll be home by twelve," Worth said; and at that moment as he looked around he was startled by his wife's face, her look of frightened determination.

"If it's only for that long"—she laughed—"I'll come too. If I may, Harold?"

Why? It was too silly, Worth thought, to believe that she was afraid Harold would lead him astray. He could not account for it.

"Please," Harold said. "I'm glad you're coming. The two of you together is what I need to get me out of my rut. I mean you people are such a team. Nuts. I mean I like you sooo." Delighted now, he made them hold the cab while he went back inside to get an extra pint.

They had been fooled and taken in, there was no doubt of that. In their moment of compassion in the bar Harold had made a demand on them they could not refuse. Who could tell what desperate thing he might do if they would not help him? He had looked so terribly wasted and shaky. Now, climbing the stairs to his apartment, his drunken unbearable arrogance was loose again. The taxi ride had given him time to drink half the pint like a happy child drinking pop.

"You might know them sonofabitching Courtneys," he said to Margaret. "You know what that bitch Alice Courtney said to me the other day? 'Harold, you're malodious,' she said. I ought to let her have it right in the mouth. So she thinks I'm a bum, so what? Forget it." He had grabbed Margaret's arm—his black fingernails pinching into the cloth of her coat—and was dragging her up the stairs at his own headlong pace, thrusting his ugly happy face toward her, ignoring her anger. "Yeah. That bitch. You know who she's playing around with while that fag husband of hers goes out with his fag pals? I'll tell you. . . ."

"Oh!"—the convulsive, revolted sigh of Margaret's breath.

It seemed to Worth that his wife would turn at any moment and march righteously toward home; and he thought later that she might have done so if they had not come then to Harold's door and into what he had always referred to as his apartment.

The shock of seeing it—the immediate acid shock—must have restored anyone from the notion that Harold was more to be blamed than pitied. There was a studio couch unfolded in the room with a brown blanket rumpled across it, crumbs and grease spots on the blue couch upholstery, and no sign of any linens. In front of the couch was a long coffee table crowded with beer cans from which the roaches poured as the light went on. Among the cans were crusts and slivers of meat. There was a chair in the room. There were three skillets and some dirty plates in the opposite corner on the floor. Something that looked like an egg had been trampled into the linoleum.

"It's lovely, Harold, lovely," Margaret exclaimed. Her voice rang with triumph. After all, her excursion over here was not in vain. To see this den of corruption was revenge for the embarrassments he had caused her. "Maid's day off?"

He stood blinking in the harsh light from the ceiling fixture. He had not counted on the room's being this way. His befuddled face suggested that gnomes must have come in while he was gone and lived the hell out of his room. "It's kind of messy," he said in a diminished voice. "Glasses. We've got to have glasses. You see any?"

"I'll look under the couch," Margaret said. While he went out to get some she asked Worth, "Are you going to sit *down* here?" She pulled her wool skirt against her hips as if it were iron that she was fitting close for protection. She moved away from the couch. It might have jumping bugs.

Worth said, "Kilroy was here. Before that Raskolnikov had this suite, I suppose. What the hell? Let's sit down and have a drink anyway. Maybe he does have something on his mind he needs to talk about. You take the chair. I'll sit on the couch."

"He doesn't need us."

"We'll see."

"Worth, doesn't this bother you? I don't understand you."

"I wouldn't want to live here. It's interesting."

"If you could tell me why. . . . It's just filthy."

Down the hall they heard Harold speaking and heard a woman's voice—a bawdy, bubbling, fat-woman's voice—answer him with a joke.

"Don't needle him about it," Worth said.

The glasses Harold brought were greasy. Beads of cold water huddled on their surfaces. He divided the whiskey and took an armful of the beer cans from the table so they would have a place to set their drinks.

"It's a mess," Harold said. "But let me explain something— it's always this way." When he laughed very heartily at his joke the laughter turned into prolonged coughing. He rubbed his lips with his fist after he coughed and rubbed his fist on the cover of the studio couch. Margaret set her glass down hard. After seeing the slime on his lips she had no intention of drinking from any of his glasses.

"Have you been doing any work, Harold?" Worth asked. "We hardly know what you're doing these days. The novel you were. . . ."

"I haven't committed it yet," Harold said. "I been thinking about it. I may make it oral." His eyes were swinging to cover every detail of the room, as though some arrangement of the papers piled on the floor, the cans, the skillets, and the milk cartons behind the door might hold a pattern which he did not yet know. "Needs a woman's touch, don't it? But nothing like I do. Pretty Sarah is the girl. That's what I have to talk to you Joes about." Again he coughed and rubbed his mouth. "Women, shmimmen. I had a babe and now she's gone."

"Sounds like a blues number," Worth said.

"Don't it? Listen I wrote some song lyrics yesterday. Tell me what you think of this." He began humming the tune of *Night and Day*. "Hell, I don't remember. It was about a guy whose girl left him and it's spring, see?"

"Never mind," Worth said. "Tell your story. You had a girl and she's left you."

Margaret's face tightened even more. She had never looked colder, more like a disapproving schoolteacher. She was carried by the intensity of her disapproval to a foolish question. "Here?"

"Here, shmere," Harold said. He was jolly drunk enough to ignore what Margaret might think of him. "You know her, Worth, old boy. You ought to know her. Found her when I came to hunt you one day. Never did find you. Found her. She works at your office. Out in the pen in front where they got this acre of pretty girls. Pounds a typewriter. Pretty Sarah LeRoy is the one I mean."

"You're joking," Worth said. "LeRoy's a kid. She can't be more than. . . ."

"Well, she's seventeen."

"Good God, Harold."

"Now wait. I ain't so old myself. Relative matter of course. I'm only twenty-seven and the baby of the family. Right, Margaret? Margaret knew me when I was a baby at the breast."

He kept on talking, a harsh croon intended obviously for himself, but pointless and perhaps impossible to him unless he had them there to sit as though he were telling them something. Worth did not listen. He was thinking about Sarah LeRoy.

Such a pretty little kid. The starched white of her blouses every
morning, the skin that kept fluctuating in color whenever he
talked to her, her pleasant eagerness to get work done just right
for him, "Yes, Mr. Hough. Yes," the hands that looked so clean
and creamy but not yet shaped like a grown woman's hands, the
smooth fall of her hair brushed neat for school, he thought, a
pretty little maid from school. His idea of her had been so fixed
that what he was hearing from Harold stabbed at him like the
discovery of a betrayal.

". . . Damn near three months," Harold was saying.
"Through the winter when it was cold. Happy as little old pup-
pies. Bang, slam, one day she hits me right in the mouth. 'Only
reason you want to marry me is you think you ought to.'
'Right,' I said. I was real smart. Whatta quick comeback that
was. So bang, slam, she let me have it while I was lying flat on
my back in bed. Out the door she goes without even waiting to
pack her douche bag. I shouldn't have said that to her because
this weather is so nice. I sure need her because. . . ."

"Please," Margaret said. "You have no right to tell us things
like that. Oh come on, Worth. I can't stand any more of this."

"Sure wish I could coax her back," Harold said. "She was so
pretty, so beautiful, so lovely." He lay over against the arm of
the studio couch, breathing heavily through his mouth. His
tongue lay for a second against his ugly lips. "Listen, Worth,
old boy, she won't even let me come near to her. I chased her
on the street one day, and she ran up to a big fat mean-looking
cop. That's a fact. You hear me, Worth? Here's what I want
you to do. . . ."

Margaret was at the door, her gloved hand resting on the
frame and her whole body inclined for immediate exit.
"Worth . . . ," she said.

"Coming."

Harold said, "What I want you to do is talk to her for me."

"I'm sorry, Harold."

"Now listen, Worth, I know what I'm talking about. She
thinks you're brains from the belly up. That's a fact. She told
me. You're her boss. Now listen, you talk to her. Tell her old

Harold's cleaned up and quit drinking. If you get a rise out of her, I will, too. Anyway talk to her sensible. Tell her. . . . I mean she's an adult. Don't give her any Sunny School guff. Just tell her old Harold. . . ." Then gently his voice stopped. His hand with the fingers spread and cupped moved caressingly over the arm of the couch. His face in their last glimpse looked sick and moldy as the room, but young, like a debauched-child's face.

Their taxi moved for what seemed a very long time through streets of velvety darkness. Over and over Worth thought, Not Sarah LeRoy. It seemed impossible to him and then impossible that he should have been so wrong about her. He had been thinking of her as he would have thought of a daughter, and she was living with a man almost his own age.

Once when they stopped at a traffic light and the cab was lit from the store windows on the corner he noticed Margaret watching him distantly. "You're not going to, are you?" she said.

"Going to what?"

"Going to talk to this tramp about Harold?"

"No. Of course not, darling. She's not a tramp, though. We mustn't jump to any judgments."

"Living with *Harold* in that sty? Oh no." He could not see her face, but he felt her shudder.

He smiled to himself. He had the melancholy and lonely notion that he was assailed from all sides by the grotesque emotions of other people. "Now, darling," he said, "love and cleanliness are not necessarily mutually dependent, whatever the soap ads say." As he spoke it seemed that the cab might as well be the basket of a balloon carrying him miles above the earth while down below the earth was twinkling with the thousand garrulous lights of April. How comic and melancholy to ride at that height saying reasonable things to the empty air.

"Love!" Margaret said. "I've heard everything now."

She went to bed as soon as they got home. "Don't stay up too late," she said.

When he saw the light go out in the bedroom he got a small

glass of whiskey from the cupboard. Something soft that the wind carried beat twice against the window. He went to the window and looked down. It was too late now for anyone to be on the street. The upreaching branches of the trees below him swayed as though they were a scaffold that might sometime— soon—collapse all at once to show him the secret and filthy processes of spring among the roots. In the meantime it seemed that this fragile scaffold was supporting him at a lonely height. If the wind rose more, he might hear the snap of branches giving way, letting him drop.

"Margaret," he called. "Margaret? Tonight *was* good-bye to Harold. Never again." He called this out jovially. He went to the bedroom door, wanting to talk to her. If the two of them could really agree and think together they might keep their lofty and precarious perch above the mess that the Harolds and LeRoys made of their lives. He peered toward the dark bed. "Margaret?"

"All right," she said. "I heard you. Please. I'm too tired to talk about it tonight any more."

But I have to talk about it, dear Margaret, he thought. Tonight all this has jarred me loose. He went back toward the window and this time, as he approached it, was sharply aware of his own reflection emerging on it—the reflection of his white shirt; his head, hands and trousers being darker hardly registered on the transparent pane. The white animate shape jiggled on the glass. Then in a trick of vision it seemed to be moving against the cover on Harold's couch, an immaculate substance on that dirty blanket. As though it were one of Sarah LeRoy's white blouses he was staring at.

Sarah LeRoy—how wrong could he be about someone? For a long time he thought he had her figured out perfectly, and he was quite wrong. From his height in the air he had never seen her as a woman at all. He had missed the simplest fact in the world. A surge of self-pity struck him, the realization that his cleverness had someway cheated him.

He drank and then without thinking lifted his hand to the pocket where the bracelet lay wrapped in its soft paper. His fingers tightened on it and he felt its spring give under the pressure. Margaret's bracelet for her thirtieth birthday. No. He saw now why he had bought this gaudy bit of jewelry. It was not for Margaret.

He was pinching the bracelet together as though he were already fitting it to someone's wrist.

"Sarah LeRoy," he whispered in amazement. "I'll be damned."

Harold seemed to him, just then, very lucky. He envied Harold everything—his enemies, his dirty room, his mammoth drunks, his cough, his Sarah. He saw now why Margaret had wanted so much to get Harold cleanly out of their way. She had been afraid sometime he might envy Harold. She had known what that envy would mean to him; she had known what he was just beginning to grasp—that envy would never lead him to imitate Harold, nor even actually give the bracelet to Sarah, but that it would swing a cold light on his own imcompleteness. He saw—or thought he saw—how every limitation in Margaret's life had been placed carefully, like a spar to shore over and hide from him his own matching frailty, and his heart was stung with a treacherous wish to wake her and tell her he understood. At the same time he knew that the time itself for such communication had been spent as ransom against his terrible need.

He opened the window a little as if the stable air of the room were choking him. A flat tongue of wind came in, sliding its secret dampness and urgency against him with a tremor, and on its motion he heard the crackle of branches breaking.

The Last of
the Grizzly Bears

BY RAY B. WEST, JR.

THE glass case contained only a glistening, irregular mound of polished bone. He had been unprepared for it, had not seen it really, until his son, Tommy, had stood staring curiously at it for a few moments, and he, Thomas, had come up behind him to see what it was had finally engaged his curiosity. In the immensity of the museum, surrounded by the dramatic reproductions of wildlife behind the long, curving glass windows, the skull was as inert as a rare stone displayed in a jeweler's showcase.

"What is it?" his son had asked.

"Why, that, Tommy—" He paused to slip on his shell-rimmed spectacles, bent forward to study the identification card; but he knew what it was without reading, for it was as though time had suddenly flowed backward, unreeled like a motion-picture film, and suddenly stood still, frozen and inert as the bone within the case. "It's the skull of a grizzly bear."

"A bear?"

There was bewilderment in the small, uncertain voice of his son, who had heard of bears only through the books he received on his birthdays and at Christmas time. "A bear, Daddy?" The question became more insistent as Thomas, trembling, leaned closer to the case to study the small printed description.

"A bear's skull, Tommy. That's the bone inside the bear's head." He paused to tap his fingers gently, first against his own forehead, then against his son's. "It says here—" He returned his attention to the case. " 'Although there are accounts of grizzlies in the folklore of states as far south as Missouri, this bear is normally the inhabitant of northern, mountain regions. This is the skull of a bear killed in the Wasatch Range, the farthest south science has any record that the bear wandered.' "

But he knew all this, had known it since he was scarcely older than Tommy, yet he didn't, even now, dare wholly believe it. Yet somewhere within the recesses of his mind a faint warming element had begun to glow.

"What does that mean, Daddy?"

His son's words came to him as though from a long distance.

"It means—"

His own words were as those spoken by another person.

"This bear was either a stranger in the land where it was killed or it had lived there a long time without anyone knowing."

"Thomas! For heaven's sake!"

With Alice's voice, the vibrating current wavered. She had been standing behind them, clutching her pearl-gray handbag to her immaculate stomach, the slim gray toes of her shoes (which were the first things he saw as turned from Tommy toward her) in elegant contrast to the scratched marble floor, her small gray hat silhouetted against the blank reflection of a case containing a bald eagle clutching an artificial limb.

"The child didn't ask for a lecture!"

"Didn't anybody know the bear lived there?" Tommy asked.

"No," Thomas replied, straightening. He took off his glasses, folded them and inserted them in his breast pocket. He took the child's hand. "Come on, Tommy. It's time for us to go."

"How did the people find the bear, Daddy?"

He felt the story seeping quietly back into his mind, still

scarcely believing it to be true. To Tommy he repeated the brief information from the card in the case as they crossed the wide, marble floor, walking a few steps behind Alice's sharp footfalls, which were really the sound of her slender spike heels, the only sound in the enormous room, except where it was picked up and repeated faintly against the cold walls which enclosed this space.

"Did somebody shoot it?"

"Yes."

"How, Daddy?"

His son's voice was like a spark—a candle flame preserved within a tomb—that ignited and blended with the warm air from the outside as they emerged and began their stroll along the pathway lined with flowering trees. The sweet scent of the blossoms and the noise of the waterfowl on the park lake, the feel of his son's small trusting hand in his own, were the warmth he had been waiting for, yet which now seemed suddenly insufficient.

He was back in the cement-floored room of the church basement, turned on one of the spoked, round-backed chairs, shouting something at Harry Leberman who sat behind him, grinning, with his dark hair tumbled over his eyes—sitting in the room that was too cold in the summer and too hot in the winter, with the steam pipes running the length of the low ceiling. When he put his hand to his face, he could smell the varnish from the chair rungs, but it was part of the smell of the room, along with the faint dust and mustiness and the oil on the blackboard against which Mr. Steelman was standing now, talking to an old man with an uneven grey beard.

"Boys!" Mr. Steelman's bulk blotted out the Bible passage which someone had scribbled on the blackboard. The old man seated himself on a chair and crossed his legs one over the other, both encased in faded, tan trousers, his arms folded neatly too, the shirt darker and newer than the pants, his thin gray hair combed in a lock that had been wet with water and

pressed down across his forehead. "Boys!" Mr. Steelman repeated in a voice not much louder than before but which
brought the room to an uncertain stillness.

"Boys. I have invited Mr. Ephraim Neger here to tell you a
story—a true story."

If anyone else had said it, they wouldn't have listened. They
might even have groaned, but everyone sat forward when Mr.
Steelman said that.

"Mr. Neger was born in Ohio. Now who knows where Ohio
is?"

Eden raised his hand. He was known as Eden then to his
mother, who had named him after his grandfather, but the boys
called him Edie, never bothering to make a nickname for him.
Later, Alice didn't like it and had him change it to Thomas.

"All right, Edie."

"It's right next to Indiana," he said.

"That's right. The other side of the Mississippi River. And
when Mr. Neger was born, even Ohio was a wilderness. Mr.
Neger came west when he wasn't much older then you boys. He
was a *real* scout, sailing up the Missouri River to the Yellowstone. Mr. Neger knew this country when there wasn't a house
on it except a few trappers' shacks and the tepees of the Indians."

Edie saw Mr. Neger then, a young man in buckskin with a
squaw wife. (Mr. Steelman didn't say this, but Edie's father had
said it.) Mr. Neger didn't look like a man who had been part
of the wilderness, but he didn't look like a man who was ready
to die yet, either.

"Mr. Neger had his most thrilling and exciting experience
right here—in Box Canyon—up the North Fork, and I've
asked him to come here and tell us about it."

Mr. Steelman wiped his wide, red face and turned to Mr.
Neger, who hawked once or twice in the back of his throat and
stood up, not feebly, but with the uncertainty of an old man.
His starched, clean, canvas trousers stood stiff, almost straight,
like the young Mr. Neger (who was known as Eph, and that
was what Mr. Steelman called him when he spoke directly to

him). "It's all yours, Eph." And Eph smiled modestly, but with a pride stiff as his trousers.

When he smiled, holding onto the table or leaning against it, his old-man mouth seemed empty, so that at first you had to lean forward to understand what he was saying, that he was pleased to be talking to boys—he liked to talk to boys better than anyone, and you believed him. But pretty soon you forgot that his words came out indistinctly, for they didn't. They became pictures, and you saw the young Eph camped up Box Canyon—not the boy Eph who sailed up the Missouri, but a younger Eph than now, still with sandy hair and a mouth full of teeth and legs that could follow a trap line all day. You saw this younger Eph sitting at his campfire at night with a dog which he said was no dog to have in the mountains, not a large fierce dog, who would really be some protection to a man, but a small terrier dozing near the fire. You saw the old man's annoyance at having such a dog, which barked (he called it *yawped*) at the wrong times, going off after a rabbit or a prairie hen, getting excited over even a field mouse, but which yawped at the right times too, waking up to growl in the night when something came in too close to the camp, and which (most important of all) looked at you wagging its tail with the love of God and man shining in its eyes, so that you couldn't really ever get mad at him, even when you were the most aggravated, and which (Eph said this several times too) was smart as a whip.

You saw Eph furrow his brow, because he furrowed it now recalling it, over what he could do about the critter which was going from one trap to another, pulling up the beaver with the intelligence of the devil, pulling up the traps and mutilating the catch, not eating it, but simply "mutilating," as Eph said, sometimes knocking the stakes clean loose, so he had to hunt around in the brush and grass for maybe a half hour before he found what was no good to him except for the trap. You saw Eph before the fire with his rifle between his knees, worrying about the bear, because you couldn't imagine this younger Eph without his rifle any more than you could see old Eph with his sandy hair and his old teeth and his strong limbs.

You found yourself imagining what you would do if you saw the whole work of a year going for nothing, and always the same thing when you ran the traps—the mangled fur where a good clean pelt had been. Even if you salvaged a few, you didn't have enough to keep your women and children (even a squaw woman and half-breeds) eating until the next season.

"I can tell you boys truthfully," old Eph said, "in ninety-odd years I never hated like I hated that old devil. And I knowed too he was close by me all the time. I seen his marks in the grass and the mud by the river and on the trees where he reached up to scratch. I knowed he was the biggest thing I'd ever come up against, and I knowed him as well as Sourdough (the terrier), though I'd never once set eyes on him."

You hated, too, joined in a communal hatred that you could feel in Harry behind you and in Slim and George on each side of you, and in Mr. Steelman up there in front, who usually preached only love and comradeship.

"I opined p'isen might do, but I hadn't none, an' b'sides, I never taken much to p'isen. I opined on traps, but no traps was big enough—leastwise, none I had."

You watch the ideas, like people, performing in the younger Eph's brain—like a man picking out a good tennis racquet, picking up one and feeling the heft of it, putting it down and taking another, plucking at the gut or sighting along the handle. You saw Eph finally leaving a chunk of venison out in the sun to ripen, hanging it by a rope from the limb of a birch within sight of the camp, leaving it hanging until even he couldn't stand the smell of it. You saw him take it right out and bury it (and you laughed at this, the way he told it), but not until Sourdough had dug it up again and rolled in it and carried the smell in and out of camp for several days. You saw the final idea come like a blossom which unfolds silently and without surprise, but which is there when you look in a place you'd have sworn there wasn't a flower before. He didn't know why he hadn't thought of it sooner, because it was too easy, and the easiest thoughts always come hardest (he said); but he recollected how such animals like sweets, and he had some preserves hidden away somewhere, and he got them out and smeared them on some bread and hung that where he'd hung the meat. That night he went to bed with Sourdough right beside him, and his hand on Sourdough. Sure enough, in the night he felt Sourdough stiffen and rumble once deep, almost in his stomach, and he awoke and pressed his fingers on Sourdough, which was a sign for the terrier to keep quiet, as much as you can ever teach a terrier to keep quiet, and he peered out across the coals of the fire toward that tree. He didn't see anything at first, but Sourdough growled again, and he could feel the hairs alive on the dog's neck; and then the next thing he could see a shape in the darkness.

He waited a moment to make sure, then he took his hand from the dog and reached for his gun. But the minute his hand was gone, Sourdough was off, yawping at the top of his lungs, but with a note of fear in it too, as though he knew he was not up against a jackrabbit this time. And the younger Eph swore, thinking surely he'd lost his bear, but the bear, he said, just sank back on his haunches and looked at Sourdough with his mouth partly open and his paws working. He looked as if he knew Sourdough was not really dangerous, even if it was annoying to be interrupted right now with the smell of that jam in his nose. He waited for Sourdough to dart in close enough so that he could reach out and bat him with his paw.

Sourdough was getting close, too, so close that it took Eph a while to figure out whether he dared shoot, so that the bear really had time to make up his mind to get out of there if it really wanted to. He couldn't see the bear's head too plain. It was moving back and forth and sidewise, because the terrier was making moves as though he wanted to get behind him, darting from side to side. But Eph finally raised his rifle, after making sure he had another bullet handy to stick in if the first one didn't kill.

He felt the bullet strike, felt it against his fingers and clear into the stock of his gun, heard it too in the roar that assaulted his ears; and the black shape rose up taller than he ever thought a bear could rear, even in a man's excitement. His fingers were

busy with the second bullet, but his eyes and ears knew that
Sourdough had retreated from that huge animal shape, still
yawping, but darting backwards nonetheless, his animal shrewd-
ness telling him what the man's eye and ear and brain was
telling him—that the bear was not only the largest he had even
seen or heard of, but that it would not be dead for a good while
yet. Manlike, Eph cursed himself for not having his second,
smaller gun handy, knowing that it would take a good clean
shot into the proper vitals to stop him now, especially if he
should come in a rush.

He could imagine the bear wondering what it was that Sourdough had done to him, who was nothing but a pesky little terrier, yawping out there in the dark, not something flat and
burning which blasted against your neck and shoulder and sent
the blood into your windpipe to cough up and taste in your
mouth. He saw the bear come down again on his four legs, roaring, to start after the terrier. He saw it at the same moment that
he felt the bullet against his fingers, not sliding cleanly into the
chamber, but jamming somehow, so that he tore his fingernails
trying to get it loose. He was beyond thought now and an equal,
really less than an equal of the bear, who at that moment must
have seen him for the first time. Less than equal, because the
bear still had his strength despite the gaping hole in the fur and
the flesh of his shoulder, but both animals in their desperate
need to destroy the other. He was a lesser animal, because he
and Sourdough together didn't make one of the bear, who had
seen him and was coming toward him so that he thought of
flight at the same moment he knew there was no place to
flee to, still pounding and tearing at the bullet (and cursing
too, though he couldn't remember it), and the bear making its
sounds of pain and anger, and Sourdough still yawping off
somewhere in the shadows.

Too late he felt the bullet yield, so late he half expected to
feel the weight of the animal upon him; but not yet feeling the
weight but only the fragile pressure of the bullet sliding into the
chamber and the sweet click of the bolt against the heel of his
hand. It was feeling too, rather than sight, which told him that

the bear had reared again and was wheeling away, distracted by the white streak which darted from the shadows to sting not once, but several times. Turning as a man turns to swat a mosquito which distracts and irritates him, the bear made a wide arc over the young Eph's head, his one paw catching Sourdough as he darted for the last time, striking him as a bat strikes a ball, sailing him in another arc out of the clearing and back into the shadows. Eph's fire was ready now, in the same moment that the great angry head swung back, so that the bullet tore this time into the soft cartilage and flesh of the mouth, through the first fragile layer of bone, to explode in the brain.

Both of them collapsed then, the bear and the man, but it was the breath of sense, not the breath of life, gone from Eph, so that he revived. In the morning, he first found Sourdough and buried him beneath the sweet-smelling layer of pine needles and fern, among the wild-hollyhock bulbs and the sego-lily bulbs, then he skinned the bear and spent the rest of the day digging a grave deep enough for him because he didn't think of finding a new place for his camp, and he knew that his traps would be safe and he would have a bearskin rug in addition to the muskrat and beaver pelts.

Old Eph's face was white, standing there with his crooked knuckles on the edge of the table, so all he could do was point toward the newspaper-wrapped bundle in the corner; and Mr. Steelman went over and lifted it onto the table, and untied the string, and spread the bearskin rug out. They all got up to take a look at it, disappointed not to see the head, which had been left in the grave. Old Eph, in his ninety-odd year, had revived faster than the younger Eph, and showed them how he could tell it was a grizzly bear by the hoar tips of the fur, though the moths had gotten into it and chewed holes here and there. He said he didn't suppose any of them would see a grizzly, leastwise not a real live one, the way he had seen it up Box Canyon, and he hoped they wouldn't.

They were to have dinner that evening at the Bob Sloefellows' in the recently built Georgian mansion set back from the road and hidden behind the rows of evergreens. They had Tommy all ready for bed when the girl arrived. He was standing beside the kitchen table holding his glass of milk in one hand, his crackers in the other, the storybook open before him. They told the girl—really talking through Tommy—"Now when you've had two stories, you'll be a good boy, won't you, and go right to bed?" He said he would, his eyes still glistening but the lids heavy from the long spring afternoon at the museum and the park. Sally put her own high-school notebook and the two thick, worn textbooks beside his on the table and shook her carefully combed coffee-colored hair and patted it with her fingers. Thomas handed her the little card with the telephone number printed on it. "We'll be here all evening, Sally. If you need anything—"

She took it smiling, not needing to say anything, then turned to Tommy and patted his head and glanced at his book. Alice came in and repeated the instructions, but Sally did not look at her. Alice said to Tommy, "You'll be a good boy, won't you?" and put her cheek down for him to kiss, which he did, and she dabbed at the milk with her lace handkerchief as she stood up again. "If anything happens, be sure to call," she told Sally, and Sally said, "Yes, Ma'am," without looking, picking up the storybook and turning the pages as Alice straightened the fingers of her gloves.

"I don't know about Sally," she said, as they were seated in the car and moving backward down the driveway.

"Why not?" He had his door slightly open to guide him along the edge of the grass. He pulled it shut and placed both hands on the wheel as they swung into the street. "She seems like a nice girl."

"She's surly."

"Not with Tommy. He likes her."

"Yes, I know."

Alice had been straightening herself in her seat, and she sighed without explaining herself, but didn't sink back against the cushions. Thomas felt suddenly tired as they turned onto the boulevard which led to the country. He wished they had not had to hurry home to dress, wished they could have remained at home and got to bed early. He had to be at the office tomorrow as usual. He was always too tired at night, it seemed, and Sundays were the only times he had really to rest. Yet he couldn't have turned Bob down, because right now he was working on the Sloefellow income-tax case. And he knew Alice had wanted to see the Sloefellow house ever since it had been completed year before last.

He drove slowly on the outside lane, not too bothered by the traffic, since most of the cars were returning to the city, not caring much whether they were late or not, yet not wanting to be too late. He had no difficulty finding the corner where Bob had told him to turn off, where the boulevard made a wide sweep to the right; but as they turned up the long lane, Alice straightened in her seat and plucked at the clothing at her hips. He remembered the time he'd been on the overnight train to New York and the couple in the berth next to him had talked in loud, intimate whispers: "For God sake, you don't mean you wear that thing on the train too?" "Of course I do. I wouldn't go anywhere without it." They were moving through the narrow gate to Bob's place now, and as they came nearer he could see that drinks were being served on the wide front porch, and someone waved as they drove past and around to the side of the house. Alice lifted her hand and smiled, the smile still on her face as she turned toward him. "It's lovely," she said.

Bob came down the steps to greet him, his large, round, but still youthful body encased in white palm beach, his blond hair that was thinning at the top of his forehead brushed across and flat against his head, a glass in one hand, the other raised toward them. He took Alice's hand, but merely lifted his glass to Thomas. "I hope you don't mind it outside. The bugs have been pretty decent tonight." He held his large white hand at the small of Alice's back as he followed her up the steps, his head turned smilingly back toward Thomas.

On the porch there were more greetings and introductions "Just a small, intimate group," Bob had said; the faces he recognized and the names he heard were from a world he had known only from the tops of legal documents and the newspaper columns. He took a drink from a tray held out to him, feeling his tiredness vanish under the nervous energy which had come to him as they stepped forward to meet Bob. He saw Mr. Burgat, his partner and his boss, and waved, then sat down where Roger Lowery and Eilain pointed to the empty seat beside a white-topped iron table.

The party was broken up into three separate groups, the largest of them centered about the old Robert Eugene Sloefellow, Bob's uncle, whom Thomas had not met before tonight, whose gaunt and lean body he recognized at once from newspaper photographs, whose bony fingers he had grasped momentarily in introduction. Old Bob, as he was called at the office, was talking, and a group of the older men, including Mr. Burgat, were listening and occasionally bursting out in brief spurts of laughter. The second group, to which Bob had taken Alice, was seated at another of the small, round tables, but far enough away that only the sounds of their voices could be heard, not the words themselves, and here it was Young Bob's voice which was heard most often.

"Oh, God," Eilain said, tossing her head toward the group of old men. "I ought to break it up, but I swear to God, I haven't the energy."

She got up and walked quickly toward her husband. Roger picked up his glass and held it toward Thomas.

"How's it going?" he asked.

"So-so," Thomas said, his stomach taut but warm from the first taste of his drink.

"Bob tells me you're trying to chisel a hunk off his tax returns?"

Thomas sipped his drink. "I don't know if we can make it stick," he said. "It's purely technical."

"You'd better," Roger said, not looking at him, but gazing across the flood-lit expanse of lawn and trees.

Thomas looked at him, wondering how serious he was. Bob's was just another case as far as he was concerned—even more routine than most of them, except that it *was* a Sloefellow case. Roger, being a relative of some kind, handled most of their routine law business, and he wondered about that.

"I don't know if anything can be saved or not."

He wanted to say—"Why do they care about saving a few thousand when they've got—well, what they've got?" He almost said it, then thought better.

"It's not what they can save. It's the principle of the thing," Roger said, looking at him now with the little smile that quivered at the corner of his mouth.

Bob came along and filled both of their glasses, then waved the cocktail shaker toward the larger group.

"Pick up your chairs and come on over here, you two barristers," he said in his loud but slightly effeminate voice. The ice tinkled in the shaker.

The other group, where Alice had been, was moving toward them, and Thomas and Roger moved several chairs into the circle of older people. Old Bob stopped talking and glared for a moment, until young Bob said, "Just moving in to make ourselves sociable, Uncle."

The old man grunted, and Bob laughed. Thomas saw Alice seat herself beside Eilain, listening intently to something she was saying. He saw Eilain wince when her husband spoke.

"You mightn't believe it," Old Bob continued in his hoarse but still somehow powerful voice, swinging his thin arms so that a little of his drink slopped onto the stones. "At the top I weighed two hundred thirty-five pounds. Had more energy than a string of mules." He tapped a bony finger against his chest. "The first time we had trouble—time I went down to see Teddy—that was the beginning—was prepared to stay till hell froze over."

He paused to stare at Mr. Burgat.

"You remember, Simon?"

Mr. Burgat laughed and took the cigar from his mouth.

"No, Bob. It wasn't me who'd remember. It was my old dad. You forget—"

"Ah—!"

Old Bob ran his bony fingers across his forehead and slumped back in his seat.

"Ah, yes," he said wearily.

Eilain came up and put her hand lightly on his shoulder.

"You mustn't get too tired, Uncle."

He looked up at her and patted her hand.

"It's not that," he said, shaking his head and taking a sip from his glass. "It's not that—it's just—"

Thomas had never thought to wonder how old the old man was. He'd outlived all of his contemporaries, but the newspapers had not mentioned the deep wrinkles which lined his face and crossed his forehead, the shrunken bony remains of the body which once might not have been out of place in the prize ring or on the docks, which had bossed gangs of Irish laying ties and rails, which (so many rumors went) had more than once destroyed a man by the force of his muscles alone. The stories Thomas had heard did not include the vague look which now veiled the old man's eyes, the invisible hands pressing against the thin shoulders.

"It's just that—there's so many things to remember."

The thin lips trembled like a child's and Eilain was bending forward, speaking softly into the brittle, shelllike ear, but loud enough that everyone heard.

"It's time for you to go in now."

"What? Yes—maybe so."

He set the glass down and rose unsteadily to his feet. He was still the center of attraction and no one spoke. He stiffened and looked about, bowed slightly with a vague and independent formality. His lips moved, but he spoke as though to himself, or to someone invisible.

"There's so many things to remember nowadays."

Young Bob stepped in and laid his fingers on his uncle's arm, but the old man shook him off. He walked slowly from the circle and did not object when Eilain helped him up the steps to the front door.

During dinner Thomas sat opposite Roger Lowery and between two women he had not met before. Roger was talking to Alice, but occasionally Thomas would catch him staring across the table at him as he listened to what the two ladies were saying, not speaking much himself and not approving particularly of what was being said to him. He was annoyed at Roger's smile which appeared occasionally, lifting one corner of his mouth or lurking somewhere in the depths of his eyes, never coming completely into the open. Bob, on the other hand, was friendlier than usual, turning from something he was saying to Louise Burgat to ask his opinion.

"What do you think, Thomas? Louise thinks the best way to handle that man is to give him enough rope—he'll hang himself sooner or later. I say we ought to fight him—give him all we've got."

Thomas knew exactly whom they meant, though he hadn't been following the conversation and didn't know the precise person—he was anyone who interfered with their management of what they considered their private affairs, though Bob Sloefellow's "private affairs" involved thousands of persons.

"Well," he said, conscious of Roger's eyes and the smile dimpling one corner of his mouth. "I say, be sure you're in the right. Then fight with all you've got."

It was an evasion, and he wished evasion had not been necessary.

"Oh, yes, of course. Be sure you're in the right," Bob agreed. "But we mustn't let him go too far. Look at the mess other countries are in. We can't let that happen to us."

"Did it ever occur to you, Bob, that it might already have happened?" Roger asked quickly.

"A grim joke, I call it," Bob said.

"Did you talk to Dale Meyrick the last time he was over?" Roger asked.

"Dale always was too radical," Bob said.

"He votes conservative."

Eilain broke in then and changed the subject by saying that she and Bob had reservations for their summer sailing, and the talk broke up again into little islands of conversation, Eilain's shrill voice penetrating the talk about food and accommodations to say what a coward she was—she wouldn't think of flying. The lady on Thomas' left showed him a diamond she said she had bought in Germany in 1923. Bob said he'd like to miss England. He hated leaving good American dollars to be squandered by a government which had no respect for the rights of others, not even of its own people.

For no reason at all, Thomas remembered the time he had been called home from school by his father's death. It was early spring and the lilacs were just blooming in the cemetery. The mountains were covered with a soft green, like moss. Already his brothers and sisters, who were all younger than he, had begun to seem strangers, so that even their common grief had not brought them together. Or perhaps there had been too little grief for the occasion. His father had opposed his going away to school, even before the long painful illness had begun, so that already it was his mother's will which had won out.

Walking back to the car he had paused briefly beside another grave, caught by the sagging, weathered marker where the name of Ephraim Neger was almost obliterated, snared by reviving memories which recurred seldom these days, but which came with the vital shock of not having been willed—came at the most unexpected moments, in bed at night or in the library or while taking a shower. The memory had been lost now for a long time, but again it seemed to him almost as though he had fought the bear, just as it had seemed that time that he had not come back to see his father buried, but to fulfill a duty to old Eph, whose bones, like the bear's, were moulding beneath the mountain earth.

It was fall, during the beet-thinning vacation at school, when they took the hike into Box Canyon. They had ridden in the truck to the camp, which had been closed since Labor Day, and which was filled with the smell of mouse-droppings and with a dampness that penetrated to the bone until they got a fire started. They retold the story of Eph and the bear, Mr. Steelman pretending he was old Eph, but not doing the way Eph could, who fought again with the bear everytime he told the story.

Edie had not had enough money last year when the troop went to Yellowstone, but this year when they got the bear's skull and brought it back to prove that old Eph knew what he was talking about, a museum back East was going to give them money, and they would use that for the trip, and everyone who helped dig up the skull and carry it back would go. Mr. Steelman showed them the map old Eph had made before he died in the winter and said how if they got an early start, they should find the grave by noon. They could dig up the skull and be back in time to get home soon after dark.

They shivered in the morning until the big cookstove was heated up (they didn't camp outside and cook over a campfire the way they did in the summer); then after that they were all right, even when they began to hike through the thick frost on the ground, and their boots and even their scout pants got wet from marching through the tall grass. Once, after the sun had come out bright, they stopped in a clearing and dried their clothes. They weren't cold again until that night when it started to rain, when they were bringing the skull back later even than Mr. Steelman had expected it to be, sloshing through the mud in the darkness to the scout camp.

Old Eph's map, which was scratched in ink on brown wrapping paper, took them to the camp site, but the canyon was silent as old Eph lying in his grave, and they couldn't believe the camp had really been here or that the fight with the bear had really taken place. By noon, when they thought to be ready to start back, they had dug up half the space surrounding the linked "X" on the brown paper, without finding anything except roots and boulders and heaps of rich, black mountain soil. They dug until they were waist-deep and had to throw the dirt as high as their heads.

The rain had begun to fall through the colored leaves when Harry, who had worked, first stripped to the waist and had then put on his denim jacket, thrust his spade against something solid, but something which did not sound like a boulder. Even

Mr. Steelman sloshed down into the mud of the grave then, saying, "All right, boys. Take it easy now. We don't want to damage it."

It was a rib Harry's shovel had struck, so they dug carefully upward, uncovering the bent spine, sometimes scratching around it with their bare hands, disclosing the folded front legs, then finally the skull, so that the white upper half of the skeleton lay finally revealed, but obscured by the muddy water and the dirt, and even by time itself.

Edie thought how it didn't look like anything he had expected, just as the labor of unearthing it was greater than they had thought; and especially when they bent down for the first time to dislodge the bulk of bone, how it was heavy as any boulder they had lifted all day, heavier with its accumulation of dirt, which had become part of it; and more especially yet how the stench rose when one of them (he couldn't remember who) had thrust his finger into one of the sockets and revealed how a kind of life had adhered to it all this time.

They tied their kerchiefs over their noses and mouths, but the corruption still filtered through, and it enclosed them even when the skull had been deposited a good distance away in the weeds and grass while they filled up the black holes. It accompanied them back on the litter of birch boughs, so that the sandwiches he had brought to eat were thrown away untasted, and he found himself off the trail once, trying to retch, but nothing coming of it except the bitter taste in his mouth and throat.

Even when the skull was wrapped in the wet, heavy canvas tarpaulin and hoisted into the back of the truck, the stench leaked out to assault them when they pushed the truck, slipping and rocking down the narrow roadway until they struck the main road at the forks. After that the wind whipped most of the smell away, and they felt better, though growing hungry and stiff from the labor and the cold.

Edie felt fine when he walked into his warm, bright house and his mother said, "Heavens! If you don't catch your death of pneumonia, I'll be surprised." But she was too busy getting the younger children into bed to pay much attention to him. He

took off his clothes (which still had the smell on them—
which she had noticed) and took a bath. Later she asked him
questions about the hike, but he didn't feel like answering, because there was no way he could say it, the way he felt, and she
became not angry but impatient, the way she became impatient
sometimes with his father. She forgot about his regular bedtime
and let him stay up a little later that night.

Sally was asleep on the sofa when they returned home, the
radio still blaring dance music and her school books and papers
scattered about on the floor. Alice went straight upstairs to look
at Tommy, but Thomas stood a moment looking down at the
girl before awakening her. He touched her first lightly on the
shoulder, calling, "Sally—Sally," first softly and then louder until finally he had to grasp her shoulders and shake them before
her eyes opened and she sat up quickly, her eyes still gentle and
full of sleep, but her mouth mumbling, "Oh, hello—Mr. Enhalter. Must have fell—must have gone to sleep." Then she was
fumbling awkwardly for her books, and he was down helping
her stuff the torn sheets into her notebook, paying her, and
telling her he still had the car out to drive her home
    Alice came in then and cut the radio off with an impatient
twist.
    "How was Tommy?" she asked. "Did he get to sleep at once?
Did you have any trouble with him?"
    "No," Sally said. "He was fine, just fine, Mrs. Enhalter."
    She was hugging the awkward bundle of books against her
young breasts, and the vagueness was disappearing from her
eyes, but she shivered slightly as she stood clutching the two
dollar bills, responding politely to this last demand.
    "Here," Thomas said, "the books."
    She smiled at him.
    "Oh, thank you, Mr. Enhalter."
    He felt awkward and somehow younger as he escorted her
out to the car, holding the car door open, and then when she
had got in, depositing the heavy bulk of books upon her lap.
She was fully awake now, and when he asked her what she had
been studying, she chatted gaily about the tragedy of tomorrow

(she called it that) when that old Miss Hoskinson would learn about her failure to complete her theme. She supposed she might get up early in the morning to finish it, but sometimes her alarm clock didn't go off, or she didn't hear it, or she turned it off and went back to sleep. He asked her what she was writing about, and she said, "Glacial Deposits of the Ice Age." She laughed. "Isn't that a silly subject? It's an assignment. Just the kind that old Miss Hoskinson would make too."

Thomas wondered briefly how old Miss Hoskinson was.

"I suppose it's worth knowing about, the ice age," he said.

The car, as they drove down the empty street, seemed filled with the life of her, not only her agreement that there might be some value in knowing about glacial deposits, but the warm, youthful vitality of her sixteen or seventeen years, the musical ring of her voice—her frank, unabashed ignorance, which was a kind of knowing. Thomas found himself wondering, as he wondered often about Tommy, where she would be, say ten, fifteen years from now. He wanted to join in her laughter about Miss Hoskinson, just as he often wanted to join Tommy in his play. He felt a kind of wisdom stirring in the back of his mind, but all that he could bring to the surface was not wisdom at all but foolish sentimentality—cliché, which he couldn't bring himself to speak, even to Sally.

He let her out before the small, white cottage where she lived with her father, who was an electrician, and which she would leave soon to enter another, similar, perhaps better, perhaps more modest. She thanked him, again politely, and he waited until she had walked up the short walk and tried the door. She turned and waved awkwardly, shuffling the heavy load of books in her arms. He put the car into gear and moved on down the street, not waiting to watch her disappear into the house. It occurred to him suddenly that perhaps there was a way to say it to Tommy, what he wanted desperately to say, thinking—"I'll do it tomorrow night. I won't wait any longer. I'll tell him as soon as I get home from the office."

They camped several days beside the lake but a long way from the bear feeding grounds. When they went over there in the evenings to see the trucks from the lodge and the hotel drive up and empty the glistening cans of garbage onto the dump, they couldn't stay long, because Mr. Steelman wanted them back before dark, and if they walked it was a three-mile hike through the woods. There were bears at their campground, one large black mother bear with a cub and several smaller black and brown bears which sat up and begged for food, but they didn't somehow seem like bears, because even though the ranger told them the bears were dangerous, these bears seemed too polite and well fed. So they went to the dump every night to watch the greedy scratching-about among the piles of garbage.

On one side of the pine rails were the bears, moving unconcerned among their ill-smelling scraps; on the other side the curious eyes of the tourists who came from all parts of the country just to stare at the bears. The tourists stood about in their slacks and sports jackets or in their too-new hiking clothes, gossiping about where they came from and where they were going, the man from New Jersey telling the lady from Oregon about the roads across Nebraska, just which route to take and where to stop for the best dinners. The man from Texas amused everyone by throwing candy life-savers at the bears, shouting at them in his loud southern voice, especially when the bright disk lodged in the fur on one bear and another came up and licked it off with his pink tongue, until the ranger came over and pointed to the sign which said, "Do Not Feed or Annoy Bears on the Dump," and the man from Texas (who was bigger even than Mr. Steelman) saying this was a free country and that he didn't think throwing the bears life-savers could be called *feeding* the bears.

One night they saw the ranger talking and pointing with a group of people, so Edie and Harry went up there and watched. They saw that he was pointing far across the dump, just inside the dark rim of pine trees, saying, "There's one now. They don't come out much farther than that. There aren't many of them, and they don't like people."

Harry said, "Grizzlies!"

Edie saw them too, ghostly shapes against the darkness of the trees, their large heads (three of them) rooting around on the very edge of the dump, their huge humped backs giving them a look of bulk, so that all of the other bears, after you had seen them, looked like imitations. You didn't want to look at them anymore—or have anything to do with them, but just stand looking at the grizzlies as long as you could.

They didn't hear Mr. Steelman and the others calling that they were going back to the camp, and they didn't see that it was getting dark and that most of the tourists were returning to the lighted lobbies of the lodge and hotel. They stood watching the grizzlies until once, even while they were watching, the three bears seemed just to dissolve before their eyes, to disappear the way smoke disappears in the air, and they had not turned and walked away, but had just gone, as though their presence had just been to remind everyone that they were still in the woods, even if Edie and Harry didn't see them again at the dump; and so far as they knew, no one ever saw them there again (the way Edie liked to think of it later).

Edie became worried then about Mr. Steelman and the others going off in the truck. They hurried down the path to the highway, but the truck had gone without them. If they walked on the highway, it was three miles to the campground and would be dark when they got there, but if they took the short cut by the lake it would be two miles through the woods and dark all the way. Harry's flashlight went ahead of them on the path, and they talked about the bears to show they were not frightened.

At first there was just the flat with bushes and clumps of willows and the lake off to the right. Then they were in the pines, and the path was a slender tunnel, with not even the sky visible above them and thick undergrowth brushing their pants, as they walked. Edie remembered the Indians who could walk so quietly not even an animal would know, wondering how even an Indian could tell that the shadows and clumps of brush did not conceal some inexplicable danger. He would know when they were almost to the camp by the rotten log which crossed the dry creek bed, the log rotted with the many feet crossing it, but still at the bottom of the gully. Knowing you were almost there would be comforting, but he still knew now that the log lay at the bottom of the dark pit (as he imagined it, because he had not seen it except in daylight). They would go down into darkness, cross the log, then climb back up into the dark tunnel again.

Harry kept the light on the path, its comforting beam disclosing in separate moments the solid, black earth, muffled by pine needles and rotten leaves and twigs which broke beneath their boots, raising the column of light only a few times to focus on a bush or a tree stump, the beam stopped always by the inscrutable blackness, held captive there by the unfamiliar object. Then they moved on again, thankful for the solid earth beneath their feet, which was all they seemed to have besides the light, telling themselves that the woods were no more filled with mystery tonight than they had been in the daylight, but knowing it was not true, at least not the way they felt.

Even the sounds were magnified, though obscured by the constant, vibrating overtones of wind and trees; and more than once they paused while a gopher (maybe no more than a field mouse) scurried rattling through the brush. The light beam's futile search revealed nothing, except once when it picked up a pair of eyes shining on the path, and the eyes turned out to be only a fresh tin-foil gum wrapper, perhaps one they had dropped earlier. And the light was no protection against the calls of birds, which were not the familiar cawing of crows or the chaotic chirpings of the smaller birds, but the furred, mournful calls of birds which belonged only to the night.

It was when they were approaching the creek-bed crossing that the first genuine stab of fear froze them in their tracks, because what they heard was not their imaginings, but something as real as the pulsing of their own blood, a rocking, rhythmic crash, the crackle of brush, not loud but distinct enough never to be forgotten. Edie saw the light extinguished before the sounds had stopped, and whispered, "Turn it on!" not knowing for sure that he had spoken or only prayed for light, because he had not heard it himself. When the light came on again, the sound had become a low grunting and scraping, so that he knew something was coming up the path from the gully—not a man, or men, but another familiar thing, a sound they had been hearing these several days but had not thought to meet alone on a narrow pathway on a dark night, something not to be attracted with cookies and sweets, but repelled somehow or escaped from.

"Shine it there!" Edie whispered, the painful sound clear enough that the sounds on the path stopped.

The beam sought out the place where the path disappeared into the dark gully, and there, when the light was on it, appeared the high, humped front quarters and the broad skull and the small glistening eyes (no gum wrapper this time); and the light wavered, and the bear shook its shaggy head to escape the beam. His hump rose even higher and his head lowered as he pulled himself the last foot or two up out of the gully and stood before them moving his angry, surprised head slowly from side to side and up and down, the boys' minds frozen too now, so that Harry's body touched him before he realized that Harry had been moving backward on the path. He did not move and Harry stopped. All Edie could think of was the bear standing there (it seemed as though he had been standing there forever), a fact, but not one clearly discerned, blocking their way to the lighted campground. What would the bear do if they turned and walked backward down the path? It seemed better to stand still. He didn't think it—will it; they just stood still. Harry's light trembled on the bear, but not on his eyes except when it touched briefly, because the bear was still moving his great head back and forth.

Then he saw that the bear was trembling, either in fear or in anger, his great body gathering for some fateful movement. He rose, wheeling slowly like some cumbersome machine, and crashed into the wall of the forest, disappeared, not the way the three grizzlies had done at the dump up on the hill, but leaving a trail of sound behind him—and a new weakness, as though the old life had been drained from the boys, so that they stood recalling the danger and reliving it, not exulting in it as they

later wished they had, not even fainting as Old Eph had when
he shot the grizzly, but fearing the danger even when they knew
it had passed and even when they were not sure it had been a
danger.

It took almost a greater courage to walk to the edge of the
gully and down the dirt path to the log than it had to stand
facing the bear, because they had time to think about it and to
debate the wisdom of going ahead or of going back to the lodge
to call Mr. Steelman. It had taken no courage really to stand on
the path, for they were not thinking then, but they knew they
would remember it as courage anyway; while the debate about
crossing the rotten log, warm with the bear's footprints, would
never be told.

It wasn't long until they heard voices, partly because they
were hurrying faster now, no longer ashamed to show their fear
to each other; but mostly because Mr. Steelman had sent some
boys up the path to look for them, while he had driven the
truck away up the road in case they had come that way.

What they had done passed for courage at first (coming by
the path when they might have stayed on the road, maybe
catching a ride—which they hadn't thought of), but they were
put on K.P. for two days, courage or no courage, and their punishment was a kind of glory in which they shone until the
memory grew confused. There were times later when Edie
wasn't sure that it wasn't a grizzly they had met on the path,
and there was one time after they had got home when some of
the boys taunted them by saying that maybe they hadn't met a
bear at all, had just said it to excuse themselves for missing the
truck that day in Yellowstone.

Sometime in the morning Thomas remembered the words
Roger had whispered to him just before leaving the Sloefellows', whispered ironically with the silent lift of an eyebrow and
the quiet smile: "You've got to choose quick, Thomas. The
barricades are going up." He had not thought it any funnier
than most of the things Roger said, but somehow he had spent
the morning weighing the rights of Bob Sloefellow against those

of Tommy Enhalter—who hadn't even the right to be called
Edie.

Just before noon he went into Mr. Burgat's office and told
him he'd like to get away for a week or two. He didn't feel at
the proper pitch, he said, sensing somehow that he couldn't
give the real reason. Simon Burgat said he had no reason for refusing. He suspected Thomas had been working too hard. Bob
Sloefellow would be disappointed, though. He seemed especially
anxious about his case.

Thomas was really most concerned about Alice, who could
understand no whims or sudden decisions, even distrusting her
own. He had been unable yesterday to say anything to her
about the skull at the museum, and he thought now that it was
because he had nothing to say. Perhaps he did not know yet, or
ever would, but he felt that he had a responsibility to Tommy,
and it was upon this impulse that he was acting.

Alice was surprised to see him at twelve-thirty, annoyed a little too, since she was going to an afternoon bridge luncheon.
She had cream on her face and her hair hidden beneath a silk
scarf. He didn't give her a chance to say much before he began.

"We're going on a trip," he said. "Get your things together.
Get Tommy."

He had little hope really of winning her by assault, but it
seemed the best plan since her own strategy was always elaborately worked out.

"Thomas!" she said. "Where?"

"Right away," he said, pretending she had said "when?"

He knew that her "where?" was a brake—a check—against
the speed of his attack.

"This afternoon. Call Tommy's school. I'll run over and pick
him up. We can just throw a few things together. We can buy
what we need when we get there."

"Thomas!"

He was checked then, but really not as soon as he had expected to be.

"You haven't even said where we're going."

They talked it over then, reasonably and rationally, "like

grown people," which was one of Alice's favorite phrases. She couldn't go. She wouldn't. That was final. She had no objection to his running off, and really (though it seemed foolish to be thinking of rushing in on his mother and perhaps frightening her to death), she had no objection to his going, if he insisted, but Tommy—!

It was upon the issue of Tommy that he was determined to fight.

"Don't you see," he said, "it's not for me—it's for Tommy. It came to me at the museum yesterday, but I didn't know it, not until this morning."

"What came to you?"

"This idea. It's a long story. I'll tell you later."

He wasn't sure that he ever would—or could.

"Thomas! You're acting like a child yourself."

"Perhaps I am," he said, and he knew he was, "but you've got to believe I know what I'm doing—what's good for Tommy. It would be good for you too, if you only knew it."

He kept at her until he saw the look of fear in her eyes. Even then he kept on until he was sure it wasn't just pretense, until she said, "Very well, if you give me a day or two to get him ready."

"One day," he said.

"Very well—one day."

Her surrender, like everything she did, was accomplished gracefully, even the artful shrug of her shoulders, but he knew he had hurt her, and it was all he could do to keep from giving her another day. He had lost nothing, forfeited only the sleep he would lose at home, which might just as well have been wasted on the Pullman. He had planned all along to outfit Tommy when they got there. He could still do that. His problem now was to remain firm for a full day, for he knew that the day's delay was partly a hope lingering in the back of Alice's mind that another twenty-four hours might bring him to his senses.

He didn't go back to the office in the afternoon, but remained at home reading a book, feeling a little like a truant, but experiencing also a little of the truant's pleasure. He wanted to get the details in his mind, so he could relate them to his son—the pioneers—the long, hot desert and the climb through the mountains—the fight to subdue the wilderness. Those were clichés, he knew, but it was exactly the emotion beneath the cliché he was seeking to recapture. Recaptured, they would no longer be clichés, and even the book he read could not express what he knew in his own mind, what he wanted Tommy to know before it was too late.

He picked Tommy up at school and had him sufficiently won over (a not very difficult feat with Alice absent) by the time they reached home, watching with gratification as his son's excitement mounted. He climaxed his account by referring to their visit to the museum—

"You remember the skull of the grizzly bear we saw yesterday? Well, never mind. I've got the best story of all to tell you about him, but we'll save that for tomorrow night when you'll be going to sleep on the train."

Tommy didn't go to sleep that night for a long time, but neither did Thomas, and he didn't know whether Alice did either. She simulated sleep if she didn't, and he must not have stayed awake too long, for the next thing he knew was when she had her hand on his shoulder and was pulling him gently. He saw that it was light and raised up. The clock said only four thirty. Alice said, "Dear, Tommy's sick. He's got a fever."

"Nonsense," he said. "It's just the excitement. He'll be all right."

"Perhaps so," she said. "But it's a hundred and one degrees."

"Is he asleep?"

"Yes, he's gone back to sleep now. I've been up with him for over an hour."

"He'll be all right when he wakes up."

Alice went back to bed, but he couldn't. He got up and made himself a pot of coffee and some toast. He read the morning paper, not knowing what it said, remembering only the time he couldn't go to Yellowstone Park.

An hour later the thermometer said one hundred and two,

and Alice said, "You wouldn't think of taking him now, I hope, knowing how I would feel with him gone. And Thomas! If anything should happen—?"

"You should come along," he said.

"We've gone over that before," she told him. "I couldn't possibly. But dear—"

Just then Tommy stirred, crying out in his sleep, and they both ran to him. He was turning and tossing on the bed. Alice put her hands on his shoulders.

"What is it?" she asked. "Tell Mommy."

He roused gradually from his sleep, his usually pale face flushed and hot, his eyes turning from one to the other of them still filled with fear.

"What was it, dear?"

Alice bent over him and he clutched her and pressed his face against her arm. She ran her fingers soothingly through his hair.

"Yes," he sobbed, clinging to her. "Yes."

She continued to soothe him until he quieted. Then she turned and placed her slender white hand upon Thomas' arm.

"You see?" she said. "Perhaps later. Perhaps we can go later this summer—when we're properly ready for so long a trip."

He didn't reply. He knew now that he had half-expected to be defeated from the beginning—that there was nothing to look forward to except defeat. His very struggle seemed now no more than Tommy's dream. He walked outside, somehow ashamed to stay where Alice could continue to accuse him with her soft words, and he was surprised to discover how early it still was. He wondered what Simon Burgat would say when he returned to the office this morning. He wondered once what would happen if he announced that he would no longer continue with the Sloefellow case. But he knew he would not say this. He could not even remember why he had been tempted to throw it up. He knew only that he needed something to do, and he supposed winning Bob's case was as good as anything else. When they went west later on, there would be nothing to frighten Tommy. He could play with the children who were growing up on the same street where Edie had grown up, and if they went into the mountains Alice would prepare a picnic basket and they would have merely to watch to see that Tommy did not go too near the river.

A Piece of Polenta

BY JORDON PECILE

JUST before leaving Italy at the end of a year on a Fulbright
grant, I visited my father's family in a country village in the
province of Udine. Except for a certain curiosity to see my father's birthplace, I had no desire to make the difficult journey
from Florence. I had already posponed it twice during the year,
following other Fulbright students to Cortina for the Christmas
holidays and to Sicily for spring vacation instead. Only the
knowledge that my father, were he alive, would be disappointed
if I failed to visit his family when I was so near made me decide
to go. In the end, the obligation which I felt to take the trip
made it seem like a reluctant pilgrimage, reminding me of the
ritual of carrying a basket of flowers with my mother to my father's grave in Wilkes-Barre every year on All Souls' Day.

I waited until the end of my courses at the university because
with each additional month in Italy I gained a better grasp of
the language, and I didn't want to fumble awkwardly for words
before my father's family. In that part of northeastern Italy, between Treviso and Gorizia, an ancient Latin dialect called
Friulano is spoken. I had heard this dialect often as a child,
when my father and his Friulian friends gathered around the
wine bottle under our grapevine. Their coarse voices as they
shouted about their work in the coal mines and about the old

country drew me away from my games to watch and ridicule as they got drunk and fell asleep in the late afternoons under our arbor.

That arbor, leaning against the back porch and the kitchen windows, was my father's strongest tie to his boyhood home. He was proud of the twisting, dark vines which each year yielded the first bunches of ripe grapes in the neighborhood. Every October he would patiently try to teach me the art of making wine from the small, sour grapes. Pretending he needed my help to turn the wooden press, he would ask me to stay home from school to watch him; but I hated his damp, spidery wine cellar and the empty barrels smelling of ferment. Ashamed of my father's alien ways, I stubbornly resisted all his attempts to teach me to make wine or to speak Friulano.

Remembering how difficult it had always been to understand my father, I knew it would be necessary to speak at least a good grammatical Italian, if not Friulano, when I visited his brothers. By the end of a year of study which started slowly at the University for Foreigners in Perugia, I finally felt that I was fluent enough to carry on simple conversations with the family, and wrote them the date of my visit which had been so long delayed.

Since my father's village is only fourteen kilometers from the capital of the province, I was certain that my uncles would be at the station in Udine to meet me when I arrived, and on the train I wondered if they still looked enough like my father to be recognized easily. Attilio and Tarcesio, the two brothers who had remained in Italy after my father emigrated, were both older than he. Through the years, they had written him several short letters, after such events as the death of his mother or the birth of another child. To every letter my father replied immediately with packages of clothing and generous gifts of money. Once, shortly after the war, he sent them a large family photograph. My brothers and I, elaborately groomed in bow ties and white shoes, were grouped around my father in the photographer's studio, against the pastel backdrop of a garden with a sprinkling fountain and swaying ferns. In order to be seen from behind her husband and three tall sons, my mother, tiny and buxom, had to stand on a box. In the photograph she looked massive, towering over our heads, but my father was pleased and the portrait was mailed.

In return, we received from Italy one of those sepia-tinted photographs which are printed like postcards, showing my father's two brothers standing together self-consciously in the center, each surrounded by his small family. Before Uncle Attilio, mustachioed and husky, sat a dark and fearless looking woman dressed in black; this was Aunt Firma, my father had explained, the handsome sister-in-law who was as strong as a rock and ruler of both households. In front of Uncle Tarcesio, an emaciated man with deep circles under his eyes, sat a frail woman clutching at a bulky, netted shawl; this was poor Aunt Clelia. There were only three children in the picture, two boys aged fourteen and ten, and a six-year-old girl. The older son, as tall and dark as I, was wearing a tweed sport coat which had once belonged to me. He was named Americo because he was born shortly after my father reached the United States, and the family hoped my father might send for him someday. A younger boy, Rino, stood stiffly at attention next to Americo; he was wearing my long-outgrown corduroy suit with knickers. Standing beside Aunt Clelia was the girl, Celesta, wide-eyed with wonder, dressed for her First Communion with a crown of flowers and a long veil over her thick, black hair. Rosary beads were entwined around her clasped, gloved hands, and white paper roses were strewn at her feet.

One son was missing from the postcard sent from Udine after the war. He was the oldest son, my father explained, and Nazi soldiers had taken him one day from his work in the wheat fields as a laborer for their salt mines; he never was found after that.

For years my father had hoped to return someday to see his brothers and his family home, but always there were more urgent uses for the small savings he could accumulate. When at one time he had saved almost enough for the round trip, my mother insisted that the money be used for my college educa-

tion, and he postponed his visit without argument. Three years
later he died, and the last of the letters from Italy was a painfully written response to my cable describing his death. My uncles expressed their own long-nurtured hope that they might
have seen their brother once more; but since God had denied
them this, they hoped that I, his first son, would be able to visit
the family in his place.

It was dusk when the local train finally arrived in Udine, and
I was tired from the long day's traveling and apprehensive
about meeting my uncles. I had little taste for the emotional
scene which was bound to take place in public on the station
platform, so I delayed descending until the other passengers
disappeared. Only a few got off, and the narrow platform was
soon deserted as the train continued on to Trieste. Standing
alone in the shadows, I wondered if my letter had been received, or if they weren't able to meet me after all. I started to
carry my suitcase into the second-class waiting room when I remembered that in Italy it cost five lire for visitors to enter onto
the boarding platforms, and no doubt my uncles would be waiting outside the station. Turning, I carried my luggage down the
stairs and through an underpass, following the *Uscita* signs to
the station lobby.

Opposite the exit I saw them huddled together, eagerly scan-
ning the faces of everyone passing through the gates from the
trains. I should have known them in any place; they were wearing the same dark suits of the postcard photograph, and though
different from my father in height and weight, had the same
high forehead with its fine fringe of light hair, the same deep-
set blue eyes and wrinkled, leathery skin stretched tightly across
sallow cheeks. I felt them searching my face for some sign of
recognition on my part, then looking at each other for reassurance before they rushed forward shouting, "Giordano!"

They grabbed me in a strong and tearful embrace. "*Che
miracolo!*" they kept repeating. "What a miracle, to see poor
Gildo's son at last!" I was given the demonstratively affectionate welcome which is so common in Italian stations and which I
had nervously anticipated aboard the train. People passing

through the lobby considerately gave wide berth to our family reunion, barely glancing at my emotional uncles who were alternately hugging and standing off to admire their nephew from America.

Embarrassed, I was relieved when at last Uncle Attilio picked up my suitcase and led me out of the lobby and across the street to a waiting car. "This is the taxi of Fagagna," he said, and proudly introduced me to the grinning, coarse old driver as "Gildo's boy, from the United States."

"Pontebabba, Guido," the driver said, thrusting out his hand. "Does he speak Friulano?" he asked my uncles.

"Why should he?" Uncle Tarcesio answered. "He speaks Italian better than we do, and he writes it too, don't you, Giordano?"

"Never mind, I speak American very good," Guido said in English, not listening. "I lived in the States for ten years, in Pennasylvania," he informed me carefully.

"That's where he earned all the money to buy his taxi," Uncle Attilio commented, beckoning for me to sit in the little Fiat while he lifted my suitcase in the trunk.

"Yes, but at what a price!" said the driver, speaking rapidly in Italian again. "I caught this asthma in the coal mines in your country and came back to Fagagna a ruined man. Here, not even the doctors know what I have, although they charge me all they can get and won't admit anything. Your good father died from it, and so will I someday. I used to work next to your father for a long time," he said over his shoulder to me as he switched on the ignition, "until I got this asthma and decided to come home. Two thousand dollars I saved in America before I returned to Fagagna to buy my own piece of land and this car!"

"And now he thinks he's a Cavalier!" scoffed my uncle.

Uncle Tarcesio got in the car and interrupted the two old men. "Let's have an *aperitivo* together before we go back to Fagagna," he said. "We could go to *Cappo Rosso's* public house, close to the station."

"No," his brother said. "We must go back as we promised;

they're waiting for us and Firma will have supper ready."

"What a shame, to come all the way to Udine and not celebrate an occasion such as this without even a glass of beer,"
Uncle Tarcesio said. "*Pazienza*, Giordano! We'll celebrate
when we get home, and again tomorrow when we go around to
all the houses in Fagagna to introduce you to the neighbors who
are waiting to see you, especially those who have relatives in
America. I hope you are as good a wine drinker as your poor
father because we will have to drink to your health many
times." He settled back then, smiling in anticipation.

Crowded into the narrow back seat with an uncle on each
side, I watched the driver maneuver his car noisily across the
piazza, honking the horn as if he were sounding ruffles and flour-
ishes for some visiting hero. He swerved around the corners of
winding side streets and soon entered the stream of bicycle
traffic on the country roads. Lowering my head to look through
the windshield, I saw in the distance, across the vine-clad plains
of Friuli, the snow-capped Alpine foothills. Against the hazy
blueness of this ridge, slender campaniles and tall, black cy-
presses stood in sharp silhouettes. In a cloud of dust we sped
past whitewashed cottages with shuttered windows, occasionally
passing the stone and tile country houses of the gentry. From
quiet pasture lands, the road led upward, lined with mulberry
orchards and long rows of grapevines. Women wrapped in
black kerchiefs walked along the chalky road, and the boys in
corduroy shorts and wooden shoes carried cans of milk hung
from poles slung across their shoulders. Lights were being
turned on in modern roadside canteens, and on each tiny farm
there was a flurry of activity around the barn. The entire spring
countryside, divided into innumerable square fields, looked as
carefully landscaped and tended as the City Park in Wilkes-
Barre, and an evening calm seemed to have settled over this
small part of the world. I began to wonder, briefly, why I had
hesitated so long before coming here.

When we finally entered the empty main piazza of Fagagna,
it was too dark to see the village clearly. Uncle Attilio leaned
across me and said, "*Ci siamo*, Giordano!" The little Fiat

passed under an arch and jolted to a stop in a courtyard enclosed by an aged, stuccoed dwelling. Uncle Tarcesio called out to a little group gathered in the dim light of an open door. There was no movement; the family remained clustered together, waiting.

"Americo," called Uncle Attilio, "come and meet your cousin! Rino, take his suitcase. Hurry, for we are hungry!"

From the group emerged a tall broad-shouldered young man with a wide grin across his face. "Ben venuto, cousin," he said and threw his arms around me.

"Holy Mary, he arrived safely," cried an Aunt; then suddenly they surrounded me and kissed me, one by one, on both cheeks, to the immense enjoyment of my uncles, who moved aside to pay the driver.

"Come, don't eat him up! Take him inside, into the light so you can see him," laughed Uncle Attilio, and amid shouts of "Ben venuto!" I was ushered into a fragrant kitchen, where Uncle Attilio proudly presented the rest of the family. Americo was brought forward first for these formal introductions, since he was the oldest son and would be my special guide during the visit. He knew all the girls in the village and promised that I'd meet them after eleven o'clock Mass on Sunday. Because we were almost equal in height, both dark and about the same age, the women were quick to find a familial resemblance. My cousin, however, was more robust than I, and his right hand, when he extended it, was almost twice the size of mine, and his grip was twice as powerful.

Rino, Uncle Attilo's younger son, was introduced next; he was a stocky bashful boy, who had just come in from the fields and was still wearing his cap and heavy work clothers. "Ciao, Giordano," he said in a deep voice, shaking hands and grinning self-consciously.

Then my uncle brought forward the women, first presenting his good wife Firma, who was afraid of nothing and did a man's work everyday. Behind her, brimming with excitement, was Aunt Clelia, who had been sickly ever since the Nazis had stolen her son. She was painfully frail and even on so warm a night was wrapped in a short, heavy shawl. Aunt Clelia put an arm around her daughter Celesta and gently pushed her forward, a pale, thin girl who curtsied with a shy smile.

Without further ceremony, Aunt Firma took charge. "*S'accomodi, Signore*," she said. "The polenta is almost ready and supper will be on the table shortly, because I know you must be starving after such a long trip." She moved toward a massive wood-stove set in a brick alcove which must have been a fireplace at one time. The top was crowded with frying pans and kettles and a battered black coffeepot. Aunt Firma opened one of the stove lids and set a copper bucket down into the red hole. Aunt Clelia, hovering nervously behind her like a lady in waiting, handed her a short wooden pole, and she started stirring vigorously in circular motions.

"Go on," Aunt Firma said to her son. "Take him to wash up, and you, Rino, can carry his valise upstairs. Quickly!" she admonished, "The polenta will be ready any time now!"

I followed Americo into a small pantry which appeared to be all that separated the kitchen from the stable. Through a partly open door I caught a glimpse of several cows and heard their restless noises as they moved about in their stalls. The pantry was as cool and sweet-smelling as the kitchen, in spite of the animals next door. Pots of basil stood on the window sill and bunches of garlic and dried herbs hung from beams overhead, filling the small space with their combined aromas. Tall baskets of onions and a small barrel of black olives stood against the wall. I washed my hands and face at a high sink by ladling cold well water from buckets which stood, brimful, on a shelf next to the cement sink.

When we returned to the kitchen my uncles and Rino were sitting at a wooden table covered with oilcloth and set with heavy white dishes. Uncle Attilio at the head of the table indicated that I should sit on the bench at his left, my back against the whitewashed wall. Americo sat down next to me and filled my glass with wine. The uncles wanted to talk about my father, whom they called "*povero Gildo*," making a heavy sign of the cross and bowing their heads everytime they mentioned his name. In detail they described the Mass for the Dead which they had requested in the Church of Fagagna after receiving my cable, naming, with some disagreement, all the people who had attended the Mass and all those who had sent flowers.

They had wanted so much to see my father again, but now they were happy enough to see his son, whom they had never even in their imaginations expected to meet. "Truly," said Aunt Firma, continuing to stir the polenta with her wooden stick, her sleeves rolled up to the elbows, "your mother must be a fine, big woman to have such a tall son." No one would believe that my mother was not the outsized woman she seemed, standing on a box behind my father in the family photograph. To decide the point, their leather album was brought out, wrapped in layers of newspaper, and I had to go over the names of my brothers and tell what each was doing now. They were eager to hear about our life in America; my father had always been so vague in his letters, they said, although of course they knew he was very successful and must have been very happy. I told them about his job as boss over six miners (*Che bravo!*), about the modern house he finally bought for us (*Che ricchezza!*), and then about his death from miner's asthma (*Che peccato!*)

We had no difficulty understanding each other; the family spoke a Venetian-accented Italian to me, lapsing into Friulano only to clarify certain meanings to one another. Americo was the arbiter in this, since he had gone to school longer and knew Italian better than any of the others.

"The polenta is ready," announced Aunt Firma finally, redfaced as she turned from the stove, carrying the heavy copper bucket to the center of the table and overturning it onto a wellscrubbed board covered with a clean cloth. A hissing cloud of steam escaped as the thick, bubbling cornmeal mixture slid down the sides of the bucket and lay quivering on the cloth in the cool air. Rising, Uncle Attilio took a silk thread from his wife and started to slice the drying cornmeal cake neatly in squares. It was a ritual I had seen my father perform at home on rare occasions like his birthday, when my mother let him make a polenta. For a moment the sight of my uncle neatly cutting the polenta with a piece of thread, and the steamy smell of the cornmeal, like Proust's tea-soaked morsel of madeleine, brought back a sudden rush of memories of our Wilkes-Barre kitchen, bright with enamel and stainless steel, and I remembered painfully how awkward my father had always felt around his own home, and how ashamed I was of his strange, alien habits.

Then for the first time I realized how lonely my father had always been and how successfully he had hidden his feelings from us. Neither his American-born wife nor his sons could offer companionship for him. But there was no need to wonder why he had left home to take his chances in another country. I looked down at the bare, trampled dirt floor of the kitchen and then my cousin Americo leaning forward with his elbows on the table, watching his father cut the polenta, and I thought that there, but for my father's courage and the grace of God, would I be also.

When the polenta was cut and pieces were passed around, Aunt Clelia served deep bowls of black-bean soup which was thick and hot and had a pungent taste. To cool his soup, Uncle Attilio poured in some wine and passed the bottle to me, motioning for me to do likewise.

"We eat the polenta with our fingers, *Signore*," Aunt Clelia said, "but if you want to use a fork, go ahead. Do not be ashamed to eat as you like and as much as you want."

"No, no," I said quickly, and picked up the polenta with my hands and dipped it in the soup.

The bean soup was followed by platters of homemade salami and *prosciutto*, thinly sliced, and bowls of a regional white cheese which we ate with more polenta and ripe tomatoes in oil and oregano. The wine bottle was passed around until it was emptied, and then Uncle Tarcesio disappeared to fill it up again. There was little conversation during the meal; everyone was concentrating on his food, and I sensed that they were all trying to eat as noiselessly as possible, in deference to the stranger at their table. When finally Aunt Clelia served strong coffee in small cups, I was so dazed by the food and wine that I was almost asleep.

The climax of the meal came after the dishes were cleared away, when Aunt Firma, followed by Aunt Clelia, carried in a long, flat cake which was placed ceremoniously in the center of the table. The cake was a baroque creation ornate with scrolls and flowers in white and pink icings and smelling sweetly of rum. Across the top, in elaborate script, were the words, "*Ben venuto,* Giordano."

Not to be outdone by his wife, Uncle Attilio went outside to some inexhaustible wine cellar, returning with another bottle, corked and covered with dust, saved for just such a celebration. It was a bottle of *Piccolit,* the sweet dessert wine of Friuli, he said, filling small glasses on a tray.

When we had all been served with cake and wine, Uncle Attilio slowly lighted his pipe and rose from his seat at the head of the table. "*Salute, Giordano,*" he said, lifting his glass toward me. "I never expected to see you in this house, and I still can't believe that you came all the way from America and are taking your father's place at our table! When your father left here almost thirty years ago, he was as old as you are now. How our mother cried that day! I wanted your father to wait until after Americo was born, but Firma herself urged him to go while he had the chance. Now we are glad that he went, and very proud that you came so far to visit us."

Amidst cheers and applause, Uncle Attilio sat down and the family lifted their glasses and drank. Then I too got up, with my head already spinning from the wine and the food, and began another toast while Uncle Tarcesio hastily refilled the empty wine glasses. Unsteadily and rather rhetorically, I said something about my father always hoping to return to die in the house where he was born. It must have been harder for him to leave this house than any of us would ever realize, I told them, for he never found anything in America to take its place. Some plants transplanted grow stronger, I said, while others whose roots are torn in the movement might grow poorly for a while, but will wither and die before their time. A matter of roots. Then I thought I had better sit down, for I was getting too maudlin. Was it the wine, I wondered, or was it for oratorical effect that I chose those words, simply to show off my fluent Italian? Sober, I could handle words, but now the soft Italian phrases were managing me, and their effect on the family supper was devastating. Aunt Clelia made a swift sign of the cross and kissed her hand toward heaven. Twisting the corners of her apron, Aunt Firma bowed her head, nodding, "*E vero, é vero!*" Sudden tears appeared in my uncles' eyes, and I felt I had better finish and sit down.

No cheers and no applause greeted my speech. Under the cloud of emotion, we drained our glasses of wine and then the aunts and Celesta started to clear the table.

The stairway to the bedrooms was outside, so Americo lighted a candle and led the way, pointing to the outhouse as we climbed the steps and telling me I had better go since it got very cold during the night. I took the candle and walked across the courtyard to the convenience, which was a narrow wooden shelter perched at the edge of one of the slopes descending gently behind the house and carefully cultivated with vines crawling along low trellises.

Later, I undressed by candlelight in the cold bedroom, clean and bare except for a huge double bed with a chest at its foot and a china pitcher and basin on an iron stand in one corner. Over the bed was a picture of the Madonna pointing to her bleeding heart, and the dried palms of some past Easter were draped around the black frame. My suitcase had been opened and placed on the chest.

"Put your shoes outside the door and Rino will polish them for you in the morning," Americo said, "and if you will fold your clothes and leave them by the door, my mother will take them early in the morning and press them for you before you wake up."

I placed my clothes on top of his by the door, then climbed into bed. Americo blew out the candle. In the darkness, he lifted himself on an elbow and whispered, "I hope to reach the

United States someday soon, Giordano. All my life I have been waiting to go to your country. My parents wish it as well; they have always wanted me to follow your father and live in America. But it's hard to get into the States now. After the War I registered with the American consulate in Genoa for a visa under the emigration quota, and I have been waiting ever since because the quota for my category is always full.

"Here life is hard, Giordano," my cousin continued. "There is nothing to look forward to except continuing to work in the half-profits fields which my father and Rino cultivate. I want to go to America and make enough to help my father buy some land for himself before he is too old. All my papers are ready; I need only the visa. I know that there are many jobs for Italians in America. I'd like to live in your house."

I waited for him to continue, but he had stopped talking. I lay in the high, hard bed looking out through the unshuttered window at the sky. I heard the steps creak as my uncle and his wife passed our door on their way to bed. A door was slammed on the other side of the house, where Uncle Tarcesio slept with his family. From down below came the occasional rustling sounds of the cows next to the kitchen. In the darkness, I wondered how it must have been for my father, night after night, dreaming the same things Americo had just described. Then I sensed how he must have felt in America, not victorious as his brothers thought, but so defeated he couldn't even complain.

Finally, I got up. I walked across the cold, unpainted floor to the window and looked down into the courtyard enclosed by the ancient, crumbling house. In the moonlight, I could see the shape of an empty wine barrel rolled against the wall. Now, when it was no longer possible, I wanted to go back and sit with my father under his grapevine and talk with him in his language; I wanted to help him make wine and tell him that I had seen his family home and understood his foreign ways.

Turning from the window, I walked noiselessly back to bed. "Stay," I said. "Stay here, Americo." But my cousin was already asleep.

Dear Friends
and Gentle Hearts

BY LESLIE A. FIEDLER

"DEAR friend," Aunt Aggie said, "dear friend," and she wept. All the while the tears kept streaming wildly across her face, her hands lay without motion in her lap, her body expressed nothing. She is a poor actor, George thought, watching her through the crook of Helen's elbow, even of what she *is*, but he did not believe it and he could not resist the pull from his safe corner into the arena of her mean skull.

"You are six," Helen had told her, "this is your sixth birthday," and the old woman had begun to cry as if she would never stop. But the innocence of her faith in tears was lost among them; she held her wet face, the eyes closed, a meaningless offering in the scant light. The rest watched from the periphery of the shadowed room, refusing commitment, simply themselves; only he endured the full terror to which the laced and withered body of Aunt Aggie was not adequate. This Helen knew, and she would not stop.

"Father," Aunt Aggie sobbed, "please, father—oh, *please!*"

He almost cried out in shame for Helen, who danced there in the floor's center with a few conventional gestures, the gross threat of the father, the imposition of will, and for himself who had to bear yet once more the indignity of the victim. How thin his wrists were, and the fist to which his fingers crumpled—nothing. He would sense when a party was moving toward this moment; into a lull Kathy would cry, "Oh, let's *hypnotize* someone! Helen is very good," hoping that Helen would choose *her* again, assert their relationship, permit her the habitual public submission.

But tonight Helen had picked Aunt Aggie for her subject, perhaps to punish Kathy for talking so long with Aaron whom she despised, or in simple malice toward the old woman who was Aaron's aunt, brought along at the last moment to betray under her affability, her company manner, a fear of them all. That fear had titillated them secretly from the beginning of the evening, had broken through at last the ennui of the unseasonable spring which a week of parties had not breached.

When they chose her, Aunt Aggie had lifted her faded hands in small anguish, but she had been glad, George knew, to escape the word games at which she had hopelessly stumbled, and they had insolently tolerated her ineptitude. When Helen, whose flamboyant unstylishness cowed her, had taken her by the hand, insisting, she could not refuse.

"It is just like going to sleep," she had repeated to herself the false assurance, "Why, yes, yes, I'll—" A little quiver of daring visibly moved her; the easy chair in the cleared circle under the arranged lamps was a guarantee of status and she sat there, her hopeless ugliness, neither comic nor grotesque, with a mincing shyness that was a kind of courtesy.

"O father," she cried now in a little girl's voice from the dead streaming face, "it's my little friend, my dear little friend—" It sounded almost as if she were saying "littoo," "littoo." Someone tittered.

"You are six," Helen repeated. "This is your sixth birthday. What is the matter, little girl?" She spoke slowly, with the unbending seriousness that made her so effective a hypnotist, though she had learned from watching a single demonstration. She carried about her a kind of magnificence: her total unawareness of the possibilities of the ridiculous in any role she adopted. The same humorlessness made George's political ideas in her mouth (since they had been living together, she had taken over with fearful thoroughness all his views, though she submitted to him in passion or ceremony never) gross, ill-mannered; in him ideas lived in an environment of self-mockery, of *play*, and no view could seem less than civilized in his tired irony. She is an American, after all, he sometimes told himself, but that was too easy, a crudity.

Aunt Aggie only sobbed in answer, and Helen tried again, softly, passionately. "What is the matter, little girl, *poor* little girl?" She would not rescue the old woman from the bitterness of recollection but trembled at the possibilities of humiliation and triumph. She would, George foresaw, be immensely excited when they got home, warm, moist and overbearing in bed, so that more than ever he would be aware of the imparity of their desire. He coughed a little to feel the narrow reverberation of his chest, and watched Helen's strong fleshy back bend to the limp subject, the exploration of power. He experienced, in an act of total recall, her odor and was glad to snuff furtively his own smell: a little too much eau de cologne for America, some-one had told him, but he relished the improbable sweetness like a private joke.

"I am your father, your father!" Helen persisted, and the of-fensive health of her bourgeois body that the mannered disguise of her dress, spinsterish, bohemian, could not conceal, played the haired belly of the father, the dark-pronged mystery beneath; the secret was out. "Tell me. Tell me!"

"I—I—I" Aunt Aggie's confession was a stammer, and she pitched forward moaning, fingering in her own shadow her moustache beaded with sweat, as if in the un-time of her agony she had confused that indignity with her sixth-year sorrow.

"Tell me—Tell me!"

It would not matter what monstrous acts he might later urge upon her heat in the darkness; he had begun thinking of them as a kind of revenge, but Helen's impregnable lack of humor protected her in bed, too, and in the end *he* suffered nausea. And yet he could not leave her; his timid nagging sensuality needed the minimum satisfaction he found it tiresome to pursue—and she had *happened* to him, choosing him for reasons he found at once trivial and shocking: that he was foreign, a poet—and a public warrant of her sexual freedom. Her programmatic concern with sex gave a grotesque importance to what he was accustomed to find a necessary, slightly deplorable incident of maturity.

"She is not deep enough under," Helen explained in an aside to the group, forestalling their mutter of pity; and stroking the mottled forehead of the old woman, she made a new start: "Sleep now. Relax. Sleep. Sleep." The compulsive stutter died under the formality of gentleness, the plausible authoritarian voice.

George could no longer abide it. "Monstrous," he shouted, rising suddenly, "it is monstrous," knowing as he cried out that his accent was, as always when he was disturbed, exaggerated, almost comic.

"Sh!" Kathy hissed at him protectively. "Sh!" When he turned toward her dark genteel face, he could see under the momentary exasperation, the residue of an almost ecstatic languor from which she would not willingly awake. He had looked at her only once during the performance, following a glance of Helen's, had seen them forgive each other in the humiliation of the old woman, and Kathy, whom either face of cruelty aroused, moved against her husband, Oliver, her haunch, in a gesture sleek as a yawn.

Once during the demonstration, Oliver had walked out of the room to the john, and in passing had laid a hand, with its faint blonded fur, its calm, on George's shoulder. It was a conspiratorial movement; Oliver understood, of course, and could not forbear that show of masculine solidarity. Under this aegis, what is male only, cool and needing no assurance of cruelty, he seemed to be saying, can prosper; but George, who had been to a boys' school in his own small country, winced a little, knowing the peril of that promise, the obverse of its specious cleanliness, remembering the mockeries and rapes of boys. On his way back, Oliver did not touch him.

"End this now! Enough!" George cried again.

Helen wheeled on him briefly her soft quivering face. "George, the *rapport!*" The serious silly word unnerved him and he made with a shrug his surrender.

But Aaron took up his cry, disturbed for all his vague hostility toward his aunt, at the threat of a scene, and flinging his hand in a proprietary gesture toward the chair, began: "Really, I think—"

"All right," Helen said, "all right, now let's *everyone* be stupid! I'm bored anyhow." Her pretended anger did not deceive George; he knew that she enjoyed the protest, their small distress.

She moved back over Aunt Aggie, grave and possessive. "When I count three I want you to wake up. When I count three I want you to wake up." Someone laughed without conviction. "One, two—*three*." She even dared snap her fingers.

George could feel himself struggling back from the total openness, the quivering submission, the female dark; there seemed no profit in waking, and he could feel how, after all, Aunt Aggie had plotted her indignity, had nursed and pampered it for this moment, and he too, improbable accomplice, had willed it for them both. The eyelids of the old woman came up sullenly, and sight baffled under the pale light, fumbled toward pain. She threw the back of one hand limply against her forehead, damp flesh kissing flesh, and she shuddered to touch herself again, "Oh, it *hurts*," she cried in her own trembling voice, "You said—"

"I could have given her a posthypnotic suggestion that she would feel well." Helen did not speak to Aunt Aggie, but declaimed to the stirring room. "*If* I hadn't been heckled—"

"She always gives me—" Kathy began, her voice slow with a kind of nostalgia.

But Aunt Aggie was asking from face to face, "What did I say? What did I do? I didn't do any—" and her stupidity seemed suddenly not her shame but theirs. They were all leaving.

In the street George could scarcely match Helen's stride; an occasional street lamp verified the face he could sense in the dark, self-satisfied, fulfilled. "Not so bad, after all," she said finally.

"Your slip was showing the whole damn time," he said. It was a lie, but more than feeble malice prompted it; somewhere there must be for her a metaphor of the absurd.

She did not even trouble to look down. "Say 'slip', '*slip*'," she told him, pronouncing precisely. "When you say it, it sounds like 'sleep'," and he could see the glimmer of her teeth biting in anticipation her moist lower lip.

Sweet Love Remembered

BY JOYCE CAROL OATES

THAT day had been a Sunday too, though not so late into
summer as this, not nearly so hot, and Amie remembered too
the slight pressure of company about the house—in the front
room, the parlor, sitting about with their casual and apparently
endless exchanges of remark, expression, pointless memory, the
clamor and suspension of their talk drawing them, she had
thought, further and further into the past, echoes within
echoes, till at last she believed they would confront her out of
some bemused and oddly polite distance of time, as though
they hardly recognized her. This was Sunday at home: and
Amie on the back porch, listening to the monotonous drone of
conversation, her mother, her aunts, and listening too for the
frequent sound of thunder, rolling through the heavy silence of
the day. She was waiting for the rain to come—the sky was dark
and overcast, the clouds had been thickening, graying, before
they had even set out the long way to church that morning—
and waiting, vaguely, for Jarley to come back. He had gone off
without dinner, probably down to the creek; and, sitting on the
top step of the porch, beside the softly rotting quart containers
for strawberries, or pears, which her mother sold out by the
road in season, Amie had watched the far bank of foliage which
marked the creek, waiting to see her brother emerge out of it.

Now the scene, which had been evoked, she thought, for no real reason, caught itself calmly and effortlessly in her mind's eye: and as she crossed the narrow street, her straw purse uplifted a little, prettily, her eyes following the convertible which passed close by her with the heavy-faced, balding, suntanned man who stared vacantly at her, and the woman with sunglasses and a new straw hat beside him, and the two children—a boy and a girl, the girl somewhat older—arguing petulantly in the back seat, she found herself drawn heavily up out of the flat and ordered memory to a sudden flashing of sunlight which made her squint, wrinkle her nose, as the automobile crept past her and the children, still arguing, the girl in a white sunsuit leaning forward suddenly to appeal to her mother, her clean, outraged cries hurting Amie's ears, both children so close she could almost have reached out and touched them.

She crossed to the sidewalk and paused for a moment, peering at her reflection in one of the shop windows. She touched her hair; she could see it gleam in the piercing sunlight; then she looked at the window, its display of watercolors, some of them so real, so beautiful, Amie felt she could stand there all day just looking at them, now and then someone, perhaps one of the tourists, stopping to look at them too as though drawn by Amie's interest, exchanging remarks with her, nodding, the two of them caught for a moment by the charm of the paintings—which were of sea scenes, mostly, with some of the land, though she liked those of the sea better because of the rich blues. But no one stopped; and she picked her way through the crowd and down the side street to the restaurant—as far away as the corner she could see clearly the sign with the clever letters, all in red dots, which said "breakfast served at all times." She was nearly there, only waiting with a look of forced, sweet patience for an elderly man to move out of her way, when the policeman stopped her: she could not remember, afterward, whether she had noticed him before or whether he had only just appeared behind her, tapping her on the shoulder.

"Miss," he said. She stared up at him; he was a young man, but she did not recognize him; he was staring back at her, his eyes beneath his fine, fair eyebrows like small wheels, metallic, blurred, staring at her as though he were trying to recognize her. "Do you have any identification, Miss?" Amie looked at him. "Any identification?" he said.

"Is something wrong?" said Amie. Now she had regained her composure, and returned his cool, impersonal look—they might have been two strangers confronting each other in some remote, lonely place, impersonal and without much care, even, she thought, and it was with a kind of apologetic indifference that Amie took her billfold out of the straw purse—it was a purse from last summer but not worn, not worn at all, the straw newly cleaned and smart and exactly like the purses the women carried about here, the women tourists—and, frowning a little, for the sunlight was quite bright, and piercing, she took out her social security card and another card, she did not remember it at first, a smudged white card, something to do with a religious organization for young people she had belonged to back home, some years ago, indeed she was embarrassed to have given it to the policeman at all. But he looked at them only briefly, and looked to her again. "That's fine, thank you, I'm sorry to bother you," he said. "I didn't think you were—there's a girl missing upstate," he said, "they told us to check everyone down here. You know, the beach and all. I'm sorry to bother you," he said.

"Oh, it's all right," said Amie. "What did she—" She hesitated; the bells of a church somewhere had begun tolling, suddenly, loudly, the church the one only a block or so away, of course, she knew where it was, she had passed it only five minutes ago. The policeman bent to her slightly, his hand to his ear. "What did she do?" Amie said.

"Do?" said the policeman.

"What did she do?" said Amie.

"She's missing," he said, looking at her. "I suppose run off with somebody. It's just a girl," he said.

The tolling of the church bells followed Amie into the restaurant, and the look of the policeman's face in the piercing light, even as she was walking unhurriedly through to the back with her expression adjusted, set, her purse swinging tightly by

its straps at the crook of her bent arm, her hand upraised above
the new silver bracelet, past the table at the window where
some of the boys were sitting with their cups of coffee and their
cigarettes, watching her, she walked through to the back without once looking around; she could feel her hair, grown quite
long now, stirring in rich, gleaming curls which must catch even
this dull light.

The boys had come in every day since the beginning of the
season; she and the other waitresses had gone out with them, in
their rust-streaked, loud cars, racing down the strip on the
beach at night, and there came to her mind as she stood behind
the counter later that day, watching the door, and the empty
table where they had been sitting, a vision of their harsh young
faces and the smell of the sea, the cold air, the roaring of their
automobiles; but she did not go out with them any more, she
did not even look at them. Outside people moved slowly past
the window with its ruffled white curtains, half-curtains which
Amie thought looked very charming indeed, people with sunglasses and tanned faces, women with their hair damp and
shapeless. From where she stood she could see her reflection in
the mirror on the cigarette machine across the way. She watched
the window, though, even when customers came in and she or
one of the other waitresses was serving them, she watched it
and the stream of people beyond it—and, as always, it evoked
within her a queer, chill sensation, a sweet hurt, the faces forever moving past and out of sight. She knew she had felt this
before. She had mentioned it to one of the other girls, but
found that though the girl professed to agree with her she had
not really understood her at all; this was something secret, it
could not be expressed, a sweet luring hurt she could not quite
understand. She had felt it so many times before, when she had
been a part of those wild and aimless rides up and down the
beach, and the snatched words, the faces, even then it had
touched her—and she felt as she waited on the people who
came in, mechanically, smiling mechanically, a sense of distance
from them and their life, their vivid, piercing looks, a sense of
isolation and a knowledge that the world was false and pain-

ful, that perhaps she would always be alone with this knowledge, that she would never be able to share it with anyone.

Toward evening the man came in, Amie had not even found herself waiting for him; she spoke of him to the other girls and to herself as her "friend"; she never called him by name. He would sit in the back and order coffee, and sometimes she would speak to him, but if the boys were there she would not; she moved about the small restaurant, cleaning the carved wooden tables with short, constrained, self-conscious circlings of her wrist, pocketing tips, smiling at customers, her head quite high, her chin a little lifted. She had met him nearly a month ago, they were together nearly every night: it was all a part of the harsh and piercing world which she could not escape, within it, so much involved with it as he was, he had no identity in himself beyond a series of gestures, the thought of him evoked within her, a response to this series of gestures, a nod of the head, a lifting of the eyebrows, a sense of the brittle splendor of an artifice contrived by lipstick and powder and her shining hair—which she washed every three days, which she brushed at least one hundred times every day—this sensation which came to her, perhaps, as she stood before the mirror in her room, touching her fingers to her cheeks, blending faint dots of lipstick into them, but only faint, only faint, at this time or perhaps in glancing at her nails accidentally, the smooth-worked enamel of her nails, a red exactly the color of her lips. Lately he had come in earlier and earlier to wait for her, to wait with his shoulders slumped a little and his expression quiet, faintly mournful, to Amie always a little absurd; he reminded her of a dog in the rain. So she would pass by him with her bright, impersonal look, talking to the other waitresses in snatches, nodding snatches of words, smiling at the many customers, at the sand they brushed off onto the floor with their noisy apologies, their teeth grinning at her, their hands big and tanned and restless on the tables. Today she moved through the clamor which began about five-thirty, a discordant ringing of silver and plates, the cash register, children's uplifted voices, and traffic from outside, aware of the fact that she hardly heard it at all, that it seemed to her—and must express itself in her face, he must notice how quiet she had grown lately, a little reserved, a little sad—she moved through a kind of dream, the vulgarity and the cheapness of what she saw about her, forever about her, and her own surrender to it, a sadness of a sweet and luring force, a tragic, inevitable surrender to the prodding of the loud world.

On the Sunday she had waited for her brother to come home—she forced the memory upon herself, something about it had touched her deeply—she had perhaps had a feeling like this too, though she had been so much younger then, of course, she had not known nearly so much. How much of her life, she saw now, had been made up of these odd lapses of time, these odd thoughts, binding one time to another! Perhaps she was a strange girl, she was not like the others. They saw the sunlight of the days and the endless crowds of people as she did, they surrendered to them, they did not as she see them in juxtaposition to anything else, and, seeing it, exult in it and in their own degradation, to have been brought so far, committed to something from which they could never return. For against the hot sunlight of these summer days and the gaudy snatches of neon light in the evenings, light and music and people, there was always the world of other summers, against this Sunday and other Sundays, when a girl might sit apart from those older persons with whom she could not communicate, with whom she did not care to communicate, sitting as she was behind their house on higher ground, in the wasted light before a storm, staring off at the sky, the horizon, at nothing perhaps, it might never cross her mind that these things and their condition would ever change, that the voices so monotonous behind her would vanish into time, the house, too, vanish for her, vanish out of her time, and the apple tree at the corner of the house, with Jarley's rope swing hanging frayed and rotting against the worn ground, this too might vanish for her, the sudden relieved downrushing of the cold rain too might have its end. She had not known she was waiting for Jarley, she would not have admitted it, she only sat, about fourteen, bored and petulant, her arms crossed, lis-

tening to the soft explosion of thunder behind the mountains.
When it had finally begun raining, and when her brother had
finally come up from the creek, running, his arms thrusting the
bushes and the high grass aside, his face snatched running
against the confusion of the rain, she watched him without any
emotion at all, she did not even care that he had come: until
she saw something on his leg, his overalls at one knee torn and
smudged with dirt, and red, and Jarley stopping every now and
then to peer down at it, prodding at it with one finger.

So she watched him coming through the rain, limping a little,
and behind him the sky gray and enormous, looking heavy, and
about him their father's land with its accustomed look,
Jarley limping up the path past the barn and toward the house,
the rain darkening his clothes, slashing coldly across his face—
until she saw him stop, simply stop in the rain, and bend to examine his bleeding knee, not moving save for his finger prodding at the accidental wound, he stopped for some time, bent,
watching the blood, watching as the rain mixed with it, and
about him the grass torn and frayed with the rain, and Amie
watching him, her waiting look of contempt already drained
away. "You, Jarley," she said. But he did not hear her: he only
stood there, his face hidden from her, poking at his knee with
the air fresh and lifting around him, fresh against Amie's face,
entirely oblivious of the rain and of her while she stared at the
scene so flat and ordered before her, thinking suddenly that she
loved her brother and that she had never told him so, that she
would never tell him so, she would not be able. Then the rain
came down harder and Jarley jerked up, as though he had been
awakened, slapped into life; he looked to her across the cold expanse of rain and, his child's face already set into an expression
of pain and self-pity, ran up to the porch with his one leg
absurdly stiff, looking to her, his face newly contorted.

Her hours had nearly ended before she even glanced, really,
at her friend; but he looked as she had expected, his eyes on her
already, his thick fingers about a cup of coffee. Now there was
no one in the restaurant save them and another waitress, and
the four or five boys at the front table, their legs outstretched,

talking loudly, laughing, shaking the ashes from their cigarettes onto the floor, the other girl with her arms folded talking with them, looking quickly from face to face. Amie listened to their talk; she stood behind the counter, quite still, looking to her friend, and only after some time did she smile in her careful, almost impersonal manner, a waiting manner, as though she did not really recognize him. There was the awkward moment when they left, and the boys now standing outside, one of them talking loudly with a foot on the sidewalk, the other absurdly in the gutter, Amie and her friend looking blankly at them and then away, not flinching before their grinning remarks, already walking quite unhurriedly through the settled heat to his car at the end of the block, the boys behind them, following for a short distance, calling to them in their loud, harsh, young voices, their footsteps scraping on the walk. "Aren't you sorry for yourself?" one of them said. "You don't have any money. Aren't you sorry?" One of the others shouted something, Amie could not make it out, and she heard them scuffling behind them, swearing, and, a few minutes later, she saw them standing on the sidewalk staring coldly and aloofly at her as she rode past, sitting beside her friend, amid what she knew to be a slow piercing gleam of chrome, of neon light streaking off chrome, brilliant and calm and precise, moving past them and out of their narrowed sight.

They drove out along the ocean road, where the great motels were, brilliantly lit, their swimming pools lit green, brilliant and superfluous beyond the clusters of people and, farther down, where the motels gave way to the beach itself with the air cooling through the open window, Amie's hand outside, her fingers apart against the streaming wind. Her friend drove with his usual loose, bovine, vaguely apologetic air, giving way to other cars, slowing so that those behind him might pass, always glancing out to them with a quick nervous jerk of his head. Amie could see this out of the corner of her eye. After a time she thought to begin speaking, and she listened to her voice, a light, easy, charming voice, she listened to hear what she might have to say. "I'm always so glad when it's time to leave, I don't like it there," she said, "always all those people, and those boys—they don't leave me alone; I don't know why. I never even look at them any more. I only do my job. But when it's time to leave—"

"I'm sorry you don't like it."

Amie felt the wind coldly against her hand. "Oh, I like it," she said quickly. "I do. I like it. I like to do things for myself."

"You could quit any time."

"No," she said. "I like it. It was just tonight. I like it most of the time."

They rode for a while in silence. "I like the evenings best too," he said. Then he went on, clearing his throat, "I mean the end of the day coming, the days here are so long—"

"Yes," said Amie, nodding. "Yes. Daytime lasts so long in the summer."

"And all this land here," he said. He waited a while; Amie believed he was worrying to think of what to say, to order his words. She saw him grip the steering wheel tighter. "I feel something in all this distance, this distance, something almost more than you could be expected to bear—the land stretches out for so far, all this flat land, and the ocean there—"

"That's true," Amie said slowly. "It goes on so far."

"All this land," he said. Amie waited to smile; but he only said: "The terror isn't in the dark, but in the light, so much light. It's more than you could be expected to bear."

"Yes," said Amie. The air had grown colder; she leaned her cheek to the window, she felt the wind touch it, touch her soft fine hair. The difficult balance of the twin visions—the vision of the old memory, and the vision of the crowded town—was at last being ended, the usual surrender impending, irresistible, the repetitive defeat a perverse exulting in the triumph of the vulgar over the beautiful. "But the summer won't go on much longer," she said. She spoke easily and with an air, still, of impersonality; she listened to it in herself. "There's only a few more weeks left to the season." She glanced to her friend. "Then are you going back?" she said.

"I don't know," he said.

She smiled a little. "You have to go back," she said.

"I don't have to," he said. Now they were out in the country, driving along the beach, but the land here was rough and sand-swept, the beach was harsh, cold-looking in the glare of the moon, this road only little more than one lane. "I don't like to keep moving from one place to another," he said. Amie waited for him to continue; she thought about this. He had told her about himself but she had listened only vaguely, she had matched her reactions with his gestures, she knew what to do, she understood the accustomed behavior. He was a teacher somewhere, he wrote things but mostly he was a teacher of some sort, she thought, though she could not be sure, perhaps a teacher in college—she could not be sure; he was separated from his wife, there were some children, Amie could not re-member, she had never really known. This was all she might play back to herself about him: beyond that he was only a face, he sat with his rather broad shoulders slumping a little, he sat with his fingers curled thickly about a cup of coffee, watching her, watching her. "I don't like to," he was saying. "Everything changes from one place to another. That's what I've learned— how everything changes. What we say has a meaning only for now, and for this place, and as soon as we go off somewhere else it all changes, it can't even be remembered correctly, it isn't simple or baffling, it's just nothing. I don't like to think about it."

"I'm sorry," Amie said at once.

"The way the laws are," he went on, "as soon as you leave one place you have to prepare yourself for the next. As soon as you leave you're already in the next," he said. "That makes it nothing, they all negate themselves. And all people the same. I don't like to think about it."

"I'm sorry," Amie said.

"Why are you sorry," he said. "You didn't make it that way."

Some time later when he stopped the car it was on a small hill which overlooked the ocean, and, behind them, what must have been a little village, its infrequent lights blinking through the still night air and the sharp sound of crickets; farther out

the low rushing of the water came as though from some depths
beneath them—a sound curiously unreal, yet sweet, discordantly
sweet; Amie listened to it, she felt her breath become one
with the murmur, a high, lost, painful murmur, the shadow
of the hot soft night about them one with the final horizon, the
melted line of division between the sea and the sky, only the
depths of the sky, the world, unfathomable space. He was saying something; she listened to him, her head turned a little,
nodding, her eyes straying to the ocean beyond the jagged
fringe of trees. When he stopped talking she heard nothing for
a moment—she waited, without looking to him, without, especially, what she believed to be much concern, and felt the piercing sweetness of the night and the ocean impinge itself upon
her, the sadness, the surrender, that flattened world of some
abandoned past and this present violation, the beauty and the
corruption, the tragedy before which she could feel only relieved, only a little sleepy, how one reflected the other, drained
into the other, how this overturned upon her! She thought of
the accidental vision of her brother again, his child's face
averted, fascinated by blood and pain, prodding at his knee, this
child and she watching him out of all time, on the brink of
time, not yet in it, aware dimly and sadly of an oceanlike
immensity which draws one to it, leads him to new relationships, new faces, new roles, as a child one prods again one's
accidental wound, and delights in the relieving pain. And the
unspoken love of that time, the beauty and frailty of that
love—

Amie jerked around. There was a bell tolling—a distinct,
solemn tolling—from the village, of course, a church down in
the village, it must be twelve o'clock and Sunday over. But she
stiffened slowly, listening to it, and, turning to the man, to his
tired, waiting expression, his thickened face, his slightly parted
lips, she stared at him for a moment, listening to the bell; past
it the sound of the surf exploded quietly, like something falling,
collapsing without end. She waited until the bell stopped, listening to it. Then the usual silence returned, rolling in to them
as they sat in the automobile watching one another, the waitress

and the middle-aged man, perhaps waiting for the shock of recognition to overtake them. "My God," Amie said suddenly. She
felt perspiration break out on her palms, a queer, itching sensation. "My God, please," she said.

The man was staring at her in alarm. "You didn't make it
that way, it isn't your fault," he said quickly, a little clumsily.
"Are you still worried about that? I'm sorry I said anything—"

Amie only looked at him. The bell had stopped tolling; there
was nothing, not even an echo. Yet she could feel a fine cold
mist rise and subside within her as though some tension, some
brink, had been passed, as though some part of her life were
over. "What you said—you said—"

"No, nothing," said the man. "It wasn't anything. Here," he
said. He made to touch her, she watched his nearing face in the
sullen light. "Here," he said, "I'm sorry I said anything, it isn't
that way. It isn't that way at all. It isn't that way at all."

As I Am You Will Be

BY B. H. FRIEDMAN

ALL the years of his young life Little Boy wanders the streets, looking at the beautiful girls and wanting them; all his young life he longs for the orgy that never comes. The conventions, the mores, the pressures of his group, they bother him; they never leave him free; they are to blame. The big experience never comes. Ecstasy is a word. Romance is paper and celluloid and Ernest Hemingway. He watches the truck drivers, the bartenders, the stevedores, admiring their broad chests and narrow hips and their lives, their lives which pulse in the night. There is something about a strange face, a double shot of whiskey gulped down without a cough, tattooed arms.

Little Boy wanders, hating his clothes—the uniform of his class—and envious of the men who don't wear ties.

The war comes—silently and secretly, like a worm eating an apple. At first he and his clique aren't bruised by the falling cards. But eighteen comes fast, fast enough so that Little Boy doesn't miss the big war. He may go marching off to camp with men, using all the strong words, hearing all about the big strong nights.

And Little Boy may get tattooed. Do you know what it is to walk into a tattooing parlor? Can you imagine choosing one label out of thousands as yours for life? Does the eagle seem to

scream? Is the battleship too large? Is the "Sailor's Grave" too
common? Is the seaman carrying the swab too cute? Would
MOTHER, in capital letters, be flattered when she saw his arm?
His eye finally lights upon a skull and crossbones with the
motto: "As you are, I once was. As I am, you will be."

Little Boy rolls up his sleeve. Swede dry-shaves his arm and
swabs it with alcohol. The stencil is applied and smeared with a
black charcoal compound. Swede picks up the electric needle,
dips it into heavy black ink, and follows the outline.

The boy holds fast on the left arm of the chair. Damp dead
sweat trickles from under his arms. The needle works in and out
on its course leaving blood in its wake, and the boy grips the
chair more tightly, thinking of the sea, and breaking with the
parental yoke, and the blood and the needle, and in and out
and in and out, and forever, which is a long time.

The needle looks caked and dirty. What about infection?
What if some sailor before him had a disease? "Ya ain't a man
till you've had a dose." "Blued, screwed, and tattooed." "Darling, don't forget your rubbers." Oh Boats, Oh Mate, Oh
Mother, Oh God.

Swede finishes shading the central portion of the tattoo with
a thicker needle which doesn't penetrate or hurt as much. He
wipes the surface again with alcohol, but this time it bites and
stings. Cool, soothing vaseline and a gauze bandage.

"That'll stay on there good. Don't pick it if it starts scab-
bing up on ya."

"Thanks a lot."

The boy gives him the three bucks and leaves.

For about two weeks the tattoo doesn't look just right. It is
scabbed in spots and indistinct in others. And then it emerges
—clean and sharp and part of you. You belong to a vast fra-
ternity, encompassing all oceans and all ports, all roads and all
jobs. When you walk into a bar in Shanghai, with your sleeves
rolled up, you acquire a dozen friends. And a dozen men want
to know you as you swim off the beach at Manila. The world is
yours, the blood, the pulse, the ecstasy, the godhead you en-
visaged in a thousand strange thighs. No longer the prep-school

frustration. You're a man of and among men. Forever, "As you are, I once was. As I am, you will be."

But the worm dies. It is the summer after the war. Seduction must replace rape and purchase. "Intercourse," "sleeping with," "going to bed with," "oh shoot," all must be forced back into the vocabulary. And oh the polite cocktail parties and bridge games.

Forget that weekend in Frisco, when the water was running cold in the bathtub on a case of beer and four fifths of rye. Three sailors with their jumpers off played cut-throat pinochle for fourteen hours (and a carton of Lucky Strikes)—waiting for the knock on the door the pimply elevator boy had promised them. He made a four-hundred hand and waiting, waiting, waiting—till finally the knock. She'd take them all on for ten bucks. They cut, and his king was high. Christ, what a run of cards.

But now Susan bids four no-trump, and he knows she's using Blackwood, asking for aces, but he wants to ask the boys to beat a full-house.

"Five hearts."

"Five no."

"Six diamonds."

"Six spades."

"Pass."

"Pass."

"Pass."

He's dummy. He gets up and looks at his partner's hand. If the finesse doesn't work she'll go down—one trick—one dollar in Panama.

She makes her contract and tells him he bid it nicely. Now they all want to go swimming, and the last one in is a monkey's uncle. So long ago he had drawn king high.

His tattoo is so-ooo cute, but really how could you? Were you drunk? God, you must have been really pickled. Cold sober? Early in the morning? In Norfolk? O priceless, priceless. Well, it really isn't so bad—I guess.

The cute little blonde, six years old, with her curls bouncing on her shoulders, runs up to him:

"What's that, what's that?"

"It's a tattoo."

"What's a taboo?"

"Tattoo, tattoo. They make an indelible picture by pricking coloring matter into the skin."

"What's indelible? Does it hurt? Does it hurt much?"

"Indelible means it never washes off. It didn't hurt much."

The president of his father's club sits down next to him in the "hot room":

"You're Mike's son, aren't you?"

"Yes, sir."

"How'd you ever happen to get that?"

"I guess I was trying . . . I wasn't thinking very clearly . . . I was drunk."

He is in the shower room with his fraters for the first time: "Ha ha. You salty dog. Why the hell did you ever get that thing? I almost got one; I'm damn glad I didn't though. A buddy of mine back home got tattooed, and his parents made him have it taken off. Has Susan seen it yet?"

He had dreamed of his return home and strutting across beaches and tiled floors flaunting his tattoo, but he found himself deliberately draping towels over his arm and buying longsleeved sport shirts. Now, in the shower, he spread the lather thickly on his arm.

The needle goes in and out, pricking beneath the skin. Superficially, at least, he had always belonged to his group. He had all the right labels from the Roman numeral three after his name to the Hunt Club and Beach Club. What had happened? It would be different if he were a nigger, a wop, or a Jew, but having a tattoo—that's such an unimportant thing.

Going to sleep at night, he would make a tacit pact with God that if the tattoo were gone in the morning he would always believe in Him. A thousand times he looked expecting it to be gone. Finally, he made an appointment with a dermatologist.

Dr. Turner looks at the slip the nurse hands him and smiles.

"I assume since you are here you have made up your mind to

have the tattoo removed. It would be useless for me to try to dissuade you?"

"Yes, I've thought a lot about it, become self-conscious; I'd like it off."

"Well, let's take a look at it. Roll up your sleeve."

The doctor looks at it, pinching and stretching the skin, and remarking that the pattern is not really offensive. He calls for the nurse, and they lead the boy to the back room. Once again the surface is cleansed. The doctor keeps up a running commentary throughout the inquisition. He will try electrolysis, acid, and injections on various parts of the tattoo. When the boy returns in two weeks, whichever method has shown the best results will be used to remove the entire thing. The various treatments hurt about as much as the original tattooing, but in the sparks of the electrolysis needle he sees regained ease, and physical pain is of only secondary importance. The little sore spots are covered with a bandage.

"Good-bye, doctor, see you in two weeks."

"Righto, good-bye."

The two weeks go by surprisingly fast. A few times he catches himself wondering which parts of the thing will be the first to go. He pictures it minus a bone or an eye, a word or a phrase. Twice he peeks under the bandage. He sees three ugly little scabs.

He is early for his appointment when the time comes. The doctor removes the bandage and scrapes away the scabs with a scalpel. He shakes his head.

"I'm afraid it's in too deep, too deep. The only way to get it off is a rather painful plastic operation."

Charlie, the lifeguard, has a cruiser anchored on his chest. Joe, the locker boy at the gym, has five or six small tattoos all over his arms. What would they think of him? And what would his ex-mates think? Just before the end of the war, he used to talk a lot about what design he would get for the other arm.

"Would you make arrangements with the surgeon, please?"

The waiting room of the plastic surgeon is extremely crowded. Women with their noses bandaged and black eyes sit looking at the words in fashion magazines and National Geographics. At last a big nurse with a little voice calls out the boy's name and he is ushered into the back office.

"Dr. Turner spoke to me about you. I've arranged for an operating room at the hospital two o'clock tomorrow. Will that be all right?"

"Fine."

"Good. Now let me see your arm."

The boy removes his coat and rolls up his sleeve.

"Not bad. Not bad. I was under the impression it was much larger. That will come off nicely. We'll be able to use a local anaesthetic. You can watch the whole thing. Don't eat a heavy lunch, and turn in at the incoming patients' desk about half past one."

He signs his name at the desk and is turned over to an intern who dresses him in a clean white nightgown and prepares his arm for the operation. A sickening smell of ether pervades the place, and "NO SMOKING" signs make the minutes pass more slowly. Promptly at two, the intern leads him into the operating room, where the surgeon waits all in white except for the horrible pink-tan practicality of his hands, hands that represent the ultimate in social aesthetics. Those hands and a scalpel will make him feel comfortable on the beach and in the shower room. They will deliver a scrap of flesh, a scrap of understanding and sensitivity, to the hospital sewage system, to the river, to its mother ocean. For a few days on beaches and in shower rooms laden with talcum powder he has known inferiority, but the pink-tan hands will cut this away. The left hand is smug and the right is complacent. The surgeon offers both, stretches them towards the boy.

The day before, the girl in the doctor's office with her new nose looked so relaxed, so completely untroubled and peaceful, almost animal. A bloodless operation. Black eyes and a swollen face for a few weeks. And then that wonderful freedom we all crave—freedom from feeling. The knife, cat-gut, anaesthesia offer this.

Cyrano, Cyrano. What a nose, what a man.

If the bullfrog had wings, he wouldn't bump his ass on the ground. If he were stronger . . . If the war . . . If society . . . If. . . .

"Ready, nurse, the novocain."

Tartarus

BY DOUGLAS FOWLER

AFTER a friend of mine had been able to do Europe alone and had developed that certain way of holding both a cigarette and a drink in three fingers of the same neuter hand, he would tell me that, alas, being a garment-district robber-baron's scion was, God, very cheap, but that it had certain advantages. Although he would be the first to admit that he hadn't seen everything ("the Hindus and Salinger have something in this reincarnation business, it's not as questionable as you may think . . . you *do* have to read in it before you can pass judgment on the private Mark Twain and his determinism") it was, by and large, a truth that the most exciting, valuable people sprang from the gilded loins of the very rich, already silver-spooned and saddle-soaped. The boy, Freddy Linz, told me with delight about a Dutch tulip-king's tawny-headed son who, to the shame and passive outrage of four Princeton doctoral candidates, interrupted traffic on Dublin's O'Connell Street for some twenty minutes by draping a pair of olive BVD's with "Joyceans, No!" painted on the flap about the statue of King Billy referred to not only in *Ulysses*, but also in "The Dead," and that this same youth talked freely and concretely of his dabbling in certain uncomfortable-sounding homosexual acts with Algerian freedom fighters and Heidelburg optometrists, and had once amazed a dinner party of industrial princelings and timid Mediterranean princesses by depositing, on his second-course plate, a forty-inch, magenta tapeworm.

I myself believed in common people. My apartment was in an unhappy section of town near our (exclusive) university, and I was proud that the landlord was not only a janitor for the mathematics building, but also had a powerful cabbage soup for dinner whose reek assured me that I was heartbroken and betrayed among the other true sufferers, the aging chimney sweeps and guttersnipes of a sooty world, just as an anchorite might keep his flagellating apparatus displayed on his celibate wall to remind the eye that he must suffer because no one else would submit his pride for the world's advantage. Our senior year was the climax of a kind of hopeless paradox certain male collegians usually are able to pick their way through scarlessly. We all claimed the total human experience as beyond judgment to be the only means of existing. Rich or poor all were "human beings, the most miraculous emperors and clowns under a skin, caught in dark webs of pain and joy, and only love separates us from the dullest beast." Just as a moth will find the crowning act of its life in the last drink of fiery opiate from a candle, my senior year was as bright and passionate as an assassin's knife, we had only to find the proper mythology to yield our minds to, the proper candle, and incessantly invoked the troubled dust of Kafka and Christ with gnawed souls and the intense, whipsaw gestures of Italian vendormen.

On a luminous spring evening I took my hundred embroidered dreams to a party held in the back-yard apartment patios of a here-to-be-undifferentiated group of friends, a whiskey-sourish, tie, and drollery affair with a close defender and admirer of mine, Alice Havens. The wind moved about in the elm boughs and gently tugged them here and there, a gold sheen drowsed over the little pond casting reflected light that hung softly in the eaves of the white house, a thrush and a star were out.

"Oh, it's going to be one of those things," Alice said.

"Alice, thank you, Alice, Sweetheart, for not saying either

'God' or 'Christ' thank you very much," Freddy said, gliding up with a brat-faced actress at his side.

"I liked your other affectation better, Freddy. If this is going to be one of those country-squire parties I will vomit on the grass."

"This is another dimension, Alice, completely another more mystic time and place; we're all changed utterly from the dull clods you knew. You'll love us all. Won't she, Brenda? Oh, allow me."

Freddy introduced us. They were both pale and lithe, Brenda black of hair and eye, a black and white nymph, Freddy her favorite fawn, with liquid eyes and the face of a bitter courtesan, a bitter child.

"Most amusing, I got a letter from the tulip prince today featuring a new snobbery against the Philistines. The whole thing is beginning to take on aspect for me. He grows slightly tiresome and annoying as he grows more familiar. But *funny?*" he leaned to kiss Brenda's submissive cheek, fashioned as exactly for receiving cocktail lips as some palms are fashioned to submit themselves for coins. "It was the funniest thing I've ever read." He laughed in a public and private manner. Ice tinkled in glasses. A few children were shouting something or other on the dissolving street as the steeds and tiered galleons of clouds followed the sun in the tallest light, while we below in the gaining shadows perhaps moved a step closer and let our voices burn a little lower, perhaps touched a little more.

"He's incarcerated in this Danish palace or ski lodge for the winter, with a very maiden aunt and two fine native fellows, one of whom he claims plays only *Clair de lune* on the piano and drinks ale out of an Alpine horn, both unthinkable prospects, while he is attempting to write this novel of vigorous social comment about a Rotterdam dowager with picket-line-induced dropsy who has this red-headed daughter forever in vain love with a blinded miner or some kind of grimy proletarian type and raped by a captain of industry. The final scene . . . let's see . . . the final scene she draws on her childhood skates and repeats to herself a little folk song . . . I think the

miner has drowned himself . . . but the supreme irony and
psychological zingo is provided when we learn that the miner
and the captain of industry are uterine brothers . . . could that
be right?" Freddy asked himself. "Well, it's something like
that. At any rate I know she sings a little song at the end. He
expects the Nobel Prize inside a year."

"Well, at least she loved the miner," said Alice, "I always
make an exception for people being in love, even in these *things*
people write."

"I can't vouch for the author's sincerity," said Freddy, "because he's only trying to put one over himself."

"But her mother got dropsy because she was a picket. Do you
get dropsy from being a picket? That's when your ankles get fat.
I hate these perverse reptiles that write stories like that. I like
stories about balloons and school children." She turned on her
heel, completely around. "Who are these people anyway? Are
they really, really made out of shirt cardboard, Freddy? I've
never known anybody who was before, but I suppose this is just
part of my fat education. Fat."

"Quiet, this is a very exclusive party," Freddy said, looking
over his shoulder, "I had to invite some filler material, though. I
cannot bear to have a bald-faced boorish party with everyone
standing around picking their nose and knowing each other."

"Well, I don't know anyone here at all. I haven't the faintest
idea who these people are, do you?" she asked me. I diverted
our little social knot by calling attention to the yellow fragments of a kite in an elm tree. "A kite-killing elm," said Alice,
and the student actress laughed, "I hope the dogs wee on it."
She smiled at me with her eyes closed. "Oh, I can't bear it," she
said, turning around again. At this moment the party had
achieved whatever maximal happiness it would have; those who
would be imitating the famously gifted inside the apartments, a
certainty held in check only by the lees of daylight still drifting
through a choir softly bewitched from the voices of students,
assistant professors, children, the hoarse and eloquent bereave-
ment of a distant locomotive, those who would be falling over
armchairs or dropping drinks or naughty stories to an audience
whose collective expression would be suffused with a kind of

dead-mackerel glaze of pseudo ennui, they were all behaving themselves and responded admirably to the looking-glass charm of garden and weather as the night fell veil on veil. A few firefly lights were burning across the airy deepness of the violet, drowning valley and flickered in regions of memory and faces were passing like Japanese lanterns across the blue and gold hour. Not one of them would have been surprised if he were offered seven-league boots to draw on, dreaming so on success and fortune with faintly gauzed eyes and twilight voices as if they waited in deepening colors, finger to musing lip, in a train station where the sun finds its last residence in the dusty glass, on the worn ticket counter, or strikes a note from an indifferent earring, and some journey waits along the flying track, some aspect of the sea or yellow field whose sight will lift the soul into its permanent and expected state of joy. They seemed to have forgotten the shadow under an eye that is the watermark of grief, the regret reflected up a face that reveals a heart as dark and spiky as a thistle.

"Isn't this lovely," said Alice, "I knew this would be nice if you didn't have to look too closely. You'd think everyone was perfectly healthy and nice."

"And brave, clean, and reverent, too," said Freddy.

Alice put her hand on his face. She had one glove on, a negroid copper calfskin. The other she had thrown into the gorge for luck. I always expected lilac shoots and so forth to spring from her soft mouth, so fair she was.

"You aren't brave and clean and reverent, no matter how lovely a party you have, Freddy, and that's your little cross to bear. But it *is* nice, even if half the people here are . . . armadillo heads or have lobotomies or something. If we stand here all night we may never see what freaks they are."

"Speaking of freaks, you should have seen this old guy who lived upstairs." Freddy pointed to a melancholy window dark with premature night. "He just died this Tuesday. His name was Donovan."

"He *did*," said Alice, shocked, "well, let's not talk about it or we'll spoil the party. Was he an old, old man?"

"Pretty old. He was some kind of poet. Fat and poetic-

looking. He practically lived off some of his friends. I think Professor Brownlee was one. Does he have a skunk-like streak in
his hair and kind of a nod when he walks? If it wasn't Brownlee, it was Winkler."

"How did he die, though," Alice asked, her voice trembling,
almost piping with fear.

"Heart attack, Train, Pow, Dead. He died of senility. I don't
know the whole story. He was pretty absurd anyway. Very
friendly with the Marshall's little boy. In fact he probably satisfied his passionate perversity on the flowery helpless towheaded
child. I think he fed him traces of arsenic and cyanide and
things to keep him sick, because no one else would speak to
him. I think he poisoned the little boy and carried him about in
the snowy fields and wept icy tears and prayed over the broken,
starlit body; think of it, the blue shadows gathering, the white
gales, heaven's vault blank and ignorant, an old man kneeling
beside a litter of childish bones. . . ."

"But this was *Tuesday*," cried Alice.

"I'll have to revise the scenario," Freddy admitted, "And I
suppose I'll have to have the little boy gassed. He won't do
alive. Besides, he's nauseating."

"You're horrible," she said, "you really are," tears in her
handsome eyes.

"Horrible?" Freddy looked at her. I could see his image swaying in the tears. "To mourn for a poor little boy who was killed
for perversity? We all come to dust, but this was unspeakable.
Wait, I have it . . . a holy bier of flowers and wheat for his
little clay . . . close-up: the old man with tears in his azure
eyes, shot of flowing grain in the sun (Freddy blocked them out
with his hands) close-up: the small, dead hand, heavy with its
burden of quenched blood . . . shot: grasshoppers emerging
from eggs, the ceaseless bounty of Nature, a new rose ponderous with crimson wealth . . . shot: old man in sackcloth, the
knife raised to plunge into himself catches a glare of bitter
light . . . shot: the old man lying across the body with a wire-
haired terrier or something chewing on his leg." At this, Alice
began to cry in earnest, and Freddy stopped. "He was just an

old man. Besides the urchin is still alive. I'm just kidding you,"
he said reproachfully. "For God's sake, I'll bring the little kid
out if you'll stop crying."

"He did *die*, for Christ's sake," said the actress, taking the
girl's side.

"Say, I'm making this movie in 411, and I bet I can use you."
Freddy took out a pair of black-rimmed glasses and studied her
face. There was a careless felicity of hair upon her white nape,
and she had a dancer's movement. "Yes, you'll do fine. Fine."

"What kind of movie is it? I don't want to be in any of these
rape movies any more. I got a bruised collarbone from being
kneeled on."

"Oh, this is on the up-and-up. It's about this ape that escapes
from the zoology labs and you're this scientist's daughter . . .
it's really a musical but we can dub that in. . . . This ape
comes after you, see. . . . I like to think of him as kind of a
bitter ape, kind of jaundiced, and he's been watching you mixing chemicals and stuff."

"Look, I don't want to be in any movie with apes and things
. . . why don't you do something sort of, you know, English? I
love Englishmen, don't you love Englishmen?"

I interrupted to ask Freddy if the old man was buried yet,
and Freddy said that he didn't know but that he had been able
to get into his room and to read all his letters and his diary. A
unicorn moved through some dappled forest of my mind, a spe-
cific detail of some charmed realm where the spider's threads
fell slowly through aquarium light and forest lakes were deep as
the blue heavens they embraced, a Byzantine mosaic fashioned
from the leaves that drifted on the waters of its face. Freddy
asked me if I would like to see the room and told me about a
friend that had been hypnotized by a professional the preceding night and would be convinced until Wednesday that his
parents were a toad and a bat.

The moon had risen, a breathless white against the Aegean of
an April sky; the thrush still sang, and its singing shadow fell
upon that visionary stepchild of the world that floated over our
garden elms, and Alice's face was created all over again between

two lights as the firmament passed darker shadows, stranger colors, upon the softly burning lawn; I could see her cheek and throat dim and waver slightly, her bright hair and eyes shimmering delicately like a disturbed harp. We heard a sudden thunderhead advancing mile on mile.

Freddy and his girl disappeared, we heard them calling, reappeared again near the porch, disappeared again into some chink of the night. An instructor in the economics department folded his wife's scarf over his head, announced that it was Veronica's veil, and said that stopping the storm by miracle would "cost ten thou. in American dollars." A girl said that the rain wouldn't stop for any damn fairy and his handkerchief, another said that her spinal cord might act as a lightning rod and that if she didn't get inside she would cry. Someone stepped on a wineglass. I knew that they would pause on the glassed porch to watch the rain walk in state across the lake, and for a moment Alice and I paused too in the comforting warmth of the close bodies and the proud, electric air. The sky was suddenly as ascetic and dark gray as some Presbyterian heaven.

"Now the rain is up to the second buoy."

"No, farther."

"I hope lightning strikes Professors Kaplan, Hastings, and Whiskey Jim Stanley."

"Or at least my Mythology term paper."

Alice and I found the stairs, warm in the rich dusk, and almost ran the three flights up. A yellow bulb in a green tin skirt hung at the door, and the black night healed up around it. A card in the door slot said "Chas. Donovan." We looked at each other across a yard of dust motes.

"This whole thing stinks of hubris you know," Alice said.

I answered that we could not disregard the one opportunity to look directly into a man's life.

"I still don't think we ought to violate a dead man's room for our personal edification or whatever," she said, opening the door, "as if we were gods or something, as if we didn't really care."

There was a faint glow of thunder down the lake. The first

thing we saw was his window and through it, the university clock tower making a chunky effort to be noble in a siege of apocalyptic black clouds. A pittance of yellow, short-winded light from the hall brought a gleam from whatever objects in the room that could afford even such a niggardly expense of themselves, save for a precious-faced clock on the mantel which shone with the kind of black brilliance an acetylene torch in daylight casts, darkly radiant like Lucifer or the hooded back of a beetle. Perhaps we expected Rouault's old king with his single flower, perhaps Juliet laid like snow between incensed tapers. There was a bottle-green rug, a seacoast in mauve and Pierian, a head-high zone of books, a desk with papers, magazines and other combustible nostalgia. The shadows seemed carefully drawn in, and a vase with an iris painted on its curving flank was of the same smoky silver and blue as a struck tuning fork. The wall was girdled with snapshots, one of which, a photograph apparently worn and grooved fragilely by the diurnal progression of light upon it, as a sundial might be traced with a relief map of the sun's progression, was a celluloid reproduction of the owner. He had a Gothic, wrinkled-linen face with an Irish racial blur, full of heavenward intentions, slantwise and shadowed by an ancient summer day, almost trivial in its self-regard, and the light on it was so harsh I thought it not to be linen so much as gold foil crumbled and seamed after I had studied it for a moment. Full flutings in the dramatic nostrils, a wide pale mouth, and something congested and furious about the eyes where the light had dissolved in their sepia and yellow which gave him the cast of a hunting bird; and yet this was modified by the lower lip, which should have been an altar boy's or some virginal, ill-equipped creature, so that the final impression (I studied it for some time) was of vanity undoing beauty, and pouting instead of wrath. A traveling player asked to reflect on a skull, an impersonation of the gallows' hour of a patriot. And yet for a moment we both, Alice and I, saw down some metaphorical corridor into a violet room, the hint of a door closing, a shadow of voices scattered along stone. . . . I say it was a black and green countryside in Greece and the approach-

ing of magnified shapes in the bird-hung mist as Laius and his
retainers pass toward an intricately calibrated crossroads . . .
perhaps Illyria with its clowns and plane trees . . . a Florentine
gentlelady's hand shaking poison through evening velvet into
her melancholy lover's cup of dream . . . or at least this:
the falling star of a moment. Alice in shadow, the dimly
thundering night, objects crowded back out of their proper dimensions by the brightness of the lamp, and Donovan's vio-
lated journal swooned open on a desk so dark my hand seemed
to sink a little into it. I think that Alice and I wanted to find
some fiercely comical ironies in them, some hollow gesture of a
fool that we could pity with relief and condescension. I know I
expected his voice to crackle up from the pages as if from a
gramophone, full of sportive eccentricity and India-ink maledic-
tion, the squeal of a plucked mandrake root, a curse concocted
of bat's blood and an old librarian's spittle.

"I hope he's one of these people that go off bang like a gun.
What I want to see is a little disaster," said Alice, "after you
and your friends have been pulling this mudlark routine all
year. Incidentally, that moron that Freddy's with told me she
always raises her hand in Drewry's seminar because it makes her
bosom move. Can you *imagine?*" She reached over my shoulder to the journal, as if to reassure it. "The way Freddy talked I
expected this to be written on satyr's skin. You and your friends
are truly the most sickening emotional lechers I have ever seen.
You and all those little people with umbrellas. You always
think everyone is useful in this stupid, poetic way, and you
think you can condescend and say everything is beautiful and
you're all the worst snobs in the world. Freddy is the bitch of
the world, but he doesn't play Salvation Army. I don't think we
should look."

And yet there are moments in the ancient curve of nightfall
when the room that is morally next door to our lives suddenly
achieves the incandescence Faust was ravished by, when the
wall is so thin it seems only a saffron mistake in the light itself,
and hell-fires and gilded serpents writhe before some magical
objective: the fairy-tale mirror with its captive princess cham-

bered in silver, leaf shadows dissolving in a curving, burnished river. Alice and I chose to look at the journal. I have seen the eventide witch-light create fawns and such loveliness in a china-berry bush, or make a king's ransom glitter in a bicycle sprocket, and I have passed through a looking glass or reversed telescope into the Swiss workings of the whippoorwill's throat, and what we wanted from Donovan was the same transubstantiation: we wanted to be in the virtual presence of suffering, we wanted to see a man die, not through morbidity, but I think for a shabbier reason, through curiosity, and here was our chance.

What follows is stolen from the diary and the coffin:

April 2—How quiet God is! All last night I lay listening to the starts of the wind. (Remembered a round lake and a black tree a long, long time ago.) The boy who lives below is sick with the flu. I am planning to get some toy. Shall I take myself in my own confidence? I want him to be my friend. Baseball bat or something. Had lunch with DeForest noon, he has written a book on Indian culture in the Southwest. Dutton or Lippin-cott? Remember to ask. Heard (last night) the weather vane creaking out the scarcely created skies of spring, and I heard the new moths drum my screen. The boy is seven or eight, Marshall. I might get him something scientific. The birds are saying their rainbows. I dislike Mrs. DeForest very much be-cause she fancies herself an intellect. Nothing but a mental bootblack for Dr. DeForest. I went down to talk with the boy (really just taking out the trout bones in a newspaper and stum-bled on the whole thing—Mrs. Marshall is sweet but protec-tive.) and he seems to like me. Maybe. We agreed on kittens, spies and how we hate asparagus "like poison," both of us. I only touched him once so they wouldn't get the wrong idea about me. It is necessary for a widower to be careful. His shirt was unbuttoned (pajama), blue stripes and that silvery, little-boy chest. I had to turn my head because I had tears all of a sudden. (Why? I want to find how this bears on Pam.) There are large dumb spaces in the night. I can hear the snail leaving his wake, and the starlight sifting on the spider's web. Or so I imagine. If you listen hard enough you can hear the worms in the ground. (Robins can, I've read). The worm-shot earth. The earth with worms like priests or kings. They never build

anything do they? When I closed his pajama top I could feel
the heart move (they needn't worry about a libidinous old
man, I am withered there anyway). I can't describe his heartbeat (the little *clock* of him there) or the unshed tears, but it
was as vivid to my thumb as a fire or a wasp. Tomorrow see
about toy. I must visit Mrs. Bartonsen's garden soon since she
promised there would be a yellow crocus any day now.

April 5—I have not decided for the present to give. Mrs. Bartonsen remembered the time so many years ago when we went
to the village theater (Import. being Earnest? Candide?) and
had a chicken broth sent up to Moser's apartment. Remembered laughing at my peach suspenders. I apparently got very
mad. She said that I'd changed and that everyone thought of
me as being the most gentle person. Is this true? She had on
blue silk today and a beautiful cameo, but laughed and laughed
so long. Brownlee called with a cake Mrs. Brownlee baked for
me. Very sweet of her, and I shall dedicate a verse to them (to
her, I think).

April 5 afternoon—Woke up uncomfortably from my nap, as
sometimes you will when the moon is on your face and causing
bad dreams, and thought for an instant the tiny moths were going at my eyes like they go at flaxen cloth. I could almost feel
the white powder they leave. I decided to get a fireman climbing a spiral pole for the Marshall boy. I will have my eyes
checked again, since the exercises don't seem to help.

April 8   Sonnet in Praise of Life

My thumb reads death and history
In childish veins, and leaves of skin,
In darling shapes the heart-sick story
Of Swift's despair and Nero's sin.
And in a crimson, vivid throb
A burning Troy, a broken Lear,
For this I must be sure as Job
And mask with fortitude my tear,
That all the living go to graves
And May's proud galleon sinks in seas
Of Winter's white, and the flower stays
But breath's aching moment till it freeze;

Enscribe, O God, in blood my dying song:
That Gabriel break my sleep, cold, low and long.

Mrs. Bartonsen has that disorder or anarchy again in her eyes.
I think she will be ill. She continues to wear her blue silk dress
and her cameo, although the dress is soiled badly. The crocus
had come and was the brightest yellow. Like a cockcrow. A real
Easter flower. Wild, too, and quite satisfying. She told me her
mother and grandmother before had planted them, and that
they grew for a whole generation. She gave me one that was almost in bloom and I planted it in the W. window. By that
chronology Pam lived half-a-crocus if a generation is twenty
years. The Marshall boy really seems to love the fireman I gave
him. It makes a noise sliding up and down the spiral pole.
There is nothing more pitiful than the last years of an old vir-
gin like Mrs. Bartonsen because she leaves nothing in the world
when she passes away. Ever since Pam died I have felt a guilt
about being a father with no children. One doesn't have to be
much of a thinker to see that having children is the most fitting
condition for manhood, and I cannot help but think I have
failed a little. There is a ghost in my veins and sometimes my
bones ring like crystal when the children are calling and war-
ring in the evenings. I must remember to see about timetables
at the depot tomorrow.

April 12—All this winter the birds died from the trees and lay
in the rotting snow with sunlight on their beaks and feathers,
and I was reminded of omens. In the whirl of a fire I found the
sleeping face of my daughter and cried myself out of a dream.
The clock struck, the fire spat and hummed and sang like
Shakespeare's Ophelia, and I wept a little in my chair that such
a beautiful thing sprang from Adam's rib, and now lay one
black fathom in the earth, in a crown of worms and roots. I
must stop this. Got a ticket for Corinth for Wednesday. The
Ponds like me and we have gotten along (although with a bit
of a strain) since that time when he called me a finger-bowl
poet and I went outside and the crippled boy had to come to
fetch me.

April 17—I got up this morning feeling better than I have for
years although my eye is now so bad. The glass glittered all
down the street, and the shrubbery was hot and moist. Saw the

Marshall boy imitating the "galvanic fists and wishbone swag-
ger" (to quote Brownlee) of some Western star. The sun
pressed on the shining wavy roof and sparrows winked by. I
stood for a moment by the wall and heard the children over
the wall. Then by the walk I saw the fireman I gave the
Marshall boy twisted in the ground by my door where I think
he knew I would see it. I went back in and listened, have been
listening, to Mrs. Marshall singing all day below, and the
slams of the door when he comes in and out but I will not go
down to the yard where he can see me and laugh.

The diary ends at that. Alice whispered something from the
couch which seemed to be adrift, and then she was borne off by
nodding dolphins of sleep; the lightning delicately scorched
window-bar shadows here and there on the innocent wall. I put
my head down on the desk, and then seemed to wake immediately to a wash of Doric daylight from the window. Alice woke
simultaneously, blinked, got up swaying a little, rubbed her
temple, and said she was hungry.

We went downstairs, Dante and a drowsy Beatrice, and at
each landing the East was kindled to a rosier quickness until at
the bottom window Alice said that we had made the sun rise,
and combed her hair till it was full of lights. Freddy stood in his
room leaning like an anxious priest over the only other conscious person and pointing at him. People had either had too
much lotus or too much gin, and curled about the furniture in
cocoons.

"Welcome to Lethe," he greeted us, "I have some cheese I
don't want that you can eat." Alice nodded, combed her hair
again, and ate a piece of cheese from the table, "Did you read
his stuff? I thought it was funny as hell," he said. The boy in
the chair uptilted his ashen face and said, "Sic transit gloria
mundi. We're tired of your platitudes, Tarzan, and all the lim-
ber little old ladies in the world won't make any damn difference mumble mumble," and sank back, apparently graveward.
Freddy looked at him and then turned his Saracen face toward
us once more. "And wait, this is the grand finale. When Donovan went to Corinth to see his fossilized friends, he had a heart

attack. Mrs. Wolrath told me they said he kept saying, 'I'd like to water my flower if you please, if you just please,' over and over."

Freddy looked first at Alice, then at me, then at Alice. The hip pocket of his pants was tufted out like a cottontail.

We went out the front door, and I last softly parted the tightness in my throat to ask her if she understood how I felt about the spark that passed through some twilight ether into our first hearts from the asylum-eyed man who was dead. I told her, with proper understatement, holding her arm as in a ballet, that I had learned how grotesque I had been. If memory serves (an old gray muse with a pince-nez), I also told her that she had learned something too, about disaster. Dawn grew in the trees, a ghostly crown of gold light lifted on shining boles of midnight wood, a sparrow's lid opened, the ditchwater struck to fire, and a coughing woman opened and closed her painted door, carrying in the abandoned milk. Alice nodded, tears matting her lashes. She fumbled with a bracelet of colored beads and suddenly it turned into a spilled sunbeam and lost itself in the gemmed grass. "Damn it," said Alice, still crying softly to herself, rubbing the faint bas-relief of the bracelet on her wrist, "damn it anyway."

The Bandaged Man

BY HERBERT WILNER

AFTER a week Daniel was finally getting used to the smell of
carbolic and ether. At times he even waited for the odor, inhaling it deeply with mysterious pleasure. It reminded him of
how the leg, which no longer pained, had been so badly hurt.
Then the Italian, bandaged like a mummy, was put in the bed
next to him. The cops came in three shifts through the day and
night to sit at the foot of the Italian's bed. The hospital began
to smell again for Daniel like a place where people with sickness
inside of them came to have the limp, infested places looked
at, and to die.

He was certain something bad was happening again inside his
leg. The doctors didn't know because they never looked beneath the bandage anymore. During the night he would die. It
brought him shame, but he could not help thinking anyway
that his mother would not be there. He felt weakened with a
delicate sorrow, and, if he did not bite his lip against it, he knew
he could cry. Even biting his lip, he felt the welling of his
eyes. He blamed all of this on the Italian in the next bed, but
he did not know why. He turned his head to look at him again,
but a shaft of afternoon sun coming through the open window
cut through the aisle between the four beds of the alcove and
fell upon the chest of the cop. He was sitting on the chair read-

ing from a magazine. The light made the silver of his badge glitter, and Daniel lay still.

After a while he raised the blanket and sheet to look down. The bandage went from thigh to shin. The leg had been painted with iodine, and now the skin was peeling in small orange flakes. He pulled at one of the strips and it came loose. He rubbed it between his fingers, then let it fall on the bed. He started to think ahead to after supper, because Matty had said he would try to come again tonight and maybe bring Flip or Dox with him. It was a good hour when any of the fellows came. They always wanted to look at the leg, and they talked about how he had gotten hurt. It was better than his parents because his mother cried all the time and said she would never let him play ball again, and his father said he would have to stop running around with that gang of hoodlums. When they had to leave to let two of the fellows in, his father would shake his head and his mother would rub her eyes with the handkerchief. But the fellows talked of how they knew something was going to happen as soon as they saw Tyrus jumping to pile on, and Danny lying there with his knee already on the ground and the rest of the leg up in the air. They said they saw the leg twist and it would have broken off if Danny hadn't turned that little bit when Tyrus dove. He wanted to laugh when they said this, so he would turn his face away and smile and say he was not sore when they told him Tyrus was afraid to come and visit him. Then the fellows would stare about the ward and look like they wanted to leave and let someone else come in. The last time Flip did that, Daniel told him to look through the glass partition behind his bed. He watched Flip as he looked, then saw him pale and rear away.

"God! How do you stand it here?"

"Get used to it." He winced a little, as though with a new pain, and Flip turned away.

But tonight the fellows would see the cop first, and then they would look at the Italian and not see anything else. It was that way for the whole hospital as soon as they had brought the Italian down from the operating room last night and a cop followed after them and sat down in a chair before the bed. The patients tried always to look at him, and they were all talking of him this morning. Even the nurses, as they hurried by, turned their heads, and the doctors had stood at the foot of the bed after breakfast talking in whispers and sometimes nodding. When they came to Daniel's bed they only looked at the chart and then went away, some of them turning to glance at the Italian once more.

The man's whole head was bandaged. There was a narrow slot for the eyes to show, and two others, smaller, for the bottom of the nose and the mouth. But whenever, now, Daniel turned toward him, he would look only at the eyes, which had opened for the first time after lunch. They always stared straight ahead, somewhere into the cop sitting on the chair at the foot of the bed and reading from a magazine. It was the eyes that confused Daniel about the smells of the hospital, that made him feel as he followed their empty stare toward the cop that he would himself never get better any more, he would not get home. Sometimes the eyes would blink closed, not with sleep, but as though the Italian could not any longer hold the weight of them. Soon, they would open again to stare at the cop who never looked back at him. An hour ago, when the nurse had come to give Daniel his shot, and he moved to his right side, the eyes of the man turned on him, big, bulging, the pupils far in the corners because he had not moved his head at all. Daniel felt his face go warm, and he bit his lip and could not think of smiling as he always did when the nurse called the place she was going to put the needle in his hip. When he looked again, the eyes were staring past his bed toward the window beside it. Then they blinked and opened on the cop again.

That was the last time Daniel had looked at the Italian. Now he wanted to look once more. He thought he would close his eyes and turn his head on the pillow and then open his eyes again. In that way he would not see the cop. But he did not turn his head far enough, and when he opened his eyes, he saw only the man's hand. It was bandaged across the knuckles and there were brownish stains on the white gauze. The middle finger was bandaged too, and against the splint it looked like white decoration on a little box. All the other fingers showed, and the one next to the splint rubbed slowly against the gauze. Daniel watched the fingers move, then turned his head away, closing his eyes. The detached motion of the one finger teased him, like pulling at the skin of his own leg.

He wondered what the Italian's face was like. He wondered if it was like a face at all any more, and if he would recognize him because the cop had said he was from Van Sicklen, or if Dox would know him because his older brother had gone with Italians for a while, if Dox would know him just by the eyes and the part of the lip that showed beneath the small slit in the bandage. But the Italian might be as old as his father. The cop hadn't said anything about how old he was.

That morning, after the doctors had come and while the Italian had not yet opened his eyes, some of the patients who moved about the ward on wheel chairs and crutches had gathered around the cop, making him look up from his magazine. They tried to keep their voices low, but they talked all at once while they looked over their shoulders at the bandaged man. The two men in the beds opposite Daniel leaned forward to hear, and even the old one who had the thing that looked like scissors' handles stuck through the bandage around his stomach, even he tried talking to the cop. But when Daniel leaned forward, something in the knee pulled. He fell back against the pillow again, listening.

"What happened to that guy?"

"Who fixed him like that?"

"What you cops sittin' around watchin' him for? He ain't goin' nowhere."

"Go on! Get back to your beds. Excitement ain't good for sick people." The cop tried to read the magazine again. He was fat and his face was very red. Like blood, Daniel thought.

"Come on. Why can't you tell us?"

"What'd he do, get in a fight with somebody?"

"He walked into a bus." The cop looked up from the magazine and smiled. He looked like a clown, Daniel thought, with

the dark blue, almost black of his shirt, the silver badge, the
very red face, and the crooked teeth of his smile.

"Yeah, sure. And I broke this leg kicking statues. Come on,
tell us straight."

"He killed a cop, that's what he did. The sonofabitch!" He
brought the magazine down to his lap, then raised it again,
pointing it toward the bandaged man.

They all turned toward the bed. Daniel's chest heaved as he
stared at the bandaged head.

"Yeah. We picked him up at his old lady's house on Van
Sicklen. She was laying there in bed howling like a cat, and that
dumb bastard was trying to hide behind her bed with half his
ass sticking up. We could've blown it all the way into the next
street."

"That don't look like it was his ass you shot at."

"Yeah, what happened to his head?"

"He try to run away?"

"Yeah, that's the way it was. He tried to run away." He
looked down at the magazine again, then raised his eyes toward
the bed where the others were still staring. "The Wop bastard!"

"Hey, why you call him Wop all the time, Mick cop?"

"What'd you say?"

"I say don't call him Wop." It was the old man with the scissors in his stomach.

"I'll call him what I goddamn feel like calling him. Don't go
saying Mick to me just 'cause you're an old man sick in bed.
Now all of you, outa here, and let me read. I don't want to
catch nothin' from you."

"Say, this is a hospital. You aint no boss here."

"Go on, all of you, scram, 'fore I put the stick to your butt!"

Then the nurses came, and a doctor too, and they hurried everyone away. Daniel saw the doctor look long at the cop, but he
was already reading his magazine. He supposed another cop
would come at four to take his place. It was strange how careful
they were about a man who couldn't move. It made the eyes—
always peering now at the cop from the white and faceless

head—even more terrifying. Daniel knew that if the Italian died, the eyes would still be open. He imagined what the cops with their clubs must have done to the face. Underneath the bandage it was wet with blood, and the eyes stayed open and stared, afraid to close, afraid to become a part of the face and the leaking blood.

At four o'clock the other cop did come. He took the magazine from the blood-faced one, and they stood whispering for a minute while they looked toward the bed where the Italian stared back at them. Then the nurse came and hung another bottle from the pole at the side of the Italian's bed. It was after she left that Daniel heard him moan for the first time.

He tried, without looking, to listen to the sound. It was different from the other hospital cries. He listened for a long time and then knew the sounds had nothing to do with pain. They came from far away, as though, behind the bandages, the Italian remembered a word and was trying to say it now, but could only moan. Daniel thought he heard something like Mahyeea, or Mahmeeya, and then he knew it was Mamamia the Italian groaned, and he knew they all did that and it was their religion, but they could say it other times too—like Jesus or Christ—and it would not be religion.

He was afraid of the Italians and did not like them. They came down the Parkway in gangs, from Avenue and beyond, from Lake and Van Sicklen. They would start fights for little reasons, and only Dox had kept them once from jumping Whistle. They tried to say Whistle, with the strange voice he had, was making fun of them, but Dox spoke of their older brothers, and they went away. He heard the Italian moan again, a little louder now. He stopped thinking of the gangs. He wondered if the Italian was speaking the Mamamia, or really praying. He would turn his head again and see. But first he wanted to look quickly at the new cop to know if he too heard the moaning and watched.

But the cop, like the other one, was reading from the magazine, almost with his eyes closed. The badge was in the shade, and the light fell on the white gun handle and the black holster.

The holster hung loosely, almost on his thigh, so that it lay partly on the seat of the chair and pointed its barrel toward the window. Daniel stared at it. Slowly he realized that the bandaged Italian had killed a cop. He would go to the electric chair. He felt his skin dampen under the sheet, and he began to listen to the moaning. He turned his head instead to the window and wanted not to hear as he looked at the leaves that had turned with the late October, swirling here and there, on the pavement.

That night, during visiting hours, none of the fellows came, but his parents did. They looked in disbelief between the still-reading cop and the faceless, motionless, still-peering Italian, who had no visitors. They tried to ask Daniel questions, but he could not manage to tell the story clearly, though he knew he could have told it to the fellows. His father went finally to talk with the cop, and Daniel tried not to look there, or at his mother either, who kept glancing back at the Italian while she cried softly. His father came back to the bed and spoke in a hushed hospital whisper.

"He's a murderer. That man's a murderer."

"Sidney, please." She put her hand on the lapel of his jacket.

"I tell you he's a murderer. He killed a policeman yesterday. He's one of those Italian gangsters."

"Sh, Sidney."

"What do you mean, shush? A murderer is in the bed next to your son." Daniel turned his face away and bit his lip when his father pointed into the bed at him. He could not look at the man's thick, clean, unbandaged fingers.

"The leg hurts you, doesn't it, Daniel?" She moved closer to the bed, her lips pursed, her head moving slowly from side to side.

He nodded.

"Well, thank God for that anyway. No more ball."

"Listen, I talk one thing and you talk another. I don't want my son in bed next to a gangster, a murderer. I'll find the head nurse."

"Sidney!"

"Aw, Dad, for chrissake."

"Listen, he can have a gun under the pillow. There can be shooting in here." He leaned over Daniel's bed, whispering dramatically.

"The man is dying, Sidney."

"You know that? Who told you? The policeman said he's like a bull."

"Daniel, why are you crying? Does it hurt so much? Should we call the doctor?" She put her hand on his shoulder and was rubbing it, the fingers reaching to his neck.

"No." He turned his face toward the window.

Before they left his mother told him the doctor said he would go home soon. He said nothing, but he did not believe her. He did not try, before they put the lights out, to look again at the Italian. He was certain he had heard everything and was staring at him now from out of the bandages with those mournful eyes. When it got dark Daniel turned slowly toward him, but he could not see his eyes, saw only the blanket rise and fall, and the light color of the bandage. He could not hear the moaning any more. He saw the cop, sitting now on the other side of the Italian's bed, his chair tilted back against the edge of the partition. He was reading from the small light above him. Daniel tried again to look hard at the bandages, then, suddenly alarmed, thinking the Italian was staring back at him in the darkness, he let his head fall quickly on the pillow. He tried to think of school and all the work he would have to make up. He wondered when it would be that he could play ball again. He tried, in the darkness, looking up at the ceiling, to worry about it, but he couldn't for long. He woke during the night many times with the noises of the hospital. Each time he thought he might look at the Italian again, but he never dared.

The tinny rattling of the wash basins woke him in the morning. He saw immediately that another cop was back in the aisle at the foot of the bed, his eyes closed, his chin on his chest, the magazine in the hand that hung below the seat of his chair. The eyes of the Italian stared at the cop. He was moaning again. The Mamamia was very plain now.

They did not bring the Italian any food at breakfast, and after it the doctors came and stood at the side of his bed, nodding their heads and looking at the chart. The fat, blood-faced cop of yesterday who came after breakfast looked up from his magazine to watch them. The Italian stopped his moaning and his eyes went up to the ceiling. Then one of the doctors picked at a corner of the bandage below the eyes, and Daniel turned away. A stretcher-wagon came, and he heard them put the Italian on it. When he turned again he saw the cop get up to follow them, saying, "Well, I can't do nothing about orders." Only one of the doctors lingered at Daniel's bed for a moment. He looked at the chart, nodded, said "Fine," and went quickly after the others.

It was about an hour when he heard the stretcher again. The two orderlies got him into the bed while the one doctor watched. The cop sat down in his chair and said loudly, "What keeps the Wop alive?" and the doctor, without looking at the cop, said, "Hate, maybe," and Daniel tried to understand that, but it didn't seem to mean anything. As soon as they left, the Italian, looking now not at the cop but at the ceiling, started to moan again. The bandage was whiter, and Daniel knew they had taken the other off to do something to what was underneath. He wondered if the face hurt as much as his leg had when Tyrus had fallen on it, and if all the skin behind the bandage was the same color his knee had been when Flip had finally pulled away the elastic of the football pants—red-blue-purple, like fish scales. But he knew the Italian's was worse than that. It was open and hanging and the red was the color of beef. Some of the bones might even be showing. He wondered what they could do to fix bones broken in a face. If he had to look at it he would be sick, and he knew again he did not want to be a doctor any more. He knew that even before the Italian came, when he had sat up and turned around last week to look through the glass of the partition behind him. The head he saw through the glass was bald. On the top of it there was a big, perfect ring of brown crust. The skin inside the circle was as white as a plate, looking like a lid to the darker flesh outside.

But the Italian's face would be worse than that. He was glad
they had it bandaged, except that it made the eyes so strange.
They were still looking at the ceiling. He wondered how many
times they had looked at him since his father had shouted last
night. He heard him moan again, this time louder still, almost a
cry. Mamamia! Even the cop looked up once.

Daniel turned suddenly to the window. What if it was his
real mother the Italian was calling for?

He tried to look out the window, but he saw nothing, only
that it was light and the sun glared. He remembered what the
cop had said about the Italian's mother, how she lay on the bed
screaming. The old Italian women wore black and had soiled
gray hair and were short and fat. This was one like that, but sick
in bed, and he was calling for her.

He could see the old woman, but could not imagine the Italian belonging to her. He had only eyes and had killed a cop. If
the mother was very old, then he could be almost forty. But
Daniel could not imagine his own father calling to his grandmother like that. He decided the Italian was young, only ten
years older than himself maybe. He saw what must have been
the black, oily hair, the dark skin. Then the Italian groaned the
name loudly. Daniel had to turn and look. The eyes—the pupils
in the corners and the watery large whites against the white of
the bandage—stared back at him. Daniel made a little movement with his head, then opened his mouth almost to say something like hello. But thinking of the cop, he reddened, and closing his eyes, turned his head quickly away. He bit his lip hard
and winced, as though the Italian should know what was sick in
him pained too. He raised the bandage and looked down at the
thick bandage of his leg. It did pain very much. He even
moaned.

During the afternoon the Italian began to move his arm.
Once Daniel saw it raise to the bandage, the splinted finger
rubbing lightly for a second against the gauze where the ear
might be, then falling to the bed again. Daniel tried not to
think of it and to read the newspaper he had bought from the
man who came through the ward after lunch. But there was

nothing to interest him, and even in the sports section there
was nothing because it was the middle of the week and the colleges only practiced.

The moaning continued, and even now, having heard it for
so long, Daniel still could not bear it. He wished very much to
go home. He stared out the window. It was only a few feet
above the street, and looking out into the middle of it seemed
to make him almost level with the tops of the cars, as though he
were out there among them. He watched the cars pass, watched
along the bike path on the other side of the Parkway, watched
for the gangs of kids that sauntered by, watched the women sitting on benches, some with their hands on the gleaming bars of
the carriages. It seemed very lovely out there, like a colored
movie almost. He wondered how the cops, when they didn't
really have to, could sit on the old wooden chair reading from
the magazines in the middle of all that smell. The Italian
couldn't go anywhere.

That evening, during visiting hour, again none of the fellows
came, and his father did not either. His mother said he had to
work late, but Daniel thought she had not let him because he
would yell again, and he was glad. She cried a little but did not
say anything about his playing ball. Once, her hand resting on
his blanket groped for his, and he let her take it and press it
tightly. It was damp, but it made him feel good and very small
once more. The Italian had no visitors again. Daniel could see
him lying very still with his eyes open to the ceiling. He moaned
the one word softly.

The next morning the Italian moved his arm more freely. He
brought it up often to rub against the bandage. But he still
moaned. He moaned the single word many times, and Daniel,
having to turn once for the shot the nurse brought, could almost not bear to look or listen. He had decided it was his
mother the Italian called for—or if not called, at least named,
for the word was not so much a cry anymore as it was almost a
remark, like you would think long enough of a name and just
say it, but without the strength to not moan—and having decided that, that it was his mother alone the Italian could think

of now, Daniel was frightened. It made him feel sicker, made
him want more to be home, and this filled him with shame.

He felt at once a whelming of pity for the Mamamia the Italian called to. He could not understand why, but it made his
eyes feel moist and he wanted again to pick the peeling flakes
of skin on his bandaged leg. When he heard the nurse at the
side of the Italian's bed, he had to look again. She brought
something yellowish in a glass with a tube in it and tried to
make him drink. She held the glass below the bandaged head
and put the tube through the little opening where some of the
lip showed. But Daniel saw that none of it went down any
lower in the glass, and the nurse had to take it away. She had
not spoken a word. She had not even tried to look at him. But
the Italian had never looked at her either. His eyes, blinking
slowly, stared at the cop, and the cop, who had heard the nurse
come, stared back. He kept the collar of his shirt open, and the
redness of his face was on the neck too.

When the moaning stopped during the afternoon, Daniel believed the eyes of the Italian had left the cop and were staring
at him. He turned his head half way. He would look at the cop
and tell from him. But the cop's chin was on his chest and his
eyes were closed. Daniel turned his head all the way. The eyes
were on him. They met his. The whole bandaged head seemed
to have moved for the first time, turned toward Daniel. He had
to lower his eyes, but he was afraid to move his head. He felt
the Italian was waiting for him to say something, wanted him
to, and he did not dare try not to.

He groped suddenly for the paper. Leaning as far as he could
and with his arm out and his eyes almost closed, he tossed the
sheets to the Italian's bed, mumbling "Here," while he tried to
smile. He looked toward the cop, but his eyes were still closed,
his head still on his chest. He turned back toward the Italian,
his mouth still pulled weakly by the smile. The newspaper was
on the Italian's chest. He had not touched it. His eyes, white
and watery, were on Daniel.

"I thought maybe you wanted the sports."

He said the words feebly, not knowing why he said them, not

knowing why he had thrown the paper. One of its sheets slipped away, slid nearly to the Italian's hand near the edge of the bed. He raised his arm slightly, then let it drop. He raised it again, letting it fall once more. He kept the finger next to the splint pointed, poking with it into the mattress each time the arm came down. Daniel turned his head away and was going to stare out the window, but he heard the Italian make a small squawking noise in his throat, and he turned back. He was doing the same thing with his hand, poking the finger against the white sheet. Daniel looked at the bandaged hand. The eyes, the pupils in the corners beneath the fringes of gauze, were still on him. They were blinking slowly, then hard, staying closed for seconds. The hand came up, the elbow resting on the mattress. The Italian pointed a finger at him, then let the arm fall. He poked several times rapidly into the mattress. Daniel could not understand. He was going to speak again, but the words stopped in his throat. He turned his head away and looked out the window. He saw the afternoon light and, vaguely, the cars, the bikes, the women, and the carriages. He turned his head back again to the Italian. He stared at the place where the bandage lumped against the nose. He was moaning again the single word, softly, drawn out. The same finger—the nail white and bloodless—pressed itself, extended, against the mattress, raising the hand above it by the length of the fingers. Trembling, Daniel turned away, trying not to see the cop. He bit into his lip hard. He needed desperately to go home.

The Italian wanted to change beds with him.

He knew it all at once. The Italian wanted to go home to where there was the old fat woman with the soiled gray hair, sick in her black dress on the bed. He wanted to die there. He would get into Daniel's bed and wait until the cop napped and then get out the window to the street and make his way down the Parkway. He wanted Daniel to make up a story for the nurse so she would wheel the beds around. She had done it once before for the man with the moustache who was always getting tests for the pains they could not find and who did not want to be near a window and look outside. They had put the

old man with the scissors in his bed. Daniel would have to tell
the nurse he was cold near the window, or he couldn't sleep at
night because of the car lights, or the sun in the morning got
into his eyes and woke him too soon. That's why the Italian had
been watching him, testing him, and knowing now that Daniel
could make many stories for the nurse if he wanted to, and he
wondered what about him made the Italian know that. But he
was afraid, anyway, even to look up. The cop had seen.

He raised the blanket and looked at his leg. His hip pained
from not being able to turn over. He hooked his good foot beneath the ankle of his bandaged leg and moved it. But it did
not change the position of the hip, and he was sad for the pain
there. He wondered when he would get home and how he would
walk on the crutches and if the leg would get better by the time
basketball started. He imagined what he would do at home before he went back to school, but his mother came always into
the little dreams. He looked out the window again, but he
could not remember with each new moment what he had seen.
Then, as though from far away, at his side, faintly, he heard the
clicking of the glass and metal. He lay perfectly still, his hands
tightened about the blanket. The nurse had come to fix the
blood at the Italian's bed. He could call to her now and make
up his story. He knew the Italian was watching him.

The blanket was wet under his fingers. He turned his head
slowly. The cop, the magazine in his hand, his fingers on the
corner of a page, was staring at him too. Daniel lowered his eyes
and rubbed tenderly with his hand on the blanket across the
width of bandage beneath. The old man with the scissors called
loudly to the nurse for the pan. Daniel heard her walk away, but
she would be back and then once more to take away the pan.
He could not look toward the window any more. He closed his
eyes, hoping the Italian would think he was asleep. He imagined the Italian, who had killed a cop, pretending sleep near
the window during the night and sitting up suddenly, crawling
to it, rolling over the sill and then out. He would stay close to
the building under the wide stone ledge so that the cop, if he
heard, could not shoot. He would be strong enough to get all

the way home, walking through the dark streets with his eyes
peering out from his bandaged head, walking with his hands
pressed against his stomach, leaking the trail of blood from one
block to the next, the white bandage getting red and wet with
it, walking in the cold night in the gray pajamas of the hospital,
walking all the way to where the old Mamamia waited. When
the cops came for him he would be in the bed with her, holding
her hand, and dead. There would be blood on the white sheet.
The cops would come back to the hospital and sit by Daniel's
bed.

He heard the nurse at the old man's bed and opened his eyes.
She was holding him by the back and getting the pan under
without looking at him. Daniel turned his head slowly toward
the cop and saw him reading the magazine. Quickly, without
thinking, he looked toward the Italian. The eyes looked back at
him and he thought he saw the bit of lip move. He heard the
nurse begin to walk, and he looked away from the Italian toward
her. She looked back at him and smiled and his mouth opened.
But she kept on walking and no words came.

He'd almost said it. He would when she came back for the
pan. He would not look at the cop. He did not turn back to the
Italian, but he nodded his head slowly, knowing the other was
watching and would understand. He closed his eyes and
waited.

He tried to count, but he lost track. He thought of what the
fellows would say when he told them what he had done and
they read of it in the papers. But then he knew he would not
tell them. He saw himself going to school on the crutches and
everyone stopping him to see the scar. He saw himself after
school practicing running on the bike path to build up the leg
again. He would walk with a limp for a long time, and the girls
Dox had started to go with would ask about him. His mother
would try to keep him from playing ball and there would be arguments and he would be angry with her for a long time. He
thought of many things and they started to get mixed and he
felt himself very tired. He saw his father many times reading his
paper in the living room after supper, the page stretched be-

tween his thick, clean fingers. He saw the cop going from class
to class with him in school, always sitting in the seat behind
him so that Flip had to stand in Biology. The cop was too fat
for the seat, and he made noises as he squirmed.

He heard the nurse take the pan away and he heard himself
telling her, but he could not open his eyes, he was that tired,
and faintly, as from far away, he heard the Italian moaning, but
he could not hear the word, it was that far away.

When his parents came during visiting hour they laughed
and said foolish things and told him he could go home tomorrow morning. He knew he was not well enough and again he
did not believe them. He told them he wanted to go home that
night. His mother said the hospital did not like anyone to leave
at night and it would only be a few more hours. He took his
mother's hand and said again he wanted to go that night, and
his father said what would be the difference? and his mother
said there must be a reason, and they stood looking at each
other and Daniel said he did not want to be next to the Wop
anymore. His father said See! See! and left to find the doctor. He
came back smiling, the bundle of Daniel's clothes in his arms.

He had to stay in bed the first three days. All the fellows kept
coming up after school, and Tyrus came finally and said he was
sorry and Daniel laughed. He was glad Matty was there when
the family doctor came to take out the stitches because Matty
bragged always about his bad knee and made it crack whenever
he wanted to. They counted the stitches together and there
were twenty-four. The doctor, smiling, holding the scissors up,
said it would be another day in bed for each stitch and they
laughed and went on counting. Then he was on the crutches,
doing tricks soon, pushing down with his arms to keep the rubber
caps in the carpet and swinging through, laughing when his
mother yelled.

The day before he had to go back to the hospital, terror
seized him.

His leg hurt again all day and he knew the doctor, when he
touched it, would feel something they had left in the knee, and
he would have to stay in the hospital again, in the same bed.

His mother annoyed him, hurrying in and out of the room all day, saying once how tired she had gotten taking care of him. But she put her handkerchief to her eyes when she saw him take the crutches to go to the bathroom. It infuriated Daniel now to see her cry over him, and he almost shouted at her. Matty came up after supper and Daniel kept him there a long time talking of the football season.

He had an argument with his mother the next day because he did not want her to go to the hospital with him. She yelled, but he said he would not go if she came. He let her walk beside him down the stairs, but he insisted he could manage and would not let her touch him. She gave him the two dollars and watched with him in the street until he got into the cab. He laid the crutches on the floor and sat in the corner with his leg straight out, the heel on the folded chair in front. He could not easily turn his head that way, and he saw only dimly the things they passed on the Parkway.

In the hospital he felt sick with the smell of the carbolic and ether. The nurse put her hand on his shoulder and said how fine he looked and asked him how he felt and he said he guessed he was OK. He sat on the bed and she said he would have to get ready for the doctor and she turned and moved her hands about the table with jars. She came back and began to cut at the bandage, a small one where the wound had not closed. She kept a hand on his thigh, and he felt ashamed. He thought he should say something so that she wouldn't know.

"How is the Italian?"

"Which one?"

"The bandaged man."

"Oh, we lost him."

"Lost him? He got a . . ." He could not say the word.

The nurse went to the jars again, dipping a gauze pad in one of them. He was not even thinking of whether it would sting. When she came back she did not say anything else.

The doctor told him the knee was fine and that he did not need the bandage any more and should begin to exercise right away. But Daniel could scarcely hear and he did not once look at the leg when the doctor rubbed his fingers on the knee. He did not want to take a cab home and decided he would use the McDonald Avenue car. He would pass Matty's house before his own and they could talk. He would stay in the candy store until Matty got home from school. His mother would worry and there would be an argument when he got home, but he did not care. The crutches, as he walked, coming down against the dry and fallen leaves, made them rattle loudly. Here and there, he knew, a woman turned to watch him. He grew tired as he made his way across the five blocks to the streetcar. He had to breathe deeply of the air, but the smell of the hospital still lingered.

Mr. Princeton

BY MARVIN SCHILLER

IT snowed the whole night before Naftoli Gold took the train to Princeton University. In the morning, the sun dazzled everywhere. Walking up the Brooklyn street Nafty was acutely aware of the fresh snow. He had taken it as a marvelous sign: it symbolized the eradication of all that was uneven in his past, not up to par. The sidewalks, transformed to coconut frosting, all smooth and white, untrammeled, stretching purely before him, portended a day that was to be marked by accomplishment, by recognition, reward for his many talents.

He batted together his gloved hands, thrilled. Within one of the gloves was hidden a ten-dollar bill, folded as small as a three-cent stamp, that his father had given him to cover expenses. His father was still doubtful about the expedition and had given in only after the insistence of his brother, Nafty's uncle, the pediatrician.

On the corner, in front of the synagogue of which Naftoli's father and grandfather were lifetime members, the *shamus* was shoveling snow, clearing a path for sunrise worshipers. The shovel, scraping the hidden sidewalk, made a hollow sound in the clear air. Noticing Naftoli, the *shamus* stopped his work and looked up, astonished.

"*Sholom*," he greeted in disbelief. "*Sholom aleichem*, Naftila.*"

At seventeen, athletic, mature from tip to toe, Nafty did not relish being accosted in the diminutive. He answered hurriedly, "*Sholom, sholom* already."

"So don't tell me you're coming to services?" said the *shamus*. He leaned on his long-handled shovel. Behind him the synagogue with its great blue dome and its thin, stained-glass windows rose from the snow with Byzantine solidity.

"Such clothes!" and "My, my," continued the *shamus*, now scrutinizing the boy, in a motherly way picking at his clothes for an inspection of tidiness. "What is—second *bar mitzvah*, something?"

Nafty brushed an invisible flake of snow from his coat lapel. "You like it?" He was pleased to have found approval.

The coat was a powder blue: $18.50 at Crawfords, Pitkin Avenue. An A.F. type, so called because it left one's bottom exposed to the Brownsville breeze. He was hatless, but his hair was cast carefully into a stiff and prominent pompadour, arrived at by employing half a jar of green "Surcurl" wave-set and an aluminum wave-clip (secretly) the night before. And he smelled desperately of Aqua Velva—his father's—the advantage of rising before the old man. And he had used his father's electric razor on the fluff beneath his nose, unafraid of waking the man; after all, this morning he had the excuse.

Now, he rubbed his nose that twitched in the cold: two thousand years to shape that projection, that teapot's spout (he accepted his fate with jocularity. He could always be a night-club comic, a Jimmy Durante, a Danny Kaye. Already the girls who thought his family was richer than most were telling him, "You got a terrific sense humor, Nafty.")

"Hey," he said to the *shamus*, suddenly inspired. "Will you say a little prayer for me today? What do you say? Something to bring me luck?"

The old man returned to his shoveling. "What's the matter? You can't say your own prayers? Yeshiva boy like you?"

Nafty blushed and knew a moment of shame—for it was true. He had been educated in a Yeshiva, had led himself, his family, and friends to believe he was going to become a big rabbi.

"You don't understand," Nafty said. "I'm going to college today."

The old man screwed up his face doubtfully. "You?"

"For an interview. You know. Big. Big time."

The old man, nodding, was obviously impressed. He tucked the shovel's handle under his chin. With an air of divinity he asked, "N.Y.U.?"

"Naah. An out-of-town college. Princeton!"

"Princeton!? For *goys?*"

Nafty knew a shock of anxiety. He tried to explain that it was different these days, 1947. "It's a new policy. They're liberal now, very liberal. You know, Finkel, because of the war. My uncle, the doctor, he knows the dean."

"That's very nice."

"My uncle says I got a good chance to get in. I got good grades, and I'm a swimmer." And as if he didn't think the man understood, Nafty started to make a swimmer's motions—his arms flaying the morning air rapidly, his head tucked neatly into his shoulders.

When the demonstration ended the old *shamus* bent once again to his shoveling. "I hope you get what you wish."

"But say a little prayer, a little *brucha* for me, huh? It'll make me feel more confident, no kidding."

Gently, the *shamus* lifted a shovel full of snow. He carried it to the hedge and dumped it. He paused to examine the narrow walk he had created as if he no longer was aware of Nafty. Then he spoke, full of wisdom. "Believe me, Nafty, believe me, if I knew a *brucha* I could say for Princeton I would say it for you. For City College, maybe; but for Princeton—this *brucha* you know better than me."

"Ah—"

The train ride to Princeton seemed without end. In his seat, huddled up in his blue coat, as he stared out at the snow-covered province of New Jersey, as he neared his destination, he grew unsettled. He was a sailor coming into port, a Daniel awaiting the first roar. He girded himself, because more than anything he could imagine, Nafty Gold wished to be admitted

to Princeton. Not so much Princeton *per se*; it could be Cornell
or Yale, even the University of Michigan at Ann Arbor—any
institution with the ability of lending him an air of unique and
desirable belonging. But Princeton especially. Princeton, what a
tradition! A name that fell musically from the lips and produced a nod of respect from one's listeners. Princeton . . .
Prince-ton, in time to the wheels over the rails: Woodrow Wil-
son, Princeton; Nafty Gold, Princeton. . . .

He tried to make the rattling wheels lullaby away his trepida-
tion but he was unsuccessful. The closer the train bore him to
his destination the more fearful he grew. In his heart of hearts
he knew he was not the master of interviews. He would either
talk too much or too little. Or else he would sit down and his fly
would yawn open cavernously. He would take out a pen to sign
a document and the pen would leak all over his fingers. The
train hurtled on. He grew unsure of his shirt—were all the buttons there? His tie, his suit, his shoes? Was there a hole in his
socks? Even his not-so-bad looks began to bother him: his
nose—it had figured in so many touchy scenes that he dreamed
about it. Once, his nostrils had been made of two overturned
red flowerpots with weeds growing out of them, downward,
drily, darkly. Another time he had walked into a cave at a
mountainside only to discover he was hiking up his own nose.
He stood now in a sweat and went rocking down the aisle. He
asked the conductor how long the ride would be, and being told
it would not be very long at all he considered journeying with
the train to Philadelphia, instead. But he pasted himself down
in his seat—the wrong seat, but he was too confused to notice
it—and he watched the telegraph poles being plucked like black
feathers from the soft down of the snowy trackside.

An hour later the train halted, panting, its white breath
columning upward against the ultramarine sky. The station was
not one of those bright toy stations with a yellow roof but was
run-down, its dark timbers even darker against the blinding field
of snow surrounding it. The campiness of the station had a
soothing effect on the explorer. But it passed, that moment of
easement, as even a lozenge passes, dissolves. Nafty Gold be-

came aware of his aloneness. What Gold had ever traveled this far afield? Even his uncle had been city bred, city schooled. Had his uncle been correct in pressing this interview on him? The train left him, his last link with the past, and Nafty looked around—not at all sure that this was the promised land. Above the platform roof, on the other side of the station, he made out the tops of the university buildings, shining like the tops of saltcellars in the distance, all silver. How did he get there? Was there a bus? Looking around, he noticed for the first time, on the opposite platform, four young men waiting for a train to New York. They stood huddled together; one was wearing a long orange and black Princeton scarf; and from time to time their voices rose in the clear air. Nafty was awed to realize that these were Princeton men. He had never been so close. . . .

"Why don't we just whip down in my Dad's Buick?" Nafty Gold overheard.

One of the young men leaped down onto the snow-cushioned rail bed and stared down the empty, glinting trainscape. He pulled the fur collar of his stormcoat around his ears, and yelled back to the coevals, "The goddam train must've busted down!" He kneeled down in the snow, immersed his pink, melony hands into it and shaped a snowball. Standing, he eased it into the air so that it landed with a dead thud on the platform roof just over Nafty Gold's head, making the boy start, as out of reverie.

"Sorry, Dad," the Princeton man called out, and Nafty, still awed, blushed, speechless, and watched the man hop back onto the platform to rejoin his dark, shivering Sanhedrin. One young man, the fellow with the scarf, kept repeating, "Why don't we just whip down in my Dad's Buick?"

"I keep telling you my girl's expecting me at the station," said the boy who had been on the tracks.

"Send her a telegram, ass."

"How can I send her a telegram? Her whole family is turning out for this cocktail party at the Vanderbilt."

How envious Naftoli Gold was of them! How desirable to

partake in that conversation! But how impossible! What mad-
ness! Buicks—cocktail parties—telegrams, even, were beyond
his manner of life. What was he doing there?

"Hey, did you lose something?"

He was aware of a voice addressing him. Focusing on the
boys again, he saw that a skinny fellow was now standing on the
edge of the platform, just across from him.

"You lost, or what?"

He couldn't find his voice. He wanted to burrow a hole in the
snow and, rabbitlike, disappear from the face of the earth.
What could he do?

"Can you tell me the way to the Admissions Office?" he finally squeaked across the tracks.

"Sure thing." And the skinny fellow relayed a series of careful
instructions that Nafty clicked into his mind with successive
inane noddings of his head.

"Cut through the athletic field," said the Princeton man.

There was something in the clarity of the fellow's voice that
made Nafty feel like a visitor to a foreign city. He was thankful
for the instructions, yet at the same time, he wished to move
away—as if it were becoming too immediately apparent that
there was something too vitally different between himself and
the boys on the other platform. Sheepishly, he thanked the fellow and trudged away.

"A tux," he heard a voice fading behind him. "She was wearing my goddam tuxedo when I walked into the bedroom. This
forty-dollar negligee I bought her was on the chair, and she was
in bed wearing my goddam tuxedo!"

Nafty's ears burned; his head burned. Was it possible that
this life could be his? Was an interview all that stood in his
way? He had begun to run and his shoes made mouths in the
snow.

He came to the main street of the town and slowed down.
He walked for several blocks amid housewives out on shopping
skirmishes with their children. Young college men were carrying
books, walking in the gutters where the snow was packed down
firmer; older persons who might or might not be professors were

getting in and out of station wagons. He felt strange to the
small town, as a decent crusader must have felt strange in passing through those distant cities. But it was attractive to Naftoli.
It was what he wanted, this small-college-town life. He prayed
that the interview would go well. His uncle had said it was the
most important step in the Princeton procedure.

He came to those gray fortresses of buildings from which
knights and monks and courtesans might properly have
emerged, on horseback, muleback, or in some gay cabriolet
rocking through the snow. Somewhere a carillon had begun to
ring. Was it to announce the triumphant appearance of Naftoli
Gold? He glanced at his Ingersoll watch and saw that he had to
hurry to be on time for his interview. Gothic archways yawned
open for him, effigies winked, windows glittering in the scintil-
lating sun were giggling in feminine conversation concerning
the search for the admissions office by young Knight Nafty, Sir
Gold. An oak door, broad and high as an ocean-going raft
caught his eye, it was his port; he was terrified, but he forced
himself to turn its handle. Within, a gray-haired lady, a
Grandma Moses so placed as to put the most nervous of would-
be Princetonians at their ease, greeted Nafty, took his coat and
told him he was just on time. He stammered and his knees
quaked, yet such was his passion to be admitted that he forced a
degree of quietness upon himself. He pointed out to the terrible
molochs in his brain that he was actually *there*, at Princeton,
that he had been, in all certainty, granted an interview, that
certainly he must have a good chance—or else why had they
sent for him?

"Mr. Gold?"

The door to the dean's office had opened, and some dark
shadowy bookcase had materialized in silhouette against the
room's far windows. Nafty stood and watched the bookcase
slowly evolve into flesh and blood, a man in a dark suit with a
vest and a trickle of gold across it, a short man with dark red
hair, a thick red mustache, a corpulent face as soft looking as a
ripe cantaloupe, with eyebrows and eyes as pale as a cantaloupe's seeds, the kind of man who would never step out into

the bright sun if he could avoid it, who spent his vacations in the deep shade of a mountain cottage. He held an index card in his hand and he was smiling like a crescent moon. "How are you, Mr. Gold?"

He extended a pudgy hand and Nafty took it weakly, mumbling something inarticulate. He had begun to shake again.

The dean ushered the boy into his office, shut the door behind them, and introduced Nafty to a chair that was to be his womb for the next twenty minutes. The boy accepted it, alert as a traffic cop now as the adrenalin began to pump through his veins. The dean sat behind an impressive desk littered with papers, and he faced Nafty squarely. The boy did not flinch. On the wall behind the dean was a painting of a man in academic robes. Built up of blacks, browns, and deep reds it gave a solemn air to the room. Nafty glanced at the other walls. They were paneled in a design that suggested hidden cubbyholes, and framed here and there were further paintings of ruddy men, some with circular gold-framed eyeglasses refining their academic eyes. On the desk was a photograph of a woman, encased in a large leather frame. Two lesser frames, of silver, displayed devil-may-care poses of a boy and a girl. Through the two windows on either side of the wall behind the desk a portion of the campus was visible, a field covered democratically by snow.

"Did you get a chance to look around at all?" the dean asked.

Nafty had to shake his head a number of times before the words fell free. "No, sir, not too much."

"You'll want to walk around. The PSO conducts a tour some time around noon. Miss Rampaw will tell you about it at the desk out front."

Nafty nodded stupidly. What was the PSO? Was he supposed to know? "I guess I would have looked myself," he began hesitantly, "only my train just got here about ten minutes ago."

"I guess we routed you out of Brooklyn pretty early this morning."

Nafty nodded. The word "Brooklyn" hung with a foreign, crisp tang in the air. It was not like the name of his home town at all. He was beginning to feel vaguely queer. The very luxury of the room—he had dreamed about having a room with paneling—seemed unreal to him. From out of doors he heard the muffled shouts of two young men at play. He saw them far away, but could not make out their game, dark specks against the blue snow, nothing more.

"How do you like getting up with the dawn on a morning like this?" the dean was saying.

"We're usually up pretty early anyway."

"I'm the kind of fellow who's tempted to hide under the covers till noon in this weather. . . ." He bent forward to straighten the silver frames on his desk. "But these kids of mine begin to tear the roof down about 6:30, regardless of the weather."

Nafty bowed his head, understanding, but embarrassed by the dean's friendliness. In his own circle, a man was always cagey on the first meeting. Maybe this interview is to find out how friendly I am, he thought. Maybe you're just supposed to be very friendly. And the idea of friendliness became immovably locked in his mind.

"Family life, though," the dean observed. "Side effect of being a father, don't you think?"

"My father is pretty strict about getting up early. Whenever he catches me lolling around after a quarter to seven he says, 'Good morning, Mr. Morgenthau, and how much is in the treasury this morning?' "

Dean MacIntosh chuckled.

"I've got five brothers," Nafty said, brimming over with openness, his eyes gleaming with friendship. "Three of my brothers are in service. The other two are in the business."

"The business?"

"My father's business. He has a wurst-casing factory in Long Island City. That's just outside New York. He wants me to study business so I can step in."

"Into wurst casing?"

"The stuff that holds the hot dogs together. We sell to everybody. Hygrade. Nathan's in Coney Island, all of them."

The dean was smiling, his teeth showing like a young girl's fine milk teeth. He looked cherubic, if you could imagine a cherub with a thick mustache.

"I guess it's not the average business," said Nafty.

"No, it isn't, but oddly enough it reminds me of a story I once heard. Let's see. . . ." The dean tapped his forehead as if he could cause to tumble into place the fragments of that old story. He smiled. "I think you'll enjoy this. It was in England, oh, about 1913, '14—they weren't in the war at the time, that's it. They were still shipping food to Germany. Among other things, wurst. Millions of sausages. They entered the war, of course, but still some manufacturers continued to export the sausages. Then one day a German Zeppelin was shot down just outside of London, and I'll give you five guesses what its skin was composed of."

"Wurst casing?"

"Right."

"That's pretty clever."

"The manufacturers were old German families. In cahoots with the German government. They were sent to prison."

"I'll have to tell that to my father."

Again the cherubic smile; then an awkward silence. Nafty waited. It was like an examination in school. You waited to see the questions written out on the blackboard and you prayed to God you knew the answers. The dean was riffling through some papers on his desk. Nafty's gaze wandered to the windows again. He was warm. He heard the shouts come, muffled, through the windows, and he could now see two boys, up to their calves in snow, ridiculously practicing lacrosse. His head swarmed with the mere fact that he was at Princeton.

"I see you've been pretty active as a journalist."

Nafty caught something different, something of a less expansive nature in the dean's voice. Was he just imagining it?

"You really enjoy writing quite a bit, don't you?" The dean looked up studiously from the report.

Yes, there *was* something different. The joking voice had become a serious voice, the falsetto was now a basso profundo.

"All forms of writing?"

"Ever since I was a kid I've been writing," Nafty blurted. He felt that he was about to get tangled up in the soft web of his own honesty and friendliness. Friendliness. He couldn't shift into another gear the way the dean did. He could hardly find the clutch. "Writing, I mean, for instance, it goes back a long time."

"I'd like to hear about it," the dean said quietly.

"It goes back to an English class I had in elementary school, around the 4A. I wrote a Mother's Day poem. It was part of a class assignment, but it was a strange thing for me to be doing because my mother had passed away the year before. I wrote it because I didn't want anyone to know I didn't have a mother. It was all about my heart being gay on this merry day; and the teacher thought it was pretty good. I had a feeling for poetry, she said, and my mother was sure to love it. 'Thank you,' I said. 'I hope so.' During drawing class we prepared cards, and inserted the poems inside them. I remember drawing three tulips on my card; or maybe we were all assigned tulips. Then we were supposed to present them to our mothers. . . ."

"That could make a touching little story. . . ."

"When I got home I didn't know what to do with the card. I think I must have cried a little. Then I hid it in my commode, under a stack of underwear. Every week I hid it under something else. I didn't want anyone to find it. It's funny, I always used to imagine my aunts snooping through my things. Not my father or brothers, but my aunts. I used to think they were trying to find out what I was like, because in those years I was very solemn. That's pretty stupid, isn't it?"

"No, it isn't stupid at all, Naftoli—"

Of course it was stupid! How did he get started on all of that?

"Naftoli—is that how you pronounce your name?"

He nodded, a quick little rabbinical nod.

"Naftoli, tell me a little more about yourself. What do you like to read?"

"Oh, I read quite a few things. I browse a lot. That's funny

too. Some months I'll pick up a hundred books and not finish
more than four or five of them. I become bored very quickly.
Magazines. I read a good many of those. *Look, Life, Reader's
Digest, Model Airplane News,* back copies of *American Mer-
cury* we have around the house, my next brother's *New Yorker,
Writer's Digest.* This is crazy. You know what I do sometimes?
I'll pick up the classified section of a newspaper and start to
read it. Right from the beginning. I mean, I don't even have
enough money to buy a war bond but I'll read all the Mer-
chandise for Sale columns. I'm not in business, but I read the
Buyers' Wants. I read the Situations Wanted, the Commercial
Notices, the Personals. Did you ever read the Personals?"

". . . ."

"I read the personals every day. It fascinates me. 'John Jones,
no longer responsible for the debts of his wife.' Or, 'S.S., please
come home. The family and Myra forgive you.' Jeezus, did you
ever wonder about those people? I mean, what's going on in
their lives?"

A buzzer sounded on the dean's desk before he could reply.
For Nafty, it was the breaking of a spell. He was left stranded
with his unanswered question, like the man taking a high dive
on a motion picture screen, when the projector breaks down and
he's left glued in place while the machine whirs incredibly fast
behind you. Nafty's heart was beating, and he tried not to
listen when the dean spoke into the phone and said he would be
out in a few minutes. Nafty tried not to hear that fatal whir.

To realize that just a small chunk of time had been set aside
for him, and that it was coming to a close—it was a death! He
was in agony. And the dean remained so unperturbed!

"It's a very difficult decision, isn't it?" MacIntosh said softly.
"Deciding what college to attend."

If it were only a matter of decision!

"I remember my father pressing me to go to Amherst because
it was *his* school."

I don't have that problem, Nafty thought, I'm lucky.

"What I mean to say, Naftoli, is that you ought to be pretty
darn clear in your mind as to what a school can offer you.

You've got a good record. Stand by it. Get in as many interviews as you can. If you select Princeton, base your selection on a particular reason. If you've got a question about curriculum, that's what I'm here for."

"I just—"

"Yes?"

"I don't think I could have a particular reason. I just feel that I want to get in. Be here. Princeton. It means something just as it is."

"Suppose we can't accept you, Naftoli? What then?"

Ugly, fantastic pictures flashed through Nafty's mind: he was a vulgar night-club comic; a pin boy in a sleezy bowling alley, a lifetime of lifting leaden pins; he was pushing dress wagons, lost in a maze that resembled streets in the garment district. He flushed, feeling a moment of anger against MacIntosh, feeling the man had tricked him, cheated him out of his secret yearnings. His voice tightened. "Do I have any chance at all of getting in?"

"I'll put it on the line, Naftoli. We're in an unhappy position at Princeton. We don't like it—I don't think anybody does. But it's going to be this way for a few years. Because of the war. GIs and so on. We've got more outstanding applications than we know what to do with. It shames me to tell you how many fellows we can accept out of every three hundred that apply."

"How many?" snapped Nafty. "Fifty?"

"Eight, Mr. Gold."

"Eight—?" Mr. Gold was hushed. And so sincerely had the dean spoken that Nafty's soul filled with remorse not only for himself but for the 291 others who would never see the light of a Princeton morning. What chance did he have, a nut like him from Brooklyn?

"In a few days I'm going to send you an application form. I don't want you to get overexcited when you see it. It doesn't mean acceptance."

Nafty nodded sadly.

"I want you to fill it out. Take your time with it. I know you can do a bang-up job on it. Tell us what you plan to do with yourself."

The earlier feeling of unreality overwhelmed the boy again. He hardly heard what the man was saying. At first he did not see the dean rise and extend his hand, and when Nafty rose he felt clumsy.

"I'm glad you got here for the interview, Naftoli."

The adventurer nodded weakly, and when he saw the dean open the door he welcomed it, his escape, his release from bondage.

"How is your uncle? I haven't seen him since the cruise we took to Bermuda before the war. How is his practice?"

"Fine, Mr. MacIntosh. He's fine."

"Good. Glad to hear it."

"He sends his regards to you." The words fell by rote.

"Give him my best," and "Good luck to you," and the door closed, he was in the outer office, the interview was ended, and he wanted to scream in anguish. It had come to nothing! No signing on the dotted line, nothing!

A secretary he had not seen before wavered into focus in front of him, holding a sheet of paper in one hand.

"If you'll just fill out this information sheet for us, Mr. Gold."

For a moment Mr. Gold looked at the paper in her hand, confused.

"It's just your name and address and so on."

Nafty shook his head.

"You could mail it in, if you'd rather. The dean—"

"I told him everything already!" he cried out, his voice rising uncontrollably. He stopped himself, for again MacIntosh was framed like a bookcase in the doorway. And Nafty felt annihilated. For the first time he noticed another young man in the room. The dean looked away from Nafty, and read from an index card held between his delicate fingers. "Larry?"—as if he were embarrassed that his greeting should be overheard by Mr. Gold. Sheepishly, Mr. Gold watched the applicant march into the dean's office. The dean did not turn to him again; and Nafty walked out without taking the paper from the secretary.

What was the sense? he kept asking himself as he walked through the snow of the campus. All bottled up with nervous energy, Nafty could not bring himself to go back to the train station. He walked past the university buildings, lost in its quadrangles. What the hell had been the sense of trying in the first place?

He came to the athletic field, a tundra of snow, barren except for a clump here and there of willowy, sickly trees, looking as brittle as rust. Low gray buildings seemed lonely and sad in the middle of the field. Then he heard shouting, and he saw them come out from behind the trees. "Hey, hey!" he heard, and, "Hey, hey, chuck it, boy. Chuck, chuck." Two young men, identically dressed in sweat pants and dark turtle-neck sweaters. A small ball was flying through the air between them. They stood a hundred feet apart now, practicing lacrosse, stamping on the snow to keep warm, swinging their bats fancily, yelling encouragement to one another.

Sullenly, Nafty approached them. He leaned against a winter-bare elm, and from a distance, he watched.

Between flings, one of the boys turned to Nafty and cried out, "What do you say, kid? What do you say?"

The kid said nothing. Even the sports were foreign to him. This strange game, with a bat like a snowshoe. Where did one get the knowledge of lacrosse? Where was it taught? In what back yard was it played? As he walked away he tried to convince himself that at the beginning these boys had probably been as unknowing as himself. There was the reason for coming to Princeton. To learn lacrosse. This was the place it was taught. And with practice he could be as they were. Lacrosse. Train rides to New York. Parties at the Vanderbilt. In later life, pleasure cruises to Bermuda. But even as he thought it, he knew he would never fill out Dean MacIntosh's application form.

He had walked back to the main street of the town. As if in a reverie he stopped to peer into the window of a haberdashery store. He did not want to go home. He stared hard into the window.

Inside, a salesman caught his attention, pointed to a striped bow tie that was featured in the display, as though to ask Nafty's opinion of it. Orange and black, the school colors of

Princeton. The salesman smiled, and Nafty, hardly aware of what he was doing, walked into the overheated shop.

"Did you like that tie?" the salesman asked.

"How much is it?" said Nafty. He walked to the window to look at it. The store was very warm, and he unbuttoned his short topcoat.

"Two bucks this week, on sale." The salesman lifted the tie from the display and dangled it in front of Nafty. "Try it on," urged the salesman, leading him to a mirror. "Going into New York?"

Nafty nodded, wondering if the salesman had mistaken him for a student.

"That's a big game this weekend."

"I know," said Nafty, though he did not follow the games. Nafty unwound his own tie, a blue wool hand-me-down from his oldest brother. Carefully, he knotted the new tie.

"That looks fine," said the salesman.

"I'll wear it now," said Nafty, and he paid for it, and stuffed his old tie in his coat pocket.

He was ready to go home now. He would wear the tie on the train and on the streets of Brooklyn. He would wear it to the synagogue where he would meet the *shamus*, turning on the outside lights because it grew dark early at that time of the year. "How do you like this tie?" Nafty would ask. "This is what all the boys at Princeton wear." No, the *shamus* wouldn't understand. Maybe he would show it to some girls. During the summer he would go away to the mountains. He would work as a bus boy. Instead of wearing those dinky black ties he would wear this one. "It's my school tie," he would explain. "It's a requirement to wear it all year around." He would buy a lacrosse bat, and he would practice against the handball courts. That's all that was needed, he felt. He had to practice, just keep on practicing and he would learn all the things a Princeton man is supposed to learn.

At the station he bought a ticket back to New York, and as he stood waiting for the train where earlier that day the four boys had stood, he thought to himself that he would make himself different, that there would be a time when he would walk into a room and people would nudge each other, sensing that Nafty Gold was different. "Mr. Princeton," they would think to themselves. "Here comes a Mr. Princeton." He turned to stare down at the empty trainscape, thinking to himself, the goddam train must've busted down. The wind came up and blew full in his face, fluttered his necktie against his collar, and froze at the corners of his eyes the tears that had begun to form there.

Twelve O'Clock

BY HARVEY SWADOS

SHE paid the counterman, stuffed her purse under her arm, and picked up the sandwich, the slice of pie, and the iced coffee. She turned gingerly, avoiding the supplicant arms of the other customers.

The clock on the wall was arrested at noon. She felt that if she were to take one step in the instant before the red second hand began its downward sweep, she would be impaled on the stiffly upraised arms of the clock, and would dangle there until her lunch hour had passed. But the long hand clicked backward, then forward, and she made her way through a fetid jungle of damp armpits, dripping chins, and whining voices choked with saliva, to the only empty booth. Its black-topped table was littered with wilted brown scraps of lettuce floating dismally in pools of coffee. She jerked a paper napkin from the metal holder, wiped the table, and sat down.

It seemed to her that if she were to concentrate with all her strength she could forget the rain, the cigarette butts underfoot, the rank odor of eggs swimming in bacon grease, and the hypnotic fan waiting in front of her typewriter on the twenty-third floor. She opened a paper-bound copy of *Walden* to the chapter on "Sounds," rested her forehead on her fist, and lifted the sandwich to her mouth.

"*Sometimes,*" she read, "*in a summer morning, having taken my accustomed bath, I sat in my sunny doorway from sunrise till noon, rapt in a reverie, amidst the pines and hickories, and sumachs, in undisturbed solitude and stillness, while the birds sang around or flitted noiseless through the house, until by the sun falling at my west window, or the noise of some traveler's waggon on the distant highway, I was reminded of the lapse of time. I grew in those seasons like corn in the night. . . .*"

"Anybody sitting here?"

She looked up angrily. A weary man and a shabby adolescent boy were standing beside the table. They both carried hamburgers and coffee, but otherwise they had so little in common that she could hardly believe they had come together.

"No," she said, "just me."

The boy slid in next to her without any further ceremony and began to wolf his hamburger. The man, who was probably in his fifties, took off his corduroy hat and settled himself on the opposite bench with a phlegmy sigh. The pressure of the hat left his graying hair matted damply at the temples. His face, hawklike and vertically lined, was that of a European intellectual, and it was accentuated by a pair of black shell glasses; but his grimy hands, scarred and spatulate, were those of a workman. The girl was annoyed to think that she could not locate him in any obvious category.

He spoke sharply to the boy in a heavily accented voice. "Jeanie, I vant to talk to you."

The boy licked a drop of catsup from his lower lip and replied, his mouth full. "Go ahead. I told you already, I ain't got much time. They don't hardly give me any lunch hour at all. They're always after me—I got to chase right out again."

"It's very important, Jeanie." He jerked off his clouded glasses impatiently and wiped them on his sleeve. The girl dropped her eyes in embarrassment and turned a page ostentatiously. If there was one thing more terrible than the loneliness of the city, she thought as she stared unseeingly at the printed page, it was this endless unavoidable eavesdropping into the private miseries of all the strangers. "You will see her this afternoon?"

"Don't I always?" Jeanie asked in his piping, messenger-boy voice. "There isn't a day goes by that I don't stop at the house. That's more than you can say, isn't it?"

"Don't get excited, Jeanie. We must be calm. I show you now what I have for your mother. This is why I ask you to meet me."

At the moment that the girl raised her eyes, she saw the man's hand stealing into his bosom. She saw an expanse of muddy-colored army underwear behind the gaping shirt front, and she watched with fascination as he drew forth a soiled envelope. Before she lowered her eyes once again, she observed that the envelope was covered with foreign stamps and speckled with exotic postmarks.

"This letter came this morning. It is from our Aunt Anna, and it is the first I learn that she is still alive. Do you know how excited your mother will be? To read the news from her aunt, her only relative besides you and me?"

The boy looked at him scornfully. "Who you think you're kidding?" His voice was suddenly infused with a weary maturity. He gulped absent-mindedly from the thick cup, as though he had been drinking coffee for many years. "If you ever went up to see her, you wouldn't talk so foolish. Last night the doctor said to me, she can't last more than a couple of weeks. I tell her she's looking better and she looks at me like a liar. Jesus, do you think a letter is going to stop the pain? Has it got money in it, so she can at least die in a decent room?"

The man held up his hand warningly and the boy subsided, shrinking back in the seat beside the girl. She bent her head further down, but the printed page was already blurring before her eyes.

"What do you think I am, a fool? I know enough from the last ten years not to expect miracles. Maybe it is a miracle that Aunt Anna is still alive, and maybe it would have been better for her to die without seeing all her family disappear. But all I say is that this letter will mean so much to your mother. It will make a little easier her last hours."

Jeanie pushed away his cup contemptuously and picked up the letter. "A hunk of paper. What the hell good is it going to do her to know that her aunt is still living? She'll never see her anyway."

"Can't I make you understand, Jeanie? Anna is the only one still living, the only one. She was your mother's favorite aunt. She used to play with you on her lap, in the days before your mother brought you to America."

"So what?"

"There is no need for you to talk cruel. The letter will make her happy. For a little, she will be very happy. That is what is most important."

Jeanie ran his fingers through his shaggy hair. "That's easy for you to say. If you think it's so important, why don't you take the letter up to her?"

"Must we talk of this again? I know what you think. You do not believe me; you think I am afraid to see her. Maybe when you are older you will understand. I have seen them die by the thousands, lined up in rows like cabbages. I am not afraid to look at my sister. But she will not like to see me as I am now. It is better if you take her the letter, and tell her I mailed it to you. It will make her happy, I swear it."

"I wanted for her to be happy. You're her brother, you know what I mean. She'd be happier if I was in school getting an education. Can I help it if I had to quit school and go to work? I wanted to get an education, I wanted Ma to be proud of me, but who'd pay the doctor bills? Who'd pay the rent? You?"

He twisted convulsively in the booth. His legs came into momentary contact with the girl's; she moved hastily to the wall and gripped the book tightly, but the boy ignored her.

"Never mind, Jeanie," the man said softly. He looked warmly at the boy. The girl felt herself growing hot as she saw the look on his face; but it was impossible for her to get up. "I know I am not such a good uncle. I used to think . . . ah, God, how I used to think, if only I had gone to the United Stages with my

sister fifteen years ago. But so soon as I find myself, and master
a little more of the language, you will go back to school. I promised it to your sister, I promise it to you."

The girl stole a glance at Jeanie's face. He was even younger
than she had thought; his beard was only beginning to sprout
along his jaws and under his tilted nose. She had time to notice
his unkempt hair growing over his ears and an ink smudge on
his chin that looked violet in the ghastly perpetual half-light of
the restaurant, and then she had to look away, because he
began to sniffle violently. She repressed an impulse to reach forward and press the dirty, half-grown hand that clutched the
coffee cup so tensely. Instead she pulled out the sugar bowl
with a clatter and leaned her book on it.

"*As I sit at my window this summer afternoon, hawks are circling about my clearing; the tantivy of wild pigeons, flying by
twos and threes athwart my view, or perching restless on the
white-pine boughs behind my house, gives a voice to the air;
a fish-hawk dimples the glassy surface of the pond and brings up
a fish; a mink steals out of the marsh before my door and seizes
a frog by the shore; the sedge is bending under the weight of
the reedbirds. . . .*"

"I told you," Jeanie said quietly. "All I want is for my mother
to die in peace. I don't want to hear any more of your pipe
dreams. I'm so *sick* of being poor. If I was rich, maybe Ma
never would have took sick. I haven't even got sixty cents to get
my shoes heeled. Every time I buy a pack of cigarettes I feel like
I'm taking something out of her mouth."

The man chuckled wryly as he slipped his glasses over his ears
with both hands. "You'll laugh at it some day, how you were
such a poor boy."

"I'm not laughing now. Maybe you can, because you're used
to being poor. But I'll never get used to it—I hate it all the
time."

"That's not why I laugh." The man pointed at the letter. "It
is because I think of all the boys where this letter comes from,
how they watched their parents die. How they died themselves.
Your life will be different from them."

Jeanie shrugged as he wiped his nose with his index finger. "You're probably glad to be alive"—his tone was heavy with an irony at once pitying and biting—"after everything that's happened to you. Maybe you'll never be able to work again. Maybe you're entitled to sit in those stinking movie shows every afternoon, instead of looking for work, or going up to see Ma. I don't know."

The man leaned halfway across the table. His narrow tie, a frazzled thing of yellow leaves against a brown background, dipped into his coffee. He brushed it aside and said tensely, "Do you think I have been joking? For myself my life was over before I came to America, and I came only to see you and your mother. Now we must do what we can that she dies properly, and that you live properly. Take her the letter this afternoon, and if I get this job that I hope, I will come soon."

"I won't be able to stay only long enough to give it to her. You don't know how they keep after me. I got to call back every hour. They think I'm joy riding in the God-damned subways, when I'm out chasing my tail off for them."

The man laughed shortly. "Don't worry about them. So soon as I make my connections, you will quit. If your mother cannot sit up, perhaps you will read her the letter yourself. If you cannot pronounce, spell out the words. She will know." He passed his hand over his face. ". . . and I will meet you here tomorrow, at the same time. And Jeanie," his fingers whitened around the envelope, "you must not lose it. It is all that connects us to the past life. It must be saved."

"I won't lose it."

"Put it inside your shirt. Use a safety pin."

"Jesus Christ, I told you already. I never lose anything. I'll put it right here. I'll be home in half an hour."

The man said pleadingly, "I mean for your good, Jeanie. I am not afraid to go. Tell her I will come soon."

"All right, all right. I better get going now."

"Don't stop on the way. Go in with a smile, you will make her happy with the letter."

"Lay off, will you? You talk to me like I was a baby." Jeanie twisted his legs free of the booth and stood up. He reached back to one of the metal hooks that curled back from the outer corner of the booth, removed a torn black oilskin raincoat, and slipped his arms into it.

The girl turned her head, as if she were looking across the restaurant, across the sour steamy air, through the thick plate-glass window that protected the opposite booths from the nervous jostling thousands who were tramping hurriedly along the subterranean stone corridor on their way back to work. But she saw none of this, any more than she saw the sunny grass and the quiet shining lake that she had been yearning for when she sat down at the table with her sandwich and her book. She saw only the boy, standing awkwardly in his castoff raincoat, at the side of the older man. His heels were, as he had said, quite run down, and he wore an odd pair of usher's trousers with a broad stripe running down the outer side of either leg.

The man blinked his eyes rapidly and smiled proudly at the boy. "Chust one more thing, Jeanie." He lifted his arm, the elbow bent and the hand curved inwards, and waved the boy silently down to him. Jeanie leaned forward until his ear was almost touching the man's mouth.

They whispered animatedly to each other, but although the girl listened so intently that the book slipped into her lap, she could hear nothing but their rapid breathing. As they finished the boy was smiling, nodding his head in approval, almost in time to the quick movements of the man's lips.

He straightened up and said aloud, "All right then. I'll do like you say."

"I knew you would. Don't forget tomorrow, yes?"

Jeanie smiled. "I'll be here. Maybe you'll have the job by then."

"Let us hope. Good-bye, Jeanie."

"So long." The boy waved farewell, turned, and walked swiftly out of the restaurant, the long raincoat flapping clumsily about his legs.

The girl sat there stiffly for a moment, suddenly aware that she was alone in the booth with the musing man. She gathered her purse and her book together with a consciously prim gesture and prepared to leave the booth, but when she raised her eyes at last she saw that the man was staring directly at her.

He wiped his forehead with a faded silk handkerchief that he drew from his breast pocket, smiled sheepishly, and said, "It is so warm. . . ."

"Yes, it is."

"I hope we did not. . . ."

"Oh no, not at all." She nodded quite soberly as she arose. She felt herself moving to the door, gliding through beyond someone's outstretched arm, clacking along the stone corridor, climbing up the stairway to the first floor of the building, carried forward by the impetus of all those who were moving in the same direction.

When she reached the main floor she stood irresolutely, with the clerks swirling around her in little waves, as though she no longer knew the way to the express elevator. Suddenly she turned and ran to the revolving doors.

She stepped out into the rain and peered up and down the darkened streets, ducking away from the ranks of bobbing umbrellas. Was that Jeanie, or was it a Western Union boy scuttling across the street a block away, his overlong raincoat blown behind him as he leaped to the curb past an advancing bus? A woman in front of her raised a newspaper over her head, a policeman blew his whistle, a row of taxicabs swung into the green light and blocked her view: by the time she reached the corner, breathless and confused, there was no sign of him.

She walked slowly back to the building, and to the job for which she was already late, shaking her head to free the clinging raindrops from her eyelashes, pressing the half-soaked copy of *Walden* to her side, conscious now only of desolation more frightening than anything she had ever known.

Biographical Sketches
of the Authors

Leonard Casper was born in 1923 in Fond du Lac, Wisconsin, and was educated at the University of Wisconsin. Today he is a professor of contemporary American literature and creative writing at Boston College; he has also taught creative writing at Wisconsin, Cornell, the University of Rhode Island, and (as Fulbright lecturer) at Ateneo de Manila and the University of the Philippines. He is a former Stanford Writing Fellow and Bread Loaf Scholar. His major publications include *Robert Penn Warren: The Dark and Bloody Ground* (1960), *The World of Short Fiction* (1962), *Modern Philippine Short Stories* (1962), *New Writing from the Philippines* (1966); over thirty stories in magazines and many poems, as well as stories in the O. Henry and Martha Foley annuals and *Stanford Short Stories* 1953.

R. V. Cassill was born in Cedar Falls, Iowa, in 1919, attended the State University of Iowa before World War II and received an M.A. degree there in 1947. He spent some time as a painter and WPA art teacher in 1941 and 1942. He taught at the Writers' Workshop at Iowa from 1948 to 1952 and from 1961 to 1965. He has also taught fiction writing at the University of Washington, Columbia, and The New School for Social Research in New York. He published his first story in 1939,

won an *"Atlantic* First" contest in 1947 and third prize in the
O. Henry Awards for 1957, and held Rockefeller and Fulbright
grants during the fifties. He has published about fifty short
stories, of which more than a dozen have been anthologized,
some of them repeatedly. During the fifties he wrote eleven
paperback "original" novels. His more serious novels include
Eagle on the Coin (1950), *Clem Anderson* (1961), *Pretty
Leslie* (1963), *The President* (1964). His stories have received
book publication in *15 x 3* (with Herbert Gold and James B.
Hall), in *The Father* (1965), and in *The Happy Marriage*
(1966).

Daniel Curley was born in 1918 in East Bridgewater, Mas-
sachusetts, and was educated at the University of Alabama.
He teaches in the Department of English of the University of
Illinois, where he has been an editor of *Accent.* He has published two novels, *How Many Angels?* and *A Stone Man, Yes,*
and a collection of stories, *That Marriage Bed of Procrustes.*
During the past year he has been in London on sabbatical
leave and has been busy finishing a novel, writing a few stories,
and working on a play.

Donald DeLillo was born in New York in 1936, has published
stories in *Epoch* and *The Kenyon Review,* and has just finished
writing his first novel.

Harris Downey lives in East Baton Rouge Parish of Louisiana,
where he was born and reared. His stories, most of them published in the literary quarterlies, have been reprinted in many
anthologies and textbooks. He has published six stories in
Epoch. Of these six, "Crispin's Way" has been reprinted in
The Best American Short Stories and in the textbook *Reading
for Life.* "The Hunters," which was rejected by nineteen publications before it was printed in *Epoch,* is being reprinted
continually in anthologies, other magazines, newspapers, and
textbooks. Its next reprinting, an Italian translation, will appear
in an anthology of American War Stories to be published by

the Mondadori Publishing Company in Milan. It won first prize in the O. Henry Memorial Awards in 1951. Mr. Downey is the author of three novels: *Thunder in the Room, The Key to My Prison,* and *Carrie Dumain,* the last named published in May, 1966, by The Henry Regnery Company.

Charles Edward Eaton was born in Winston-Salem, North Carolina, in 1916. A Phi Beta Kappa graduate of the University of North Carolina, he studied philosophy at Princeton and taught English in Puerto Rico. He returned to this country to take his M.A. degree at Harvard, where he studied with Robert Frost, upon whose recommendation he was awarded a fellowship at the Bread Loaf Writers' Conference. After leaving Harvard, he taught creative writing at the University of Missouri for two years, and for four years thereafter was Vice Consul at the American Embassy in Rio de Janeiro. He taught creative writing at the University of North Carolina for several years. His poetry and prose have appeared in over fifty publications here and abroad, including *The Sewanee Review, Harper's, The Saturday Review, The Reporter, The Virginia Quarterly Review, The Yale Review, The Atlantic Monthly,* and others. He has published four volumes of poetry: *The Bright Plain* (1942), *The Shadow of the Swimmer*—winner of the Ridgely Torrence Memorial Award (1951), *The Greenhouse in the Garden* (1956), and *Countermoves* (1963). His volume of short stories, *Write Me from Rio* (1959), included "The Motion of Forgetfulness Is Slow," which was anthologized by Martha Foley in her *Best American Short Stories.* Mr. Eaton has read his poetry at many universities and colleges; recordings of his poetry are in the permanent collections of American poetry at the Library of Congress, Yale University, and other universities. At present, he is living in Woodbury, Connecticut, where he is working on a novel and a fifth volume of poetry.

George P. Elliott was born in Knightstown, Indiana, in 1918, and moved with his family to Southern California when he was ten. He received A.B. and M.A. degrees from the University of California at Berkeley. Since 1947 he has taught English, with three years off on fellowships for writing. He has published three novels—*Parktilden Village, David Knudsen, In the World*; a number of short stories in literary magazines and ten in *Among the Dangs*; a number of poems and one book-length narrative poem—*Fever and Chills*; and several essays, some collected in *A Piece of Lettuce*. He is now completing a full-length play, which he has been writing on a Ford Fellowship. He intends next to alternate a long narrative poem with a book on nihilism. He is a professor of English at Syracuse University.

Leslie A. Fiedler was born in Newark, New Jersey, in 1917, received a B.A. from New York University in 1938 and the M.A. and Ph.D. degrees from the University of Wisconsin, the latter in 1941. He served as a Japanese Interpreter with the United States Navy in 1944 and 1945 in Hawaii, Guam, Iwo Jima, China, and Okinawa. He did post-doctoral work at Harvard in 1946 and 1947. He taught at Montana State University from 1941 to 1963, when not on leave, serving as Director of the Humanities Course and for two years as Chairman of the English Department. During leaves, he taught at the Universities of Bologna, Rome, Venice, Athens, and Princeton. Since 1964, he has been Professor of English at the State University of New York at Buffalo. He has lectured widely throughout the United States, as well as in Canada, England, Italy, Germany, Greece, Yugoslavia, Turkey, and Israel. In addition to countless critical articles and reviews, he has published many short stories and poems, both here and in other countries. His principal books include *An End to Innocence* (1955), *The Art of the Essay* (1958), *Love and Death in the American Novel* (1960), *No! in Thunder* (1960), *Pull down Vanity and Other Stories* (1962), *The Second Stone: A Love Story* (1963), *Waiting for the End* (1964), *Back to China* (1965), and *Last Jew in America* (1966).

Douglas Fowler was born in Columbia, Missouri, in 1940. A graduate of Cornell University in 1962, he taught in the New

York City public schools, and is now in Officer Candidate School of the U.S. Army. He is at work on a 300,000-word novel.

B. H. Friedman was born in New York City in 1926 and has lived there almost all his life, except for two years in the Navy and three at Cornell University from which he graduated in 1948. He has written fiction, poetry, and criticism. His first novel, *Circles,* was published in 1962; a second, *Yarborough,* was published in 1964; and *One-Man Show,* a collection of short fiction, is scheduled for publication early in 1967.

James B. Hall was raised on a farm near Blanchester, Ohio, and was later a merchant sailor, and a Chief Warrant Officer (Recon) in World War II. After schooling at Miami University and the University of Hawaii, he had a literary education at Iowa State University, where he received his Ph.D. degree. He has published three novels and two collections of short stories. He taught at Cornell University and at the University of Oregon and is presently a writer-teacher at the University of California (Irvine) and director of the Writing Center there.

Steven Katz was born in 1935 in New York City. He has an M.A. degree from the University of Oregon. He has lived in Idaho and in Nevada, and has spent three years in Italy. A book of poems, *The Weight of Antony,* was brought out in a limited, hand-printed edition in 1964 by the Eibe Press. The story in the present volume is one of five from a group called *From the Childhood of Marcus Morocco.* His work has appeared in *Epoch, Midstream, Chicago Review, Northwest Review,* and elsewhere. He has two poems in the new anthology, *Modern Occasions,* edited by Philip Rahv. The recent 20th anniversary issue of the *Chicago Review* contains a large sample of *The Exaggerations of Peter Prince,* the novel he is presently finishing.

Julius Laffal was born in New York City in 1920 and was graduated from City College of New York in 1941. He received the Ph.D degree in clinical psychology from the University of Iowa in 1951, and since that time has been working as a clinical psychologist in the Veterans Administration. He has published a few short stories and numerous technical articles; his book, *Pathological and Normal Language,* was published by the *Atherton Press* in 1965. Most of his writing is in the domain of psychology. Currently he is working on a book which gives a picture of a psychiatric ward largely through the eyes of patients on the ward.

John Logan was born in 1923 in Red Oak, Iowa. He was educated in the Red Oak schools, received a B.A. from Coe College in 1943 with a zoology major and an M.A. from the State University of Iowa in English. He has been an instructor at St. John's College (1947–1951), assistant and associate professor at Notre Dame University (1951–1963), Chairman of the Department of World Classics at St. Mary's College in California (1963–1965), Visiting Professor of Poetry at the University of Washington (1965), Visiting Professor of English, San Francisco State College (1965–1966), and is now Professor of English at the State University of New York at Buffalo. His books of poetry include *Cycle for Mother Cabrini* (1955), *Ghosts of the Heart* (1960), and *Spring of the Thief* (1963). His poems have been anthologized frequently. His short stories have appeared in a number of magazines, and he has written many critical articles and reviews. He has also published a book of fiction for children, *Tom Savage.*

Joyce Carol Oates was born in 1938 in Lockport, New York. She received a B.A. degree from Syracuse University and an M.A. degree from the University of Wisconsin. She has published short stories widely in *Mademoiselle, The Kenyon Review, The Virginia Quarterly, The Transatlantic Review, Prairie Schooner, Cosmopolitan, The Atlantic Monthly;* several have appeared in the O. Henry Awards anthology and in the *Best American Short Stories* anthology, and in other places. Her books are *By the North Gate, With Shuddering Fall,* and *Upon the Sweeping Flood.*

Jordon Pecile grew up in Hazelton, Pennsylvania, graduated from Cornell University, and received a Fulbright grant to Florence—which led to "A Piece of Polenta." Since then he has served in the Navy in the Antarctic and at Annapolis. At Annapolis he wrote "The Barrel Lifter" which was an "*Atlantic First*" winner in 1963 and was televised in 1964. He started work for his Ph.D. degree at Princeton, but since he could not bury his interest in writing, he shifted to the Iowa Writers' Workshop in September, 1965.

Thomas Pynchon was born in 1937 on Long Island. After a hitch in the Navy, he graduated from Cornell University in 1959. He wrote his widely-acclaimed novel V. while doing technical writing for Boeing Aircraft in Seattle. V. won the Faulkner Award as the best first novel of 1963. His most recent novel is *The Crying of Lot 49* (1966). Short stories have appeared in a number of magazines: one, "Under the Rose," received second prize in the O. Henry Awards of 1962. He has lived in recent years in Mexico and California.

Faye Riter (Kensinger) is by birth a midwesterner, by marriage (and travel orders issued by the Air Force) a wanderer, and now by family choice a North Californian. She has published many stories during the past twenty-five years in literary quarterlies and large-circulation magazines.

Philip Roth was born in Newark, New Jersey, in 1933. He received a B.A. degree from Bucknell University in 1954 and his M.A. degree from the University of Chicago in 1955. He taught at the University of Chicago, the State University of Iowa, Princeton University, and the University of Pennsylvania. His first book, *Goodbye, Columbus*, published in 1959, won the National Book Award for Fiction, the Daroff Award of the Jewish Book Council of America, and a grant from the National Institute of Arts and Letters; his second book, a novel, *Letting Go*, was published in 1962. He has also been the recipient of a Guggenheim Fellowship and a grant from the Ford Foundation for work in the theater. He is at present living in New York City, teaching at the State University of New York at Stony Brook, Long Island, and completing a new novel. His stories have appeared in *Epoch, Commentary, Paris Review, New Yorker, Esquire, Harper's, Playboy,* and elsewhere; they have been reprinted in Martha Foley's *Best American Short Stories 1956, 1959, 1960* and in *O. Henry Prize Stories 1960* (Second Prize).

Marvin Schiller was born in New York City in 1929 and was educated there. He did graduate work at Stanford University where he was a Creative Writing Fellow (1952). He has spent several months at both Yaddo and the Huntington Hartford Foundation, writing. He lived in Europe in 1962, working on a second novel; the first, *Country of the Mind,* appeared in early 1966. His stories have appeared in the *Paris Review, New World Writing, Epoch,* the *Antioch Review,* and *Stanford Short Stories.* In the advertising business, he lives in New York.

Harvey Swados was born in Buffalo, New York, in 1920. He received a B.A. degree from the University of Michigan in 1940. He has published three novels—*The Will, False Coin, Out Went the Candle;* three volumes of short stories—*A Story for Teddy—and Others, Nights in the Gardens of Brooklyn, On the Line;* a book of collected essays—*A Radical's America;* and two anthologies—*The American Writer and the Great Depression, Years of Conscience: The Muckrakers.* He is presently teaching at Sarah Lawrence College and Columbia University and working on a long novel.

Jan Wahl was born in 1933 in Columbus, Ohio, was raised in Toledo, Ohio, and is now living in Brooklyn. He received a B.A. degree from Cornell University in 1953 and his M.A. degree from the University of Michigan (where he studied under Austin Warren) in 1958; he was awarded a major Avery Hopwood Prize in fiction in 1955. A Fulbright grant took him to the University of Copenhagen in 1953 and 1954 to study Danish folk literature and film. He returned to Denmark in

1957 to be secretary to the late Isak Dinesen during the writing of her *Last Tales;* he has also worked in movies in Denmark with Carl Th. Dreyer. He has published stories and poems in a number of the quarterlies, including *Epoch, The Prairie Schooner, The Transatlantic Review,* and *Audience;* and also five children's books—*Cabbage Moon, Pleasant Fieldmouse, Hello Elephant, The Howards Go Sledding,* and *The Muffletumps,* as well as a bestiary, *The Beast Book* (1964). Harper will publish soon a long fable, *How the Children Stopped the Wars.*

Ray B. West, Jr., born in Logan, Utah, in 1908, was educated at Utah State College and at the University of Utah. He obtained his Ph.D. degree at the State University of Iowa. He is now a professor of English at San Francisco State College after teaching at different Utah colleges, at Montana, at the University of Kansas where he was Director of Creative Writing, and in the Writers' Workshop of Iowa State University. He edited *The Western Review* from 1937 to 1959. He has also taught at the University of Innsbruck in Austria and in Ankara, Turkey. He has published several books on American literature, Rocky Mountain writing, and modern fiction, as well as many short stories in magazines.

Herbert Wilner was born in Brooklyn in 1925; he was educated at Brooklyn College (B.A.), Columbia University (M.A.), and the University of Iowa (Ph.D.), and is currently teaching at San Francisco State College. His stories have appeared in such literary magazines as *Epoch, The Sewanee Review, The Western Review,* and *Furioso* and in such large circulation magazines as *Esquire, The Saturday Evening Post,* and *Redbook.* Stories have appeared in O. Henry and Martha Foley collections, and in *The Esquire Reader.* His first novel, *All the Little Heroes,* was published in June, 1966.